Anne Melville, daughter of the author and lecturer Bernard Newman, was born and brought up in Harrow, Middlesex. She read Modern History at Oxford as a scholar of St Hugh's College, and after graduating she taught and travelled in the Middle East. On returning to England, she edited a children's magazine for a few years, but now devotes all her working time to writing. She and her husband live in Oxford.

By the same author

The Lorimer Line
The Lorimer Legacy
Lorimers in Love
Lorimers at War
Last of the Lorimers

ANNE MELVILLE

Lorimer Loyalties

GRAFTON BOOKS
A Division of the Collins Publishing Group

LONDON GLASGOW
TORONTO SYDNEY AUCKLAND

Grafton Books
A Division of the Collins Publishing Group
8 Grafton Street, London W1X 3LA

Published by Grafton Books 1987

First published in Great Britain by
William Heinemann Ltd 1984

ISBN 0-586-06613-6

Printed and bound in Great Britain by
Collins, Glasgow

Set in Times

Contents

THE LORIMER LINE

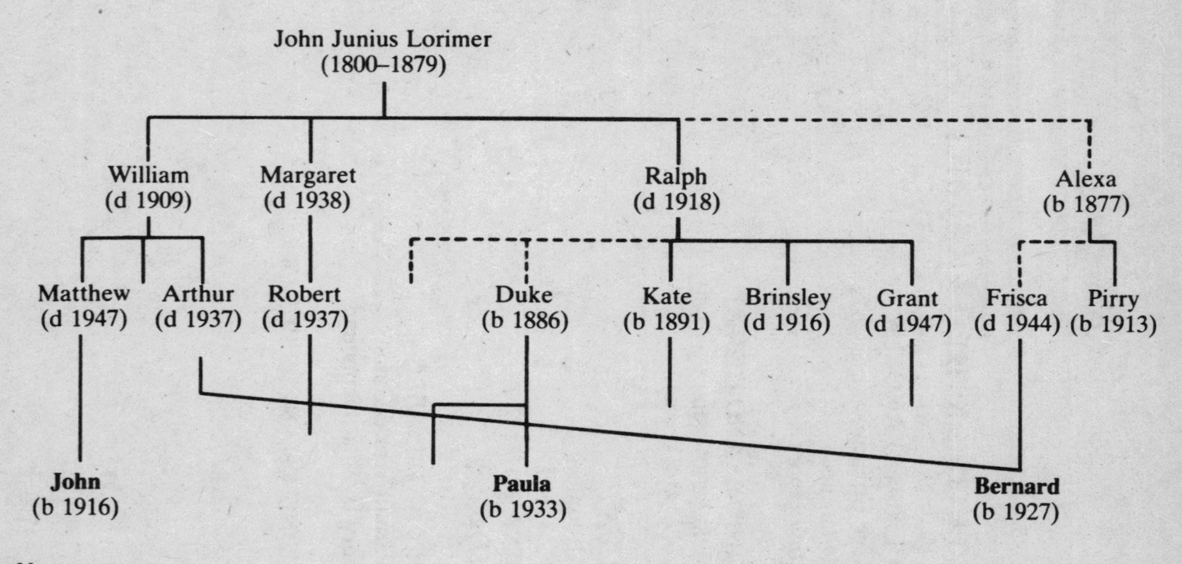

Note

Dotted lines indicate illegitimacy.

Three Cousins
1953–54

1

Outside the iron gates of Dame Eleanor's College an elderly Rolls-Royce waited in dignified patience. Around it swirled the normal end-of-term chaos as those undergraduates who had ordered taxis to take them to the station fought familiar battles with the drivers about the number of passengers legally allowed to share the vehicle and the amount of luggage which could be physically stowed aboard. Calm amidst all the flurry, Paula and Helen and Angela waved goodbye to two of their friends who would be cycling home and strolled towards the car which Lady Glanville had sent to drive her Christmas guests to Blaize.

Any stranger watching the three young women as they handed their suitcases to the chauffeur and stepped into the car would have assumed an immediate understanding of the situation. Every highly-polished inch of the Rolls proclaimed its owner to be a member of an aristocracy endeavouring in 1953 to maintain pre-war standards of gracious living whilst reeling under the twin blows of capital taxation and never-ending repair bills. Angela, plump and untidy, could not be regarded as an appropriate passenger. By constrast, it was obvious that Helen must be the daughter of just such a family. Her straight blonde hair, the calm expression on her pale face and the long-legged thinness which a suit of Harris tweed only partly disguised, all combined to make it clear that she would be at home in a stately country house.

Equally obvious was the fact that she must have invited to join her for Christmas a fellow-undergraduate who had no home of her own in England. True, Paula was completely at ease as she settled into her seat. Her clothes, although not expensive, were smart, and her narrow hips and exceptionally straight back helped her to wear them with a sophisticated air. Her dark brown eyes were intelligent and alert and the poise of her small, neatly-groomed head gave an immediate impression of confidence. She was at home in Oxford, at home in the spacious car. Yet there could be no doubt that she was a foreigner. For Paula Mattison had been born in Jamaica and, alone amongst the undergraduates of Dame Eleanor's College, she was black.

Whatever conclusions the casual onlooker might have drawn from his observations would have been wrong. It was certainly true that Angela would be travelling only a short distance in the car, having been offered by the others a lift to the station. But for all her lack of style, Angela was the daughter of a duke, and the only one of the three who had been brought up to take expensive cars for granted. Of the other two it was Helen – whose missionary parents worked in Africa – who had no home in England. And it was Paula, a regular visitor to Blaize, who had been asked by Lady Glanville if she would like to bring a friend to stay with her for Christmas.

'I did warn you, didn't I?' checked Paula after they had dropped Angela and were making their sedate way along the Thames valley. 'Lady Glanville won't be at Blaize herself. She spends Christmas with her son in the south of France. There won't be much action unless we set it up for ourselves.' Paula knew that she need not apologize for the lack of amusement. The eight weeks of each Oxford term were so tightly packed with social excitements that all serious reading was left to the vacations.

Helen, like herself, would expect to spend the next few weeks studying.

The car turned off the road between two stone pillars. The wrought-iron gates which once bore the Glanville family arms picked out in gold and red had been melted down for the war effort more than ten years earlier and would never now be replaced: Paula had seen them only in photographs. But the house itself had survived both war and the years of austerity outwardly unchanged. 'Gracious!' exclaimed Helen as they rounded the last curve and Blaize came into sight.

'We'll be slumming it in the west wing,' Paula told her. It was a reassurance rather than an apology, for the wide Tudor frontage suggested the presence of great banqueting halls and long galleries but not much in the way of hot water or central heating. The two wings which had been added a mere two hundred and fifty years ago were equally spacious, but lighter and far more comfortable. 'Most of the house has been taken over by a school of music. It's tough, isn't it, that no one can afford to keep up a grand house as a family home any more.'

'I thought you came from one yourself,' said Helen. 'I remember being impressed by your address on the freshers' list before I ever met you. Bristow Great House!'

'I'll tell you, compared to Blaize, Bristow is a cottage.' Then Paula's voice changed abruptly from disparagement to surprise and pleasure. 'Oh, glory! Bernard's here!'

No one would ever call Lady Glanville's red-headed grandson well-dressed, she thought as he strolled, smiling, towards the car. Although he was only twenty-six, he already wore the crumpled look of a scientist too deeply engrossed in his work to bother with the mundane details of ordinary life. He was a shy young man – but not with Paula, who had the knack of making friends with men as well as with women and had set herself from their first meeting to make him feel at ease with her.

'Do you plan to spend Christmas here?' she asked, as they greeted each other. 'If so, the vacation is looking up.'

Bernard shook his head. 'I'm going skiing on Tuesday,' he told her. 'But Grandmother asked me to come for the weekend and welcome you in, since she wouldn't be here herself.' He was looking over her shoulder as she spoke. Paula could see admiration in his eyes as he waited to be introduced to her friend.

'Helen, this is Bernard Lorimer. Bernard, Helen Langton.'

'How do you do, Mr Lorimer.' Helen shook hands politely while Paula and Bernard spoke at the same time to put her right.

'Sorry,' said Paula. 'Inadequate introduction. He's really Sir Bernard, if you're going to be formal.'

'But you're not,' said Bernard. 'You're going to call me Bernard so that I can call you Helen.' He was holding her hand for longer than was strictly necessary as he smiled at her.

'That's very impressive – a knighthood so young!' exclaimed Helen.

Bernard continued to smile as he explained. 'Only a baronetcy, I'm afraid. The sole qualification is to be fatherless. Let me help you with your bits and pieces.'

Paula could hardly restrain herself from laughing out loud as she thanked the chauffeur and followed the other two into the house. She had never believed that such a thing as love at first sight existed. But Bernard's expression was too transparent to leave any room for doubt. In the space of about thirty seconds he had been completely bowled over by Helen.

He was at a vulnerable age, of course – orphaned many

years earlier and quite probably by now ready to abandon his bachelor flat and embark upon family life. He needed a homemaker, someone to look after him, but at the same time he was too clever to feel any interest in a stupid girl, however beautiful she might be. He would be justified, though, in taking it for granted that any of Paula's university friends must be intelligent – the competition to get into Oxford made sure of that. If he was looking for a girl, Helen was just the sort of girl he needed to find.

The role of matchmaker did not come naturally to Paula. Nevertheless, as the three young people lingered over their after-dinner coffee at the end of that day, she could not resist the temptation to look at Bernard through Helen's eyes and wonder what her friend was thinking. There was no doubt at all that the baronetcy would have made as immediate an impression on Helen as Helen's own blonde good looks obviously had on Bernard. At Oxford she belonged to the Conservative Club – not because she had any interest in politics but because that was the best way to meet all the Eton and Christ Church men who would one day be barons or merchant bankers or both. When she discovered that Bernard was wealthy as well as titled, the fact would do him no harm in her eyes.

It was not really that Helen was a snob. She was a clearsighted young woman who was aware of her own talent for orderly efficiency. Undaunted by wealth, she would have the taste and ability to preside over an establishment of any size in the same effective style with which Lady Glanville ran Blaize, should anyone offer her the opportunity.

She was addressing Bernard now with all the earnestness of a young woman who had been taught that the best way to appeal to a man is to show interest in his own enthusiasms. For a second time that day Paula was tempted to laugh aloud. She could guess exactly what the question would be.

2

Bernard knew what was coming. From the moment when any new acquaintance discovered that he not only owned a research laboratory but worked in it himself, the conversation became completely predictable.

'What are you working on at the moment?' Helen asked.

It was a question which Bernard found difficult to answer in female company, although there was no good reason why he should feel embarrassment in revealing that he knew a good deal more about the workings of a woman's body than most women did themselves.

On this occasion Paula came to his rescue. 'Still working on the baby-blocker, are you?' she asked, grinning.

'Yes.' He met Helen's eyes squarely. They were clear blue eyes, interested and sympathetic. 'I'm helping to develop a new method of contraception.' In spite of all his determination to control it, he could feel a blush spreading over his freckled face. 'It will be a pill for women to take, with an almost hundred per cent certainty that it will prevent them from becoming pregnant. When I say it will be, it actually exists already, but we're still testing it on animals. To make sure that it doesn't cause any nasty side-effects. If all goes well, we hope to start clinical trials on human volunteers in about two years.'

'You won't be popular with novelists,' laughed Helen. 'No more plots about young girls being ruined or young men being trapped into marriage.'

'And what will happen to college discipline?' demanded Paula, who always enjoyed a spirited debate. 'Would you believe this, Bernard? If any member of Dame Eleanor's is found not to be on the premises after the magic hour of eleven at night, except with special permission, she's sent down without right of appeal. So long, and don't come back. How about that for sex discrimination! If I were to be caught in one of the men's colleges at midnight, the young man might be fined, but my Oxford career would be finished. And what's the difference? Just that the young man isn't about to get pregnant. The Principal and Fellows are using the fear of their punishment to protect us from ourselves. But your pill will do that instead, won't it?'

'Rather more efficiently.' For some reason Bernard never felt any embarrassment in discussing the subject with Paula. Perhaps it was because she approached every topic as the journalist she hoped one day to become, without taking his answers personally. 'For one thing, it will protect you at four o'clock in the afternoon as well, when presumably your rules are off duty. Do you all in fact obey the rules?'

Paula laughed aloud. 'One or two of our year keep the rules because they have naturally law-abiding natures. Like Helen here. That's not sneaking, I hope, Helen. Others keep the rules because they're afraid of the consequences of being caught. And there are others still who calculate the odds and take the risk. I did the social gossip column for *Isis* in my second year. If I'd been tucked up in my cot by eleven every night there would have been a good many blank spaces.'

'You're talking just about rules, though.' Helen did not dispute the category into which she had been placed. 'What Bernard's research is liable to turn upside down is the whole ethos *behind* the rules.'

'That's right.' Bernard was pleased that she had taken the point so directly. 'If it works – and I believe it will – it's going to be one of the greatest social revolutions of the century. Far more important than landing on the moon. Every woman will be able to decide whether she *wants* to have a baby. Every baby will be a wanted child.'

'So if the whole human race comes to an abrupt end in about eighty years from now it will be down to Sir Bernard Lorimer, will it?' asked Helen teasingly.

Bernard knew that he should in honesty admit that there were others working in the same field; the idea had been in the air for years. But he could tell that Helen wanted to be impressed and, with an intensity that he did not wholly understand, he wanted to impress her.

'I imagine there'll always be some women who want to have children. It may lead to smaller families. No more accidents! In terms of the individual, what it will offer is the power to make a choice. That must be good, mustn't it?' He struggled to put his passionate belief into words. 'If you think, as I do, that a major cause of war is overpopulation – people desperate for food and land and having to burst their national boundaries to find it – and if you look at the forecasts of population growth in places like India and China – well, it's terrifying, don't you think?'

He checked himself before he could launch into a boring lecture and offered liqueurs all round from his grandmother's selection as a gesture towards changing the subject. The two girls began to exchange good resolutions about the timetable of study which they intended to observe during the next three weeks. Listening, Bernard wondered whether the idea developing in his head was brilliant or ridiculous. Not until later, after they had dispersed to their bedrooms, did he make up his mind and set out in search of Paula.

Paula was looking for him at the same moment. They met in the corridor as though they had planned a midnight rendezvous, and giggled as the realization occurred to each at the same moment.

'I have a favour to ask you,' said Paula.

'And I have an invitation to offer you.'

'Invitations take precedence over favours. Tell me.'

There was a window seat at the end of the corridor. They sat close together so that they could keep their voices low.

'This skiing holiday of mine,' Bernard said. 'I'm going with a party. Friends from my Cambridge days, mostly. I wondered – well, I wondered whether you and Helen would like to join us.'

Paula threw back her head and laughed. Bernard had known that she would laugh, but oddly enough he didn't mind. He had a lot of time for Paula. He admired the extraordinary speed with which she had learned to combine the cool observation of a foreigner studying a society from outside with a vivacious participation in its internal debates. He enjoyed the warm friendliness with which she made it clear that she enjoyed his company without ever prompting him to wonder whether she expected him to flirt with her. She was the most quick-witted girl he knew – there had never been any chance that she would fail to guess what lay behind his suggestion – but her amusement did not make her unkind.

'That's a great idea,' she said. 'But not for me, with Finals only six months away. I wouldn't say that I've *wasted* the past two and a half years, because I've packed them full of what I wanted to do. But it is just possible that Politics, Philosophy and Economics, in the examination sense, haven't had their fair share of my time. Helen's reading Greats, though. She has another year to go after I'm through. The pressure's not on her yet. I don't know that she's the sporty type, but I should think the après-ski would go down very well. Why don't you ask her?'

'It would leave you stuck here without any company.'

'When I work, I work,' said Paula. 'Truly. Bringing Helen here was for her sake more than mine, because none of her folk live in England. You go right ahead.'

That was another of the special things that Bernard had discovered about Paula. She was honest. If she said that she didn't mind, then she didn't mind. He had noticed before what a high value she set on friendship. Whenever she could see that some small sacrifice on her part would benefit a friend, the action ceased to be a sacrifice and became genuinely a pleasure. Yet at the same time she was by temperament self-sufficient, capable of being alone without being lonely. It was curious, he thought, that he should know Paula so well and like her so very much without even considering the possibility of falling in love with her, whilst the mere touch of Helen's hand, the steady smile in her blue eyes . . . Bernard pulled himself together and remembered that there was to be another side to this conversation.

'Thanks, Paula,' he said sincerely. 'You said you had a favour to ask?'

'Yes. It was an idea I had while you were talking earlier. About there being too many people in the world. And what you were doing about it, in the course of your work. I could write a great series of interviews – with people who are pursuing ordinary professional or commercial careers but who are going to finish up by changing the face of society. Not by preaching revolution. Just by insidiously leading people to take quite new concepts for granted. Would you let me do a piece on you for a starter, Bernard? Then I could sell the idea to an editor, and the paper would give me the backing I'd need for the other interviews.'

Bernard hesitated for a few seconds, but then shook his head. 'Sorry, Paula,' he said. 'I'd like to help, but – it's too soon, you see. When people read about this sort of thing, they expect it to turn up tomorrow.' He thought for a moment, feeling guilty about refusing her when she had made it clear that she would help him to get to know Helen better. 'I could give you an introduction,' he said. 'To a cousin of mine who might fit into a series like that.'

'What does he do?' asked Paula.

'Anything with concrete. Specifically, pre-fabricated housing. He must have made a fortune since the war covering bomb sites with ready-made homes.'

Paula gave a mischievous sigh. 'Yet another rich Lorimer!'

'Well, as a matter of fact, that's an interesting thing. He may be doing nicely now, but he was brought up poor. I don't know exactly how it happened. But it's left him with a large chip on his shoulder. You might find him quite a tough nut to crack. The thing is, though, because he spent his childhood in some kind of slum, his ambition now is to provide central heating and constant hot water to the whole population of the British Isles. Would that be revolutionary enough for you?'

Paula's face expressed a certain lack of enthusiasm. 'I'll think about it,' she said. 'What's his name?'

'John Lorimer,' Bernard told her.

3

The Lorimers, with few exceptions, were tall; it was in the genes. But in this respect – as in almost every other – John Lorimer was not a typical member of the family. Malnutrition in childhood had checked his growth as permanently as other forms of deprivation had stunted his emotional life. There was no way in which he could make up for his lack of family life as a child. Since the day when he discovered that his mother had lied to him throughout his boyhood about the father he believed to be dead, he had been unable ever to trust a woman's word. He enjoyed the conversation of intelligent women and he enjoyed making love to beautiful women; but he did not expect sincerity from any of them and for that reason was never completely sincere himself. He had never been tempted to surrender his privacy to marriage because he had never found, or expected to find, a woman honest enough to reveal her own secrets or to make promises and keep them.

In other respects it was easier to turn his back on the past. For the dirt and hunger of those boyhood years he could compensate now by dressing smartly, eating well and bathing obsessively. His prosperity, though, could do nothing to increase his height. He would never be taller than five foot three.

It didn't bother him. Sitting behind the chairman's desk in the Lorico offices he ignored his lack of inches with all the self-confidence of a man who had left school without a penny on his fourteenth birthday but was already, at the age of thirty-seven, well on the way to becoming a millionaire. For the Lorimer genes had not proved completely ineffective. John had inherited a businessman's good judgement from all the generations of Bristol merchant princes who made a fortune in the slave trade and increased it by investment in shipping, docks and banking – but he acknowledged no debt to any of them, accepting nothing but his name from the Lorimer family. He was his own man: in family terms, a loner.

Nevertheless, reminders of the past could still trigger

off old family memories. One such reminder was handed to him by his secretary on an April morning in 1954.

The letter came from Blaize, Lady Glanville's stately home. John knew the house well – it had been the setting for one of the most humiliating experiences of his childhood. The writer of the letter, Paula Mattison, had not briefed herself very well if she believed that the die-stamped address and her claim to be a friend of his cousin, Bernard Lorimer, would help her to obtain the interview she was seeking. In any case, John never gave personal interviews. He had no liking for journalists and submitted himself to their questions only when some new business project required publicity for its launch. His secretary, anticipating his shake of the head, was already holding out a hand to take the letter back and write a polite refusal.

But John took longer than usual to consider it. The name Mattison, in a Lorimer context, had a place in a remote corner of his memory. He had heard it spoken in his years as an apprentice draughtsman with the Lorimer Line shipbuilding company before the war. Even that alone might not have caught his interest, but there was a phrase in the letter which combined with this background knowledge to arouse his curiosity. She was a friend of Bernard's, was she? Only a friend? He nodded at his secretary. 'I'll see her next week.'

Punctually at her appointed time Paula Mattison came into his office. If she expected him to look surprised, she was to be disappointed – John was already sure that she would be black. He studied her with interest as they shook hands. She was younger than he had expected, and very good-looking. Although her skin was dark and her closely-trimmed hair was black and tightly curled, her features were smaller and more delicate than might have been expected from her Jamaican origin. John smiled to himself at this confirmation of half-remembered gossip from his time in Bristol. He knew how Paula Mattison had come to inherit that neat mouth and most un-African narrow nose.

'You wrote from Blaize, Miss Mattison,' he reminded her as he indicated a seat. 'What's your connection with Lady Glanville?'

'Remote.' Paula's educated accent, he noticed, owed nothing to her West Indian heritage. 'Before I came to England three years ago, a friend of my father's offered to give me a home in the university vacations. Dr Kate Lorimer, a niece of Lady Glanville. But the week I arrived in England she was sick. Lady Glanville didn't care for the idea of a young girl being on her own in a strange country. She told me to regard Blaize as home.'

'Kind of her.' John found the explanation more interesting than Paula could have realized.

'Yes. And she did it in a nice way, you know. Just the one offer, and then no fuss. Mr Lorimer, I'd like to ask you – '

'Just a minute,' said John. 'You didn't mention in your letter which paper you work for.'

'Does it matter?'

'Of course it matters. Every product has to be presented correctly for a particular market. Even an interview.'

'Even the truth?' asked Paula. She was smiling with the mischief of someone who expects to be found out, so John guessed the situation without needing to be told.

'Answer my question,' he said nevertheless.

Paula sighed, her dark eyes twinkling. 'Strictly freelance,' she confessed. 'I'm still up at Oxford. I've done a lot of university journalism. Editor of *Isis* for two terms, that sort of thing. I take my Finals in June and so I'm looking for a job. I want to go straight to Fleet Street without wasting time on a provincial paper.'

'In other words,' said John severely, 'you're practising on me.'

'Yes,' agreed Paula. 'And I'm sure, Mr Lorimer, that you've only allocated a very short period of time to me today. If I may say so, it's unfair of you to waste so much of it asking me questions when you ought to be letting me ask mine.'

'Just one more,' John said. 'Why me?'

'I have a series of interviews in mind – to make up a kind of portfolio which I could present to an editor. What I'm looking for in each is someone whose ordinary day-to-day work will result in some kind of social revolution.'

'And you think that churning out pre-fabricated housing units comes into that category?'

'Yes, I do. Bernard told me about your company to start with, and I've read everything I can find. Isn't it true to say, Mr Lorimer, that you've done as much as anyone since the war to change people's expectations of comfort in council housing? And if today's luxuries are tomorrow's necessities, you're redefining standards of living. It's the consequence of that in terms of happiness, health, strikes, political re-alignments that I'd like to talk about.'

John hesitated. He had granted the interview to assuage his own curiosity, not Paula's. But it seemed that she had taken the trouble to research her subject and that she did not propose to ask the kind of personal questions which he would have refused to answer. She was intelligent, and she had put her finger straight on to the aspect of his work which gave John most pleasure. Almost to his own surprise, he gave a quick nod and allowed her to take control.

As a man who admired efficiency he noted that she had structured her questions with sufficient precision to bring them to an end at exactly the moment when his secretary, by arrangement, rang through to interrupt. It was he and not Paula who extended the visit.

'What set you off on this subject?' he asked.

'Do you know what Bernard's doing now?'

John shook his head. If Paula thought that he knew or cared about the other members of the Lorimer family, someone had misinformed her. He listened to her brief summary of his cousin's work.

'So if Bernard has his way, women will have the sole power to decide whether or not a child shall be born,' he checked. 'And men may not even know when the choice is made. I do see that that will constitute a social revolution.'

'Bernard sees it as being important in overpopulated countries. He thinks that if poor women are offered something that's cheap, easy to take, hygienic and fool-proof, they'll simply stop having babies.'

'Your phrasing suggests that you have a different viewpoint.'

'I see it more as a moral revolution,' said Paula. 'Is sin sinful if it has no consequences? For an unmarried female like me, fear of pregnancy is the most powerful sanction with which I can be threatened. Take that fear away, and what do I have? Fun!'

They laughed together. John was impressed by the sophisticated ease with which she talked to him. Most twenty-one-year-olds were either too cocky or too earnest to be interesting.

'So that gave me the idea,' she continued. 'But then Bernard wouldn't let me write up that subject in case it built up people's hopes too early. I guess he gave me your name as a sort of compensation.'

'What's your relationship with Bernard?' John had submitted himself to the interview mainly so that he could ask this question casually.

'Relationship?' She seemed puzzled.

'You obviously know him well.'

'He visits his grandmother at Blaize and in vacation I'm there as well. That's all.' She spoke with a firmness intended to deny any suggestion of romantic entanglement. But it was not that possibility which John's impertinent question had been designed to explore. He knew – as Paula herself clearly did not – that, her black skin notwithstanding, Paula was a cousin of Bernard Lorimer; and, indeed, of John himself.

They were all great-grandchildren of John Junius Lorimer, the Bristol banker whose elder son had inherited a shipping company and whose younger son became a missionary in Jamaica. It was interesting that no one had told Paula the story of that missionary's escapades before his marriage. Duke Mattison, whose birth was the result of one of Ralph Lorimer's liaisons, had inherited his father's property although not his name and might have been expected to tell Paula whose granddaughter she was. And even though Bernard Lorimer might not know the truth of the situation, his grandmother certainly did: she must have deliberately kept it from the person most concerned. A more mischievous man might have been tempted to stir up trouble by dropping at least a hint. But John's lack of family feeling was such that he did not volunteer the information even when Paula gave him a lead.

'You asked me earlier on why I chose to interview you, Mr Lorimer. I'd like to ask why you let me.'

The true answer was that they had in common the state of being Lorimers by blood yet both outsiders in the family. Instead of that he said, 'I remembered the name of Duke Mattison from my time in Bristol. Your father, perhaps. He used the Lorimer Line to ship sugar and bananas from his plantation.'

'He's just about to give that up,' Paula told him. 'He

doesn't see me taking over a plantation. He's going to sell off the land and convert Bristow Great House into a hotel. But what has that to do . . .'

'Only that from the combination of your name and the Lorimer contact I guessed you were Jamaican. It can't be easy to break into English society from outside. I'm an outsider myself. I've had to make my own way. I thought you deserved encouragement.'

'I appreciate that.' Paula shook hands. 'When I pick up my first pay cheque as a journalist, I shall remember that you helped me on my way. Thank you.'

John found himself smiling as she turned to leave, her slim, poised body firm with energy and confidence. Both physically and mentally she attracted him. Had she been a few years older he would not have allowed her to walk out of his life again after such a short encounter. But although he never formulated his views in words, even to himself, his romantic relationships were regulated by a curiously precise set of rules. Because he did not trust women to be honest, he would not allow them to think of him as reliable. All his affairs were with women who were confident enough in their own careers or marriages to enjoy his attentions for a little while and then to remain as friends when they returned to their own lives. Although Paula gave an impression of maturity, a young woman of twenty-one who was only just preparing to make her way in the world must be regarded as vulnerable. It was because he liked her that he must not risk hurting her.

So probably he would never see her again – but he suspected that it would not be long before he saw her name in print. The day might come when he would boast with amusement that Paula Mattison, the journalist, was his cousin. In the meantime, she presumably had one more hurdle to clear. 'Good luck with your Finals,' he said.

Paula and Angela

College Friends 1954–56

1

The last examination paper had been handed in, the last trunk packed. Waiting for midnight, Paula stretched herself out on the floor of Angela's room, an empty champagne glass balanced on her forehead. Just for a few hours she could enjoy the feeling of being in limbo. This was her final night at Oxford, affording her the opportunity to relax after the strain of the past weeks and to take a deep breath before submitting to the different stresses of the real world.

Her four closest friends sprawled around her amongst the debris of a party. Angela had held open house for the whole third year of Dame Eleanor's College to celebrate the end of Finals, but only this more intimate group had been asked to stay on after the others left. They would be leaving Oxford early the next morning. If Angela was to celebrate her twenty-first birthday in their company, it must be as soon as the day began.

For the moment, resting after the chatter of the over-crowded earlier party, they remained companionably silent. The silence was regretful, even sentimental. They all recognized that their closeness during the past three years would not survive their dispersal unaltered. Even in the last few weeks they had noticed changes in each other as they revised for examinations. Only Helen, the classicist, who still had a fourth year of study ahead, remained as calm and well-ordered as ever. Angela, naturally plump, had fed her anxiety with non-stop nibbling and was now resignedly considering what kind of shock diet would be most effective in removing her excess weight. Ingrid, on the other hand, working long into every night, had become too thin. Her long dark hair, strained severely off her face, emphasized her paleness. Lindsay, the fourth of Paula's special college friends, offered yet another contrast. She was a natural athlete, small but strong and well-coordinated, who had been persuaded to finish her education before embarking on the career as a tennis player that was her heart's real desire. The need to spend a whole summer at her books when she should have been keeping fit and practising her shots had made her nervy and irritable, convinced that she was now too old ever to be any good at the game. Even Paula herself had briefly succumbed to the tension building up all round her at the beginning of term, but then had deliberately shrugged it off. Agility of mind was more important to her than academic qualifications – that, and the friendships she had made.

Across the quiet Oxford air came the sound of the first midnight chimes. Paula stretched a hand under the bed.

'I thought we were one short,' said Angela, looking at the bottle of champagne which emerged. 'Couldn't you trust me to take precautions?' She produced another bottle from the back of the wardrobe and opened it, filling each glass generously.

'Angela! Many happies!' Their eyes smiled with friendship as they toasted their hostess.

'We should fortify this,' said Lindsay. 'Champagne cocktail.' She felt in her handbag. 'My parents gave me this bottle. Medicinal brandy, they kept calling it. They're both teetotallers. I think they honestly believe that medicinal brandy isn't brandy.'

'Do you have a jug?' asked Paula. 'That sherry I

brought could go in as well. To add a touch of *je ne sais quoi.*'

'And this.' Ingrid had half a bottle of Bols to contribute.

Angela sipped the result doubtfully. 'Is this wise? I feel halfway drunk already.'

'Everyone should get sloshed once,' pontificated Paula, perhaps not wholly sober herself. 'How else do you learn where to stop? You have to count to a hundred before you know it comes after ninety-nine. And tonight's the perfect occasion, right? A good reason to celebrate and nothing to do which could be spoiled by intoxication. We can all put each other to bed. To us!'

They drank together. Ingrid looked quizzically at her glass, while Lindsay spluttered. 'If anyone gets drunk on this it will be a triumph of determination,' she said. 'It's the Bols that's filthy. Is there anything that would kill it?'

Angela groped again inside her wardrobe and produced cherry brandy. The improvised punch turned to a rich coca-cola colour.

'My last Oxford midnight!' said Lindsay sentimentally. 'All my best work for the past three years has been done in the small hours. My brain doesn't function before midnight. Yet my parents go to bed every night at half past ten. All those wasted hours!'

'It's a form of boredom with life,' Paula suggested. 'We may be as bad by the time we're forty.' She didn't believe that for a moment.

'That was a game I was going to play while the others were here,' said Angela. 'But then I decided not to. The cherry brandy improves this, I think. It's quite good.'

'What game?' Lindsay refilled Angela's glass.

'The "when-I'm-forty" game. I was going to ask everyone to write on a bit of paper what sort of life they expected to be leading on their fortieth birthday. Then we'd have shuffled up the papers and read them out and tried to guess who wrote each one.'

'What made you change your mind?' asked Ingrid.

'It might have been depressing. To read "Novelist with flat in London and country cottage" and know that it was Isabel and that in fact she'll be teaching history in a grammar school and perhaps writing the odd review of other people's books for her local paper.'

'What would you have put, Angela?' asked Lindsay.

'I'd have been all right. I'm not ambitious. On my fortieth birthday I shall have a house in the country, two horses, two dogs, two cats and five children.'

'And a husband, I trust,' suggested Ingrid.

'And a husband. What about you?'

'I shall be a don. Professor of Modern Languages at one of the new universities they keep talking about.'

'Not Oxford?'

'Who wants to be a woman at Oxford! No, somewhere where they've heard of the twentieth century.'

'I shall be an ex-Wimbledon champion,' said Lindsay. 'A depressing thought. Sad if it's true and even sadder if it isn't. Paula?'

'I shall be a prime minister.'

'You seriously want to go into politics?' Lindsay was startled.

'No, not seriously. When I was a kid – right up to the time I came here – I planned to go back and stir things up in Jamaica as soon as I had my degree. But I've developed a taste for England, and England isn't ready for a prime minister like me just yet. Black is bad enough, but female! So I shall be a political commentator instead, telling the government where it's going wrong. You're very quiet, Helen.'

'It's difficult to get excited about a career with another year to go here still. I'm interested, though, that none of you has mentioned marriage – except Angela who had to be pushed into it for the sake of the five children.'

'Marriage isn't a career,' Ingrid pointed out.

'I don't see why not. If you marry someone who's doing a worthwhile job and devote yourself to making him happy, with his domestic life running smoothly . . . I mean to say, what actual use is Latin and Greek going to be to me or to society? I can teach it, or I can go into the Civil Service and forget it. That's about all. I might be more useful supporting someone whose work is more valuable.' Her fair complexion flushed as she caught Paula's eye.

Paula leaned over to refill her glass. 'To Bernard!' she said. She had not failed to notice the starry-eyed state in which her friend had returned from the Christmas ski-ing holiday. Helen's blush deepened, but the others had not noticed the exchange.

'We seem to have played the "when-I'm-forty" game after all,' Angela was saying. 'So we must check it out. On my fortieth birthday you will all be expected to come to dinner and report progress. No further invitation will be issued. You know the date, and it's up to you to find out the address.'

'Only if you promise to keep the five children out of the way,' said Ingrid. 'I don't approve of all this procreation. You've been given an education which is only offered to the top half per cent of the female population. Don't you feel any obligation to use it?'

'I shall use it to improve the minds of the five children,' Angela claimed. 'If everyone did that, the laws of geometric progression would produce a nation of geniuses in a couple of centuries. You'd have more right to carp if I only wanted one child. Helen agrees, don't you, Helen?'

Helen's sleepy smile suggested that her view of the

future was indeed not far removed from Angela's; but Ingrid pressed sternly on.

'But you ought to have some kind of career, Angela. I know you don't need to – ' Angela's father was one of the biggest landowners in England – 'but you *ought* to.'

'You seem to forget that I'm the only person in this room who has the firm offer of a job.' With a dignified display of indignation, Angela poured more champagne into the heady mixture and passed the jug round. 'Three cheers for the British Council! I hope the Egyptians will appreciate my profound knowledge of Beowulf and the poet Keats. I feel a fraud. I'm really going to Egypt because I have a romantic yearning to sit on the banks of the Nile and daydream.' She sighed happily. The concoction they were drinking was beginning to show its effect on her, but she poured herself another refill without appearing to notice. 'My best memory of these three years will be the river. Sitting under a willow tree early on a Sunday morning, watching the mist rise from the water and hearing the sound of church bells across the meadow. All those church bells. That's Oxford!'

'Fiddlesticks!' Paula had heard the exclamation on Lady Glanville's lips within an hour of her first arrival at Blaize and had delighted in using it ever since. 'Oxford is people. A thousand men and women will leave Oxford today. Young, inexperienced, useless. But in thirty years' time they'll be running England. I shall know a quarter of them, and for the rest it will be enough to say, "But we must have been up together!"' Paula was filled with a sudden energy. 'Wake up, you-all,' she exclaimed. 'There's no more to drink and we need fresh air. We're going to take a walk.'

'We can't go out of college now! It's against the rules.' No amount of alcohol could wholly subdue Helen's law-abiding nature.

'What use is a rule without sanctions?' Through a haze of champagne Paula remembered that she had made the same remark quite recently in another context. To John Lorimer, was it? Or Bernard? She shook her head to clear it. 'Even if we're caught, we can't be sent down, because we're down already. We've taken our exams. Nothing can prevent the results coming through. And there's nothing in the law of the land to prevent five citizens from taking a peaceful stroll in the middle of the night.'

'I'm due to come back here next year,' Helen reminded her. 'Anyway, someone must clear up all this mess, and it oughtn't to be the birthday girl. You go ahead. I'll see you all at breakfast.'

Paula hesitated for a moment. From now on the paths of the little group were bound to diverge, but this was an abrupt start to the process. She recognized, though, that she could not change Helen's submissive and tidy temperament – and the other three, although pretending to grumble, were stirring themselves into movement.

Five minutes later, their party sandals exchanged for sensible footwear, Ingrid, Lindsay and Angela assembled in Paula's ground-floor room. With a silence which spoke of careful maintenance for the purpose, the bottom window was slid upwards. Scented air from the June garden outside floated headily in.

'There we are,' said Paula. 'The last apron string untied. Who's going to take the first step into freedom, maturity and adult life?'

Angela happened to be nearest. Shivering a little in the night air, she climbed out of Paula's window.

2

For Angela's sake, because it was her birthday, they walked by the river. Paula could feel the cold air going to her head. In the stuffiness of the party room she had been intoxicated only with the champagne; but now her mind tingled with the excitement of being alive and young and walking in the darkness.

Angela, rolling slightly, took her arm. Paula reflected that she was very fond of Angela, who was both privileged and unsophisticated. Three years earlier, coming from a stately home run by indulgent parents and a small army of servants, Angela had seemed in danger of being overwhelmed by the new experience of living in a community. The first lesson of her university education had been how to make cocoa and how not to expect her cup to be miraculously clean again by morning. It was Paula, the foreigner, who had instructed and protected her then; and who still felt protective now.

The wind rippled the water and shivered through the willows. A bird, alarmed, startled them all by the sudden beating of escaping wings. The silence of the night was too deep to be disturbed by such details; but somewhere in the darkness, nevertheless, there was a sound.

Paula strained her ears to hear. Her eyes as well, as though the two senses were connected – as though she could catch the sound more clearly in the moments when the moon was not obscured by long wisps of cloud. The noise came nearer. Somebody was singing.

Four figures, their arms linked together, appeared round a bend in the towpath. It was not really wide enough to hold them – the outside man had to be jerked back from time to time as his foot slipped down the bank of the river. They swayed rhythmically from side to side as they walked and sang. Paula wondered whether this movement was for musical effect or because they couldn't help it. She had by now recognized not only the Eton Boating Song but also one member of the quartet. He was tall and dark-haired, his skin tanned by a summer spent on the cricket field rather than in the library. The cravat tucked into his open-necked shirt and the cummerbund round his slim waist gave him a Byronic handsomeness. Paula did her best to control the bumping of her heart at the unexpected encounter. 'Laker!' she exclaimed.

'Paula! Well met by moonlight.' He raised her hand ceremoniously to his lips. 'We missed you tonight. Do introduce me to your friends.'

'Only as long as my friends don't take an introduction as a guarantee of respectability. Ladies, meet James Laker-Smith, Robin Woodford, Clark Addison. And . . . ?'

'Simon Abbot.'

'And Simon Abbot. Angela, Lindsay, Ingrid.'

Laker shook hands with each of them. The other men bowed unsteadily from the waist.

'How do you manage it, Paula?' asked Angela. 'Is there anyone in Oxford you don't know?'

'Well, Simon Abbot for one.'

'I have a more pertinent question,' said Clark. 'How does it happen that we have known Paula for almost three years without ever being allowed to discover that she has such gorgeous friends?' He stared appreciatively at Lindsay's trim figure as he spoke.

'Self-preservation,' said Paula lightly. 'Who would give me a second look in such company?' She could tell that the four men were in a mood to prolong the accidental meeting, but decided to frustrate them. Laker always held his liquor well but Clark, who now was staring with interest at Angela's see-through blouse, was unmistakably tipsy. 'We ought to be getting back to college,' she added.

As they turned to cross the river, Laker fell into step beside Paula and took her arm, holding her close to his side. They loitered, allowing the others to move ahead, and came to a standstill in the middle of the bridge.

Laker kissed her and Paula, who had been waiting for this to happen from the first moment of the unexpected encounter, was happy. Afterwards they turned to lean over the parapet, still close together. Neither of them spoke. They had been friends since the day when Paula was deputed by the university magazine to write a profile of Laker as an *Isis* Idol – but she knew that beneath this friendship, and only this one, lay a river of passion into which she would one day throw herself. The love which they felt for each other surged through their bodies, although neither of them had ever said 'I love you.'

The sound of Angela laughing, too loudly, distracted Paula. She looked round and in the bright moonlight saw the little group moving away from the river bank, taking the shortest route back to Dame Eleanor's. Ingrid and Simon were ahead, talking earnestly. The others were bunched together. Clark was pawing at Angela, and Paula was disturbed to see that her friend made no attempt to evade a touch which normally she would have found distasteful.

The clarity of mind with which Paula had started the night walk seemed abruptly to have disappeared and her earlier muzziness had returned. But Angela must be protected. 'Laker. Catch them up, will you? Look after Angela. She's suffering from her twenty-first birthday.'

'What am I supposed to do? Give her a birthday present? I'm not interested in Angela. Only in you.'

'You'll see me again.'

'Love me, love my friend, is that it?'

'That's it.'

'No,' he said. 'I don't think so.'

'But I say so.' She turned him round and gave him a little push. Like a clockwork toy wound into action he staggered slightly and then rolled on his way without further protest. Hustling Clark to one side, he put his own arm round Angela's waist to steady her. He turned his head to make sure that Paula was watching. Then the group moved on.

Paula lingered on the bridge, as happy now to be alone as a few minutes earlier she had been happy in Laker's kiss. She sighed, reluctant to move on from the moment, but then began to stroll towards the college. Not, naturally, to the front entrance. Angela, left to herself, might well have been innocent enough to make a direct approach to the unlocked window, but Laker had escorted Paula home after hours often enough to know the way through the tradesman's entrance of the property next door. If he was taking care of Angela, she would be all right.

Paula had not walked far when the rest of the party appeared round a corner, coming away from the college again.

'We can't get in,' said Angela. She was giggling. 'The place is under police guard. They won't let us past.'

'What are you talking about?' asked Paula.

'There's been a prowler round your college,' said Clark. He had managed to get Angela back into his grasp again, Paula noticed. 'A couple of girls had hysterics when a bathroom window suddenly opened, and the bursar sent for the police. There are six of them on patrol, and they won't let anyone in.'

'Fiddlesticks! One of them will be Bill. He knows me. He'll turn a blind eye.'

'Not tonight,' said Ingrid. 'Clark asked one of them. He said they'd naturally take no notice of anyone who rang for admittance at the front door, but they couldn't allow anything else.'

Paula shook her head from side to side in an attempt to clear it. She was tired and confused, but this couldn't be right. 'Did you hear that for yourself?' she demanded.

'No. Simon thought we should stay out of sight.'

'Get quit of the men and leave this to me,' said Paula. 'We'll be back in our rooms within ten minutes. Anyhow, as I said before, there's nothing the college can do to punish us now.' Even as she spoke, she realized that Ingrid – who hoped to be awarded a research fellowship at Dame Eleanor's next year – might be reluctant to earn a black mark.

'I've got my own flat,' said Simon. Alone amongst the men, he appeared to be sober. 'You'd all be welcome. We'll make coffee. You can go back after breakfast and no one will be any the wiser.'

There was a general murmur of approval; six of the group moved off together. Only Laker stayed behind with Paula.

'We don't have to go with them,' he suggested. 'Come on.'

'I'm not going anywhere.'

'Don't be so stuffy. It's our last night here. A special occasion. You can't kiss me like that and then turn a cold shoulder. I adore you, Paula. You know I adore you. Come on.'

'Uh-uh.' Paula shook her head.

'Why not? One good reason.'

'You're trading on the fact that I'm pissed,' said Paula. 'But that's as clear to me as it is to you. The only sober thought in my head is the one which tells me: when intoxicated, always say no.' She hesitated briefly, wondering whether she dare kiss him again. But no, it would be too dangerous. Instead she blew him a kiss from a safe distance. 'I adore you too,' she said. 'See you!' Turning away, she walked briskly towards Dame Eleanor's.

One of the policemen outside gave her a smile of recognition. 'Bit of an argy-bargy tonight,' he said. 'I'd go carefully if I were you. You may find your wardresses on the prowl.'

'Thanks.' Paula frowned to herself. But she had known all along that Clark must have been exaggerating. She waited until Bill obligingly began a stately patrol and then slipped quickly along to the tradesmen's door, through the gap in the hedge and across the college grounds. Five minutes later she was in her own room. Another five minutes and she was asleep.

She was awakened by the sound of her window closing. 'Sorry,' said Ingrid. 'I tried to be quiet.'

'It's okay.' Paula shook her head to clear it and groaned at the consequences. 'Do you have the time?'

'Half past six.'

Paula groaned again. Only now did she realize that she had not undressed before falling asleep; she was both mentally and physically crumpled. 'How do you get to look so fresh?'

'Five cups of black coffee,' said Ingrid precisely. She sat down on the edge of the bed. 'I like your friend Simon.'

'Not my friend,' Paula reminded her. 'Never seen him before in my life. Laker's friend, I suppose. So what's he like?'

'He has a *very* good mind. A double First. Now he's studying for his D. Phil. He'll be in Oxford next year as well, so if I get a fellowship . . .' Ingrid paused happily.

'We discussed Nietzsche. He has interesting theories. But I think he's based one of his ideas on a mistranslation. I've promised to send him a better version of the passage.'

'Frivolling away the night with small-talk!' teased Paula. 'The others must have been fascinated.' She sat up in bed, suddenly awake. 'Ingrid. Where's Angela?'

'No idea.'

'But wasn't she with you?'

'No. Simon invited everyone in. But Clark suggested something else and the others seemed to drift away.'

'You should have stayed together. Angela – '

'Is twenty-one today. You can't cluck over her for ever, Paula.'

'Sure, I know. But I don't trust Clark.'

'I'd agree with that. But Lindsay was with her. She's probably fast asleep in bed.'

'She's too clumsy to get in without waking me.'

'Then she'll be waiting till after breakfast, as Simon suggested. Stop worrying. And tell me about your Laker. The name seemed familiar. James Laker-Smith, did you say?'

Paula laughed. 'These people who spend all their time holed up in libraries! You must be the only member of the university who doesn't know Laker. He's been President of the Union. And a cricket blue.'

'I thought he seemed charming.'

'That too. A charmer. Well, I must get myself organized. I hope you get your First.' Ingrid would need a good degree if she was to pursue an academic career.

'Thanks. And you.'

Paula shrugged her shoulders. She didn't expect to get a First and she didn't much care. It wasn't worth bothering about now. The papers were already written; the results were determined although not yet known. She had a quick shower before completing her packing. Her trunk was to be stored at Blaize while she first of all visited her father in Jamaica and then found somewhere to live in London. Once again Lady Glanville had promised to send a car to collect her and her accumulation of possessions on condition, this time, that she could undertake to be ready very early in the day. Lady Glanville was so meticulously punctual that the car would not only arrive but would leave at precisely the time arranged, whether she was in it or not. Five minutes before she was due to depart, she knocked on the door of Angela's room.

There was no one there. Helen had done a magnificent job of tidying away all the party debris. She had smoothed the bed cover, and no one had disturbed it since. Well, it was still early, and it showed good sense on Angela's part to wait until the flurry of dispersal began. It didn't matter. They would meet again when Paula returned from Jamaica. She had not been exaggerating when, on the previous evening, she defined the value of her time at university in terms of the people she had met there. Oxford had given her a dozen or more close friendships, and she did not intend to let them go.

3

Bernard Lorimer and Helen Langton were married in the summer of 1956. They had announced their engagement almost a year earlier. But Helen, determined to perform her new role perfectly, decided to complement her Classics degree with a three-months brides' course at a domestic science college. For some weeks after that she was ill, and a perfectly healthy appendix was removed before the trouble cleared up as mysteriously as it had begun. There was yet more delay while she waited until her parents could travel from Africa to be present; but now, in the last week of June, she had become Lady Lorimer at last. Paula, naturally, headed the guest list of both bride and groom.

Lacking a home in England, Helen had chosen to marry in Oxford, so it was in the familiar garden of Dame Eleanor's College that her friends assembled after the service. All her friends except one: Angela was not there.

'You invited her, of course,' said Paula accusingly.

'Well, of course,' agreed Helen.

Bernard, with his arm round Helen's waist, looked puzzled. 'Have I met Angela?' he asked his new wife.

'Not yet. Today should have been the day.'

'Why couldn't she come?' asked Paula. 'Has she gone abroad again?'

'The letter had a Kent postmark.' Helen was clearly hurt by Angela's absence. 'She was very sorry, but terribly tied up. She sent an expensive present, but I'd rather have had her company.'

'At least you had a letter.' Paula too had been hurt by the withdrawal of her friend. 'She's cut off communication with me. When she first went to Egypt she wrote once a week. Then there was the crash, and the letters stopped. Never to start again.'

'What crash was that?' Simon came up to join them with Ingrid, visibly pregnant, holding his hand.

'Surely I told you,' Ingrid said. 'Or perhaps – yes, of course, it was before we were married – in the Christmas vacation after Angela went down from Oxford. She had a job in Egypt and her parents flew out there for Christmas. When they flew back a fortnight later, there was a bomb on the plane.'

'Good heavens, yes!' exclaimed Simon. 'I remember that. All the passengers were killed. But I didn't associate them with anyone I knew.'

'Angela's father was a duke,' Ingrid told him. 'I suppose we never introduced you properly. She's Lady Angela really. Have you seen her at all since then, Paula?'

'Once. We talked on the phone when she flew back for the memorial service, but we didn't meet then. She said she was having to spend all her time with lawyers and accountants, but I guess the real reason was that she was too upset to socialize. It must have been a terrible shock.'

'If she was an only child, the business about seeing lawyers would have been true as well,' suggested Bernard. He had himself been orphaned at an even earlier age than Angela. 'Did she inherit everything?'

'A castle in Scotland went with the title, to an uncle,' said Paula. 'But that still leaves her with Wetherly Hall and all the land round it. Yes, she must have had her hands full. She went back to Egypt to finish her contract; by the time she returned to England the estate duty bill was in. We met for lunch – that would be about this time last year – and she was almost in tears about it. Her father was only forty-five. He hadn't made provision for death duties. She looked to me like a girl who was heading for a nervous breakdown – pasty and fidgety.' She had eaten five bread rolls during that lunch, Paula remembered, crumbling each without pause into pieces and seeming not to notice as they found their way into her mouth.

'And that's the last time you've seen her?'

'Yes. I was in New York for nine months, remember. Since I've been back, I've tried to propose myself for a weekend at Wetherly. She can't be short of room – and however destitute she may be by ducal standards, there must be the odd servant around. But she's always found an excuse.'

Lindsay had joined the group while Paula was speaking. 'Well, she mustn't do it again. Paula, I'm making you responsible for getting her to *my* wedding. And I have two Wimbledon seats for you. Bring Angela. Tell her it's Monday or nothing if she wants to see me play. I'm not likely to survive the first round.'

'Right.' Paula did not mention the Press pass already in her wallet. With two extra tickets she could invite both Angela and Laker. 'I'll go tomorrow, uninvited and unannounced, to line her up for Monday and bully her about your wedding. Just remind me of the date.'

'October the third,' said Laker behind her. 'Clark's booked me to be best man. Complaining bitterly that he has to wait until the tennis season's over. It's odd, isn't it?'

'What's odd?'

'That evening two years ago when we all met on the towpath. Out of the eight of us, you and I were the only couple who knew each other already, but the encounter has had – well, consequences. Weddingwise.'

Paula considered the score. Simon and Ingrid were already married and Clark and Lindsay would soon follow their example. But Robin Woodford had already been engaged to a Scots girl at the time of the walk along the river; and Angela was still, presumably, unattached. 'I wouldn't call four out of eight statistically significant,' she said.

'As the result of a first accidental meeting?' Laker slipped a hand under her elbow and tugged her gently away from her group of friends and towards the marquee. 'We need some more champagne,' he said in excuse, and waited until they were out of earshot before adding, 'and the statistics may not be final. I have a statement to make. Which is that you're the most stunningly beautiful woman in this whole assembly. And then I have a question to ask. Benedict Townsend.'

'That's not a question.'

'I'll try again. Benedict Townsend?' His voice slid interrogatively upwards.

'What about Benedict Townsend?'

'That's what I'm asking you. Coupled with the secondary question of why you're always out these days when I try to phone you. Don't tell me that he's just a useful contact.'

'He's an editor,' Paula pointed out. 'I have to cultivate editors. Just as you, I'm sure, cultivate prospective prime ministers.'

'But prospective prime ministers are never female.'

'You're not jealous of Ben!'

'Of course I'm jealous of Ben.'

'He's forty-two,' said Paula.

'An age which young females seem to find peculiarly attractive.'

'And he's married.'

'I know he's married. Does *he* know he's married?'

'Are you taking over the role of father-figure, Laker?'

'Far from it. Ah, here's the champagne.' He paused while their glasses were refilled. 'It's true – I'm conscious that the first flush of youth is fading. All my friends are getting married. Simon last summer, Robin in spring and Clark at any moment. One becomes aware of moving from one stage of life into another. There's a time to flirt and a time to make love. Not to mention a time to marry.'

Paula stared at the bubbles bouncing their way to the top of her glass. When she lifted her head, her eyes rested first on Bernard as he moved round the marquee, holding his bride by the hand. Helen did not need the dignity of her wedding gown to give her elegance, but not even a well-cut morning suit could make Bernard look smart. As soon as the service was over he had run his fingers through his sleeked-down hair, restoring his red curls to their natural exuberance. He lacked the aloofness which was perhaps an essential element of being a well-dressed man. Instead, his expression was one of adoration as he gazed at Helen, squeezing her hand. He was so much in love, so delighted to be married, that his happiness communicated itself to his friends. Paula turned her head to look at Laker. For once he wasn't smiling.

'Weddings are dangerous occasions for the unmarried,' she said lightly. 'Matrimony is contagious.'

'I've run out of small-talk,' Laker told her. 'I just want you to say first of all that Benedict Townsend means nothing to you. After that, that you'll marry me.'

'Benedict Townsend means nothing to me,' said Paula promptly. It wasn't true, so the promptitude was necessary to lend conviction to her words. But there was a sense in which she was speaking the truth. Without admitting it, she had been waiting for Laker. He wasn't a man who could be chased. Even to show him that she was waiting might have wrecked the relationship – for this was the first time he had ever mentioned marriage. But Paula had known almost from their first meeting that he was the man with whom she wanted to spend her life. It would be crazy to let him drift away because of something as temporary as her affair with Ben.

That didn't necessarily mean that she would be wise to jump at his proposal. In twenty-four hours, away from the champagne, Laker might regret his impulse.

'Don't tell me!' she exclaimed with mischief dancing in her eyes. 'You're going to be interviewed for a constituency with a safe majority.' She knew it was Laker's ambition to enter Parliament. 'You need a steady family image. The promise that you'll acquire a house in the area and a wife to open ward bazaars.' The thought of the shock which a selection committee would feel at the sight of this particular prospective wife made her laugh aloud with such merriment that other wedding guests, smiling, turned to look at her.

'Come with me,' said Laker, taking her by the hand. But their movement towards the door of the marquee was checked by someone who stepped forward to intercept them. 'Good afternoon, Miss Mattison,' said John Lorimer.

4

John knew that he had been invited to Bernard's wedding, as to every Lorimer wedding, christening and funeral, because he was on the family list. He also knew that his non-acceptance would have been taken for granted – he had made clear enough in the past his reluctance to mix with the relations he hardly knew. And a wedding reception was the most tedious form of party, with its inescapable routine of speeches, photographs and obscure fertility rituals. The need to wear fancy dress was another reason for staying away. John's lack of inches made him look ridiculous in morning dress – but although he had cut himself off from the social class into which his father had been born, he was not a man who deliberately chose to shock by refusing to wear the appropriate uniform for any occasion.

All these excuses would have given him good enough cause to answer the invitation with a polite regret. He had accepted it for one reason only: he was curious to see Paula again.

He had followed her career with interest during the past two years. The series of interviews which followed her visit to himself had impressed him by its originality, and she had written a well-argued article of her own at the end about the social changes revealed by the interviews. Later, her weekly columns from the United States had proved that besides being intelligent, she had a sense of humour. Until he read them, it had not occurred to John how invariably in the past such commentators had been both white and male. Paula's experiences were startling as well as funny. Since her return she appeared to be wasting her talents on a gossip column; but perhaps she saw it as a part of her apprenticeship. He would like to ask her about that. He wondered, too, whether by now she had been let into the secret of her place in the Lorimer family.

She recognized him at once and smiled with warmth and pleasure. 'Mr Lorimer. Great to see you again. Meet James Laker-Smith. Laker, this is Mr John Lorimer, who gave me my first break. I only found out afterwards, Mr Lorimer, that you usually mash journalists up and eat them for breakfast. No one understood why I'd been given such a scoop.'

'Couldn't resist your bright eyes,' John said lightly, and was rewarded by seeing them sparkle with pleasure. At that earlier meeting she had seemed sufficiently at ease; but as he chatted to her now he was aware of a relaxed happiness about her body, as though she were stretching herself in the warmth of an invisible sun. The contrast made it clear that she had after all felt some nervousness about that first approach.

It did not take long to recognize the cause of her present contentment. Paula's companion was not the kind of young man to whom John instinctively warmed. The few words with which he acknowledged the introduction were enough to identify him as an Old Etonian. John – who had left his own village school at fourteen – had a prejudice against the breed as great as his dislike of talking to a man almost a foot taller than himself. But he had to admit that Laker was not arrogant but polite and friendly. He was outstandingly good-looking, in the mould made fashionable by Hollywood films. But unlike some handsome men he did not seem to take it for granted that all women would adore him. On the contrary: he could hardly take his eyes off Paula, and anxiety mingled with love in his expression. He was obviously head over heels in love with her – but equally obviously he was not sure whether Paula was in love with him.

To John, watching the two young people together, the situation was easier to read. It was love which had infected Paula with lazy contentment. Her lips were ready to be kissed, her body was waiting to be caressed. She showed no impatience, perhaps savouring the anticipation of the time when she and Laker could disappear together from the marquee, but gradually John realized that he had interrupted a discussion which was important to her.

Tactfully, then, he brought the conversation to an end, smiled at them both and turned away. Had she known that she was his cousin, he could have kissed her goodbye, but it was clear that she was still ignorant of the relationship. He laughed at himself, acknowledging how ridiculous it had been to hope for a tête-à-tête with her. It had only been curiosity, after all, which had brought him here to meet her again. His sudden wish to stroke her smooth black skin, to hold her firm straight body and feel her pulsing energy startled him and must at once be dismissed. How could he expect a young woman like that to feel any interest in someone sixteen years older than herself? She would naturally be surrounded by men of her own age and very soon, no doubt, would marry one of them – James Laker-Smith, by the look of things. And then – John, who many years ago had decided never to marry, found it easy to cure his disappointment with cynicism – before too long she would begin to cheat her husband with lies and infidelities. The day would come when Laker would wish that he had adored Paula a little less, had been content to enjoy her body without putting the whole of his life at her mercy. All women, thought John as he looked for Bernard to congratulate him on the radiant beauty of his bride, were deceivers at heart.

5

'You seem to have made a conquest there,' said Laker.

Paula, watching John Lorimer plunge into the crowd with the purposeful air of a man who does not expect to find any familiar faces, laughed lightly. 'Fiddlesticks!' she said.

'Not fiddlesticks at all. I know a lecherous look when I see one.'

'Idiot. He's ancient.'

'Rather younger than Benedict Townsend,' Laker teased. 'Come on. Let's explore the gardens. I'll get rid of your glass.'

In the moment while Laker was away from her side Paula set herself an exercise; first to think about Ben, and then to stop thinking about him. But Ben was not the only problem.

As an undergraduate, Paula had found the blackness of her skin an advantage: it made her conspicuous. It was the same with her life as a journalist. There was no one in Fleet Street quite like her and so everyone knew who she was. Paula had read about racial prejudice and had written about it, but had never in England suffered its effects.

Laker, though, lived in a different world. He came from a country family and his parliamentary ambitions were important to him. What would his parents think of a Jamaican daugther-in-law? And although the first thought of it had made her laugh, it was a serious point that not every constituency committee would regard a black wife as an asset to a prospective candidate. She didn't care for herself, but she loved Laker so much that she cared passionately about anything that might hurt him.

'Fiddlesticks!' she thought to herself abruptly, tossing away the problem. Her colour was not some terrible secret which had to be divulged, or not, before a wedding day; and Laker was not a child to be protected from himself. If he wanted to marry her, he would ask her with his eyes open. She made no protest when he returned to take her hand and lead her across the lawns.

As though to make it clear that their stroll had nothing to do with any wish to admire the flowers, he came to a halt on the tennis court. 'You were right about weddings,' he said. 'An undesirable atmosphere. Frivolous and sentimental at the same time. I've been mouthing sweet nothings at you for four years. In a setting like that, how could you realize that I suddenly want them to mean something?'

'I wasn't entirely joking, though,' Paula said. 'An MP needs a certain sort of wife, who'll always back him up. As a journalist, I may sometimes disagree with you – and I couldn't promise to keep quiet about my own opinions.'

'It's a choice a man has to make,' Laker said. 'He can marry a woman whose career, whose sole interest, will lie in being his wife. That's what Bernard has done, and I'm sure he and Helen will be very happy. Or he can choose an independent woman – with her own career: a life of her own. I know what I want. It's just a question of making it clear. To other people and to ourselves. That I am not responsible for you and you are not responsible for me.'

'To someone only an hour away from the sound of the wedding march, that doesn't sound precisely a definition of marriage. I promise to love, honour and live my own life.' Paula laughed to herself but then looked up, serious again. 'There's one other thing, Laker. Important. I don't want children.'

'Because they'd be khaki?'

'No. Because I want to lead my own life, not somebody else's. I couldn't bear ever to be introduced to a stranger as little Johnny's mother. I don't want to be frightened because I've brought a child into a world of nuclear bombs. And I couldn't stand to have a child of mine ask why he was born. Where a baby is concerned, the responsibility can't be dodged. I *really* don't want one, Laker. You mustn't hope that I'll change my mind.'

She had made him pause. They had never discussed the subject before and perhaps he had a wish for parenthood as strong as her own refusal to consider it. The suspense was unbearable. Then he laughed.

'Such a parade of reason and argument! There's no reason to it. I love you the way you are. If you were different I might not love you as much. It's kind of you to give me all these warnings, but all I want you to say is "Yes, I love you too".'

'Yes,' said Paula. 'I love you too. I've loved you all the time.'

Laker kissed her; she could feel his body shivering with relief as well as excitement. When at last he relaxed his embrace there was gaiety in his eyes. 'Come on. Let's go back to the wedding. I want to announce our engagement before you have time to change your mind.'

'We ought to wait until Helen and Bernard have left before we say anything,' Paula insisted. 'It wouldn't be right to steal their thunder.' She looked directly into Laker's eyes. 'You needn't ever worry about me changing my mind. I keep promises. I don't let people down. I can't offer you a subservient wife. But I can promise you a loyal one.'

6

Bernard was looking for Paula. It had taken him only a few minutes to change out of his wedding gear, but Helen was certain to need longer. He had already searched the marquee and the gardens around it without success when he saw her walking towards him hand in hand with Laker.

It took Bernard less than a second to recognize what had happened as he looked into Paula's shining eyes. He had seen just the same expression on Helen's face as she joined him at the altar earlier that afternoon.

'I want to thank you, Paula,' he said. 'If it hadn't been for you, I should never have met Helen. You're entitled to feel personally responsible for what's going to be the happiest marriage ever known. Or perhaps you'd prefer me to say, one of the two happiest marriages. If it's a secret you can pretend you didn't hear that remark.'

'Bernard! How did you know?'

'How does a doctor diagnose measles? It's written all over you. Congratulations to you both.' He kissed Paula warmly, hugging her with a brotherly affection. On a day like this he would have liked to show his happiness by embracing all his friends, and Paula was one of the most special. From the moment of her arrival in England she had seemed to be almost one of the family.

'Did you see that John Lorimer is here?' he asked, reminded of an actual member of the family.

'Yes. You sound surprised.'

'As a rule he can't bear to be reminded that he has relations. He won't even include the name of his father in his *Who's Who* entry. I haven't seen him since one of my aunts died eighteen years ago. He was fond of her, so he came to the funeral – but he's got no use for the rest of us.'

'You might have told me that before you sent me off to interview him on the strength of my friendship with you,' Paula protested.

'I thought you got on well with him.'

'Yes,' she admitted. 'I liked him. And he liked me. But I could sense there was something important that he wasn't about to tell me. If I'd had a clue – '

Bernard was no longer listening. He had seen Helen appear in her going-away outfit and his heart was bursting with love for her. Sincerely as he wished Paula well, he suspected that her marriage might prove not to be roses all the way. Laker was too sophisticated, too much a part of a man's world, to be faithful to one woman all his life – and Paula, too, once the honeymoon period was over, might object to being regarded as the private property of any one man. Bernard knew that his own case was quite different. Any impulse to experiment, any need to boast of success could be satisfied in the laboratory. He had promised that afternoon to be faithful to Helen, and as he hurried to join her now he knew that he would have no difficulty in keeping his promise. Their marriage would be for life.

7

On the day after Bernard's wedding Paula drove into Kent to call on Angela. Was her friend's apparent withdrawal from society caused by shame at an inability to cope with her new responsibilities, she wondered. The mere day-to-day maintenance of a stately home might well have proved an overwhelming burden. Paula remembered Wetherly Hall as she had last seen it: Adam rooms kept immaculate by a band of indoor servants, the Georgian fabric of the house maintained by the outside workers on the estate, the formal terraces and lawns and flowerbeds cared for by gardeners and under-gardeners – all surrounded by a huge area of parkland. Might Angela, for the first time in her life, be short of money? Quite apart from problems created by estate duty, it was possible that some of the family income, like the castle in Scotland, was entailed to stay with the title. There must be something to explain why Angela had cut herself off from her friends.

It was easy to picture the house and grounds as they could have become after a year or two of neglect, but as Paula drove up the long approach everything seemed much as she remembered it. Deer still grazed in the park, the lawns near the house were mown to a velvet smoothness, the sun glistened on polished window panes and the grey stone of the house and terraces was free from cracks and weeds.

At the side of the mansion was a large courtyard, surrounded by a long coach house, a stabling block for horses and rooms for outdoor staff. Paula parked her car nearby and paused to glance through the wrought-iron gates. In the middle of the courtyard a small naked girl was jumping in and out of a shallow paddling pool, shrieking with delight. Her fair-skinned plumpness reminded Paula of Angela. This couldn't, surely, be Angela's child? Was this the skeleton which had caused her friend to keep the cupboard door so firmly shut – an unsuitable marriage of some sort; a husband who couldn't be introduced to anyone? Or, worse, no husband at all?

No. The dates wouldn't fit. This little girl must have been born while Angela was still at Oxford. She must be the child of one of the servants. But before Paula had time to turn away, a second child emerged from the coach house, whooping loudly. He was followed by two younger children, staggering but triumphant as they practised their newly-discovered ability to walk. They were the same size, but could not be twins, since only one of them was dark brown.

A young woman wearing a white apron was the last to come through the coach house door. 'Ssh!' she called. 'You'll wake the babies.'

The toddlers stopped yelling and looked guiltily across the courtyard. Following their glance, Paula saw a row of prams lined up in the shade. She counted them with increasing surprise. Nine.

It was time to find out what was going on. She ran up the stone steps of Wetherly Hall and pulled the bell chain. 'Is Lady Angela at home?' she asked the young woman who answered the summons.

'I'm afraid not.'

'Oh. Well, will you give her a message? When she answered the telephone seven minutes ago, the heavy breathing act was by her best friend, Paula. Tell her that now, will you? I'll wait.'

A little doubtfully the girl showed her into the drawing room. This was as beautifully kept as the garden, with no speck of dust to be seen even on the ornate gilded frame of the Chinese Chippendale mirror. Paula had to wait for ten minutes. Then, silently, Angela appeared.

She was enormous. Not just plump; not just fat. She had become huge. Emerging from a cotton dress which bulged like a barrel, her arms were as thick as an old caricature of a washerwoman, whilst her neck seemed to have disappeared. There was no longer any need to wonder why she had hidden herself from her friends. But Paula was careful not to reveal her shock. 'Wonderful to see you,' she said. 'It's been far too long.'

'You just happened to be passing, did you?' Angela managed a smile.

'No. I'm sent as a messenger with a Wimbledon ticket. Lindsay expected to give it you at Helen's wedding. You've got a lot of explaining to do in that direction, Angela. Unless you'd prefer me to do it for you and tell all the gang that you appear to have given birth to thirteen children since you went down. What exactly is going on here?'

She was right to be brisk. Angela, who had been waiting to look ashamed, smiled with pleasure at the question. 'I've turned the stable block into a mother-and-baby home,' she said.

'Why? How? Tell me all about it.'

'It was an unexpected consequence of the bomb, of my parents' death.' They sat down, smiling at each other. 'I got a bit run down. Not straight away. It took a little while to hit me. I spent a couple of months in hospital. The nurses were wonderful. Cheering me became a kind of campaign; and they were all so bright and smiling that it worked in the end. Then one night the most cheerful of them sat down on my bed and burst into tears. She was pregnant. And unmarried. The idea didn't come all at once. To start with, we just held hands while she wept on my shoulder. But then – it was like a jigsaw, with each new piece fitting perfectly into place. She wanted to keep the baby and go on working, but where could she live and what sort of job could she get? Well, I remembered that our local hospital had just closed its geriatric ward for lack of staff.'

'So you offered her a job?'

'It wasn't mine to offer. I asked if she'd be interested. There was a problem, though. I mean, I wanted to help, but not to the extent of looking after her baby! I asked if she knew anyone else in the same boat. So that one could go out to work and pay the other to look after both babies. Believe it or not, she came back the next day with four names. All from the same hospital!'

'I believe it,' said Paula.

'Well, it staggered me. All those antiseptic young women. You'd think they'd know! Anyway. Two of them had already had their babies and left the hospital. The others were in the club. They got so excited when they heard about this. It's been more than just making the best of a bad job. They've got work to do, and companionship, and a bit of money, and somewhere to live – they've got their independence back. And getting it all fixed did something for me as well. I seemed to be suffering mainly from a kind of fear of the future. I couldn't get myself to face the rest of my life. But as soon as there were detailed plans to be made – well, I just got out of bed and came home.'

'So how many nurses are there here?'

'The hospital had to be sure of five regulars before it would re-open the ward. So we needed ten mothers to form an economic unit. Two to look after the babies all day. Three more to do domestic work – two of them do it for the mothers and one does it for me, as a sort of rent contribution. Five to bring home the money. They can change around. All the wages and social security benefits go into a pool which pays their expenses – food and heat, that sort of thing – and builds up a fund for equipment for the babies. They share what's left.'

'One girl's labour is a cheap rent for ten women and ten children.'

'They help to keep the place warm,' Angela pointed out. 'I had a lecture from the surveyor when I took over, about what happens when property is left cold and damp. And I like to hear people chattering and laughing. I couldn't live here on my own, Paula. When I inherited, everybody – lawyers, the estate manager, the trustees, the accountant, everyone – said that the only sensible thing would be to move into a flat and let Wetherly to some rich Americans in the hope that they'd install central heating and an adequate number of bathrooms while they were here. But I'm fond of Wetherly. I wanted to stay. This may not make a profit, but it doesn't cost anything – and it's made me very popular locally.'

'Keeping the hospital going, you mean?'

'More than that. We've started another unit now, of new babies. With the extra workers we run a nursery group which is open to outsiders. Also, we offer a home nursing service. That's easy for the girls to manage, with a built-in baby-sitting system. This must be one of the best-nursed areas in England.'

'Are all your girls nurses?' Paula enquired.

'Not all, no. There are two physiotherapists, a radiologist, a dietician, and two orderlies with no medical training. But they've all worked in hospitals – that's the network which leads them here. It means that they're used to community life and have certain routines of hygiene in common.' Angela glanced at her friend in sudden doubt. 'Paula. We are just chatting, aren't we?'

'What an extraordinary question. Chatting as opposed to what?'

'Well, it just occurred to me.' Angela looked embarrassed. 'I've seen your column. And you're asking a lot of questions.'

'Because I'm interested.'

'That's fine, then. I – I just wanted to be sure that you were here as a friend and not as a journalist.'

'As a journalist I could give you publicity. It might bring in extra help.'

'We don't need help,' said Angela, not embarrassed now but firm. 'We're getting along splendidly. You know how any publicity would finish up. "Duke's daughter runs doss-house for delinquent mums".'

'I'd give you a better headline than that,' laughed Paula. 'What would you do if I sneaked on you?'

'I should never speak to you again.'

'What a dire threat!' Paula took her friend's hand affectionately and pulled her to her feet. 'Don't worry. When I dropped in on you, nothing was further from my thoughts than snide paragraphs about the fruits of sin growing in stately homes.'

'You didn't know before you came,' said Angela. 'You know now.'

'I said not to worry. Let's go into your beautiful garden.'

Still holding Angela's hand, she led the way through the open french windows. A double flight of stone steps led down to a terrace; beyond that was a formal rose garden. A young woman moved between the roses, spraying them from a cylinder slung across her shoulder. Paula wondered whether she too was an unmarried mother. But for the moment she was only concerned about her friend. 'So you've brought hope and happiness to twenty anxious mums and twenty howling brats,' she said. 'What about yourself?'

'I'm doing fine as well,' Angela assured her.

'Good. Then I have two instructions for you. One, that you are to attend the first day of Wimbledon, to see Lindsay play. And two, that you are without fail to turn up for her wedding.'

'She wrote to tell me she and Clark were engaged,' said Angela. 'Will it work, d'you think?'

'I wouldn't care to say,' Paula confessed. 'There's something . . . You know how some people have an aura of success about them even when they're young. Simon, for example. He'll be a professor one day, and the confidence of that is there already. But Clark seems to reckon that the world has given him a good education and the world is therefore obliged to give him a good life to follow it up. I guess he and Lindsay will be okay if everything goes well for them.'

'A big "if",' said Angela, and Paula could not deny it.

'Well, to get back to the wedding. In Stratford on October the somethingth.' She began to search for the date in her diary.

'I'm sorry, Paula. I'm afraid I can't manage it.'

'You're booked up for the whole of October?' Paula raised her eyebrows. 'Fiddlesticks! I'm here, I should say, as a deputation. I was almost glad to find that I wasn't the only person you'd cut out of your life. I was hurt about that until I found that we've all been getting the same treatment. There must be a reason. Tell Auntie Paula. What's the skeleton in your cupboard?'

'What do you mean?'

Paula was startled by the sharpness of Angela's reaction. Almost as though she were frightened. She realized, no doubt, that she could not evade questioning any longer. 'Why are you shutting yourself away here? Why didn't you come to Helen's wedding?'

For a moment Angela was silent. 'Isn't it obvious?' she muttered.

'Spell it out,' Paula commanded. 'No secrets between friends.'

'Well, look at me! Not much strain on anyone's spelling.'

She was right to claim that it was obvious. There was a change in kind, not merely in degree, between the girl of twenty-one who had always been a little on the plump side and this young woman who was obese to the point of grossness. She was nearly in tears, but now that the conversation had started it seemed important to press on.

'How did it start?' Paula asked.

'I can't stop eating. At least, it actually started when I was ill, after my parents died. Perhaps it's still the same illness. I don't know.'

'You've been to a doctor?'

'Yes. He gave me pills. They made me depressed and sleepy, so I stopped taking them. Then I went to a psychiatrist. He made me feel positively suicidal, so I stopped going there as well.'

'May I try to help?'

'What's the use?' asked Angela. 'It doesn't matter here. It makes relationships easier. Nobody envies me.'

'Sure it matters,' said Paula. 'You're only twenty-three. In twenty years' time you'll look back and wonder what happened to the good years. Please let me help.'

'How?'

'First, by taking you to Wimbledon. If you stay home because you don't like the look of yourself, that's a dead end. But if you decide absolutely for sure that you're going somewhere whatever you look like, and going somewhere else the next week, then little by little you'll feel the incentive to do something about it.' From amateur psychologists, thought Paula as she spoke, good Lord deliver us. But a professional had tried and failed, it seemed, and possibly by being definite she could dent Angela's feeling of hopelessness. If her own certainty faltered, Angela's flicker of confidence might well be doused for good. She went on talking. 'I'll give Laker my Press pass for the day and you and I can sit together in Lindsay's seats.'

'Laker? You didn't tell me he was coming. It's odd, isn't it? I mean about Ingrid marrying Simon and Lindsay planning to marry Clark. I suppose you all went to lots of parties together while I was in Egypt. I haven't seen any of that foursome we met on the towpath since that night. Tell me about the other two: Robin and Laker. Have they got the aura of success, like Simon?'

She was babbling on through nervousness, Paula decided, while she tried to think whether or not to accept her friend's help. It was reasonable that she should need a few moments. To accuse her of changing the subject would not be fair.

'Robin's gone into estate management in Scotland – looking after several thousand acres of timber and grouse moor for his father-in-law. He plans to have six children and he's notched up one and a half of them already. He was at Simon's wedding, but his wife stayed north. I guess that will be the pattern of the marriage.'

'And Laker?'

'In great form at the moment. The most beautiful woman in the world has just agreed to marry him.'

'Paula!' Angela, who had been leaning forward over the terrace wall, twisted round so abruptly that a small stone urn rocked and almost overturned. 'Paula – who?'

'Me, idiot. Didn't you recognize the description? Sorry to startle you – were you scared on my behalf?'

'Well, I did wonder. I mean, you told me ages ago that you'd marked him down to marry one day but then I didn't hear any more, so – '

'Did I tell you that? How indiscreet of me.'

'Only because I asked,' said Angela. 'I was in Egypt then, so you probably reckoned that I was well away from the general stream of gossip. Anyway, congratulations on getting him to the point at last.'

'Convention is on my side,' laughed Paula. 'He's realized that it's the done thing to marry at his age. I had to wait for him to put on the pressure so that I could be clear about little points about carrying on my own career. He'll be a success for sure. It smells stronger on him than on anyone else I know. That's enough about that. We're discussing Wimbledon, arrangements for.'

'No.' Angela looked upset again. 'Sorry, Paula, but it's too soon.'

'Well, Lindsay's wedding, then. That's over three months away. A firm promise for Lindsay's wedding. Even if you weigh thirty stone.'

'All right,' said Angela. 'I'll be there. But – '

'No buts. Determination is what you need.'

'But it won't go away. Perhaps if I make an effort to stop nibbling I can stop putting on more weight, but that won't get rid of what's there.'

The young woman in the rose garden gave a final murderous squirt at a surviving greenfly and turned away. 'What was she?' Paula asked. 'A hospital gardener?'

'No, she's a physiotherapist. The hospital only needs her part-time.'

'Nurses, physios, dieticians,' murmured Paula thoughtfully.

Angela looked puzzled. 'We've changed the subject, have we?'

'No. Hold on a moment.'

It was a long moment, in which the tiny seed of an idea began to germinate in Paula's mind. She tried to guess what objections Angela might raise. It was odd, Paula thought, that she should still feel protective about her friend, who for the past year had clearly been displaying considerable qualities of organization. But there was no doubt that such a feeling did linger on. Neither her love for Laker nor her dedication to her career could alter the unswerving loyalty to her friends. Angela needed help, and Paula thought she could see a way to give it. 'Come inside again,' she said, her old habit of organizing her friend's life taking precedence over Angela's position as hostess. 'I have a plan to propose to you.'

Assignations 1972

1

Sir John Lorimer had gone to ground. Paula Mattison was not the only journalist who, in the last week of June, 1972, was trying to track him down. He was the chairman of a committee of enquiry whose terms of reference might seem to confine it to an investigation of construction standards in local authority housing. Paula, though, had no doubt that when the report was published on Saturday it was as likely to expose corruption as incompetence: there would be a story in it. John had no wife or children to be flattered into indiscretion and his housekeeper and secretary had both refused to reveal their employer's whereabouts. As she drove herself to Wetherly Hall on Thursday afternoon Paula had nothing but a hunch to inspire her plans.

'Happy birthday!' she said, opening the door of her friend's office. It was indeed Angela's thirty-ninth birthday, but Paula had not been expected to appear for it. Instead, she was due to arrive in twenty-four hours' time for a weekend visit. Angela looked up in pleasure.

'Paula! Surprise! It surely isn't Friday yet.'

'No. Still safely Thursday. But your birthday.'

'You sent a card. Have you driven down just to help me blow out the candles?'

'Not exactly. You look very busy. How are we doing?'

It had been Paula's idea, sixteen years earlier, which had solved three problems at once: the upkeep of a house too large for normal life; the provision of paid work for an increasing number of young women, most of whom had some medical training; and the reduction of Angela's own weight and size. 'A health hydro!' she had exclaimed, and before the year was out it was a going concern.

As well as contributing the idea, Paula had toured similar establishments as a journalist, picking up suggestions and noting difficulties. She arranged for a Swedish masseuse and a Hungarian beautician to train some of the unmarried mothers. And when the hydro was ready to open she circulated details to all her wealthiest acquaintances as well as planting mentions in the press. Angela had done all the work apart from that, but insisted on regarding Paula as her inspiration and paying her a percentage of the profits.

'Booming,' she said now. 'I feel quite guilty. It's been marvellous getting all the repairs done and bringing the heating and plumbing up to date, but last year we didn't have any major expense and the result is a whacking great profit. I've been wondering – have you ever heard of Sir Henry Peacham?'

'I've never met him. Henry Peacham?' It took Paula a moment, but her mental filing system was one of the attributes which over the years had carried her to the top of her profession. 'Oh yes. The tax expert. Is he teaching you how to fiddle the books?'

'Of course not.' Angela was as law-abiding at thirty-nine as she had been at twenty-one. 'Just providing friendly advice. He helped me through all the tax complications after my father died, years ago, and we've kept in touch ever since. He comes to stay occasionally – privately, not for treatment. He's here this week. We were talking about money, and I began to wonder whether I could turn Wetherly into a charity.'

'In whose interest?'

'The children's. Most of my girls get married in the

end, but sometimes the husband wonders why he should pay for extras for someone else's child. I thought we might have a trust fund to help the children through some kind of training after they leave school. It's all in the air. You must meet Henry and put your ideas into the pool.'

'You'll have the League of Purity on your tail,' laughed Paula. 'The wages of sin will become too attractive in this part of the world. Is Lady Feacham staying here as well?'

'They're divorced.'

'Yes, I suppose a tax expert *would* be divorced. The only sensible way for a high earner to live. I'd be delighted to meet your Henry. But the reason – '

Angela interrupted. 'He's not *my* Henry.'

'Sorry,' said Paula, surprised by her friend's edginess. 'But you know me. Incurably nosy. I hoped for a moment you were going to introduce me to your love life.'

In spite of the wish she had once expressed to have five children, Angela had never married. No doubt for some years her obesity was sufficient explanation for that. But the opening of the health hydro, as well as turning her into an efficient administrator, had transformed her appearance. Long hours of hard work left no time for nibbling and the satisfaction of establishing a successful business restored her normal cheerful temperament. She acted a guinea pig for the diets and treatments offered to her guests and her determination that they should succeed made them work for her, so that within three years she became smart and self-confident, and was far more attractive in her thirties than at twenty. It was difficult to believe that her kind nature and comfortable good looks had not attracted many suitors, but she had never shown any sign of considering marriage.

Sometimes Paula had wondered whether her friend might be carrying a torch for a married man. There was something she said once, when Paula made a remark critical of one of the unmarried mothers. Angela was always quick to defend her protégées, but on this occasion she spoke more sharply than usual. 'It's easy for you to talk, Paula. You fell in love and there was nothing to stop you marrying the man. Not everyone's so lucky. Sometimes another woman has got there first.'

Perhaps Henry Peacham – but Paula shook the speculation out of her head. 'I was about to apologize for turning up a day early. Is there a room free? I feel in need of a little treatment.'

'You don't *look* in need of it,' said Angela. 'You never do. In the sort of book I read as a girl, every hero was described at some point as having not an ounce of superfluous flesh. You always remind me of that phrase. No superfluous ounces.'

'But a lot of nerve-ends. I need a morning of being pinched and slapped and covered with mud and left to unwind in the dark.'

'Your weekend room's free already,' Angela told her. 'Have dinner in the flat with me tonight. We'll play some bridge afterwards. Henry will be there, and a friend of his. I promised I'd find a fourth.'

'Done.' Paula hesitated, her conscience pricking. 'Guess I ought to come clean. It's true about the unwinding business. But I do have another reason for coming early. I'm trying to track down someone who's done a disappearing act. He might have come here.'

'What will you do if you find him?'

'Only talk. Ask a few questions.'

'For your paper, you mean?' Angela shook her head disapprovingly. 'Why did you tell me? I'd rather not have known.'

'Stupid, wasn't it? Especially as it's only a wild guess that he might be here. It suddenly hit me, that you're the only person in the world to whom I always tell the truth.'

'Not to Laker?'

'I never lie to Laker. But there are sometimes things that I leave unsaid. It's one of the pleasure of a friendship that isn't a marriage: there's no danger in being frank.'

Angela reluctantly laughed. 'In this case I'd prefer frankness to be tempered by discretion. Don't tell me the victim's name, there's a love. Or I might feel bound to protect him.'

'Do you tell the truth to me, Angela?'

Angela's smile was not quite whole-hearted. She looked down at the figures on her desk, as though anxious to return to her accounts. 'What secrets should I have?'

'How could I know? Sir Henry Peacham, perhaps.'

'I'm not interested in marrying Henry, if that's what you're getting at. I'm aware that for nine months he's been unattached, and I enjoy his company, but that's all. I suppose people tell you ten times a day how they're just good friends. You'll have to make it another test of friendship, that you not only speak the truth but believe it when you hear it.'

'Sorry,' said Paula.

'Nothing to be sorry about.'

'I'm sorry I teased and I'm sorry I pried.' Angela seemed to be upset, and Paula couldn't see what in the conversation had caused this. Perhaps the lack of interest in marriage was on Henry's part. But speculating about a stranger was time wasted. Paula took her suitcase upstairs. Then she went to the reception office and asked Rowena for the register. As a journalist she would not have been allowed to see it, but her status at Wetherly was almost that of part-proprietor. She took a quick first glance down the week's guest-list. No Lorimer.

Paula had recognized from the start how long the odds must be against John choosing this particular hiding place. Yet her hunch was not entirely fanciful. Angela had never allowed Wetherly to become merely a refuge for the overweight. With her para-medical staff she could accept convalescents who were helped by excercise and diet to recover from illness or operations. And her clients could, if they chose, enjoy Wetherly simply as a hotel. Like house guests in a stately home they could play tennis or croquet or billiards, ride or jog round the lake, or fish or swim in it. They could watch television, relax in the library and enjoy the meals provided by Angela's magnificent cook. A good many people who came first for treatment returned later for pleasure.

John Lorimer knew what Wetherly Hall offered because he had been one of the acquaintances to whom Paula sent the hydro's first printed brochure. And obviously he had not put the leaflet straight into the waste paper basket, for several years later he had spent two weeks of convalescence there after a heart attack which almost killed him. More important as a precedent was the fact that he had returned incognito for a second visit to Wetherly at the time when his knighthood was announced – to avoid journalists in search of interviews with the newly-honoured. So it was not impossible that he might now have taken refuge again in an establishment which was luxurious and discreet but convenient for Saturday's press conference. Paula applied herself once more to the list of guests, this time studying it in greater detail. She had not progressed far before her eyebrows shot up in recognition of a familiar name. Benedict Townsend.

For a moment Paula held her breath. She hadn't spoken to Ben for sixteen years – not, indeed, since the day when he sat on the edge of the bed and watched her pack her things and move out of his flat. From time to time since then she had caught sight of him at parties or press conferences, and even such fleeting and distant glimpses were enough to stir the memory of the infatuation she had once felt. Like an alcoholic she was aware that the first sip is the one to fight, and had always kept her distance.

She could do so still. The register informed her that he was due to leave on Saturday morning. This evening she would be in Angela's flat, and on Friday, by studying the treatments book, she could discover where he was likely to be at any hour of the day, and avoid the area. The only difficulty would arise if he turned out to be Sir Henry Peacham's bridge-playing friend. Or if he had come to Wetherly for the same reason as herself, in professional competition for an early interview with Sir John Lorimer. Ben had moved from the newspaper world into that of television, but current affairs were still his field – and John most emphatically qualified as a current affair.

That thought took her back to her study of the register. Angela's treatments were as useful to men as to women, but more women had time to spare and were attracted by the fringe benefits, those parts of the therapy which were beauty treatments rather than health aids. Only ten clients this week were male. Paula eliminated most of them quickly. Benedict Townsend could be ruled out at once, and so could two gentlemen with names obviously Arab, while Rowena confirmed that Nelson J. Finkelmann III was as American as he sounded. Of the ordinarily British names, five had written full postal addresses in the column provided for this information. Only one had scribbled 'London' and left it at that: John Lindsay.

Paula's eyes sparkled with optimism. The same initials, so that nothing on his luggage or handkerchieves should give him away. The same Christian name, so that he should not rudely fail to answer if some new acquaintance addressed him by it. It wasn't yet certain that her hunch had paid off, but she was hopeful and smiling as she closed the register, thanked Rowena, and went off to bathe and change.

At half past seven she came cautiously downstairs again to observe, although not to join, the guests assembling in the drawing room for their cocktail of vegetable juice. Angela had made a flat for herself on an upper floor in order that all the main rooms of the house could become part of the hydro. Her ancestors, men of sporting instincts and hearty appetites, would have turned in their graves to see their dining room occupied by fifty mainly overweight men and women doing their best to regard half a grapefruit as a meal. The music room, too, had come down in the world. In it, each morning, guests dressed in bathing trunks or leotards puffed their way through a series of exercises to the rhythms banged out on an upright piano.

The drawing room, however, retained its former dignity. Without formal prohibition, it was recognized as out of bounds to anyone lounging about in a dressing gown. Its sofas and writing tables were reserved for those prepared to make a sartorial effort. Paula, although smartly dressed, did not go in. Instead, she let herself into the conservatory. Through a window almost obscured by a climbing geranium, she could see into the drawing room without being noticed herself.

Ben was there already. Paula held her breath for a moment. The passing years seemed to have made him more attractive rather than less. He was plumper – but when he was young he had been far too thin. His hair had turned completely white, but it was as exuberantly thick as ever, the colour emphasizing the healthy tan of his face. He lay back in an armchair, his long legs stretched out; completely at ease and confident of his power to please. There was another respect in which Ben hadn't changed. He was surrounded by women – half a dozen of them, all with unnatural vivacity trying to impress him.

With an effort Paula turned her attention to the other males in the room. But she was disappointed. Sir John Lorimer was not there.

At eight o'clock she left her hiding place and walked up the curving double staircase and along the corridor to Angela's flat. 'What gorgeous flowers!' she exclaimed as Angela let her in.

'A birthday present from Henry. Orchids are his hobby.'

For a moment Paula felt guilty. But Angela wouldn't have expected a present from her – they had never developed the habit of exchanging gifts. She followed her friend to meet her fellow-guests, who rose politely to their feet. Sir Henry Peacham was a craggy man with an aquiline profile and bright, darting eyes; he shook hands with a firm grip. Angela drew breath to perform a second introduction, but already Paula was grinning broadly as she held out her hand. 'What a delightful surprise to meet you again,' she said to Sir John Lorimer.

2

John recognized Paula as soon as she came into the room. At any other time he would have been delighted to see her again; but as it was, his first reaction was one of suspicion and annoyance. He did not for a moment believe her expression of surprise, for her smile could not disguise the flash of triumph in her eyes. She had been looking for him.

During the years since their last meeting, John had

continued to keep track of Paula's career. He had approved when she left the gossip column to join a team of investigative journalists, and more recently had noted her promotion to her own by-line as a commentator on national affairs. The report of his committee would certainly fall into her sphere of interest.

At first it seemed to him that their hostess must have set up the meeting. But Angela was completely at ease as she poured drinks, showing none of the embarrassment or curiosity which would suggest complicity in a plot. And it soon became apparent that she and Paula were old and very close friends and that Paula was a regular visitor to Wetherly. John reminded himself of something he had forgotten in the first shock of seeing Paula. It was through her that he had first learned about Wetherly Hall. She had sent him a brochure when it opened, and were he to be honest with himself he ought to admit that he had kept the leaflet – and, later, made use of it when he needed convalescence – precisely because it came from a young woman who attracted him. While recognizing the unlikelihood of finding Paula on the premises during that first stay, he had nevertheless hoped for it. So it was unfair of him not to recognize now that Paula – who could not possibly have known that he would be there – would have made her arrangements for purely personal reasons.

That there was indeed a reason for the visit – and one which had nothing to do with John's presence – soon became clear; and as the two women laughingly explained it, his suspicions began to fade.

'Every year at this time Paula's husband goes off to Oxford for his college Gaudy,' Angela told him. 'So his grass widow needs company.'

'Don't you have a Gaudy of your own?' John asked

Paula, remembering that she was an Oxford undergraduate at the time of their first meeting.

'I never go. Reminiscing about my long-lost youth doesn't appeal. Reunions aren't a female vice, are they? Maybe because very few females ever set out deliberately to get sloshed at a party. Laker – my husband – is very abstemious as a rule. For a politician, that is. But I'm sure he regards every Gaudy as a failure unless he has to be carried to bed. The Gaudy dinner is on Saturday. Laker will come here for tomorrow evening, and then back again for Sunday lunch. Angela makes a regular routine of entertaining us for every last weekend in June.'

'What's Laker doing now?' asked Henry Peacham.

'He's determined to get a ministry after the next election – assuming the right people win. So he's started an elaborate programme of fact-finding. He's been picking my brains recently about immigration – but I get the impression that politicians don't sincerely want to have their theories upset by inconvenient statistics.'

'Like journalists?' suggested John, by now relaxed.

'Unkind!' Paula's laughter was friendly. She too seemed at ease, with no expectations more than of a happy birthday dinner. So John enjoyed the meal and the bridge which followed it. When Paula at last tossed in her pebble to ripple the conversational pool, he was too relaxed to recognize its nature immediately.

By that time they had thanked their hostess for the evening and said goodnight to Henry, whose room was next to Angela's flat. Paula came to a standstill outside her own door. 'Will you come in for a few moments?' she asked. 'There's something I'd like to ask you. Cousin John.'

John laughed. 'So they let you into the secret at last?' Amusement and curiosity drew him into the room after her.

'I didn't like to mention it in company. You may not want it known that the skeletons in your family cupboard are black ones,' she said.

'I've told you before; I've no interest in the Lorimers as a family. But to be able to boast that Paula Mattison is my cousin – that's another matter. How long have you known?'

'I was told on my wedding day. But you've always known, haven't you? That interview you gave me – you knew then?'

'True.'

'I could tell at the time that you were holding something back. But I thought it was something about yourself, not about me. You should have told me.'

'Should I? It wasn't my business. It would have complicated your relationships with people you obviously liked. You'd have wondered why Bernard, for example, never acknowledged any family link.'

'They all wanted to tell me long before,' Paula said. 'As soon as ever I came to England. It was my father who made them keep quiet.'

'Why?'

'People in Jamaica remember my white grandfather as a saintly man. No one ever knew that my father was the pastor's son, so I couldn't know that I was the pastor's granddaughter.'

'But someone did tell you.'

'Well, my father's dead now.' She looked John straight in the eye. 'The others had a reason to keep quiet. But you don't go along with the rest of your family. You could have told me.'

'As a boy I was in much the same situation as yourself,' John said. Anger choked his throat. For twelve years he had not known who his father was. 'Born into the Lorimer family, but not acknowledged by it.'

'Then you should have been sympathetic. I had a right to know the truth.'

John did not try to justify himself. Logically he should indeed have become a passionate defender of the need for truth in human relationships when he first discovered how his mother had lied to him. But instead, his anger had two quite different consequences. He despised women – even those he loved – for the deceitfulness which he believed to be a general female characteristic: that was the reason why he would never marry. And at the same time he had chosen to regard any information about his personal life as his own property, protecting it from others by either silence or untruthfulness. Only rarely did he feel any qualm of conscience – but Paula's case was one of those exceptions. He had liked her, and he ought to have been frank. 'I'm sorry,' he said now.

'So you'd agree that you owe me a moment of truthfulness.' Her eyes, which had been firm, softened into a smile.

'You know everything now.'

'I'm not talking about family any longer,' Paula said. 'There are other questions I'd like to ask you.'

With a silent groan John came back to earth. In the course of a pleasant social evening he had forgotten his earlier suspicion that Paula Mattison, the journalist, was on his trail. He looked at her coldly. 'You can't possibly expect . . .'

'Of course I can't,' agreed Paula. 'I'm not looking for any kind of scooped indiscretion. "Sir John Lorimer reveals . . ." Not my line at all. You know the kind of thing I write.'

'Go on,' he said grimly.

Paula sat down and indicated a chair to him, but John remained standing. 'You're releasing your report on Saturday,' she said. 'Giving the Sunday papers first crack at it. As you can imagine, you're not popular with the dailies. We shall print a summary on Monday, but it will be stale by then. So I've written an article to appear on Saturday.' She paused, but John was not prepared to comment. 'The article's a forecast of what your committee has almost certainly discovered and what you probably propose should be done about it. If it's an accurate guess, the editor will put a mental tick by my name. I'd rather take credit for intelligent anticipation than for somehow squeezing a leak.'

'So what exactly do you want?'

'Will you read the article tomorrow morning and make sure that I'm not too far off course? From your own point of view, I'm sure you don't want to see the waters muddied by half truths or the repetition of accusations which you may have disproved. And for myself – well, no one likes to look a fool in public.'

'You're asking for help on the strength of a family relationship?'

'Of course not,' protested Paula. 'I only mentioned that to hold you back for a moment. You have a reputation for evading journalists. And for accusing them of inaccuracies and distortions. I'm giving you the opportunity to remove any mistakes from an article which will appear whether you agree or not. The fact that I'm your cousin has nothing to do with it – except that, as I said a minute ago, you owe me.'

John took a long time to answer. He was still angry, but now he recognized that his anger was with himself at being caught. He did not, after all, feel resentment at Paula's behaviour. He liked her – it was as simple as that. He didn't believe for a moment that she had any greater regard for the truth than had any other members of a trade which he despised. But in a way he was amused by the skill with which she had decoyed him into a sense of obligation. 'All right,' he said.

There was a tap on the door. John opened it without pausing to remember that this was Paula's bedroom. Angela looked surprised to see him. 'Sorry,' she said. 'I was going to tell Paula . . . but it can wait till tomorrow. Goodnight.'

John stepped out of the room after her, to explain that he was just leaving, but collided with a tall man who was hurrying along the corridor. Now it was John's turn to apologize, but the stranger ignored him, instead staring through the open doorway. 'Paula!'

'Ben, hi!' Paula was smiling, but John felt sure that she was disconcerted in rather the same manner as Angela a few seconds earlier. He almost laughed aloud. It was one of the many advantages of remaining a bachelor that he could not be embarrassed by any bedroom farce. He turned towards his own room so that the others could develop their encounter. But before his fellow-guest had time to step forward, Paula's door was firmly closed.

3

The next morning Paula propped her draft article against the coffee pot on Sir John Lorimer's breakfast tray. Then she pencilled her name into the hydro's appointment book wherever there was an attractive vacancy.

The treatment rooms were below ground level, converted from the old kitchens. Paula went first to the sauna, while the paying clients were occupied by their exercise class. She stripped and showered and lay in the heat until her head began to swim. If Ben should come in now . . . Three times she cut him out of her thoughts and each time he insinuated himself back again.

They had never quarrelled. When Paula, all those years ago, announced her decision to marry Laker, Ben accepted it with regretful sympathy. There was no reason why they shouldn't now regard themselves as friends. Except that even last night's brief glimpse had been enough to remind her that she still found him too attractive to make an ordinary friendship manageable. Paula sighed to herself and punished her thoughts by throwing her body straight into the icy plunge pool.

For an hour in the massage room one of the girls rubbed her skin with oil and slapped and pinched and kneaded her flesh, before passing her on to a beautician for a facial. A tight bandage held back her curly hair while her face was creamed and steamed. Her eyes were covered with pads of cotton wool so that a chilled cucumber poultice could be applied to the rest of her face. Another bandage was fastened over her eyes to keep the arrangement in place. Then she was left alone for half an hour.

She lay in her personal darkness, luxuriating in the coolness of her head and the warmth of her naked body beneath the blankets. Her mind relaxed into blankness – until the moment when she heard the door open and close.

'I've read your piece,' said John's voice. 'I'll give you my comments verbally.'

'Then please first give me a pen and paper,' Paula asked, immediately alert. 'My bag's somewhere around.'

'Can you write in the dark?'

'There was a time when all my best stories were scribbled below table level at dinner parties'. She felt the Biro presented to one hand and her notepad to the other. A chair creaked as John sat down.

'I admired your article,' he said. 'You've done your homework well. Of course, I'm sure you don't need to be told that your fourth paragraph would lead you straight into a libel action. That kind of accusation can only be made from a position of legal privilege.'

'Has it been made by your committee?'

'That information doesn't come into the arrangement we made, which was that I should prevent you from being caught out in too many inaccuracies. I'm prepared to mention three points – '

His meticulous voice, with its vestiges of a Midlands accent, dealt with each point in turn. Paula, making brief blindfold notes, allowed her mind to consider the five west-country councillors whom she had named as guilty of corruption. Certainly she knew that the paragraph couldn't be printed as it stood. She had included it for the sole purpose of judging whether John's reaction would justify the more careful wording dictated by the paper's libel lawyer.

'I'll put your notebook back for you.' John, his comments over, was standing up, his hands reaching to touch hers. But Paula held on to the notebook, not wishing him to read her jottings. He must have been on the point of moving away when Angela came in.

'Is that Paula under that disguise? No, don't let me interrupt you.'

'I was just leaving,' said John. The door closed behind him.

Paula turned her poulticed face in Angela's direction. 'Does that worry you?' she said. 'I mean, that it might worry John?' She began to tug at the bandage which held her eye pads in place.

'Leave it alone.' It sounded as though Angela was laughing. 'Why should John be worried? And if he were, why should that worry me?'

'I don't know,' said Paula. 'What an admission for a journalist! You ticked me off for dropping hints about Henry, so I hardly dare wonder about John. All I meant was, suppose he was in love with you – or not even that, just trying to make a good impression on you – he might have been upset to be found closeted with me not once but twice. So since there was a simple explanation, he might prefer me to give it, to prevent him from seeming to excuse himself; and you might like to have it. Golly, what a rigmarole!'

'You should be writing fiction,' said Angela. 'Sloppy romances, instead of political commentaries.'

'I like to get things straight. I find it disconcerting that suddenly I don't know what the situation is. Your situation. And yet we've been friends for so long.'

'Laker has been your friend for even longer, but he doesn't understand *your* situation.'

'Laker? How does he come into this.'

'He's the reason for my badly-timed interruptions,' Angela explained. 'He phoned at half past one last night. Ostensibly to tell you that he could get away early, so that he'll be here at about three this afternoon. But what he *really* wanted to know was whether you were actually spending last night here, or using me as an accommodation address. It sounded like a simple case of husbandly jealousy.'

Paula grimaced in indignation, cracking the mask round her mouth. 'He doesn't have the right to do that. It makes my job impossible. Obviously I have to spend nights away from time to time.'

'And obviously you know how you spend them. No need to feel guilty. I don't expect he was really suspicious. Just wanting to be reassured.'

'So I hope you reassured him.'

'I might not have done,' Angela teased. 'I could have

mentioned these assignations with John. Or – ' Her voice was not laughing any more. 'Or was he the victim you came here to track down?'

Paula nodded.

'So I led him straight into the trap.'

'He didn't mind.'

'*I* mind,' said Angela. It was not often that Paula heard her speak so firmly. But she did not press the subject. 'You're supposed to be relaxing under that mask. I'll leave you to it.'

She went, but Paula did not long remain alone. Yet again the door opened and closed. Two hands encircled her throat. 'Ben!' she said.

He laughed in the lazy way she remembered so well. 'I thought I could murder you and you'd never know who was doing it. Obviously I reckoned without my aura.' His fingers began to explore under the blankets, sliding over her bare shoulders and down towards her waist.

'Good God, woman, aren't you wearing anything at all? You haven't changed, Paula. You're still adorable. I adore you.' He covered her breasts with kisses, embracing her passionately.

Paula needed all her willpower, as well as her strength, to fight him off. 'Be sensible, Ben. The girl will be back at any moment.'

'I suppose so.' He touched each nipple in turn lightly with his lips. 'Very well, then. I will desist. Upon conditions.'

'What conditions?'

'That we meet again. In a more private situation.'

'Laker will be here in a couple of hours.'

'I can wait. I could even turn a screw or two. You might prefer Laker not to know that you were entertaining a gentleman in your bedroom at two o'clock this morning.'

'Don't be crazy, Ben.' Paula tore the bandages and

cotton wool pads away from her eyes. 'You know who he is.'

'True. He's due to appear on my programme. I've had to spend the past three days pretending not to recognize him. I'm not allowed to take unethical short cuts like you.'

'Well then. It was an interview; that was all.'

'I'll believe you,' said Ben. 'Millions wouldn't.'

'Laker would.' Even as she said it, she wondered. Angela's report of his telephone call was unsettling.

'Well, perhaps. But when he arrives this afternoon and meets me in the hall, will be believe it's an innocent coincidence that you and I spent last night under the same roof?'

Paula tried to laugh. 'There was a time when you relied on your own charms rather than blackmail.'

'The blackmail is for your benefit, my darling. So that you can assure yourself you had no choice. Tonight?'

'I told you, Laker will be here tonight.'

'Tomorrow?' His hands resumed their exploration. 'Tomorrow.'

'I have a condition too,' said Paula.

'Yes?'

'That you're out of Wetherly before half-past two today.' Laker wouldn't study the register, but he would recognize Ben if they met.

'Done,' said Ben. 'Dinner at eight tomorrow. My flat.'

'Not possible. I can't come till late. Angela has the whole day planned.' While Laker was on his way to Oxford, she and Angela would spend the afternoon at Wimbledon, watching the tennis: they always did. In the evening they had tickets for a play which was conveniently having its preview at the Wimbledon Theatre.

'Girl friends only exist to be jettisoned in favour of boy friends.'

'Not this girl friend.'

Ben sighed. 'It will be two o'clock or worse if you come to London after all that. I'll take a room in the motel down the road. See you.' He lifted each hand in turn to her lips. Then at last Paula had the room to herself.

For a few moments, in an effort to control the excitement which Ben had aroused in her, she forced herself to think about the girl friend whom she would never jettison. The protectiveness she had felt towards Angela both at Dame Eleanor's and in the setting-up of the hydro had never completely faded away, but it had long ceased to be necessary. Angela was doing very well. She was running a successful business and – far more important in her own eyes – was continuing her charitable work for unmarried mothers so unobtrusively that even the beneficiaries were hardly aware of it. This efficient, self-confident Angela was even better company than the dreamy and impractical undergraduate whom Paula had first met when they were both eighteen. Paula's long love affair with her husband naturally provided the most important human relationship in her life, but her deep affection for Angela ran it close.

Did the conditions of her rendez-vous with Ben suggest that she was more loyal to Angela than to Laker? It was an unexpected thought. But Paula reminded herself that she had no intention of keeping the appointment. It had been a way of getting rid of Ben, knowing that he wouldn't be cold-blooded enough to stir up trouble if she let him down. She had pretended to go along with him only to prevent an accidental meeting between the two men.

By three o'clock that afternoon she had revised her draft article and phoned it through. But Laker did not, after all, arrive at that time; instead he came in the evening, when she had originally expected him. This confirmed her suspicion that he had used the message about an earlier arrival only as an excuse for checking on her whereabouts.

Nevertheless, she smiled to herself as the distinctive sound of Laker's Ferrari brought her to the window of her room just as she was about to take a bath before dinner. He looked up and waved before swinging himself athletically out of the car. Since she first met him he had changed surprisingly little. His hair – longer now than twenty years earlier, and fashionably cut – was as thick and dark as before, and he kept his figure trim with regular games of squash and a careful – though never acknowledged – control of what he ate and drank. He would enjoy getting drunk at tomorrow's Gaudy all the more because he took pains to remain sober at other times.

Also unchanged was his charm – the charm of a man who had never known any serious disappointment. Success at school and university had carried him seemingly without effort into a parliamentary seat which he had won so easily and held so comfortably that he had never needed any other career. Almost certainly he would be a cabinet minister before he was fifty; and although Paula was never likely to reach 10 Downing Street in her own right, as had been her youthful ambition, it was quite on the cards that she would one day find herself the wife of a prime minister.

Nor was there any dark side to Laker's character. Paula's work had taught her that many successful men who were abrasive and ruthless in their public life proved to be relaxed and sentimental at home – and that, by contrast, men whose public personality oozed charm could be tyrants to their wives. But Laker's behaviour was all of a piece. His wife, as well as his constituents and political colleagues, could enjoy his easy good manners and serious consideration of problems. He was as considerate – and as passionately loving – to Paula as when they were first married. It was love, presumably, which inspired his occasional eruptions of jealousy.

Nevertheless, he was not a perfect husband, as Paula was to be reminded that evening. 'Before I forget,' he said to her in the course of dinner, 'I'll be away next weekend. Rita thinks I ought to present prizes at the inter-schools sports day.'

'But we're going – ' Paula checked herself. Laker would not have forgotten the plan they had provisionally made for the weekend. Undoubtedly he had chosen to make his announcement in front of Angela especially to prevent any domestic argument. He might not know that Paula had discovered the closeness of his relationship with Rita, who was his constituency secretary, but he must have a guilty conscience about it.

Paula's silence concealed a real resentment. She was neither a nagging wife nor a jealous one. But it seemed unfair that she should be expected to take his words at face value when only a few hours earlier Laker had checked on her whereabouts in a manner which clearly suggested that he did not believe what she had told him. The indignation of being suspected when she was innocent urged her irresistibly to deserve his implicit accusation. At the moment when she arranged to meet Ben she had no intention of keeping the rendez-vous. But she had wished to do so; and now, as anger and desire mingled in her blood, she could feel her eyes flashing with a dangerous brightness. Tomorrow, while Laker was at Oxford, she would keep her appointment with Ben.

4

'Coffee!' called Paula. She smiled at Ben as he emerged, yawning, from the bathroom. The past sixteen years had changed him more than she had recognized at the first glimpse. At forty-two he had been in his prime but now, although his charm was undiminished, he was beginning to tire. The discovery increased Paula's affection. They could be friends again, she thought.

Still rubbing his eyes, he joined her at the table. 'How do you manage to look so smart at – my God, Paula, it's only just past six! On a Sunday morning!'

'Sorry.' Paula poured his coffee. 'But I didn't want just to slink away. And I must get back to Wetherly before seven.'

'Why? Are you expecting Laker to turn up?'

'Heavens, no. He won't have got to bed in Oxford much before three. At this moment he'd be dead to the world. But Angela goes to early service and brings me a cup of tea before she leaves.'

'So?'

'She's a hopeless liar. Loyal but transparent. If she knew I hadn't made full use of her hospitality she'd make such a performance out of covering up for me that the cat would be out of the bag in no time. Besides, why should I expect her to lie for me?'

'So you're going to sneak back through the dormy window before the rising bell goes. But suppose she's missed you during the night?'

'Why should she? What *are* you insinuating, Ben?'

'The house might have burned down.'

'In that case I'm dead.' They were talking for the sake of talking, their coffee cups empty.'

'Would you be interested in working for me?' asked Ben unexpectedly. 'I'd like to have a woman interviewer on the programme. You've got the background knowledge, the ability, the personality, the looks – '

'And I'm black.' Grinning, Paula completed the sentence for him.

'That too. The ethnic bonus. What about it? You'd have to fix your editor, but we credit the paper.'

Paula thought for some time. 'Ben,' she said at last, gesturing towards the bed. 'This isn't going to happen again.'

'There's no connection,' he said. 'Women I merely love get a dozen red roses. My reputation's on the line every time the programme goes out. I pick my team on merit – a different kind of merit.' He paused. 'But why?'

Paula shrugged her shoulders. 'Same reason as last time. Laker.' She stood up to go. 'May I think about the job? I'll call you.' He was not really upset, she realized as he kissed her goodbye – not even surprised. He had grown out of his love of complications.

The air outside was clear and fresh; it was going to be a beautiful day. Paula drove lazily back to Wetherly Hall feeling no guilt but instead a kind of satisfaction. Something had been properly ended which before had only been interrupted. And it was easier to forgive and forget Laker's jealousy now that it was justified.

She had borrowed the conservatory key before leaving and now used it to let herself into the silent house. She went quietly up the stairs and opened the door of her room. Angela was sitting on the bed.

It was a shock. Paula had hoped to avoid any need to explain. And there was something odd – almost unfriendly – about the way Angela was looking at her.

'Where have you been?'

'Out. You're up early, Angela. Are you just off to church?'

'I asked you where you'd been.'

It was the first time that Paula had ever seen her friend angry – that was perhaps why she had failed to recognize the mood at once. Even now she did not understand it. 'Admiring the countryside,' she said, hoping to avoid the truth without telling an outright lie. 'It's a glorious morning. Why the inquisition?'

'Was it a glorious morning at two o'clock as well?' Angela was more than simply angry. Her cheeks were pale and her eyes unsteady, as though she were only just able to keep desperation under control. What had she to be desperate about? Paula waited in silence for information.

'Laker phoned at two. He wanted to speak to you.'

'Showing, no doubt, the signs of a convivial evening.'

'Yes. He was drunk. But he still wanted to speak to you.'

'You should have hung up. He'd no right to get you out of bed at that hour. It would have been perfectly reasonable that you should refuse to wake me.'

'I didn't know there was any need to be perfectly reasonable until I tried to find you.'

'What did you tell him?'

'Oh, I covered up. But he went on talking. As though . . .' Angela seemed near to tears. 'There were other people there, men, listening and interrupting. I think they may all have been taking turns to phone their wives. For some sort of bet. I could hear them laughing. The second time – I mean, when I went back – Laker pretended that he was talking to you. He didn't use your name, or mine, but . . .'

Now Paula understood. Angela, no doubt, would be

unfamiliar with Laker's language of love: shocked, possibly, by his vocabulary, bewildered if she believed it to be directed to herself and hurt if she realized that it was not.

'Did he know?' asked Angela abruptly.

'Did who know what?'

'Laker. Did he know about this other man, whoever he is? Paula, it wasn't John, was it? All the time you were pretending – '

'No,' said Paula. 'No to both questions.'

'Would he – Laker – have minded if he did know?'

Paula let out a vigorous puff of breath. It was tempting to tell Angela to mind her own business. But it was only two days ago, wasn't it, that she had claimed always to tell the truth to her closest friend. If she was puzzled now, it was because she did not understand her interrogator's mood. She knew that one of the secrets of Angela's success with the unmarried mothers was a refusal to indicate that she was ever shocked by anything at all. 'Laker has a constituency secretary called Rita,' she said. 'Earnest and efficient and reasonably attractive. He spends one weekend a month in his constituency and Rita has felt it her duty to tell me that he makes use of his opportunities. I suppose she hoped – well, it was a shock. I was upset at first. Then it occurred to me that Laker had never let me suspect anything. He's always been a great support to me in my job, a great companion in our social life, a great lover. Marvellous. Well, none of that had changed. That seemed the important thing. Adultery is only a slap in the face when the adulterer chooses to make it so. Some men do secretly want to be found out, but Laker didn't. He wanted to go on being married to me. As soon as I had that clear in my mind, Rita didn't bug me any more. I never told Laker about her call.'

'So this man was a sort of revenge for Rita?'

Paula shook her head. 'I told you, I wasn't angry enough or hurt enough to think in terms of revenge. Sure, Rita's informer act may have changed my attitude. I've never been short of invitations to bed. Before Rita, I'd say No automatically. After Rita, I stopped to think. It's good for the morale, feeling able to choose. Usually I said No just the same. Last night – well, I suppose people always kid themselves that the circumstances are special. To answer your question, of course Laker would have minded if he'd known. Nothing would have happened if he hadn't been away. I'm sincerely sorry that you became involved. But you don't have to worry about us. Our marriage is a happy one and we both know it.'

Angela stood up. 'We'd better move into my flat.' Her voice was toneless and unhappy. 'There'll be a phone call for you soon.' She looked directly into Paula's eyes. All her anger had disappeared, leaving only distress. 'There's bad news, I'm afraid, Paula. I wasn't sitting here just because Laker phoned. There was another call at five o'clock. From the police. There's been an accident.'

Paula stared back at Angela, her throat suddenly dry. 'Go on.'

'There were five men involved. Two cars. One of the cars was Laker's Jaguar. Four of the five are dead.'

Paula's legs abruptly refused to support her. She sat down on the bed. 'And the fifth?' Her lips formed the question but no sound emerged. Again. 'The fifth?'

'Undergoing an emergency operation. Serious head injuries.'

'But which one?'

'The police couldn't tell me that. They weren't even sure who all the five men were. They assume Laker was one, because they checked the number of the car. They phoned your home and the housekeeper gave them this address. I told them that Simon and Clark might have been with him, so they were going to check the rooms at Christ Church. I don't know anything about the second car. It was travelling in the other direction.'

'Oh God!' said Paula. 'Oh God!' She felt Angela's arm round her shoulder.

'It may be Laker, the fifth man. Pray that it's Laker.'

'Do they think he'll live, whoever it is?'

'I asked the policeman, but he didn't know.'

Paula took one more deep, shuddering breath. Then she stood up with a little of her usual vigour. 'Come on, then. Why in God's name did you keep me talking so long?' She hurried towards the stairs.

'The police are going to phone here as soon as they've identified . . . you'll know sooner if you wait.'

'What difference does knowing make? The dead are dead. Later or sooner, it makes no difference when we find out. But one's alive. If it's Laker, but if . . .' Her voice choked as she made for the car.

Angela caught up, panting. 'I'm coming too.'

'I'm going to drive fast.' Gravel spun beneath the tyres as the MG launched itself down the long drive like a rocket.

'I'm sorry I yelled,' Paula said, knowing that the apology was unnecessary. 'If Laker was driving – he was drunk, I suppose.'

'I think he must have been. It sounds as though the accident was soon after he phoned and – yes, he was drunk.'

'Did he know it was you? When you went back to the phone after looking for me, you said he talked as though it were to me. But – '

'I think he knew. Unless he was too drunk to listen. I didn't pretend to be you. He was the one who was pretending, so that his friends would think . . .' There was no need for her to finish the sentence. Paula could imagine the scene as half a dozen inebriated men jostled in a telephone box or porter's lodge, taunting any one of the party whose wife proved not to be a patient Griselda.

So there was only one more question to be asked, but as the car roared along the deserted country roads Paula could not bring herself to put it into words. How successful had Angela been in her attempt to cover up Paula's absence? There had been no need for Laker to use his car at the end of the Gaudy dinner; he had a room for the night in college. Had he – jealous as well as drunk – decided to drive to Wetherly in the middle of the night to check on his wife's movements? Or had Clark and Simon, calling the bluff of his telephone conversation, demanded to see Paula at Wetherly themselves? Angela was probably right to suspect that money had been staked on it. There seemed no other reason for Laker to be on the road or for the others to be with him. And if that were the case, that he was driving because his wife had not been in the right place to take a telephone call, how could Paula ever free herself from the blame for what had happened?

Visiting Hours

1

For all her haste on the journey, Paula was slow to leave the car after she had driven into the hospital courtyard. She was conscious of Angela's impatience on her behalf, but her limbs were too heavy to move. Through a glass door she could see Ingrid and Lindsay inside the reception hall, bending over to write something. Their presence must confirm that Simon and Clark had been involved in the accident as well.

They turned, about to leave. Paula put her clenched fists up to her eyes. These two women had once been amongst her closest friends, but she could not bear the thought that one of them might be happy now. If there was only one survivor, it must be Laker. Their footsteps approached and she forced herself to look as they walked past without noticing her. Ingrid's face was white. She held her head stiffly and her eyes stared unblinkingly ahead. Lindsay had been crying. Her eyes were red and swollen; she dabbed at them as she walked. Paula felt a shameful bubble of hope rising into her throat. Now the chance was one in three.

As she walked with Angela towards the entrance, the receptionist met them at the door. 'You can't leave a car there.'

'I've come to see my husband. James Laker-Smith.'

'That space is reserved for ambulances. You must move your car at once.'

Bewildered, Paula stared at her. Why were they talking about cars?

'Give me the keys,' said Angela. Paula had left them in the ignition. Deducing this from her silence, Angela went back to move the car. Now the receptionist was willing to listen as Paula repeated her husband's name. She made an internal call and then stood up again. 'Come this way, will you?' She led the way from one building to another, from one level to another, passing the smells of sickness and disinfectant and food. Paula found herself at last announced at the door of a small room in which a man in his shirt-sleeves sat at a desk.

'Mrs Laker-Smith? Please sit down.'

Even from so few words Paula's sharp ear for voices, which many years ago had helped to make her own indistinguishable from that of an Englishwoman, caught the foreign accent. She identified this one as Austrian and then wondered why she should care. 'I thought I was coming to see my husband,' she said.

'A little later. I wished first to have a word with you.'

'May I know who I'm speaking to?'

'My name is Franklin. Neuro-surgeon. At four o'clock this morning I operated on your husband. Please, won't you sit down?'

But there was one more question to ask – the only one that mattered. 'Is he alive, Mr Franklin?'

The silence seemed to go on for ever. Paula stared into a pair of grey eyes; honest and compassionate and very tired. The surgeon stared back as though his answer could depend as much on her attitude as on the condition of her husband. At last he nodded his head.

'Yes,' he said. 'He's alive.'

2

Three hours later Paula returned to the reception hall. Angela was sitting on a leather bench, looking as pale as Ingrid earlier. Paula slumped down beside her.

'Nobody would tell me,' said Angela. 'For God's sake, Paula, let me know quickly. Is he alive?'

Paula knew by now why Mr Franklin had paused for so long before answering the same question. 'He isn't dead,' she said. 'He's part of a machine. It breathes for him. If there's a power failure and the emergency generator fails, he's dead. For the moment he's alive. Mr Franklin is his god. Mr Franklin can turn a switch and Laker will die. Mr Franklin can write a chitty and Laker will live.'

'What sort of life?' asked Angela. 'Is he going to live *really*? To get better?'

'I don't know,' said Paula.

'What did the doctor say?'

'I don't know.'

'But you've been there for hours. He must have said something.'

'Yes,' agreed Paula. 'But I don't remember what it was.'

'Oh Paula, don't be ridiculous. You *must* remember.'

'He talked and talked,' Paula said, 'and none of it seemed to have any connection with the man we had breakfast with yesterday. Was it yesterday? And then it didn't seem to have any connection either with the man I saw in the bed. So I've forgotten what he said.'

She buried her head in her hands. Angela was right – it was important that she should remember. Someone – a nurse – took her by the shoulder and straightened her up, putting a cup and saucer into her hands. The tea was too hot and too sweet. 'I don't take sugar,' she said.

'It's better for you this way,' the nurse told her. 'Drink it up, there's a good girl.'

'She needs to see Mr Franklin again.' Angela's voice was anxious.

'Yes. Tomorrow.'

'No, she needs to go back now. She doesn't remember what he said.'

'She's in shock,' said the nurse. 'It would only confuse her to do any more talking today. There's nothing she can do. Her husband's still unconscious. We shall look after him. The best thing for her now is to get some rest. Could you bring her back at four o'clock tomorrow afternoon? The situation will be clearer then.'

As though I were a baby, thought Paula, listening to the voices above her slouched shoulders. She wondered whether babies in their prams were able to listen to the adults who talked above their heads as though they weren't there – whether they understood and resented but then absolutely forgot. Like a mother with her baby Angela would wheel her off now to bed, and wheel her back tomorrow, and there was nothing that she could do herself. She was incompetent to help Laker in any way. The nurse was just in time to catch the cup before it fell.

3

'The accident was eight weeks ago,' said Mr Franklin. 'But as you've seen for yourself, your husband remains in a vegetative state.'

'He's still alive.' Paula had not seen Mr Franklin since a fortnight after the crash. Since then her enquiries had produced the regular answer that the surgeon needed time to complete his observation. Now he was about to deliver a verdict.

'You could say, it's a mistake that he's alive.'

'How do you mean?'

'I'm afraid I have to tell you, Mrs Laker-Smith, that there is no hope for your husband. On the night I operated, I was almost sure that this was the case. But it was necessary to allow for the one chance in a thousand, the little miracle. And it was then that the decision had to be taken, whether or not to use our respiratory machine while he recovered from the operation. I know now that we made a mistake.'

'You couldn't have condemned him to death!'

'He was almost dead already.'

'"Almost" is a large word, Mr Franklin.'

'Of course. That's why the mistake was made. I'm not saying that we could have done anything else in the light of what we knew at the time. Merely that with the hindsight we see how much kinder it would have been to let events take their course. It would have made no difference to the outcome. You would have had a worse shock, but you were expecting it, yes? Now you have it still to come. I have to say that I'm sorry. I made a choice: you must live with its effects.'

'I don't see that you *had* any choice.'

'I'm glad that you don't blame me,' Mr Franklin said.

'Blame you?' Paula felt as though she were groping her way through a wall of cotton wool. They were talking without establishing communication. 'I'm *grateful* to you. Thanks to you, he's still alive.'

'What I'm trying to tell you, Mrs Laker-Smith, is that it would be better for you – and would make no difference to him – if he were not.' His vowel sounds were unnaturally pure, un-English, as though he were carefully reading a part in a play.

'There must be *some* hope as long as he's alive. I've read about people who lie unconscious for weeks, months, but recover in the end. Maybe that's only one chance in a thousand, but that one chance . . . After all, his condition improved from the first day. You were able to take him off the respirator.'

'In some cases,' said Mr Franklin, choosing his words one at a time, at pains to be exactly accurate. 'In some cases, after an injury of this sort, the surviving parts of the brain may, to a limited extent, take over the functions of other parts that have been destroyed. That is why I have waited for so long before discussing the final situation with you. As you say, there was a slight improvement in the beginning. But that progress has not been maintained. There will be no further improvement in your husband's condition. It's always a temptation to blur the outlines of an unpleasant fact. But my duty – the only kindness – lies in helping you to accept the truth.'

'Kindness!' Paula brushed the irrelevance aside. 'He's alive. That's all that matters.' Then a gap opened through the cotton wool: they were approaching the point of the interview at last. 'You can't abandon him!'

'Please, Mrs Laker-Smith. Don't excite yourself. There's no question of abandoning your husband. It may be that I made an unwise decision to preserve his life with the respirator. But having made it, I – like you – have to live with the consequences.'

'Well then, I don't get it. What *are* the consequences?'

'I'm going to ask you a question in a moment, Mrs Laker-Smith. I don't want you to answer at once. You could send me a note. Or come to see me next week.'

Paula waited. The surgeon patted together a pile of paper, tapped the head of a pen on his desk, as he assembled his words.

'Your husband will remain in our intensive care unit,'

he said at last. 'The direct results of the accident are known and we have specialist nurses who can look after his breathing, his heart, his kidneys, his nutrition. No treatment which has started will be withdrawn.'

'But . . .' prompted Paula. She recognized this kind of pause.

'But sometimes it happens, however great the care, that there may be an infection – something so slight that a healthy person would hardly notice it, but a killer to your husband. His body can't fight for itself. So we – the medical staff – must choose. We can use antibiotics or whatever is necessary to control the infection. Or we can continue only with the care which his accident has made necessary.'

'And allow the infection to kill him.'

Mr Franklin shrugged his shoulders. 'Then it is in God's hands.'

'I don't believe in God,' said Paula. 'The only god my husband has at this moment is yourself.'

'If to make any decision at all is to play the part of God, then a doctor must be as prepared as any other man to accept the role. In your husband's case, you could say that I've done so once. But that was in an emergency. The situation now is different.'

'But you are going to decide – '

'It's not necessarily I who must make the choice.'

'You don't *have* a choice,' said Paula. 'You have a duty.'

'I have a duty to someone,' he agreed. 'I have to do the best I can. But I may know less than others what the best would be.'

There was no more cotton wool between them. Only a sword, its double edges sharp, which one of them must clutch. 'Let me get this straight,' Paula asked. 'Who will be responsible for this decision if the occasion ever arises? You or me?'

'The medical responsibility is mine,' said Mr Franklin. 'But I take my decision in the light of the circumstances. And you are the circumstances. In order that you may be well-informed, I've made my professional opinion clear. Your husband will not recover. He will never again be capable of independent life.' He stood up and came round to her chair. The interview was over. 'I hope I haven't seemed too brutal, Mrs Laker-Smith.'

'Oh no.' The cotton wool was closing again round the steel. 'As you say, it's necessary to be clear.' She shook hands, realizing that she was being signed off. In the past eight weeks there would have been other tragedies, other widows, other wounds. Mr Franklin's time belonged to today's emergencies. 'May I visit my husband now?' she asked.

'Of course. You may find it better to come less frequently in future. It means nothing to him and it could be disturbing to you.' The surgeon hesitated. 'I said earlier that you could come to see me again. But you may need longer. If you should decide one day that it would be best to end your visits entirely, I should understand that message. Until then, you needn't confine yourself to the visiting hours of the general wards. Have a word with Sister.'

Stunned by his ultimatum, Paula made her way to Laker's room. To her surprise, Angela was sitting there. She had been crying.

'I'll go now.' Angela stood up clumsily as the door opened. 'Sister told me you were in the building, so – oh Paula, I didn't expect it to be like this.' She began to cry again.

Paula hugged her until the sobbing stopped. 'Let's get some air.'

'But you want to sit here with Laker,' said Angela.

'I'll come back later. I can visit any time.' She put her arm round Angela's waist and led her out. All days seemed the same inside the hospital, but outside the sun was shining. Without speaking they walked across the park and sat down on a bench near the river.

'I had to come to Oxford to pick up an unmarried mum,' said Angela. 'I got here early, so – '

'You don't have to explain,' Paula told her. 'I'm glad you're here.'

'What a shock it must have been for you on that first day! Seeing him, I mean, on top of the first shock of the news.'

'It was worse then. There was blood. And a sort of froth.' Her mind was not on the words. Even in memory she dared not return to the horror of that first glimpse. 'Did he know?' she asked abruptly.

'Know what?'

'When he phoned that night and asked to speak to me, did he realize that you couldn't find me?' This was her continuing horror, that her betrayal might have been the last thing he knew.

'Of course not.'

'What did you say? Exactly.'

'That I'd been to your room but I couldn't rouse you. So I assumed you'd taken some kind of sleeping pill.'

'Did he believe that?'

'He was drunk, Paula. How can I tell what he believed? There was no reason why he should think I was lying.' But Angela wanted to discuss the present, not the past. 'When I first saw him today, I thought he was dead.'

'How do you define death?' asked Paula. 'How do you know? With machines to pump the heart and inflate the lungs, a man can be dead at one moment and alive again the next. Medical definitions aren't valid any longer.

What do we put in their place?' She answered her own question in silence. Death was absence without end. Simple.

'Is he going to die, Paula?'

Paula heard the question, but not as part of a conversation in which she was involved. She remembered instead another conversation in this same city. A long time ago, on Helen and Bernard's wedding day, Laker had spelled out the way that he and Paula would live. 'I am not responsible for you and you are not responsible for me.'

The system had worked better than they had any right to expect. Living together, but independently, they had loved each other from choice and not from habit. The infidelities and quarrels hadn't been important: only the reconciliations. It was because there had been no time for reconciliation . . . But Paula again closed her mind to the possibility that her disloyalty had been discovered.

Now a stranger was forcing responsibility on her. At their first interview she had been aware of Mr Franklin only as a skilled pair of hands, a sympathetic voice, someone to whom she was grateful. That was eight weeks ago. Today she hated him. How dare he force her to take a decision which could rob her of happiness and her husband of life? He was a professional. He understood the situation without being emotionally involved in it. He could have taken a course of action without letting her know that there had ever been any alternative. He had refused to accept the role of God for a second time, so what right had he to ask *her* to play the part?

Paula checked her self-induced indignation and turned the argument round. Mr Franklin was a professional and could have made a decision on medical grounds: start again from there. He must have had a reason for involving someone who in this sense was an amateur. His insistence that the wife should play a part in the decision must be because he had no way of knowing if she could stand an indefinite period of strain with such a very small hope of a happy ending. It must mean that the small hope existed. There had, after all, been that first improvement. The moment had come, as with a new-born child, when Laker had taken his first breath and ceased to be merely an attachment to a machine.

I can be tough too, thought Paula. Grimly she accepted the phrase which her own paper, or any other, would use. A human vegetable. But alive. Or at least, not dead. So there was no real choice. To say 'Let him die' was to assume a responsibility which she had no right to claim. To say 'He must live' was to preserve Laker's own right to resume responsibility for himself one day. It was settled. She put a hand on Angela's knee. 'I must get back to the hospital.'

'You didn't answer,' said Angela. 'What does the doctor say? Is Laker going to die?'

Paula shook her head. 'No,' she said. 'He's going to live.'

4

Another hospital. Another world. Helen's private room was full of flowers. By the time Paula was able to visit her, four days had passed since her hysterectomy. She was very pale and it was clear that movement pained her. But she was sitting up in bed, smiling, talking. Laker, in his long-term intensive care unit, was still alive five months after the accident; but not in the way that Helen was alive. 'You're looking marvellous,' Paula told her.

'Liar! Everyone keeps telling me that to cheer me up.

Little do they know that I smuggled a hand mirror in with my toilet things.'

'Why should you need cheering up? Bernard told me when he phoned what a bad time you'd been having for the past couple of years. Once you get out of here you'll take on a new lease of life.'

'Perhaps. In the meantime it hurts like hell. And yesterday I wept without stopping for six hours. Nurses came in relays to mop me up and try to make me smile. They must keep a book of bad jokes specially. Nothing worked. I just dripped steadily on.'

'It's an effect of the anaesthetic, isn't it?' suggested Paula.

'I hope so. Or it might mean that my hormone system has been put out of joint, which would be rather more permanent. It could even be that I have reason to be miserable. It's a very ageing thing, a hysterectomy. Especially coming within a week of my fortieth birthday. Makes it too clear that middle age has set in.'

'You're only a week older than you were last week. Nothing's changed.'

'Oh yes it has. I've lost the major advantage of being a woman. I can't ever have children now.'

'You surely – ' Paula bit the question back, but Helen answered just the same.

'No. Of course not. A first baby at forty would be ridiculous. And Bernard . . . All the same, for years I've been able to feel that I had a choice, and now I haven't any longer. You're right, though. No practical difference. I read your article on social security fiddles this morning. Fascinating. I never knew such things went on.'

The wife of a man as wealthy as Sir Bernard Lorimer would hardly need to know, thought Paula to herself; but even as she accepted the change of subject she looked more carefully into Helen's eyes and saw that her friend was indeed distressed. Post-operative discomfort would not alone explain the tears which still flooded her eyes. Helen was rich and good-looking and married to a man who had loved her for twenty years and would arrive in a few moments to say that he loved her still. Paula had reason to envy her that. And yet she was not completely happy. Helen, the perfect wife, had always secretly hoped to be a perfect mother as well. Paula knew Bernard's views about the over-population of the world well enough to guess that these, and not Helen's health, were responsible for the fact that the marriage was childless. In fact, with less time to think about her own body, Helen might not have needed to visit so many doctors.

Bernard arrived at that moment, and again Paula experienced a twinge of envy as he kissed his wife, tempering his usual vigorous hug to an embrace which would not hurt her. He passed on messages from neighbours and reported on changes in the garden since his visit the previous day. Then he opened his attaché case.

'I picked up some travel brochures this morning,' he told Helen. 'Thought you might like to choose a spring holiday. I can get away in February, so we might look for somewhere warm. I rather fancy India myself. I've wanted to go there for a long time.'

'Why there especially?' asked Paula as Helen riffled through the leaflets without much energy.

'My father spent his working life there. I've seen photographs, heard stories. Well, there's no solid reason. Just curiosity.'

'Your father?' queried Paula. Bernard's father, Sir Arthur Lorimer, had surely spent all his life in Bristol, managing the Lorimer shipping line.

Helen laughed aloud and then grimaced: clearly laughter was not yet a comfortable activity. 'Hasn't Bernard ever confessed to you that your rip-roaring grandfather in

Jamaica wasn't the only Lorimer to stuff a few skeletons in the family cupboard. Like your father, Bernard was born on the wrong side of the blanket.'

'Not in the same way,' Bernard pointed out. 'I was born into a marriage, which made me the child of that marriage. However, it's true that my mother's husband wasn't my father.'

'Did he know?' asked Paula, fascinated.

'Yes indeed. He was delighted. He couldn't have children himself, but desperately wanted an heir for his fortune and title. Mind you, I have doubts about whether I have a legal right to the baronetcy. My grandmother was careful not to tell me the true story while I was young – she was afraid I'd renounce the title and spoil Arthur Lorimer's plan.'

'She waited till he was married.' Helen laughed again, less painfully this time. 'She probably reckoned I was so tickled at being Lady Lorimer that I wouldn't let him give it up.'

'It wouldn't have been worth the fuss anyway,' Bernard said. 'Having a title doesn't make any difference to anything, except that charities always expect larger donations. And making a song and dance about it would have set all the gossip columnists on my track.' A thought seemed to occur to him. 'Paula!' he said warningly.

'Don't worry. My muck-raking days are far behind me. Family is sacred anyway. Who was your true father, then?'

'Robert Scott. A cousin of Arthur's. It was all within the family.'

'And he worked in India?'

'Yes. Apparently that was why my mother didn't marry him. She wouldn't go out there and he – he was in love with India.'

'Is that possible, to be in love with a country?' It had

always been people rather than places which provided Paula herself with excitement.

'I never knew him,' Bernard confessed. 'But according to my grandmother, Robert thought there was some kind of magic about India. It was a passive country, he said – never asking for anything, just waiting, accepting what was offered or enduring what was imposed. And casting some kind of spell. It didn't ask to be loved or hated, yet everyone did love or hate it. Robert thought that, anyway. He was one who loved it.'

'You don't really believe in spells and magic!' Helen protested.

'Of course not. But that's what's odd, that *he* did. A down-to-earth engineer, but he gave up the woman he loved because of it.'

'Well, I'm not sure . . .' Helen pushed the brochures away. She looked suddenly exhausted, unable to sustain the effort of being bright and chatty. Paula, preparing to leave, suspected that Bernard had been unwise to talk about holidays now if his wish to visit India was as serious as it seemed. No doubt he thought that the promise of a treat would cheer Helen up. But a woman who still could not move without pain might be daunted by the idea of exploring a hot country in only three months' time.

Bernard also recognized Helen's need to rest and caught up with Paula before she reached her car. 'How's Laker?' he asked.

Paula shook her head wordlessly. Almost every day she was asked that question by somebody. She could never force herself to answer it, although the answer was always the same. No change.

Bernard put his arms round her and hugged her close in sympathy. He was not only her cousin but the first friend Paula had made in England. For a moment she allowed her control to slip. Half groaning, half sobbing, she turned towards him and pressed her face into his chest. His silent understanding would have been a comfort were any comfort possible. But there was nothing to be said and nothing to be done. Paula sighed once and took a grip of herself.

'Sorry,' she said, and made an attempt to smile. 'I expect I'll see you again here soon. But just in case we miss each other, have a good time in India.'

Bernard
and
Gitta

A Package to India 1973

1

It was odd, thought Bernard as the car approached Heathrow's Terminal Three on a grey February day in 1973, it was odd that he should feel so particularly excited about the prospect of visiting India. He had failed to prepare himself properly for the trip by reading guide books or histories, so it was not the thought of exploring any particular city or historic site which made his eyes sparkle with anticipation. Nor could he pretend to be a traveller as opposed to a tourist. It puzzled Helen that he should endure the restrictions of a package tour when he was rich enough to buy his own air tickets and book his own hotel rooms. It was difficult to make her understand that after a year of taking business decisions and accepting responsibilities within the company he owned, the thought of leaving someone else to provide the framework of his trip and to deal with the inevitable hassles of travel was a pleasure in itself. But even that did not explain why he should feel that he was stepping into an adventure.

Curiosity, no doubt, was at the bottom of it – curiosity about an unknown land and curiosity about the spell it had cast over the father Bernard had never known. Whatever the reason, it was enough to overcome the only regret he felt about the holiday: that Helen was not, after all, coming with him.

Although four months had passed since she left hospital, her normal strength and energy were proving surprisingly slow to return. When the time came to confirm the holiday booking she had decided that she would not be able to stand the heat and the food and all the travelling – adding for good measure that she was putting on weight and that her muscles had grown slack: she would prefer to go to her friend Angela's health hydro to be starved and pummelled back into shape. Such a variety of excuses made it clear to Bernard that she would feel no enthusiasm for visiting India even if he were to postpone his trip – while he would never dream of submitting herself to a slimming regime. So, agreeing to share a more leisurely holiday in the summer, they were for this brief period going their separate ways. At Helen's suggestion he had asked Paula whether she would be interested in joining the party, but although a break might have done her good, he was not surprised to hear that his cousin could not bear to travel too far away from Oxford. Eight months after his car crash, Laker was still lying unconscious in the Radcliffe Infirmary, and at every meeting Bernard noticed the increased strain on Paula's face. He would have enjoyed her normally stimulating company as much as Helen's calmer companionship: but now that it was settled that he should go alone, this too added a disloyal strand of excitement and freedom to his departure.

'Be good!' Helen clung to him tightly as he kissed her goodbye. She was anxious, no doubt, to show that her unwillingness to accompany him did not mean that she loved him any the less. With no children to distract them from their devotion to each other, they were still as much in love as at the time of their marriage.

'When am I ever anything but good?'

'There could always be a first time. Every other member of the party may turn out to be a widow looking for an unprotected man.' But she was smiling, unworried.

Bernard smiled back. Somewhere within the airport now were nine strangers who by the end of eighteen days would have become acquaintances. He might even develop a casual holiday friendship with one or two. But there was no danger of any of them proving a threat to his marriage. Bernard was utterly loyal to Helen. He gave her one last kiss.

'Keep in touch with Paula, won't you?' he said. 'It's a hard time for her.' There was no real need to remind Helen. Paula was her friend as well as Bernard's cousin. She nodded, and waved him goodbye. Now he was on his own. The garish orange labels provided by the travel agency made it easy to identify his fellow-travellers as they assembled in the departure lounge. Bernard was not good at remembering names; he concentrated hard as introductions were made. Helen had been right to promise him widows as companions, for there were two travelling together. Mrs Farmer was tall, smart and blue-rinsed. Mrs Mostyn was short, plump and mousily fair. The tall, straight-backed man in his sixties with thick white hair and toothbrush moustache was Colonel Alderton, almost certainly ex-Indian Army. His daughter Daphne, a solidly-built young woman in her early thirties, was no doubt being taken to see where her father had won the war. Ten years ago she must have been pretty, and not all the prettiness had faded. Now there was a hopeful anxiety in her expression as her eyes flickered over the other members of the party. She was hoping for company of her own age, no doubt – and especially for an unattached man.

Perhaps Dr Ibbotson would fit the bill: a Yorkshireman, ten years younger than Bernard and also travelling alone. There was no other possibility, for only two more males arrived to join them. Mr Hunwick was very definitely half of a married couple, while Stephen Clyde's unsuitability for Daphne was of a different kind. Bernard, shaking hands, studied his appearance with frank enjoyment. He was beautifully dressed in a suit which graduated from rich purple at the shoulders to pale pink at the ankles. He wore purple suede shoes with stacked heels and his blond hair had been permanently waved. It came as a surprise to hear him say that his wife would be joining the party as soon as her flight came in from Ireland.

She arrived only after the others had taken their seats in the plane. Stephen Clyde's face lit up with pleasure as he rose to greet her. Had he not used the word 'wife' himself it would have been difficult to guess the gender of the new arrival. Even as it was, Bernard wondered whether Stephen might put his own meaning to terms.

In the end he accepted that she was a woman; nearly flatchested but not quite. She wore a black sweater and slacks, sensible for travelling but not becoming. She was older than her husband, and far less beautiful. Her straight black hair appeared to have been cut with the help of a ruler. Its thick fringe, touching her eyebrows, gave her face a flattened, primitive appearance. She wore no make-up. None of the other members of the party had struck Bernard as out of the ordinary, but about Mr and Mrs Stephen Clyde he felt very curious indeed.

'Gitta Clyde.' She introduced herself to him in a low, dark-textured voice as she sat down opposite him. The plane was one in which half the seats faced backwards. Bernard, in the front row of the non-smoking section, was looking straight at the first row of smokers. The handshake she offered was a firm one, her strong fingers clasping his own rather than allowing themselves to be encircled.

'Bernard Lorimer.' Because Helen liked being Lady Lorimer, Bernard never concealed his title when they were together. But an inherited baronetcy was nothing to boast about; he saw no reason to emphasize it on occasions such as this.

'Are you travelling alone, Mr Lorimer?'

'Yes. My wife's recovering from an operation.' He spoke loudly enough for other members of the party to hear, glad that Gitta Clyde's question had given him the opportunity to make his marital status clear so that he would not have to bother about it again. 'I enjoy travelling, but she's not so keen, and she felt the heat would be oppressive while her health is still below par.'

'Why do you like to travel?' The question was blunt to the point of aggressiveness. Bernard stared at Gitta Clyde for a moment without answering. He indulged his own curiosity as much in social life as in the laboratory – he had always been a man who asked questions. His companions on this tour were interesting to him now mainly because he knew nothing about them. One of his minor pleasures would be to study them and consider what made each of them tick. So he ought not to resent interrogation of himself by someone with an equal curiosity. 'I find travelling restful,' he answered.

His inquisitor gave a quick, hard laugh. 'Then you haven't read the itinerary! All those flights at five o'clock in the morning!'

'Mentally restful, not physically. Nothing important is going to happen. I spend most of my working day making decisions and choices and every decision has consequences – sometimes important ones. But nothing I decide to do in the next eighteen days will have any permanent consequence at all.'

'Everything that happens has a consequence,' she said. 'When you board the plane for the flight back, you won't be the same person. You're bound to have changed.'

'Not all changes have significance,' he suggested. 'But I grant you, by then I shall no longer be a man who's never seen the Taj Mahal.' His tone, although light, discouraged further discussion, for the tool of his own curiosity was observation rather than direct questioning. As the plane took off and turned he began to read his book. Opposite him, Gitta sat without occupation. Whenever he glanced up, she was staring at him. No doubt it was only the position of his seat which condemned him to her scrutiny, but awareness of her continuing gaze was a distraction, interrupting his concentration. Gitta's face lacked mobility. All its character came from her dark, almost black, eyes. With them she seemed to be considering him feature by feature. When she lowered her gaze it was only in order to consider more of him than his face, studying him almost as an artist might study a model. He tried by the force of his own look to turn her eyes away from him; and failed.

The plane flew steadily through the night over city lights, mountain snows and black, invisible deserts. Bernard made no attempt to sleep. He accepted the drinks and meals which were offered and then relaxed in the darkness without fretting at his wakefulness. On his left, the two widows turned from side to side in a restless doze, while the doctor and the beautiful young man in two of the facing seats slept soundly. Gitta, opposite him, continued to stare.

Bernard closed his eyes and thought of Helen. Helen, elegantly beautiful at last night's party, warmly beautiful afterwards in bed, and still beautiful now, no doubt, amongst the fat women at Wetherly. Only when he opened his eyes, startled by some shudder of the plane, was the picture of his wife and his love for her pushed aside by the personality of the woman who faced him. The blackness of Gitta's clothes and hair and eyes made her almost invisible in the pale light of the cabin, but he could tell from the position of her pale face that, like himself, she was making no attempt to sleep. No doubt her dark eyes were still staring at him, but he was no longer irritated by their aggression. The holiday had only just begun. Soon he would know as much about her as she had already discovered about him. When he ceased to be curious, she would have no further power to disturb him. He closed his eyes again and waited for India to arrive.

2

Bernard's choice of India for a holiday had been prompted by curiosity about his natural father's attachment to the country, but he had chosen this particular package tour for the diversity of sightseeing it promised. So he was pleased on the first morning in Delhi to be led by the local guide on a lengthy exploration of the Old City. By the time the group had explored the grounds of the Red Fort and the Mogul Gardens, lingered in the bazaar streets off Chandni Chowk and made their way to the great mosque, the sun was high in the sky and they were beginning to flag in the heat. Mrs Mostyn and Mrs Farmer took a cursory glance at the mosque from a distance and demanded refreshment. The guide pointed out to them a silk factory which would offer tea as well as sales talk and then hurried to catch up with the rest of his flock and prevent them from misbehaving. 'Take off your shoes, take off your shoes! This is Jama Musjid, mosque of great holiness. All must take off shoes.'

Mrs Hunwick gave a screech of protest. Long before he arrived, Bernard had decided that to be fastidious in India would be pointless, but he sympathized with her disgust on this occasion: Helen would certainly have shared it. Between the street and the raised courtyard of the mosque was a flight of steps, lined by rows of beggars who vigorously waggled their amputated stumps as they chewed and spat. Birds, roosting on an archway above the steps, contributed to the general uncleanliness, and a small boy, covered with sores, was at this moment urinating on the bottom step. Mr and Mrs Hunwick decided to join the tea drinkers in the silk factory.

Those who remained were given a short lecture on the mosque and then allowed time to explore it. Bernard chose to climb one of the minarets, although the blackness and narrowness of the shaft around the steep spiral steps proved claustrophobic. Emerging into the dazzle of daylight, he discovered himself on a flat platform with no guard rail except for the four slim pillars which supported a pointed canopy. Anyone who took more than two steps forward from the stairway would immediately find himself on the way down again. The view of the old city was magnificent, but the swirling movement of its population increased his insecurity to the point of vertigo. In the narrow streets immediately below, women in bright saris flitted like butterflies round the bazaar shops, thin men in white hurried on busy errands and boys wobbled on bicycles through the crowds. Seen from above, the movement seemed purposeless but continuous; if one individual came to a halt, his stillness was immediately concealed by the surrounding bustle.

In an attempt to steady his head, Bernard searched for a stationary object on which to fix his eyes, and caught sight of Gitta Clyde. Alone amongst the thousands of moving people she was sitting quite still in an open area just outside the courtyard of the mosque, the fixed centre of a shifting circle as small boys surrounded her; begging, selling or offering their services as guides. She appeared to be taking no notice of them. Instead, she stared up at the top of the minaret. If he were to wave, she would see him. But waving was a gesture which assumed a more light-hearted friendliness than they had yet had time to establish. In addition, it would disturb his balance. He began a careful descent; wondering, as his foot felt for each step, why Gitta had not come inside the mosque since she had apparently rejected the rival attractions of the silk factory.

It was a relief to return to the open courtyard, in which Stephen Clyde was taking photographs of small children. Outside its precincts Bernard put on his shoes and gave a coin to one of the four beggars who claimed to have been guarding them.

Gitta Clyde, from her position at the bottom of the steps, watched with an amused smile. 'You're letting the side down,' she said as he went over to join her. 'The colonel insists that we shouldn't give anything to anybody.'

'I haven't the temperament to give money to a beggar as a reward for nothing but begging,' Bernard admitted. 'But I'm prepared to pay for anything which can be described even remotely as a service. By the standards of these people I must be immensely rich. It doesn't cost me much to offer what may mean a lot to them.'

'It costs you your privacy. You've established yourself as a honeypot, so here come the flies.'

'I shall concentrate on talking to you and refuse to notice them,' he said. But this was not as easy as it sounded, for small hands plucked at his arms and shrivelled women who were perhaps still young thrust their puny babies in front of his face, muttering words that he could not understand, although their import was clear enough.

'Why do they do it?' he asked, honestly amazed. 'Millions too many people here already, and so much poverty! Why does a woman like this bring another baby into the world with no hope of supporting it?'

'Perhaps she doesn't know how to prevent it,' suggested Gitta; but Bernard shook his head.

'That would have been true twenty years ago. In the villages it may still be true now, for all I know. But Delhi is the capital city of a country committed to a birth control programme.'

'You may be giving India credit for more efficiency than it can achieve. Or for more intelligence amongst its people than they possess. You may even be assuming a wish – in the family, not the country – that doesn't exist. It can't be easy to change overnight a belief that has held a society together for centuries – that the main purpose of a woman's existence is to bear children.'

'When a woman is as poor as this and it's so obviously in her best interest – ' began Bernard; but Gitta was shaking her head.

'This isn't a sphere in which logic rules,' she suggested. 'Women need to have children. All women, unless they're cowardly or selfish, recognize that need. They need to create and they need to possess. It's rich women, not poor ones, who can afford to acquire substitute possessions and who can think of other things to create. A poor woman – a *really* poor one like these – may never possess anything in her life except her own baby. And it's the only thing she's able to create that requires absolutely no capital investment.'

Bernard stared at his companion, but her flat, expressionless face gave no clue as to whether or not she was seriously putting forward what seemed to him an extraordinary point of view.

'I can't accept that,' he said. 'I think you were nearer to the truth earlier on, when you talked about the attitudes of society. I agree that in very many societies, certainly including this one and until recently our own as well, the pressure on women to have children is strong. So strong that many of them may well feel they have no option. But if a woman is given a true choice, as happens more and more in England nowadays – if she has the same opportunities as a man – then she's just as likely as a man to decide that what she wants is a career rather than a child.'

'Not many men make that decision,' Gitta pointed out. 'Most men decide to have both a career and a child. And most women might well decide exactly the same if they were truly given the opportunity. But how many of them are? Most have to make a choice. And most choose to have children, even when the choice seems to their disadvantage.'

'But not all,' Bernard said.

'We may be defining choice in different ways. Do you have children yourself?'

'No.'

'And if that's from choice, would it be impertinent of me to ask whose choice?'

Yes, the question was impertinent. Bernard saw that it emerged logically enough from their conversation, but there was a stiffness in his voice as he answered. 'My wife and I agreed, naturally.'

'You agreed finally, I'm sure. But one of the two of you would have to raise the subject first. I can see that I *am* presuming. So I won't press the question. I'll guess instead. "My dear," you said, "there are too many people in the world already. It would be selfish of us to add to their number. Anc we could live more comfortably without encumbrances." And your wife, because she loved you – and because a reluctant father is a blight on any child and its mother – agreed that you were speaking the truth. She did not, however, suggest that you should have a vasectomy, because secretly she hoped that you might one day change your mind. Nor did you yourself volunteer for the operation, which might have proved inconvenient or even briefly painful. Instead, you expected her to go to the family planning clinic, and trusted her never to risk your anger by proving forgetful.'

This exercise of the imagination came so near to the truth and was expressed with such contempt that Bernard stood up angrily, brushing off the beggars who surrounded him and the boys who were trying to clean his shoes. Gitta did not move, but looked up at him, her black eyes momentarily enlivened by mischief.

'I've been unpardonably rude when all you expected was a little holiday chit-chat,' she said. 'You must put it down to the classic resentment of the woman who is childless by accident for those who are childless by choice. You'll find the rest of the party in the silk shop over there. Tea and Seven-Up are being served.'

Half a dozen small boys prepared to tug him into either the right shop or one of its competitors. Bernard allowed himself to be borne away, and did not look back. For the rest of the holiday, he promised himself, he would find a less prickly companion than Gitta Clyde.

3

By the fifth day of the tour Bernard had learned as much as he wanted to know about most of his companions. He had been quick to decide which of them were to be avoided whenever possible: Mrs Hunwick, perpetually grumbling about Indian standards of hygiene, and her husband who – pleasant enough in his own right – rarely escaped from her: Mrs Mostyn, always the last to arrive and the first to flag, demanding seats and drinks: and Mrs Farmer, interested only in shops and prices and incessantly discussing both in a high-pitched Kensington voice.

Stephen Clyde at least was quiet. His only fault as a member of a group was his devotion to photography: he tended to lag behind the party when it was on foot and to ask for the car to be stopped when they were on the move. Bernard did not greatly object to the delays. The reason why he had made no effort to establish any kind of relationship was the resentment he still felt at the rudeness of Mrs Clyde.

Of the others, Colonel Alderton had proved to be a surprisingly congenial companion. Far from displaying a know-all authority, he was reticent, almost shy – even confessing in an endearing manner that he was at a complete loss how to treat the hotel servants. It no longer seemed right to shout at them in the old way – but no other approach, he pointed out regretfully, produced any results. Bernard enjoyed his company – but to sit with him for a meal or in a car meant accepting Daphne as well.

By now, over a glass of duty-free whisky with the colonel, Bernard had learned the details of Daphne's domestic situation. Her husband had left her to set up a separate establishment with his receptionist, and for the past two years she had been sustained by anger. But now that the divorce had come through, her husband had remarried while she had no new partner. Her attempt to put a brave face on the situation concealed but did not cure her depression.

Bernard could sympathize with a woman who felt herself to be unlovable. It was her need to establish a pretence of intimacy, no doubt, which resulted in her compulsion to touch. She lost no opportunity to take

Bernard's arm, or Dr Ibbotson's; but even when she appeared to be flirting, her manner was tentative. She posed no danger to Bernard's peace of mind, for she would not risk a new rejection and she knew that he was married. Even if she hoped for a brief holiday affair to restore her battered self-esteem, she would wait for him to make the running.

She would wait in vain. It would take more than a week or two of absence to make him forget Helen. Gitta Clyde had come uncomfortably near the truth in her cutting picture of their decision to remain childless; but there was another side to it – having made such a contract, both Helen and Bernard recognized its special obligations. They had worked throughout the seventeen years of their marriage to keep it alive and exciting, and nothing in their lives was more important than their loyalty to each other.

Daphne offered no temptation to disloyalty, so it was for her sake rather than his own that Bernard, while not rudely avoiding her company, did not allow himself to be seen seeking it. It would be a pity to raise her hopes, that was all. Whenever possible he sat with Dr Ibbotson, a GP whose comments were pleasant and practical and who also recognized that there was no need to talk all the time.

After two days in Agra, there was to be a day trip to the temples of Khajuraho. Bernard was ready early and was enjoying the coolness of the hour before sunrise when Mr Hunwick also appeared in the garden.

'The wife's staying behind today,' he said. 'Not feeling too good. This dysentery thing, you know. Delhi belly, the colonel calls it. It's the heat and the strange food, I suppose. And the dirt. It gets the wife down a bit, the dirt. I've a bad conscience, as a matter of fact. Dragging her out here. No one really enjoys a holiday for someone else's reasons, I suppose.'

'What *were* your reasons?' asked Bernard. He had already decided that the two widows had come to India so that they could say they had been to India – this was just one in a series of expensive holidays with which they passed the time. But the Hunwicks were clearly less prosperous.

'My father was a medical missionary in Bombay,' Mr Hunwick told him. 'Long time ago – gave it up when I was born. But never forgot the years he spent here. Talked about it all the time. I wanted to see for myself. That's why the dirt doesn't worry me as much as it does the wife. The more filth I see, the more right it seems that my father should have worked here. God knows, they need doctors badly enough.'

'Someone ill?' asked Dr Ibbotson, joining them in time to hear the end of the sentence.

'Not so as to bother you. Though I must say, I'm surprised you admit to being a doctor on your holiday.'

'We were talking about our motives for coming to India,' said Bernard. 'Why did you choose this trip, Dr Ibbotson?'

'The same reason as the colonel. Drawn irresistibly back to a place which infuriated me for almost every moment of the time when I lived here. I don't know what it is about India. Some kind of spell. Sooner or later it seems to pull everyone back.'

Bernard was startled by two elements in that statement. According to his grandmother, his father had used almost exactly the same phrase when talking about India. But for the moment he pursued the more obvious cause of surprise. 'I didn't realize you'd been here before.'

'Well, never to Agra. And only for a day in Delhi, getting off the plane. I came through VSO just after I qualified, and didn't have any money to travel around. Picked up a lot of experience, though. There was a famine that year, just as there is now.'

'Is there?' The statement came as news to Bernard.

'The doctor I worked for fifteen years ago told me so, when I let him know I'd be passing his way.'

'Are you likely to become involved again?'

'No, thank God. I'm here as a tourist, to see the sights I missed before. And speaking of tourism, our cars seems to have arrived.'

Two hours later, as the group walked from the airstrip at Khajuraho into the grassy area which was scattered with stone temples, Bernard glanced at Mr Hunwick and smiled. His guidebook described the temple sculptures as erotic, but Mrs Hunwick would certainly have regarded them as disgusting and might well have forbidden her husband to look. The attack of Delhi belly had done him a good turn.

Every inch of the outer wall of each temple was covered with carvings. Bernard hardly listened to the guide, but studied what appeared to be a definitive set of illustrations, in stone, of all possible positions for copulation – including those for coupling with animals. Not every example was of practical use in modern society, for some required servants to hold one partner up in the air, head down, whilst other poses looked to be attainable only by contortionists.

Stephen Clyde was having a field day. He had brought a tripod and the largest of his many cameras. His devotion to photography might well be his reason for choosing the trip, for India offered plentiful contrasts – it was easy to feature a beggar and a palace in the same shot.

As for Mrs Clyde, she had perhaps – like Mrs Hunwick – come to keep her husband company. Bernard considered that thesis and rejected it. Quite apart from the fact that the Clydes were rarely seen together, Gitta hardly seemed a woman to borrow anyone else's reason for anything. She must have some purpose of her own – but just as he began to speculate about it, she came up to join him.

'I owe you an apology,' she said abruptly. 'Last time we spoke together I was very rude. You haven't let me get near you since, to say I'm sorry – and I'm not surprised. It was unforgivable.'

'That's all right.' Bernard saw no reason to be effusive in accepting her apology.

'I live in a remote part of Ireland,' she said, as though this accounted for her behaviour. 'Monday to Friday Steve works in London. So I'm on my own most of the time. I haven't been on a package tour before. That first day in Delhi, it came as a shock, realizing that I'd be tied to the same group of people for the next eighteen days.'

'We were the crowd who upset you, were we, just the nine of us? Not the millions of Indians all around?'

'I can escape from them. They have no curiosity about me. But you and the others, I'm attached to you and you all want – well, I've got the feel of it now. But you caught me when the lack of mental privacy first hit me. I shouldn't have taken it out on you. I'm sorry.'

She turned towards him as though appealing to him to accept the apology. She was not a woman who used her mouth for smiling, and her face was almost as devoid of expression as at their first meeting; but the dark blackness of her eyes had been replaced by something he could interpret as sincerity. He nodded, prepared to start again with her, because he was still curious. 'Why did you choose to travel with a group?'

'Money. One really has to be very rich to travel independently to a place like India. This whole package –

hotels, food, guides, transport, the lot – doesn't cost much more than an air ticket alone.'

'And what made you pick India?'

'There are things I want to see,' she said. 'Visual impressions to imprint on my eyes and transfer to my memory.'

'Like the Taj Mahal?'

'Well, *not* the Taj Mahal. But that sort of thing.'

'Why not the Taj? A visual impression if ever there was one.'

'It's dead,' Gitta said. 'Beautiful, but dead. That's understandable, I suppose, considering its purpose, but it makes the effect unstimulating.'

'What does it lack?'

'Movement, I think. Energy. Or at least the kind of tension that suggests two equal movements held in balance.'

'You talk like an architect.'

'I don't know anything about architecture.'

'What *do* you know about? Do you have a job? What do you do?' It seemed that only by asking questions directly could he satisfy his curiosity. But Gitta, it appeared, was determined to protect her privacy.

'You're expecting me to put myself into a category for you,' she said. 'If I were to tell you that I was a milkmaid – or a judge – then from that moment you'd see me only in terms of your own picture of a milkmaid or judge. I don't care to be labelled by my profession.'

Gitta spoke with the same brusqueness which had annoyed him in Delhi, but he was becoming used to her manner. This was not the moment, though, to continue a conversation which distracted them from what they had come to see. They walked together, staring up at the carvings, until their guide brought the group to a halt beside the largest of the temples – a cathedral of stone rising in a series of domes and pinnacles to a tower and spire. The guide led the way into a dark chamber, its inner walls as richly decorated as those outside. This building, he announced, was dedicated to the god Siva.

'Who is Siva?' asked Mrs Mostyn. Bernard gave a mental sigh. Quite apart from the fact that this information had already been provided in both Delhi and Agra, all their local guides were over-educated young men, taking any work they could find while awaiting their opportunity to become professors of philosophy. Mrs Mostyn's question was an invitation to practise a lecture.

'Siva,' began the guide, leaning himself comfortably against a statue in a manner which confirmed Bernard's fear, 'is one part of the Hindu trinity of gods who together form the Trimurti. This I believe is a concept easy for you as Christians to understand: one in three and three in one. All life is divided amongst these three gods. Brahma is creator, Vishnu is preserver, Siva is destroyer. Translating this to the elements, Brahma is earth, Vishnu is water and Siva is fire.'

'It seems odd to worship a god of destruction.' Mrs Mostyn, having provoked the lecture, was now interrupting it.

'Was not your own god Jehovah a destroyer?' asked the young Indian. 'Only from the destruction of chaos could the earth be created. And it must be understood that Siva destroys evil as well as good. He is the destroyer of disease, and for this reason is worshipped also as the god of medicine. His sign is the bull, and in this form he tears away the curse of infertility. To destroy is to create the opposite of what is destroyed.'

Bernard allowed his attention to wander and studied those of the interior carvings which could be seen in the dim light. They reminded him of a possession of his own – a relief of Siva dancing which he had inherited from his mother. That carving had been taken from just such a temple as this, he supposed, and sent to England by Robert Scott, the man who had loved India more than Bernard's mother. Bernard – who was so interested in discovering why everyone else in his group had chosen to come to India on holiday – was reminded that part of his own reason was the wish to understand Robert's obsession. So far he had had no success. His holiday was full of interest, but he was an outsider, a foreigner, cut off from the life of the country: he observed it but did not feel its pains or excitements. Whatever the fascination was which had drawn back Colonel Alderton and Dr Ibbotson – and Robert as well, in the year of Bernard's own birth – it had not revealed itself to him.

Disturbed by what he saw as a lack of receptivity in himself, and oppressed by the darkness of the temple, Bernard abandoned the guide and his lecture and groped his way out into the bright sunshine. Stephen Clyde had not interrupted his photography to follow the group into the temple: when Gitta came out on to the grass only a few seconds after Bernard, she glanced at her husband but did not disturb his concentration.

'A time for using one's eyes rather than one's ears,' she commented as she moved past Bernard with her heavy, unfeminine tread.

'What's the guide on about now?' Bernard quickened his pace to walk beside her.

'Elaborate parallels with the Greek and Roman gods to show that there's only one religion in the world. Siva is Pluto, god of the underworld, lord of the spirits, dancing on the bodies of the slain. But I mustn't mock. I take it that Siva is your patron – the god of medicine.'

'I prefer to claim the protection of Vishnu, the preserver,' Bernard said. 'I doubt whether Siva would accept me as a votary if he were to discover how many millions of contraceptive pills my factory turns out each year.'

'Ah yes, you're the anti-fertility man.' But her attention was not on the conversation, but on the sculptures. Bernard moved with her round the temple, which was more richly ornamented than any of those which they had studied earlier. Gods and goddesses, kings and queens, soldiers and their horses, musicians and dancers, all marched in friezes round the group of towers. Lovers experimented in even more complicated postures than had been seen outside the smaller temples. Stone courtesans, often wearing nothing but a necklace, primped and powdered and enticed.

'Do you think there was ever a time when Indian women had breasts as enormous as that?' Gitta asked. 'The young girls nowadays all seem so slender.'

'The breasts on display in *Playboy* every month represent one man's taste,' Bernard pointed out. 'There can't be many girls with such a figure, and yet the magazine's readers may have come to think it the norm. For all we know, these amorous ladies could all be carved from one favourite model of the sculptor – or they could represent his own ideal. What puzzles me more is whether, if there *was* a model, she was expected to take up every pose. This one, for example.' He pointed at the image of one particularly well-developed female who had bent her leg up behind her and leaned her shoulders back until she could grip her ankle, apparently in order to study the sole of her foot. 'Could a woman bend back like that?'

'Easily,' said Gitta. She considered the stone figure of the courtesan. Then slowly but smoothly she moved into the pose and held it. Her blouse, pulled tightly across her chest, revealed nothing which even remotely compared with the two unnaturally round, high globes on which she had earlier commented; but her long cotton skirt fell from her waist in the same line as the stone drapery of the carved figure, making her briefly as graceful as the woman she was imitating. Just for a moment, as she continued to hold the position in perfect balance, she seemed to Bernard to have become a different person from the ugly woman he knew. He had thought her clumsy, because of the heavy way she walked, but the movement of her arms and body was delicate and perfectly controlled as equally slowly she returned to a normal standing position.

He struggled for a moment to put a name to what he had recognized in the unexpected combination of grace and muscle. All his curiosity about Gitta had returned. She was the only member of the party whom he did not yet understand at all. He might not have much interest in, say, Mrs Farmer, but he found it easy to imagine her way of life. He could see her visiting a certain type of shop, could guess at the standard of the bridge she would play in the afternoons, the theatres she would choose to visit in monthly outings. Her entertaining habits, the library books she read, the drink, carefully occasional, with which she cheered an evening of depression – all these details were part of a pattern which he did not need to have explained.

Gitta Clyde, by contrast, from the moment of their first meeting muddied her own pattern with every word she spoke. But that last silent moment perhaps held a clue. He put his guess as a question. 'You moved then like a ballet dancer,' he said. 'Did you have that training when you were young?'

Gitta briefly hesitated. Then she said, 'Yes, I did,' with an abruptness which made it clear that there were to be no supplementary questions, and walked away.

Bernard enjoyed his small triumph. It was always a

good moment when he felt able to put a label on a stranger. This one, of course, was incomplete. Gitta Clyde was clearly not a dancer now – probably not for many years. One fragment of information about her past life did not reveal much about her present activities – nor did it, in itself, make her interesting to Bernard, who never went to the ballet. But it was a start, a small crack in the shield she held up against the curiosity of strangers. Sooner or later, he would begin to know her better.

4

Udaipur, the colonel promised as the group boarded a plane at Jodhpur, Udaipur would be different.

By this time, twelve days after the beginning of the holiday, everyone was beginning to tire. There had been so many five o'clock calls for six o'clock departures; so many long journeys in cars which were ovens when the windows were closed but filled with dust if they were opened. The places on their itinerary – Fatehpur Sikri, Jaipur, Amber – had been chosen for the beauty of their palaces but were equally memorable for heat and dirt. Udaipur, however, would be different.

'Why?' asked Bernard as the little plane flew south.

'Water. Udaipur stretches along three lakes, and the water gives the city a kind of sparkle. I came up here for a leave once. Invited by the Maharana to stay at the monsoon palace in the hills. Hunting, you know. His grandson's gone into the tourist business, they tell me. Converted half a dozen palaces to hotels. Well, he had enough to spare.'

The flight was short and a local guide was waiting to welcome the party, mentioning nervously that there had been a change in the choice of hotel. His nervousness was justified. Mrs Farmer spoke for the group as she demanded an explanation. From the beginning she had appointed herself guardian of the typed itinerary, each day checking their actual visits against what had been promised. Her meticulousness did not stem from particular knowledge of the places which from time to time she found to have been omitted, nor to any special enthusiasm for them; but she believed in getting what she had paid for. She pointed out now that the party had been promised accommodation in the luxury hotel – once a palace – which stood on an island in the middle of a lake, that this represented the high point of the tour and that no change would be tolerated. The rest of the group was on her side, although glad to leave the argument to one person. The guide flung out his hands in partial surrender.

'We will go first to the hotel to which you have been transferred. From there you will see the difficulty. If any of you wish to change, there will be no problem.' He hurried them into the waiting cars, which drove through a line of foothills and then steeply up to a high plateau before pulling up outside a brilliantly white building, their revised destination. Like the lake hotel, it had at one time been a palace. The party stepped out on to the terrace, no longer sure whether to maintain the complaint. It was clear that they would be comfortable in this spacious accommodation, and cooler on the ridge than down at lake level. Only the colonel was in a position to say whether the lake palace hotel would have been better.

What the colonel said at that moment was 'Good God!' The others came up to join him on the edge of the terrace. 'The hills should be green,' he exclaimed. 'Never seen those hills when they weren't green. Never been as bad as this even at the end of the hot season – and that hasn't begun yet. And as for the lake – Good God!'

He did not need to point the contrast between expectation and reality. Bernard remembered how his guide book had enthused over the lakes which curved round the wall of the city, describing them as the jewelled necklace of Udaipur. The lake palace, a cluster of white marble domes and courtyards which covered the whole of a small island, should have seemed to float like a pleasure ship on the sparkling water. Instead, it was now surrounded by mud. The lake was empty.

'Two weeks ago we have taken a group to the lake palace hotel,' the guide told them. 'They have complained of flies and the smell. Also of stealing, because now children may reach the hotel by walking when it is dark. We have made this change for your convenience, but there was not time to tell your agency in London.'

Graciously Mrs Farmer withdrew her objection. Dr Ibbotson came to stand beside Bernard. 'I'm spending the rest of the day with the medical officer I worked under in my VSO year,' he said. 'He moved here five years ago. He's taking me to see his hospital in the afternoon and for a meal with his family in the evening. But to start with he'll be having lunch with me. Would you care to join us?'

Bernard accepted with pleasure. During the previous twelve days his contact with the people of India had been restricted to shopkeepers, waiters, taxi drivers and guides, and he welcomed the prospect of conversing with a professional Indian.

Dr Chandra was a plump, jolly man whose English had been perfected while he was qualifying at the London Hospital. He roared with laughter when the curry which Dr Ibbotson had ordered to be prepared in his guest's honour proved to be a disaster – chunks of tough meat in a tasteless and watery sauce. 'The last legacy of British rule!' he exclaimed, thinking it a fine joke. 'Young boys who were taught by officers' memsahibs to make brown windsor soup and pink blancmange are now the senior cooks in our tourist hotels. They provide European food to avoid complaints and have never expanded their repertoire. Naturally, they do not eat the meals they cook. In the evening they go home to a good curry prepared by the women of the household. Vegetable curry, not meat. In Udaipur we grow fine vegetables, fresh and full of nourishment. In good times, that is.'

'Tell me about the water,' Bernard said. 'Is the situation as bad as it looks?'

'Worse. Worse.' The smile faded from Dr Chandra's face. 'At this time of year the depth of water in our lakes should be twenty-four feet. The hills should be green and the goats grazing in the high pastures. Well, you have seen how it is instead.'

'How has it come about?' asked Dr Ibbotson.

'Three years ago there were only twelve inches of rain in the monsoon instead of thirty-five. That was bad, but because of the lakes, we in Udaipur can survive such emergencies. But the next year, two years ago, the monsoon failed absolutely. Nothing. Such a failure occurs one year in perhaps thirty. It is always a disaster, but a man need expect it only once in his working lifetime. And then last year, the real catastrophe. Five inches only of rain. Enough to make the seed sprout, but not to let it grow. And because of the past years, there are no reserves of food left.'

'So what will happen?' Bernard asked.

Dr Chandra threw out his hands in a gesture of hopelessness. 'I estimate that before the end of September twelve per cent of the people in my area will be dead. Of these, some are already old and would die in any case. But ten per cent will die of famine.'

Bernard, appalled, could think of nothing to say – and

even before the discussion began he had lost his appetite for the meal.

'I have spoilt your pleasure,' said Dr Chandra, noticing this. 'Forgive me, please. We have an agricultural problem, you see, and a medical problem, but also we have a political problem. Every province might fight all the others for its share of relief. For many weeks I have been pressing my claim to the government in Delhi – compiling statistics, submitting reports. I have a duty to put a case as strongly as I can. So the subject is always in my thoughts.'

'What you say is horrifying.' Bernard could hardly believe the scale of the impending tragedy. 'You know, if twenty people in England are killed in a coach crash, or fifty youngsters die in a disco fire, the newspaper headlines shriek "Disaster!" You are saying, I take it, that hundreds of thousands of your people will die of starvation: a genuine disaster – but no newspaper in England has even mentioned it.'

'And when it happens, it will probably rate half a column and then be forgotten,' Dr Ibbotson added.

Dr Chandra shrugged his shoulders. Now that he had stated the position, his own passionate involvement seemed to fade. 'Every question must be considered from two sides. I have said that twelve per cent of our population will die, and this is true. But we all must die, and none of us can know when. Who can claim as of right that he should still be alive next year? Those who die in the hot season of this year will not need to die in the hot season of the year after. When the end is the same, the time is not of any importance.'

'That's not a point of view which you can expect any European to share,' suggested Dr Ibbotson.

'Because Europeans are afraid of death,' Dr Chandra reminded him. 'For many centuries we have despised you for this, and so we have no right to come now on our knees, asking you to help us postpone for a little while the deaths of some of our people.'

'That can't alter the reaction we're bound to feel,' Bernard said. 'It seems wrong that we should come as tourists to stare at the country and then go away.'

'Not at all. The government has decided not to beg for charity. We hope to earn help from outside on a business-like basis. We need your tourist money – desperately we need it. It is the lack of foreign currency which will kill my twelve per cent. The food exists in the world. There is wheat, too much. There are powders made from milk, from soy beans, from fish, even from oil. What we lack is the ability to pay for it. So – ' He smiled, as jovial again as though no problem existed. 'You must be happy while you are here. We hope that you will visit our shops and buy our gold and jewellery. And when you return we want you to tell your friends what a beautiful place this is. That is why – although unfortunately we cannot conceal the mud in the lakes or the dryness of the farmland – we shall do our best to keep our dying children out of your sight.'

The lunch lasted far longer than was justified by the food, and by the time the two doctors left for the hospital, the rest of the party had already been taken by car on a city tour. Bernard decided that he could cover the same ground on foot. Although the sun was still dazzlingly bright, there was sufficient breeze to make it seem a pleasant afternoon for walking.

He had reckoned without the appalling smell. Long before he reached the bottom of the slope it became clear that the citizens of Udaipur had probably for centuries been using their lakes as public lavatories and that the temporary absence of water had done nothing to change their habits. Once inside the city wall he abandoned his plan to keep near the lake and instead plunged into the labyrinth of streets. Somewhere in this area there was a palace which had been converted into a museum rather than a hotel. Bernard turned in its direction and came face to face with Gitta Clyde.

Her appearance was a surprise only in the sense that he had not known she would be in that spot at that time. It had become clear early in the tour that it was almost impossible for any member of the group to escape from the company of the others for long. Using the same transport to take them to the same places, they all had the same list of what they wanted to see. Gitta and Bernard both chose when possible to explore on foot and alone, but the smallness of the areas in which tourist sights were concentrated inevitably made their paths cross.

Today Gitta seemed pleased to see Bernard, if only to communicate her excitement. 'Isn't this a wonderful place!'

'Is it?' Bernard was taken aback. Even away from the lake, the city stank. He associated the smell with dirty, wind-swept subways or the darker corners of shabby tenements. Feeling that he was walking through a slum, he had hardly bothered to use his eyes. His concentration had in any case still been on the conversation with Dr Chandra.

Now, commanded by Gitta's sweeping hand, he studied the street in which they were standing. On the dazzling white walls of the simple mud houses, he noticed now for the first time, pictures had been painted. It was these, apparently, which so much delighted Gitta.

'This one is to celebrate a marriage,' she said, pointing. On either side of a door was a fantastic animal, painted in bright, clear colours but decorated so elaborately that the subject was not immediately recognizable. 'The elephant is for happiness and the horse is for prosperity. And look over there.' Above the door of a similarly humble house across the street a large clay relief was attached to the wall. It depicted a man and a woman and a variety of birds in primary colours liberally outlined and dotted over in black. Both the modelling and the colouring were primitive, but the effect was certainly striking. 'Everywhere else we've been shown old glories in decay.' Gitta's excitement added an unusual animation to her voice and eyes. 'But this place is alive! Have you been to the shops yet?'

'No.'

'Come with me, then.' She strode out to lead the way. Bernard looked around curiously as they turned a corner. He had observed before that many shops of a single trade tended to group in the same area. This was the first time, though, that he had seen a whole street devoted to nothing but brightly-painted toys.

'I should have thought they might be over-estimating the city's demand for playthings,' he suggested. Each of the long row of open doorways displayed toy soldiers and puppets, miniature rocking cradles and pop guns, nestling dolls and tiny farm animals.

'These are workshops,' Gitta said. 'Factories more than shops. Traders come from all over India to buy. Just watch this old man.'

They stepped inside one of the tiny shops. The young boy whose rose to greet them squatted down again in response to Gitta's gesture. She must already have spent some time on the premises, for she held aside a curtain and went further inside. In a workroom at the back of the building a very old man, his skin stretched tightly over his bones, had almost finished carving a small horse. With great care he was patterning the mane to give the impression that it was plaited.

'You see,' said Gitta. 'The whole town is busy making things. Creating unique objects. Don't you think that's exciting?'

Unwilling to admit that he failed to share her excitement, Bernard picked up a finished carving which stood waiting for someone to paint it in the bright yellow, red and black of the goods in the shop. 'Not unique,' he said. 'This one is exactly the same.'

'Not *exactly*. It's got a wicked look in its eye instead of a docile one.'

Bernard studied the two horses again and still failed to see any difference. 'You were right to call this a factory,' he said. 'Hardly a fast-moving assembly line. But the old chap is making copies of a prototype just as a Ford worker does. An object can be hand-made without being a work of art. Give this to a child and he wouldn't care whether it were mass-produced on a machine or carved like this at the rate of four a day.'

'It may not matter to the customer,' Gitta argued, 'but it matters enormously to *him*.' She nodded her head in the direction of the old man. 'He's *making* something. Not just pushing a button for money. Maybe he's run out of new ideas now, because he's old: but he still has the craft to make an object that's going to be loved. There's pride in that.' She gave a quick laugh. 'We have a different mood, you and I. I'm high and you're low. I can tell that we're not going to agree.'

'Does he speak English?' asked Bernard.

'No. The boy in the shop can manage a little, but not the old man.'

'Then I'll tell you why I feel low. It's because I've just learned that before six months are out this old man will almost certainly be dead.' He passed on a part of what Dr Chandra had told him. It seemed to make little impression on Gitta.

'He's very old,' she pointed out. 'Even if they'd had a good harvest last year he might not survive the next few months. But what I'm trying to tell you ought to make you less gloomy on his account. This man is a maker. A creator.' She took the unpainted horse from Bernard's hand and began to stroke the smooth wooden flanks with her thumb. 'When he goes, he'll leave behind him sons, and a grandson; and thousands of wooden toys which wouldn't have existed without him. No one completely dies if he has something to leave behind. It's the thought of that kind of survival which makes life worth living. And it's the people who don't think life is worth living who most resent death. If you were to tell this man now that his death is approaching, you might even find that he would be contented.'

'Your attitude has a lot in common with Dr Chandra's. I'm afraid it doesn't convince me, though.'

'Because you've never made anything!' exclaimed Gitta. 'Not even children. There's never been a moment when something has taken shape which could never have existed except for you, and when you've been able to call out, "This will last after I'm dead, and because of that it doesn't matter if I die tomorrow."'

She spoke with passion, and the silence between them as she ended was charged with tension until she broke it with a sigh. 'I'm sorry. That was unfair. Of course you've made things. Cures for diseases. I can see that this talent seems a small one to you. All I'm trying to say is that to him it's probably very important.'

'Yes,' said Bernard. He was impressed not so much by what she said as by the fervour with which she expressed herself, but it was hard not to take offence at the personal attack. Turning away, back to the shop, he picked up a bright yellow pop-gun, dotted with black in the local style. A push on the handle forced out a cork on a string with a satisfactory pop. Helen had so many god-children that one was bound to be of an appropriate age, and a purchase would represent a kind of rent for the use of the workshop as a debating chamber. 'Have you visited the City Palace yet?' he asked as the gun was wrapped.

'Yes. I was on my way back from it when we met.'

'Then if you'll excuse me . . .'

'Of course.' They were polite strangers again. Bernard was glad that he need not continue in her company. Gitta appeared to have no normal middle-of-the-road conversation: she was either silent or aggressive. There had been no need for him to care about the artistic significance of a small wooden horse; but now the consciousness of violent opinion beneath Gitta's flat, expressionless face, would prevent him from enjoying a tourist meander with her beside him. As he strolled towards the palace, he was glad to be alone.

5

Bombay had a character of its own, offering the tourists little beauty to distract their eyes, but rather the realities of life lived on the borderland of death. Sharing a taxi with Mrs Mostyn and Mrs Farmer, Bernard sat in silence during the headlong drive between shanty towns which edged the road from the airport – decrepit huddles of corrugated iron and sacking surrounded by foetid swamp water. In none of the cities they had so far visited had he felt any touch of the magic which had apparently held his father in thrall to India. Bombay was to be their last stop, and it seemed unlikely that this sprawling, overcrowded city would be able to cast any such spell.

'We shall be able to do some shopping here,' said Mrs

Mostyn as the taxi left the shanty towns behind and hurtled through a shopping area. Bernard did not bother to listen as the two women resumed their familiar click-clacking comparisons of goods and prices, but he was glad of the reminder. He had picked up various small trinkets for Helen as he went along, but she would expect one larger present. Should he choose jewellery? Or would a sari be more acceptable?

In the end, on the afternoon of the next day, he bought both. With a pair of gold ear-rings in his pocket and two lengths of gold-flecked silk in a packet under his arm, he sat down to rest on the edge of the Maidan – for the temperature was in the nineties and the humidity uncomfortably high. There had been a letter waiting for him at the Bombay hotel, written a week after he left London; he re-read it now as an excuse for inactivity. Helen had lost five pounds in her first week at Wetherly Hall, she wrote. Snow had cracked two panes of glass in the greenhouse of their Cambridgeshire home and brought down the branch of a tree across the drive. There had been a crisis in Laker's health – he had picked up some bug in his hospital bed and for three days it had been touch-and-go. Paula had spent the whole time at his bedside and had just arrived to stay with Angela for a weekend in a state of near-collapse.

Bernard mopped his forehead. Laker and Paula and snowstorms seemed to belong to a different world. Even Helen – but he was able to conjure up a mental picture of Helen, beautiful Helen, cool and uncrumpled, with gold ear-rings dangling and wearing a dress made of the silk he had bought. The strength of his desire to be with her at that moment was disconcerting. To control it, he set himself the task of making plans for the remaining three days of the holiday. These, according to the itinerary, were to be spent at leisure in Bombay. But the city did not appear to offer much entertainment to the tourist. He had visited the Elephanta Caves with the rest of the party that morning. What else was there to do?

The memory of Elephanta provided a possible answer. Throughout the morning's trip their guide had referred to other caves and other statues: larger, more artistic, covering a more extensive area, altogether more impressive. Ajanta and Ellora were the names most often repeated – not close to Bombay, but accessible. Bernard moved off in search of a tourist office.

The young man behind the counter was smart and helpful, agreeing that this was an expedition which should on no account be missed. 'But is only one flight each day, sir. Leaving at ten minutes past six in the morning for Aurangabad. And to return, the same plane departing from Aurangabad at 7.40.'

'That's fine. I'll go tomorrow and stay two days.'

'I regret, sir, that tomorrow's flight is fully booked. Half an hour ago I have endeavoured to find a seat for another passenger, but with no success. In three days' time I can obtain for you a seat.'

'In three days' time I shall be in England. Phone the airport.' Now that he had decided to go, he was not prepared to be obstructed. The young man shrugged his shoulders and did as he was told. The flight was still fully booked.

'How long does the journey take by train?'

'Unfortunately, sir, there is no direct connection. It would be necessary to change from one train at one o'clock in the morning and wait until four o'clock for the train on the narrow gauge. You would have insufficient time for your sightseeing in Aurangabad.'

Cross with himself and with the Cambridge agency – because they should have suggested the expedition before he left England and booked the flights in advance –

Bernard walked out of the air-conditioned office without a word. Then he was ashamed of his ungracious behaviour. The young man was not to blame and had been helpful. But Bernard did not retrace his steps. Instead, still annoyed, he made his way back to the hotel.

His irritation with the small frustration was not assuaged by a pre-prandial drink in his room. It increased his annoyance to find that the hotel had set aside a single table for the group's evening meal, so that he could not even nurse his bad temper in silence. It was sufficiently obvious for Dr Ibbotson to ask what was bothering him.

'A hiccup in the tourist system,' Bernard told him. 'I spent the afternoon trying to get myself out to Aurangabad tomorrow.' Already he had forgotten how very recent was the idea, how unreasonable his expectation that empty seats should be waiting for his use. 'But it can't be done.'

'Why not?'

'The plane's fully booked. There are hundreds of empty hotel bedrooms waiting for tourists, apparently, but only one small daily flight to fill them. And I must say I don't fancy another three days in Bombay. I find the humidity oppressive. Still – ' Putting his annoyance into words to some extent helped to relieve it. He changed the subject and joined in the general conversation with a determined show of cheerfulness.

At the far end of the restaurant a band began to play a Western quickstep and at once Mr and Mrs Hunwick rose to their feet. The rest of the party watched in surprise as they proved themselves to be stylish ballroom dancers. Dr Ibbotson looked across at Daphne. 'I can't match that,' he said. 'But would you – ?'

Daphne was on her feet before he had finished the invitation. On Bernard's right hand Stephen Clyde also stood up – but not, as Bernard at first supposed, to dance with his wife. Instead he murmured something in her ear and left the restaurant.

Bernard turned his head to look across the empty place and found Gitta staring at him thoughtfully. She was just about to suggest something to him. Making a guess at what it might be, he thought it only gentlemanly to get the question in first, and asked her whether she too would care to dance.

'I don't dance,' said Gitta in her usual blunt style.

Bernard looked at her in surprise. He moved into the seat which Stephen Clyde had vacated, so that they need not shout. 'When we were at Khajuraho you told me that you were actually a dancer.'

'A scientist ought to be more precise about attaching an answer to the question which preceded it. I agreed that I'd trained as a dancer. But that was years ago. I haven't danced since I was seventeen.' She looked into his eyes with the directness which he found so disconcerting. 'I don't look like a dancer. I don't move like a dancer.'

'When you took that pose, copying the statue, you moved in an unusual way. Like a woman who knows where her muscles are and what each one can be expected to do. Not many people understand their own bodies in quite that manner.'

'So you labelled me as a professional dancer?'

'Not now, of course.'

'Of course not.' Her laughter mocked herself as well as him. 'Well, now or then, you were wrong. Something heavy fell on my foot when I was seventeen. Ever since then my left shoe has been filled with metal. It's a serviceable foot. I can stand on it indefinitely. I can walk on the level as far as anyone else. I can climb stairs and ladders, more slowly than other people. But I can't swirl effortlessly round in waltz time. And if I were to tread on my partner's toes by mistake, he'd feel it.'

How could he have failed to notice, Bernard asked himself. He had certainly observed that she had a firm stride, heavier than that of many women, and less graceful – but it was in keeping with her personality and not unusual enough to be remarkable. What he should have realized was that he had never seen her legs, for she invariably wore either trousers or a long skirt. And when the rest of the party took off their shoes to visit a mosque she had always stayed outside.

While he was considering this, Gitta returned to the subject which clearly had been on her mind before he interrupted her. 'I've got a spare seat on that plane,' she said abruptly. 'If you're really keen to go, you could have it.'

'You mean that you're not using it?'

'We had a ticket each, Steve and I. It's the place I'm most anxious to visit – almost the whole point of the holiday – so we arranged the trip through the agency before we left England. I shall be going tomorrow. But Steve – Steve's found himself a boyfriend. He had his hair done yesterday and was swept off his feet by a beautiful sixteen-year-old barber. He asked me this morning whether it would worry me to travel alone. So his ticket is up for grabs. Would you like it?'

'Very much. Very much indeed. You don't seem very bothered. About your husband, I mean.'

Her flat, sallow face turned towards him, enlivened for once by a glint of mischief in her eyes. 'Well, it's not the first time.'

'You don't care?'

'People have different sorts of marriage. This is the kind that suits Steve and me. Me more than him, in fact. I don't regard marriage as important. But Steve is useful to me, as well as being my best friend. A marriage contract is as good as any other kind for keeping our interests together.'

'Are you trying to shock me?' Bernard asked. 'I don't believe any woman is as cold-blooded as that.'

'Perhaps you only know nice women. Most women are givers. I happen to be a taker. It's important to recognize one's category honestly.'

'I don't agree with your generalization. Most women are takers.'

'That's nonsense. You're talking about money, but money's not important – and you're out-of-date anyway. I give Steve money, but that doesn't make me a giver. I'm talking about emotions. Almost all women have an emotional need to give. That's why they hang on to their men, so that they have someone to give to. One can take from anyone, casually, but one can only give within a relationship.'

'Give what? Take what?'

'Anything,' said Gitta. 'Love, sex, friendship, inspiration, support, sympathy. Anything that needs a human being as its vehicle. I take it all and move on. So I can't complain when Steve does the same. It's better than that, even. He knows that tomorrow's trip is important to me. But he also knows that its importance doesn't depend on his presence. He's acknowledging that I'm independent.'

Bernard did not bother to understand what she was talking about. Instead, he smiled at her gratefully. 'Well, as far as I'm concerned, you're a giver. A good fairy, making my wishes come true. Waving your magic wand.'

'You're laughing as though you don't believe in magic!'

'Well, of course not.' He looked at her, startled. 'Do you?'

'I have an Irish grandmother. How could I not believe?' She was teasing, but only just. 'Well, I do believe that wishes of a certain kind come true. There's a degree of spiritual intensity which earns its own reward.'

'I'm not sure that I deserve this particular reward. Two days ago I'd hardly heard of Aurangabad. There can't be much spiritual intensity in a sudden whim to go sightseeing in a particular place.'

'The intensity may come afterwards. Who knows what may be waiting for you in Aurangabad! Perhaps the caves, Ajanta, Ellora, are wishing to see you even more strongly than you wish to see them.'

'You're the one who's talking nonsense now.'

By her laughter she seemed to agree, but then reminded him that he would need to rise at four-thirty the next morning to catch the plane. He saw the sense of going early to bed – but found himself kept awake by the questions which swirled through his mind. He wanted to understand Gitta Clyde and found it frustrating that she should so deliberately refuse to give him any clues. How much – like the metal foot – had he not until now even suspected about her? What did she do with herself all day in Ireland while her husband was amusing himself in London? Why had she refused to answer that question when he put it to her directly? What was the aspect of her life which would explain everything about her but which he had not yet been allowed to glimpse?

As a young man Bernard had held the theory that central to every human being was some ruling passion, which might inspire to great achievement or, frustrated, be a cause of misery – something which could be dulled or suppressed by age or circumstance but could never altogether die. Later, he had begun to wonder whether this view was fashioned too particularly by the undoubted talents of his relations, and had tacitly begun to exclude women from his generalization. The passions of most women, he suspected now, were for people, or else were of brief duration. Helen was the perfect wife, and he would not have changed her in any way, but she had devoted herself to ensuring his happiness without giving the impression that she had any ambition or enthusiasm of her own to be sacrificed to this way of life. But Gitta had nothing in common with Helen. She would be more easily fitted into his earlier theory – yet he was quite unable to identify any talent which might provide the clue to her character.

Even when at last he fell asleep he was unable to escape from Gitta. In the Elephanta caves that morning he had seen a carving which represented Siva, vertically divided to be male on one side, female on the other. The androgynous figure had disturbed Bernard, who preferred people to be unmistakably of one gender or the other. Now, in the troubled darkness of his dreams, he seemed to see Gitta Clyde's flat and unstimulating body moving backwards into a shadowed cave to merge into the carving of Siva as though she, like the god, was at the same time male and female. She was behind the stone, or inside it, and thrusting to burst out again. Bernard supposed himself to be watching, powerless to help but unable to leave. He was conscious of a throbbing of energy within the dead grey stone of the carving. Then with a crash the metal foot kicked its way through and the stone shattered into pieces. The telephone was ringing by his bed to tell him that it was half past four.

Episode At Ellora 1973

1

Tired after his restless night, Bernard was in no mood to chat to Gitta as the plane rose from Bombay Airport into the darkness. Only as the sky flushed with a delicate dawn light did he shake himself awake and ask about the programme she had arranged.

'The two sets of caves are in different directions,' she told him. 'We'll do one trip each day. A guide should be meeting us at the airport with a car. Since we're having breakfast on the plane, I'd prefer to drive straight to Ajanta rather than waste time checking into the hotel. Would that suit you? It would mean that we could get the driving over before the heat really builds up.'

Bernard nodded his agreement: he could sense her excitement and eagerness to be on her way. Without understanding the intensity of her mood, he realized as they settled into the waiting car that what they were soon to see was what primarily had drawn Gitta to India.

The road across the Deccan plateau was lined on each side by women who split large rocks with hammers again and again to make piles of small stones. The bright colours of their saris and the animation of the children who carried away the flat baskets of stones made the sight resemble an unusual form of picnic: but this was relief work, the guide told them. A family working together could earn three rupees a day, just enough to buy its ration of food.

'The soil looks rich,' commented Gitta – for the fields

they passed were furrowed with black volcanic earth. But the guide, while agreeing, pointed at a dry river-bed, its course marked by a crazy-paving of mud which had baked and cracked in the sun. Beside it cows and goats still wandered, impelled by a distant memory of past lushness to drop their lips towards the bare soil. He explained that these stone-breaking women were the wives of small farmers who in normal times were prosperous but had been reduced to poverty by the failure of the monsoon for the third year running. The cotton crop had survived, but there would be no food for the summer. Already the village wells were empty and for the next four months, as the sun grew steadily hotter, the only water would come from government tanker lorries.

Bernard remembered Dr Chandra's statistics in Udaipur. But tact and sympathy restrained him from wondering aloud whether the same forecasts applied here. One couldn't, in cold blood, ask someone what percentage of his own friends, relations and neighbours would be dead before four months had passed.

The car came to a halt on the edge of the plateau, where the land fell dramatically away before stretching to the horizon as a flat, parched plain two thousand feet below. It was from here, the guide told them, that a party of British officers had seen the panther they were hunting spring down the edge of the plateau and disappear into the cliff face of a river gorge.

Although it was already possible to see the caves which had been discovered when the hunters pursued their quarry, there was a good deal of driving to be endured before they reached the spot. The road zig-zagged down through a wild, stony area.

'What made you so anxious to come here?' Bernard asked Gitta.

'Different reasons for the two separate expeditions,'

she told him. 'What excites me about the paintings we shall see today in Ajanta is that they existed for centuries without anyone knowing about them. For thirteen hundred years no one saw them, but they were there all the time. Don't you find that fascinating?'

'And tomorrow?'

'Ellora!' Gitta spoke the word with awe and repeated it once as though it were some kind of spell. 'Ellora!' Then she spoke more briskly. 'Tomorrow is tomorrow. Don't let's spoil today by thinking about what we're going to do next.'

They arrived at Ajanta, leaving the car beside a deep gorge which a river, now dry, had cut into the shape of a horseshoe. A steep climb brought them to a point half way up the side of the gorge, where a railed path had been built out from the cliff. Bernard looked curiously at the long line of carved stone doorways along the cliff face. 'They don't look like caves,' he said.

'It's a misleading word,' Gitta agreed. 'They're man-made. The stone was cut out from the rock to form Buddhist temples. As no doubt our guide will tell us in detail.' They stepped through the first elaborate entrance into a huge dark space carved out by Buddhist monks almost two thousand years earlier. Holding up electric lamps with large reflectors so that his clients could examine the paintings which covered the temple walls and ceilings, the guide described at length the religious precepts or princely ways of life which they illustrated. Gitta wandered away, preferring to see the work through her own eyes. Bernard, politely continuing to listen, wondered how long the paint would survive the invading atmosphere of human breath and sweat.

By the time they had visited all the temple-caves and reached the far end of the gorge the day had become very hot and they were tired. By now, too, the area was crowded with Japanese tourists enthusiastically photographing everything in sight. It took Bernard and Gitta some time to edge their way back along the narrow path so that they could relax in the shade of the tourist restaurant.

'You were describing the delights of discovery,' said Bernard, sipping a cool drink. 'I suspect you left out the chief one. It's not just seeing something for the first time. It's having no one else around when you do it. But I'm annoyed with myself for not knowing about these caves before I left England. I would have read up about them.'

'When you *did* hear about them, at Elephanta, why did you want to come? And have your expectations been fulfilled?'

'I have no feeling for art,' Bernard admitted. 'And very little for history. I had no true expectations.'

Gitta laughed. 'Then why on earth go to the extra trouble and expense?'

'Because I'm a proper tourist. A rubbernecker. I can rest or go shopping just as well in London as in Bombay. I come on holiday to be entertained, and a long journey's only justified when the entertainment is something which couldn't be found in any other part of the world. Looking at pictures or palaces is only an excuse for taking a break from my work – but I like the excuse to be genuine. Ajanta qualifies triumphantly. And from the respectful voice in which you mention it, I suspect that Ellora may be even better.' But Gitta was still not prepared to be drawn on that subject.

Another hot and dusty drive brought them at last to the hotel in Aurangabad. Although he was tired after his short night and all the travelling of the day, Bernard decided not to take a siesta but instead to have dinner at the earliest possible time and then go straight to bed. So while Gitta disappeared into her room, he lingered for a moment outside his own door, looking round.

The old colonial hotel, with its spacious, easy-going atmosphere, fitted his mood exactly. A wide balcony, shady and cool, ran in front of their rooms on the upper floor of the two-storeyed building, serving as a corridor as well as a sitting-out area: pots of flowers alternated with pairs of old but comfortable cane chairs. The very shabbiness of the hotel made it easy for him to relax in it, throwing off his tiredness and feeling himself alone. Gitta's nearness did not impinge on his solitude, because she was not sufficiently interested in him to be intrusive. He could seek her company or ignore it, and she would hardly notice.

The run-down appearance of his bedroom would have had Mrs Hunwick organizing a group protest; but it was clean enough, and large. All the same, even to Bernard it seemed a pity that the hotel did not show off its country's crafts. Why were there not beautiful local rugs on the well-scrubbed floor instead of narrow strips of worn green carpet; sheets of fine lawn instead of roughly-laundered thick cotton; woven curtains from cottage industries instead of drooping squares of Lancashire print; a hand-made pottery ash tray instead of a gimcrack circle of moulded glass?

Well, that was not his business. He opened a door on the far side of the bedroom and discovered a huge and cobwebbed bathroom. The water in the roof-top tank had been too thoroughly warmed by the sun for his shower to be refreshing, but it removed the dirt and sweat of the journey. By the time he had dressed again, in clean clothes, he was in tune with the atmosphere of an unhurrying country.

Later, strolling through the hotel gardens, he found the remains of a tennis court. The grass had long since died, but the earth had been meticulously raked level before the sun baked it dry. Frayed snakes of wire dangled sinuously from each green Slazenger post, but he felt sure that there had been no net for many years. Far from seeing this as a sign of inefficiency he accepted as reasonable the thought that no one in his senses would come to this particular spot in order to chase little balls in the eye of the sun.

In other respects the hotel's gardeners had made an effort not rivalled indoors. The brown lawn was patterned with flower beds whose roses and bougainvilleas, stocks and African marigolds, were – in spite of the drought – being treated at this moment to bucketfuls of water. Just round a corner, a pair of appreciative goats whose tethering strings trailed broken behind them nibbled a row of newly-watered ferns. Bernard wondered whether to shoo them away. Then he mentally shrugged his shoulders, as doubtless the gardeners would have done, and went inside.

Dinner that evening proved not to have been worth the effort of staying awake. After a single mouthful Gitta put down her fork, although Bernard continued for a little longer to explore the stew in the hope of finding something edible.

'Don't you feel guilty about leaving food when there's so much hunger outside?' he asked.

'The more I leave, the better the cook's children will eat tonight, I imagine.'

Bernard remembered how calmly she had listened – both in Udaipur and again this morning – to the details of the drought. 'It doesn't worry you, does it?' he asked.

'What?'

'The fact that a famine is on the way.'

'If I could prevent it, I would,' Gitta said. 'But I can't carry all the failings of nature on my own conscience. I'm not an engineer, capable of building dams. I'm not an agriculturalist, able to plant trees. I see the need. But I'm personally incompetent to do anything about it. When I get back to England I shall give money to famine relief, but perhaps you don't count that.'

'No,' said Bernard. 'That's a practical reaction, and very admirable. But you don't *feel* anything, do you? Thousands of people are going to die here, and you don't really care.'

'Death is built into life. If nobody ever died, there would be no room for anyone to be born.'

'That's the sort of thing I mean,' said Bernard. 'Those are simply words. I was talking about feelings. You don't care.'

Gitta considered the accusation. 'I suppose you're right. My life is self-regarding. No man's death diminishes me.'

'We're not talking about one man's death, but thousands.'

'I'm not affected by numbers.' Gitta spoke definitely. 'No individual can die more than one death, however terrible the famine.'

'It isn't dying that's the terrible thing,' Bernard suggested. 'It's losing. Bereavement.' He thought of Paula, back in England, obstinately refusing to accept the inevitability of her widowhood and insisting instead that the man who had now lain insensible in a hospital bed for eight months would one day recover. But that was too personal an example. 'If you were a mother,' he said instead, 'watching six of your children die one after the other, you wouldn't feel like that.'

'If I were a mother, I wouldn't be me,' Gitta retorted. 'And who are you to talk? You're the man who doesn't believe in creating.'

'I try to preserve.' Bernard pushed his plate to one side, donating his share of stewed mutton gristle to the starving millions outside and accepting without enthusiasm a helping of red jelly.

'Yes, of course.' Gitta was anxious not to quarrel and yet reluctant to abandon her argument. 'But if nothing was ever created, there would be nothing worth preserving. Or you can put it the other way round. If something is worthy of preservation, it was right that it should have been created in the first place.'

'Oh come, where's the logic in that? I may disapprove – I *do* disapprove – of large families, and especially if the children are unwanted. I make pills which I hope will have the effect of limiting the number of births. I support every attempt which is made to discourage feckless women from producing their seventh, eighth, ninth child. But on the day the ninth child is born, it has the right to claim the support of my laboratory in keeping it alive.'

'You're sentimental!' Gitta was laughing at him, although not unkindly. 'Do you think the coffee will be worth waiting for?'

She stood up, taking his answer for granted. They went straight to their rooms; but in spite of his tiredness Bernard walked up and down the shabby strips of carpet for a while, ruffled by the conversation. It had been a mistake to discuss an important topic in personal terms – especially since their personal knowledge of each other was inadequate. Gitta obviously did not realize that the development and testing and production marketing of a new drug was itself an act of creation. Something existed as a result of his work that had not existed before. With that gap in her understanding, she could not legitimately attack him.

His information about her was even less complete. Had she any creative talent? Women often compensated for childlessness by making cakes or gardens, church hassocks or flower arrangements. Any discussion concerning relative values was meaningless until he knew what she believed to be important.

The next day might provide a clue, he told himself as he turned off the light and went to bed. He remembered the special voice in which she had spoken the word Ellora. Perhaps tomorrow she would allow him to understand her a little better, if only by accident. And if she didn't, that was not important. In three days' time they would be back in England and he would never see her again. Such a thought had carried Bernard through many tedious holiday moments in the past. However boring or infuriating his fellow-travellers might be, the moment inevitably came when he could say goodbye to them for good. With that thought to cheer him, he could be as infuriating in return as he chose. Not that he wished to annoy Gitta. It would be enough if he could find out why she had come to India.

2

The drive to Ellora next day was shorter than that to Ajanta. This time the road passed by ruined palaces, crumbling forts and whitewashed tombs with onion domes. Above one steep hill whose sides had been cut away to form a cliff, massive stone walls surrounded a castle, decayed but dominating. Bernard leaned forward towards the guide.

'Can we stop here for a moment?'

'On the return journey is better, sir. When the tourist bus arrives at Ellora, the temples will be crowded. If we journey straight on we shall have an hour there before this time.'

That made sense – and Bernard could tell that Gitta was in a hurry to get on. Her anticipation filled the car with an impatient energy, pressing the driver to make haste.

'What's the difference between Ajanta and Ellora?' Bernard asked her half an hour later. They were waiting in a bleak, deserted area while the guide bought their permits. The atmosphere was disturbing, even a little eerie. The air was too quiet, too still. Somewhere nearby, presumably, the guide was chatting with the guardian of the place, passing over money and perhaps accepting refreshment, but in disappearing he had left behind no impression that he would ever return. Bernard waited for Gitta to reply. What he really wanted to discover was why today's visit was more exciting to her than yesterday's, but he judged that the more impersonal question was likelier to reveal the answer.

'At Ajanta the temples were cut from the middle of a vertical cliff as caves,' she reminded him. 'But the Ellora temples have been carved down from the top, as well as inwards, out of the solid rock. The people who made them could leave a roof on the main part of a temple but cut away the rock all round, from above, to produce an open courtyard – and then excavate the inside of the temple. So that what looks like a free-standing building is actually all chiselled from the rock, working from the top downwards.'

'And what's the significance of that?'

'Who's looking for significance? Different styles, that's all. But it does have one consequence. At Ajanta, where nothing was exposed to the weather, the decoration was in the form of painting – which has in fact deteriorated. Here, it's carving – and the Deccan rock is very hard. It should look much as it did when it was newly carved.'

'Something else that was hidden, waiting to be discovered?'

She glanced at him as though she agreed, but suspected that he might not have intended the interpretation she put on his words.

'The finished temples have always been known. But – ' she paused. It was not that she was unsure of herself but, rather, doubtful whether or not to share a secret belief with her companion. 'You could say, I suppose, that everything in nature – a piece of stone or a human being – has its own potential hidden inside it. Quite often the development is botched. But when the true potential emerges – when the relationship between the second stage and the basic material is perfect – there's a special quality, a special atmosphere. Ellora has that reputation, for a kind of perfection. Not necessarily perfect carving in any absolute sense. But a perfect transformation from a rocky hill to – well, to what we're just going to see. Here's our guide back again.'

They followed him along the dusty path, but Bernard felt the conversation to be unfinished. 'And why should the prospect of seeing a perfect transformation be so important to you?' he asked.

Gitta shrugged her shoulders. 'Different things inspire different people. A painter may have a special model. A poet may need a Muse. What *I* find inspiring is the sense – ' But she abandoned her answer as they arrived on the brow of a ridge and looked across a narrow valley. 'Here we are,' she said, breathing the word softly again. 'Ellora.'

In spite of what she had prepared him to see, Bernard's eyes widened at the unexpectedness of the sight. As at Ajanta, the temples curved along the side of a cliff, but the resemblance ended there. Of the many facades, in a variety of elaborate styles, one in particular caught the eye. Near the centre of the curve a flight of steps led up to a row of pillars which flanked the dark entrance to a cave. A huge Hindu figure, as high as the pillars, lounged nonchalantly at one side. A frieze and a row of smaller pillars continued the facade upward for a little way, but above that the face of the cliff remained uncut. From the foot of the steps, no one would be able to guess what lay inside.

From this high viewpoint, though, they could see the complete temple. As Gitta had explained, the top of the cliff had been cut away to form a courtyard, leaving a complex of towers and chambers in its centre. Stone elephants ornamented the courtyard, and around it two-storeyed galleries were cut into the stone. As a building erected in the normal way from the bottom it would have been impressive enough: as a single piece of rock carved out from the top it was almost unbelievable.

'This is Kailasha.' The guide could guess what they were studying. 'Twice the size of Parthenon of Greece. Now we go down.'

He led the way into the valley and up the other side. Bernard would have preferred to go at once to the Kailasha, but was outvoted. The guide was anxious to work along the row in order that his clients could appreciate the chronological development of styles; and Gitta, like a child, chose to save the greatest treat until last.

The crowd which came on the tourist bus had been and gone again before Bernard and Gitta at last stepped inside the courtyard of the Kailasha and studied the temple's carved outer walls.

'Do you like the style?' Bernard asked.

'Which style?' Gitta seemed happy but not exactly satisfied. 'It's such an extraordinary mixture. The mass of the temple presses down, but the towers float up. There's a whole wall carved with a military campaign, which must have been intended to be educational, and yet those stone monkeys leaping about on the roof are a light-hearted joke. What I can't feel here is a sense of the religious centre. The other temples were less impressive, but they did have an atmosphere of worship. Perhaps it will be different inside.'

Side by side they walked into the first chamber and came to a standstill in front of a relief carving. It showed the same androgynous Siva that they had seen two days earlier depicted in the Elephanta cave. For a second time Bernard was disturbed by the concept.

'You don't like it?' asked Gitta, sensitive to his mood.

'I prefer people to be one thing or the other.'

'Yet none of us, surely, is wholly masculine or wholly feminine. We're all in various shades of grey.'

'It's fashionable to say so. But misleading, I think.'

'What sort of god do you worship?' she asked. 'All male or all female? Or do you not see a difficulty? If you started to write down the attributes you considered male or female, you'd realize how much you're influenced by temporary or geographical fashions.'

'You'd hardly deny a physical difference.'

'I'd deny its importance,' Gitta said. 'Except in the limited spheres of copulation and reproduction and suckling. And there are grey areas even there.' She did not wait for him to comment but moved on to a second chamber, and a third, each darker than the one before.

The last and highest of the halls overwhelmed them by its size. The solid rock ceiling was cut to represent wooden beams, pressing heavily on the rows of pillars which pretended to support them. The stone floor, polished with wear, reflected a little light near the entrance, but the further end of the chamber was dark.

'If you will please be keeping to one side, I will illuminate the Siva lingam,' said the guide, and obediently they moved away from the doorway. A large mirror outside was lifted and turned to catch the sun, directing its light into the chamber. Gitta and Bernard, keeping to one side of the beckoning silver path, followed it in. They stopped at the same moment as a dark recess at the furthest end was revealed.

For a moment neither of them spoke. Bernard was embarrassed to have a woman beside him as he stared at the phallus in the centre of the shrine. It was three feet high, cut from the same rock as the rest of the temple, but startling in its smoothness in a place where all available surfaces were intricately decorated with carving.

Gitta's silence, he felt, had a different cause: she seemed to have been struck dumb by awe. 'We've found the centre at last,' she whispered. 'The eye of the temple.' Stepping forward, she moved her hand softly over its surface. Bernard found the gesture insupportable.

'Don't touch it,' he said – and then apologized for his sharpness. 'I'm sorry. But it's obscene.'

'What's obscenity?' asked Gitta. One finger still rested on the stone but – perhaps in deference to his outburst – she checked her stroking movement. 'Something intended to shock? This may be shocking to us, but was it intended so? I doubt it.'

Bernard could not answer her question. He was excited, with an excitement which had no object. There was nothing about Gitta, whose behaviour here was as matter-of-fact as usual, to stimulate him. The lingam's obscenity lay in its startling ability to arouse a purposeless lust which had no possibility of satisfaction.

'It's the paint,' he said unconvincingly, since she seemed to be waiting for an answer. Three thin lines of red encircled the top of the lingam like a necklace. He moved forward on the pretence of examining them more closely, but also in the hope that at close quarters the stone would prove to be nothing more than a shape. 'Or is it blood? Whatever it is, it's not old. Do you think this is still used for something? I could imagine . . .'

He did not like to finish the thought, but Gitta looked up at him and laughed. 'Yes, I could imagine as well. Shall we go?'

'One question. Is this the thing you came here to see?'

Gitta shook her head. 'No. I don't know exactly what I expected to find. I just hoped . . .' She allowed the sentence to fade away. 'Well, whatever it was, I haven't found it. The atmosphere is here, but . . .' She made an effort to laugh at her disappointment.

The guide, watching from the entrance to tell when they were ready to leave, swung the mirror to show the way out. This time the brightness of the reflected sunshine moved round the outer wall. Bernard felt Gitta's hand suddenly gripping his arm, holding him back.

'It's here after all,' she said softly; and then called to the guide. 'Will you point the light back here? That's right. Hold it!'

There were a few seconds of unsteadiness as the guide propped up the mirror at the angle which Gitta had requested, so that he need not stand holding it. When he moved away, the beam pointed straight at a stone figure on the wall.

It was Siva again – the twentieth representation, probably, that they had seen in the past three hours. It was not the most beautiful or even the most perfect – in fact, it had been mutilated. It reminded Bernard strongly of the stone relief which had been his christening present from Robert Scott, for that too was imperfect, cracked in a manner which added an element of slyness to the mouth of the god. But even if it had lacked that element of familiarity, Bernard would have understood why it should arrest Gitta's attention.

It was the pose which made such a dramatic impact.

Siva was dancing, his body arched backwards to a degree which was humanly impossible. The carving – in depth less than a statue but more than a relief – was simple, even primitive. No sculptor who took the human skeleton seriously could have portrayed such a position, yet into it he had injected a controlled energy which pierced its way out of the dull, hard surface. Within the pose was concentrated the power which surrounds an arrow in a drawn bow, with all the stillness of a cat in the second before it pounces, when the movement is already assembled in its body. Bernard's own muscles tensed as though to resist an attack. Only after a little while did he realize that this might be a reaction to his companion's fierce grip on his arm. Gitta herself appeared to be in a state of trance.

Bernard studied the carving in detail, until he was able to isolate the element of shock. Siva was male, but the pose he held was female. Gitta might not have agreed, but Bernard found the figure more disturbing even than the one in which a physical difference had been marked by a central line.

'An even more impossible position than the one I set you at Khajuraho,' he said. 'I don't imagine you could bend like that, could you?'

The only light was that reflected on the wall. In spite of her closeness, he could hardly see Gitta. But he was aware of her reluctant return to awareness of his presence as she looked in a new way at the carving, studying its lines.

'I should need support.' She was still gripping his arm just above the elbow. Now she moved her hand down until it held his, and brought it to the small of her back, the palm flat against her spine. 'If you move, there'll be a nasty bump,' she warned him.

As she arched her back, Bernard needed to press

against it with all his strength. With a controlled, yoga-like slowness she forced her shoulders backwards. He had asked her to do it, but now could not endure the movement. His reason told him that he did not want Gitta but – so soon after the sexual stirring aroused by the Siva lingam – she was too close for him to be sure of remaining reasonable.

'Stop it,' he said. 'You'll hurt yourself.' He pushed her upright again, disturbing her balance so that she staggered slightly. 'I need some fresh air. I'll wait for you outside.'

Hurrying into the courtyard, he sat down on the stone foot of an elephant to wait until Gitta – pale, but apparently unflustered – emerged from the shadows. 'Let me ask you again,' he said as they drove away from the site. 'You didn't know what you were looking for. But you knew when you found it. What was it you found? And why did you look for it here?'

'Ellora!' She had spoken the word before with exactly the same tone of incantation. 'Haven't you ever had magic words in your life? Someone wrote a poem about that sort of thing. I can't quote it, because I've never been able to remember the words that were magic for him.'

'Chimborazo, Cotopaxi.' Bernard understood at once what she meant, but allowed her to complete the explanation.

'That's it. Well, Ellora was one of my words. The seed has to be sown very early in childhood, I think – so far back that one forgets. I've certainly forgotten how I heard of Ellora. At first, it was just the music of the name. Later, I read books, studied pictures. All my life I've wanted to come – but this was the first time I could afford it. When you long for something for years, it's tempting to invest it with significance. To expect more than just another trip. You're sure that you're going to find something special at the foot of the rainbow, even if you haven't the faintest idea what it may be.'

It was unusual for her to speak with such excitement. What she was trying to explain was surely caused by more than the fulfilment of a childhood ambition. 'And that particular carving?' he pressed.

'Oh, I don't know. Haven't you ever looked at someone, a woman, a stranger, and felt winded? Without any rhyme or reason?'

Bernard did not answer. Had they genuinely shared an emotion, or had the reaction of one infected the other? He was glad when the guide interrupted to ask whether they still wished to visit Daulatabad.

'What's that?' asked Bernard.

'The hill fort you were noticing this morning, sir. This city was fortified in the fourteenth century. The Shah Tughlak forced one million of his subjects to march here from Tughlakabad, the Delhi of that time, so that this should become his capital.'

'And what happened to it?'

'Sir, after seventeen years there was no more water. They marched back to Delhi again.'

Bernard was tempted to comment that the Indian people seemed fated to be victims, whether of a mad shah or an implacable climate. But he only said that Yes, he would like to stop.

Gitta left him to climb the hill alone. Perhaps the path was too steep for her. As he explored the abandoned city, Bernard found himself unable to bring it to life even in his imagination: his ignorance of its history was too complete. The huge walls and steep streets were impressive, but no more than that.

Turning back towards the car, he saw Gitta standing in a river-bed – as dry as all the others – which must once have acted as a moat. She was surrounded by a group of small boys trying to sell her something. Each held out an old tobacco tin whose contents rattled as they were shaken. As Bernard approached, she dismissed all but the eldest boy. A bargain had been struck. She handed over money and received what seemed to be money in return. Bernard came close to look.

She had bought two coins. One was of silver, elegantly decorated. The other, which looked much older, was a coppery brown and very thick.

'This is from the reign of Shah Jehan,' she said. 'You know, the Taj Mahal man. And this is from Shah Tughlak, who built this place. Or so the boy says.' She held the coins flat on the palm of her hand, passing the fingertips of her other hand over them to encircle the edges and touch the surfaces as though she were reading Braille.

'Do you collect coins?' he asked.

Gitta shook her head, continuing to stroke her purchases.

'Then what's the attraction? Do you use them psycho-metrically? I mean, do you feel now that you're in touch with Shah Tughlak?'

She shook her head a second time. 'Not with him. I don't imagine he ever touched this. But perhaps with the man who lost it in the river. Or even with the boy who found it.'

Bernard looked at the boy. He was dressed as well as any Indian village lad not actually in school uniform, wearing clean although faded blue shorts and a green short-sleeved shirt. His back was very straight and his thin legs, bare-footed, were planted on the dusty ground in a definite manner, a little apart. His brown eyes were alert as he watched his customer, trying to calculate whether the transaction was at an end or whether a word at the right moment would produce further benefits.

In that brief second, when the boy was balanced and ready to move, but remained still, Bernard felt for the first time that he was on the verge of understanding Gitta. As though he were in a dream, all sound receded and he found himself looking at the Indian through Gitta's eyes. Then the boy moved. The energy which had been momentarily pent up was released as he offered another coin from his tin.

'Memsahib, memsahib, this coin of Aurangzeb, very fine, very old.'

Gitta flicked him aside, breaking the spell. Something in the dry river-bed had caught her eye; she bent down to pick it up.

'What have you found?' asked Bernard.

As she held out her treasure he stared curiously at the ugly brown object. It looked like a potato – a potato attacked by blight. If he were to hold it and squeeze, its rotten intestines would squirt over his fingers in a brown and foul-smelling stream. Common sense told him that it could not in fact be any kind of vegetable; but still he was reluctant to touch.

'Take it,' said Gitta.

His fingers closed on it lightly, careful not to press. But it was hard – a pebble, like all the others in the river-bed. Its shape was in no sense beautiful – just a vague roundness with a surface broken by an acne pitting and a warty knobbliness. He handed it back, his eyebrows raised in question.

'You don't recognize it?' asked Gitta.

'As what?'

She knelt down in the river-bed and set her discovery on a flat rock. Using another rock as a hammer and a thinner flake of stone as a chisel, she split the pebble with a single neat tap. Before the two sections could fall apart, she pressed them back into their original roundness.

'You've seen the Taj Mahal,' she said, standing up again. 'And so have thousands of other tourists. But nobody has ever seen the inside of this stone. You're the first. It's been waiting millions of years just for your eyes. And if you were to destroy it, no one would ever see it again. It's a private present for you.'

She put the stone into his hands and closed his fingers round it. Bernard looked down at the ugly object. Then he moved the two halves apart. The centre was hollow, but inside the brown shell was a stratum of many-faceted pyramids which glinted in the fierce sun – almost, but not quite, like a bed of diamonds. He tilted the two halves from side to side so that the pointed teeth sparkled with light.

'What is it?' he asked for a third time.

'Quartz. Do you like it?'

'It's extraordinary,' he said. 'That it should exist at all, and that you should find it inside something that looks like a bad potato. Are you a geologist?'

For a moment, as Gitta's strong fingers closed his own over her gift, there had been a current of friendship between them. Now her laughter annoyed him into realizing that he had spoilt the moment with his question.

'You're still looking for the label to stick on me, aren't you? No, I'm not a geologist any more than I'm a dancer. When you meet a woman travelling with her husband, isn't it enough for you to think of her as a wife?'

'No,' said Bernard definitely. 'At least, not in your case. Mrs Hunswick is a wife. A housewife. I'm sure she polishes the furniture and cleans the bath and arranges flowers and cooks nutritious meals for her husband and loves him in a cosy way: and for her that's enough. You have a different aura – as you're well aware. I told you before, you could stop my guesses by telling me. I'm only trying to understand you.'

'Perhaps I don't want to be understood. I know who I am and what I am. Why should it matter to me what you think?' Once more she took his hands in her own. The two halves of the stone lay open on his palms. 'The quartz was there all the time, whether you recognized it or not,' she pointed out. 'It didn't make any difference to its nature when you thought it was just an ordinary stone.'

'You mean that the facts aren't altered by the label even when the label's wrong. But surely that makes it all the more important to get the label right. When I first saw you with your husband, I suppose I might have thought that you were just a wife tagging along; in the same way that I thought this – ' he looked down at his open hands – 'was merely a potato, ugly and diseased. But I would have been as wrong in one case as in the other. And with that sort of misunderstanding between us, how would we ever have been able to communicate?'

'You have a nice line in comparisons,' she laughed. 'You've decided that I'm a stone, and hard – although still ugly and not even good to eat. But I could say that I was a stone all the time. It wasn't the fault of this – ' she touched the quartz briefly before dropping her hands back to her sides – 'if you looked at it from too far away.'

'We're still not in communication. To talk about a stone is as misleading in its way as to talk about potatoes. How does one find out whether it has a core of quartz?' He kept his voice light, but he intended the question seriously and he sensed that Gitta recognized this. She did not answer at once, but began to walk towards the car.

'It's a dangerous proceeding,' she said at last. 'You can't be sure by looking and you can't be sure by touching. You have to close in and crack down. And then you could find yourself with nothing but a broken pebble – or, of course, a broken hammer.'

She turned towards him and smiled, as though to say that he should not take her seriously. Bernard found it difficult to smile back. She was warning him away. He could assure himself that the warning was unnecessary, but the fact that she had pointed out a danger tempted him towards its edge. As a member of a tourist group Gitta was insignificant: ugly and stand-offish – but only because she did not care to present herself as interesting. Now, alone with him, her rejection of any camouflage made her strength of character as conspicuous as the ugliness. He was certain that such a strength must derive from a core of identity to which he had not yet penetrated. But how could he come closer to the truth when she would not allow herself to be approached by questions?

They had reached the car by now. The driver rose from the patch of shade in which he had been squatting and opened the door for Gitta. Bernard went round to the other side. He wrapped the quartz carefully in his handkerchief so that it would not chip, and put it into his pocket. The car jolted back on to the road.

3

After a late lunch, Bernard took a siesta. With a whole subcontinent slumbering around him, this manner of passing the afternoon was not laziness but correct behaviour. Waking at five o'clock, he ordered afternoon tea for two to be brought to the balcony. The request for a meal he had not taken for years – and a drink that he mildly disliked – gave him for a second time a sense of appropriate action.

The tea tray had arrived before he appeared, showered and dressed, outside his room. Gitta sat beside it, wearing the sleeveless white blouse and floor-length wrap-around skirt in which she would spend the evening.

'Will you pour?' he asked, checking the tray as though he were playing Kim's Game: teapot, milk, sugar, cups, saucers, spoons. In this country one could not take anything for granted. But it was all there, complete with two greyish slices of Madeira cake.

'No. You.'

Her off-hand rejection of the woman's role ruffled him and he picked up the metal teapot without reflecting that the handle might be hot. Gitta, meanwhile, had raised a pair of binoculars to her eyes.

'What can you see?' he asked, shaking his burned fingers. Somewhere nearby were the minarets and dome of the mausoleum which Aurangzeb had built for his wife. But Gitta's target was closer to hand.

'Birds.'

At first Bernard thought she meant the huge kites which hovered on ragged wings above the hotel garden. Then he saw that all the trees were crowded. Green long-tailed parakeets darted between the leaves which they exactly matched. A wagtail nodded on the bare finger of a frangipani; a tiny weaver bird rested on the top of a mango tree. There were others which he could not identify.

'Those are bulbuls.' Gitta passed him the binoculars so that he could see the flashes of red beneath their tail feathers. 'And there's a peewit in the same tree. At least, that's what I'd call it – I suppose it may have another name here.'

'Do you make a special study of birds?' he asked her, recognizing without the help of magnification the golden feathers of an Indian pheasant which was making its leisurely way across the drive.

'I love the shape of birds. Cormorants. Eagles. Marvellous.' She looked at him mischievously. 'But I'm not an ornithologist either.'

Bernard smiled back. 'It's all right. I think I've given up.'

To save them from pursuing that subject, three crows landed clumsily on the railing of the balcony. Their blue-black feathers were glossy with health, their black beaks strong, their bodies plump. Bernard – remembering all those human bodies which would soon lack food altogether – was shocked when Gitta tossed a piece of cake towards them.

There was no fighting. One crow caught and stood on the prize, arching its body in profile to the onlookers as it bent to eat. One of its companions turned to stare directly at Gitta, its black eyes demanding rather than pleading. The other, more indignant, opened its beak in half-profile to complain. They were briefly still: a set-piece. Bernard laughed at an incongruous thought.

'Joke?'

'It's as though they're posing for a bust. Do you know that painting of Charles I? The head from three angles?'

'Yes, I know it.' She looked at him as though he had said something to surprise her. But when, after a silence, she spoke again, it was Bernard's turn to be startled.

'I'm going back to Ellora. I want to see that temple again. The Kailasha.'

'It's impossible,' Bernard exclaimed. 'If you don't catch tomorrow's plane to Bombay, you'll miss the flight for London.'

'There's tonight. I could go now.'

'It's half-past five. By the time you've found a car and driven there, it'll be dark.'

'It will be more exciting in the dark. A different atmosphere. I'll borrow a torch from the hotel.' She stood up, and the long skirt swirled around her ankles with the same energy which flashed from her eyes. Bernard, alarmed, stood at the same time, to stop her.

'Gitta,' he said, and his use of her Christian name for the first time passed unnoticed by them both. 'I don't think you should. The guard won't let you in. And it's a lonely part of the world. You could find yourself in trouble.'

'The guard will settle down for a quiet night in front of his fire,' said Gitta. 'If he does see me, he can be persuaded to let me pass. His job is to make sure that nothing is harmed or stolen. I don't mind him keeping an eye on me. As for trouble, I don't think so. I find the nature of the Indian people unaggressive. I should be surprised if rape were their daily diet.'

Her confidence briefly checked Bernard's doubts: but then he remembered the eeriness of the atmosphere in the empty hills even in full tourist daylight. 'I can't let you go alone,' he said.

'But I am going. You have no responsibility.' She went quickly into her room, leaving Bernard torn on the one hand between disapproval of the whole ridiculous idea – coupled with a reluctance to return to a place which had so greatly unsettled him in a first visit – and, on the other hand, an old-fashioned compulsion to chaperon a female through a tricky situation. Gitta's indifference did nothing to resolve his uncertainty. In the end he decided that his anxiety on her behalf would be greater if he waited at the hotel alone than if he were with her.

Half a dozen taxis were parked hopefully outside the hotel, though it was difficult to imagine that the night life of Aurangabad tempted many tourists out after dark. The sun was already setting as they left and, by the time they reached the deserted range of hills which contained the caves, night had fallen. The driver looked uneasy as he asked how long they would be.

'Not more than one hour.' Gitta had no sympathy for his loneliness as she switched on her borrowed torch. The sound of the taxi's radio followed its passengers for a little way as they walked cautiously along the steep track. As it faded, a new sound took its place: the mournful wailing of a single pipe. Gitta switched off the torch as the flickering light of a small fire came into view.

'It's best to be open,' Bernard said definitely. 'Trying to sneak in would be asking for trouble. He may even be armed. I've got enough money to sweeten him. Leave it to me.'

'You take the torch then, and walk straight up to him. I'll be behind you as far as the Kailasha. If he refuses to co-operate keep him talking for as long as you can, while I'm inside.'

Accepting her instructions, Bernard approached the guard noisily. The man rose to his feet, suspicious, and proved to speak no English. This was the first time Bernard had encountered this problem in India: he applied himself to solving it. 'Looking round' was too vague a concept; so he produced a notebook and pencil, indicating with a crude sketch of an elephant that he wished to sketch in the Kailasha. He handed over money as a fee rather than a bribe, taking agreement for granted, and indicated on his watch the half hour period which he wished to buy.

The guard replied fluently and incomprehensibly. Bernard deduced a general agreement and they shook hands on whatever had been arranged. Leading the way to the Kailasha, the guard unlocked an iron grille which was fastened across the entrance, and disappeared in barefoot silence. The sad sound of the pipe began again.

'Thank you for fixing it.' Gitta appeared from behind a pillar.

'He hasn't got much to worry about,' Bernard pointed out. 'There's nothing that anyone could pick up and steal, since it's all part of the solid rock; and he'd hear if anything was broken or defaced. I'll hold the torch for you. What do you want to see?'

'The inner chamber.' Gitta led the way in. She moved slowly round the walls, sometimes only looking at the carvings which covered them, sometimes stopping to feel them. When she reached the relief of Siva dancing she stopped, moving her hands over the surface as though she could absorb its shape through her finger tips. Bernard waited uneasily. He could resist the eeriness of the temple as a whole; but in this innermost chamber he was acutely conscious of the existence of the Siva lingam, even though it was invisible now in the darkness. The single section of stone which absorbed Gitta was exciting to him as well, just as it had been in the morning.

'What is it about this?' The darkness had changed Gitta's voice, which now was soft and wondering. 'It's not beautiful. It's not even perfect.' Her fingers touched the rough edge where one of Siva's arms had been chipped away at some time during the past twelve centuries. 'And yet . . . You feel it too, don't you, Bernard?'

'Yes.'

'And the pose. As you said, it's barely possible. Unless it was that I needed a firmer support than you could give me.' She took a step back, out of the light, 'Or perhaps to show a god dancing needs more than a physical position. It's a state of mind. And Siva is only one aspect of the god – only a third of the whole. You'll have to be part of the dance, Bernard. Vishnu, the preserver, working to keep things as they are. Those who are alive, you will help to live longer.'

Emerging hynotically from the darkness, her voice flickered as erratically as her shadow, whose movements reflected the trembling of Bernard's hands. He put the torch down on the floor. He knew what he wanted, although not why; but until Gitta summoned him he was unable to move. By the light reflected off the wall he saw her step backwards into the alcove, where the Siva lingam stood as an obscene altar.

'Which part should I take?' she asked. 'Brahma or Siva? The creator or the destroyer? Or are they the same? And if I lead, will you follow? Because this is a dance that I haven't forgotten.'

Using the Siva lingam to support her back, she began for the second time that day to copy the pose of the carving. The slowness of the movement increased its mesmerism. Her shoulders arched backwards. Both arms raised themselves over her head and continued until her fingers pointed down towards the floor, straining to extend the tension of her body. Her long wrap-over skirt fell apart from its fastening at the waist. She was wearing nothing beneath it.

Bernard took a step forward. This was why she had come. As he fumbled with his zip he tried to pinpoint the moment when he had known, but there was no time. Already he was pressing forward. She gasped once as she accepted him and then let her head fall back between her arms. Her stretched body was hard, like the stone she was imitating. There was no softness or tenderness; nothing womanly except the fact that she was a woman.

Somewhere in the distance the wailing of the pipe faltered. When the sound resumed it was close, and coming closer. Gitta raised her head a little and her arms came round to encircle Bernard's waist with a fierceness equal to his own. Excitement and panic brought a bitter surge of sickness to his throat as the impulse to finish quickly and escape fought with the desire to extend as long as possible something which could never happen like this again. But in fact he had no choice. He was imprisoned by the force of his own passion, by the unyielding strength of Gitta's arms and even, ludicrously, by the trousers crumpled round his ankles. The music came closer and stopped. Bernard surrendered at last to Gitta and did not after all care that the guard was certainly watching.

Afterwards, Gitta was gently businesslike. It was she who retrieved the torch, who gave the guard a second tip, who took Bernard's hand and led him up the dark path towards the taxi which waited to drive them back to the hotel. On the balcony outside their two rooms she said softly, 'Thank you, Bernard,' and touched his shoulder with her hand.

Gitta closed her bedroom door, but Bernard, unsettled, remained on the wide balcony, a foreigner in his own life as well as in a country more easily reduced to a tidy map. For a little while he stared up at the black starlit arch of the sky. Then he turned one of the shabby cane chairs to face the window of Gitta's room, and sat down. The skimpy curtains did not meet perfectly, so from time to time he could see her, bare-shouldered, crossing the room. Motionless in the darkness, he tried to collect his thoughts.

'Who knows what may be waiting for you in Aurangabad?' Gitta had asked in Bombay. Had she known the answer even as she asked the question? No, it was not possible. It was the place, that one particular spot, which had imposed a kind of demoniac enchantment upon them both. It might have been true that Gitta had been hoping to discover the magic of the place, but she had not known in advance that she would succeed.

'Wishes come true,' Gitta had said as well, when she

was trying to disguise her belief in magic with a varnish of rationality. But how could this evening's events possibly have fulfilled any wish of Bernard's? Except, of course, that one of his motives for coming to India had been a desire to understand the man who was his true father: Robert Scott, who had claimed to find India even more bewitching than the beautiful woman who loved him. Robert had spoken of enthrallment; and Bernard, hearing his grandmother repeat the word, had been unable to understand it. But he had chosen to come to India – even when it entailed a temporary separation from Helen. Had he, without knowing it, wished to be bewitched?

No, that answer made no sense. And Gitta's behaviour was equally impossible to understand in terms of wish-fulfilment. At home in Ireland, booking her flight to Aurangabad, she had not even known of Bernard's existence. But then, it was doubtful whether she had been aware of him as an individual that evening. In a particular place and for a reason that he did not understand, she had needed a man and he had been on the spot. It should have been a humiliation, but that would come later. He had not yet escaped from the spell of the cave.

The light in Gitta's room went out. Could she see him through the crack? Was she bothering to look? He stared at the closed door, struggling to steady his emotions. Had he intended to be unfaithful to Helen in the course of his holiday – and no such idea had been in his head – he would have expected to take the initiative. The reversal of roles by which it was so definitely Gitta who called the tune was one of the most disquieting aspects of an unsettling day. What had already happened was beyond recall, but now the situation was back under his control. He could choose to follow Gitta into her bedroom. Or he could stay outside – and that, too, would be his own choice.

Half an hour passed in which he did not move. Then he stood up, a crumpled man with a crumpled face, but his own master again. A little stiffly he walked to his own room and closed the door. The holiday was over. In the morning they would rejoin the party in Bombay and later in the day would fly to London. Within thirty-six hours he would say goodbye to Gitta Clyde, never to see her again. Helen would never discover his disloyalty. The episode at Ellora was over.

Paula

The Reunion 1973

1

'Is that Paula-in-person?' Helen's voice expressed surprise over the telephone, as well as a hint of crisp efficiency. By the summer of 1973 she had completely emerged from the lethargy which had been a consequence of her operation six months earlier. 'I'd begun to think I was doomed to a permanent relationship with your answering machine.'

'I've been covering a series of trade union conferences.' Paula tried to conceal the tiredness she felt. During the eight months since her last interview with Mr Franklin she had been working flat out: it was the only way she knew to push to the back of her mind the picture of Laker's body, unmoving in a hospital bed.

'Well, I hope that nobody will be conferring on June the twenty-first,' said Helen. 'I'm phoning to make sure you remember that you have a date.'

'Do I?'

'It's Angela's fortieth birthday,' Helen reminded her. 'Nineteen years ago she said that she'd be expecting us to turn up without any further invitation. I thought it would be fun to take her at her word.'

'Without mentioning it to her?'

'Given the set-up at Wetherly Hall, we're hardly likely to be sent away hungry. If she's forgotten and gone away, I'm sure the cook will take instructions from you for a banquet of scrambled eggs. And if she's arranged a different party she'll just find herself with four extra guests. I've got Lindsay and Ingrid lined up already. You can make it, I hope.'

For a moment Paula hesitated. At the inquest on Simon and Clark it had become clear that they were only passengers in Laker's car at the time of the accident. Had Laker been fit to face a trial, he would have been prosecuted for causing their deaths by drunken driving. Ingrid and Lindsay, leaving the courtroom together, had cut Paula dead as though she were responsible for her husband's actions. They could not have known how near that came to the truth; but Paula knew.

'They both said they hoped you could come.' No doubt Helen could make an accurate guess at one reason for her friend's hesitation. But there was another reason less easily explained. Paula had not returned to Wetherly since that last, disastrous visit because she was unable to face the scene of her meeting with Ben.

Well, sooner or later she would have to summon up the courage to go back, and perhaps a reunion of this sort would lay several ghosts at once. Paula looked in her diary. 'Yes,' she said. 'I can make it.'

Three weeks later, on the morning of Angela's fortieth birthday, Paula didn't bother to go to bed. Yet another trade union conference – this time in the Midlands – had ended with a ball which thudded its way into the small hours. The occasion lacked glamour, but was useful for the way in which all the gossip behind the formal decisions filtered its way between drinks and dances. Paula stayed until the end of the last waltz.

When it was over she went to her hotel bedroom and typed out her article about the union. Then she spent more than an hour making hand-written entries in the set of notebooks which were the main tools of her trade. By the time she had finished it was four o'clock.

She had intended to arrive at Wetherly in the early

evening, but now she changed her mind. The roads would be empty at this hour and, if she presented herself for a late breakfast instead, there would certainly be a bed on which she could afterwards make up for lost sleep. It would be easy to discover whether or not Angela had forgotten the nineteen-year-old arrangement. If she had, Paula felt sure that she would be able to clear the evening without spoiling Helen's surprise.

Before changing into clothes suitable for driving, she took a cold shower. It failed to refresh her, so she promised herself a cup of coffee at the first service station. Not that even coffee was likely to wake her up completely. She was tired all the time these days.

On the empty motorway she accelerated until the needle flickered round a hundred. The memory of her husband's accident, instead of making her cautious, tempted her into increasingly greater speeds. Like a woman who takes an overdose of drugs, but not quite enough to kill, so Paula never positively steered herself into trouble: she merely pressed her foot down on the accelerator and didn't care what happened. Not even the police took any notice.

The car park at the service station was almost empty. But as Paula turned in, a young man jumped down from the cab of a lorry. He shouted up his thanks for the lift to the driver. Then he turned round and Paula saw his face. She trod on the brake and the car screamed to a halt beside him. The young man turned a startled look towards her and Paula stared back. At Laker.

The likeness was so extraordinary that she almost believed in a miracle – that her husband had suddenly come back to life. But it would need to be a double miracle. This was not the man she had last seen inert in a hospital bed, with a scar running from his forehead to hide in his hair. This was Laker as she had first known him twenty years ago.

Nonsense. It wasn't Laker at all, now or then, but just a young hitch-hiker on his way to London. A stranger. And the stranger was staring at her in surprise. Paula managed to produce a perfectly ordinary smile. 'Looking for a lift?'

'If you're going south . . .' Laker at twenty had been already sophisticated, ambitious, a young man of the world. This boy was shy.

Paula smiled again. 'Where exactly are you making for?'

'Well, eventually to a village called Wetherly. You won't have heard of it – it's only a tiny place. If you're going to London, that would be a fantastic help. I say, are you all right?'

Paula was not all right. The words thudded through her head: a village called Wetherly. Angela and this boy both lived in a village called Wetherly. Somewhere in the situation there was a coincidence, an accidental crossing of paths, but there couldn't be more than one. Paula had turned into a service station and a boy who looked like Laker was standing there: click. But Angela living in Wetherly and the boy living in Wetherly wasn't a click at all. It must be part of some old story that perhaps everyone knew except Paula herself.

'Yes, fine,' she said. 'But tired. Do you have time to wait and have a cup of coffee with me first?'

'Sure. Thanks.'

She parked the car and they walked together to the cafeteria. It was the sort of place which Paula normally loathed, offering a choice of tasteless drinks in scruffy surroundings, but now she hardly noticed what she drank. She needed to pump her companion without making him curious in his turn. He volunteered the first fact, that his name was Tom.

'And you live in Wetherly, do you?'

'A mile outside the village. I'm away at Rugby most of the time, actually.'

'But your home's there, and your parents?'

'Just my mother. It's her birthday today, as a matter of fact. That's why I'm going. To surprise her.'

Paula hardly needed the confirmation. Angela could not have lived by chance in the same village as Tom without at some time mentioning to Paula the extraordinary likeness. She had kept it a deliberate secret, and there could only be one reason for that. It was a reason Paula found almost impossible to accept. Honest, straightforward, *innocent* Angela. When had it happened?

'How old are you?'

The question was too abrupt. There was a very slight note of resentment in his voice as he answered. 'Eighteen. Why?'

She hadn't meant to offend him and retrieved the situation in the first way that came to mind. 'I wondered whether you could drive,' she said. 'I mean, I'm sure you *can* drive – I wondered whether you were likely to have a licence.'

'The Porsche! It would be a pleasure.' His eyes sparkled.

'Fine,' she said. 'Because I really am very tired. Are you just eighteen, or nearly nineteen?'

'Eighteen and a quarter. Still at school. But not for much longer. I've just finished my A-levels. We're allowed a day off after the last exam, to celebrate.'

'You've got to get back today?'

'Yes. Before nine. That's why I started so early. But I wouldn't stay for the evening anyway. My mother's got a dinner planned for some of her old trouts.'

'Her *what*?'

'Friends of her own age, I mean.'

The fact that he felt no need to apologize suggested that he didn't link her with his mother's age group. She wasn't bothered about that in any case. Her mind was occupied with a little simple arithmetic. Eighteen and a quarter plus nine months equals nineteen. Nineteen away from forty equals twenty-one. She sat very still, remembering Angela's twenty-first birthday. Then she stood up. 'Excuse me just a moment.'

The sickness she felt was all in the mind. Out of sight in the ladies' room she retched once, twice, but nothing came. She splashed her face with cold water and breathed deeply for a moment. Then she went back to the table where Laker's son was waiting for her and nodded that she was ready to move on.

He drove carefully to start with, and Paula watched him equally carefully. This was not a gesture she had intended to make; the car was powerful and she was not by nature a good passenger. But he seemed competent, and his road manners were good.

'Keep inside the speed limit, won't you?' she said. She was able to relax her body and to keep a tight control over her mind. But her emotions were less amenable to discipline. The physical presence of the boy in the driving seat smothered her. He *was* Laker, in a way that the body in the bed would never be again. She wanted to look at him, she wanted to touch him, she wanted him to hold her so that for a moment she could be young again, and in love.

It was all impossible, of course. For her own sake, for Angela's, for the boy's, she must get out of his life quickly and unobtrusively. He might mention to his mother that a black woman had given him a life in a Porsche. Paula could not change her colour. But the car was new; Angela had never seen it. It would be necessary to arrive at Wetherly in some other vehicle, borrowed or hired, and make sure that her hostess noticed what it was. Paula's hands clenched as she tightened up her selfcontrol. She pulled a pair of dark glasses from her bag and put them on. Beneath their shelter she could allow tears to flood her eyes, although not to fall. Luckily Tom was concentrating on his driving. He kept to a steady sixty-nine and was perhaps glad that he wasn't expected to talk.

Angela would have taken care to keep him out of Paula's way. Probably she had sent her son early to boarding school – and all Paula's visits, she realized as she thought back on them, had taken place within the school term. Even in Tom's pre-school years there would have been no problem. It had always been part of the Wetherly system that some of the unmarried mothers should care for the children of the others. Angela could have produced a variety of reasons for including Tom in the playgroup. The other mothers, even if they guessed that their benefactress was in the same boat as themselves, would have sympathized with her wish to keep the truth from her friends.

'Your father – ' Paula cut off the question as abruptly as she had begun it. Did she really want to know what Tom had been told? But he answered easily.

'My father died before I was born; in a plane crash in Egypt.'

Paula nodded to herself, remembering how Angela's parents had been killed by a bomb explosion as they flew back from visiting her there. Simple lies were always the best. She didn't consider for a moment that she could have misunderstood the situation. If Angela had had a baby by any other father, she would have confided in her closest friend. Her silence was for Paula's sake, not her own, and it must have cost her a good deal in loneliness.

It had cost Laker something as well – the son he had always wanted. 'Do you play cricket?' she asked.

'Yes.'

'In the team?'

'Yes.' He hesitated. 'The captain, actually.'

'And squash?'

'A little. I prefer rackets.'

Probably he wondered why she should ask, but Paula said nothing more. Laker would have been proud of a son like that. Would he have married Angela if he had known? Yes, of course he would. It would be the gentlemanly thing to do, and he had been brought up to be a gentleman. To marry a duke's daughter, good-natured and intelligent, heiress to a fortune and a stately home, might not have presented itself as too much of a sacrifice.

All this Angela must have realized. For Paula's sake again she had denied Laker the knowledge of his child's existence. Later, perhaps, she had wondered whether she was right. Everything began to fall into place. The long silences of the year in Egypt; the period in hospital and the nervous over-eating which followed it; the way in which she had cut herself off from her friends.

There had been clues, if only Paula could have understood them at the time. She remembered now a question in one of the early letters from Egypt. 'I went to an Embassy party last week and met someone who'd been at school with your friend James Laker-Smith. Are you still keeping in touch with him?'

Paula remembered too the answer she had sent, as casual as the question had seemed to be. 'Sure, I'm keeping in touch with Laker,' she had written. 'I plan to marry that man one day. He's not aware of the fact, so you'll oblige me by not mentioning it if you should happen to run into him. He's a man who'd want to feel it was his own idea.'

The tone was joking but the statement was true. Angela had recognized its truth and left the field open to her friend. Yet she was in love with Laker – not only then, but now. This truth in turn startled Paula with its certainty. It wasn't something which could be proved, but it made everything else fit.

It helped to explain, amongst other things, why Angela had become so slim in the past year. Paula's own semi-bereavement had given her a gaunt look, she knew, but Angela – her face and body thinned by strain – had become handsome. Paula knew that she was not the only one to notice this. Angela had confessed, during their last lunch together, that Sir Henry Peacham was pressing her to marry him. But he had recently moved to Switzerland, taking his own advice on the best way to minimize tax demands. Angela had claimed that she wasn't prepared to abandon Wetherly; and Paula, then, had believed the statement.

Now she didn't believe it any longer. She could never believe Angela again. Her doubts became general and then centred on the assurance which, above all others, she needed to trust. What had Laker thought in those last moments before the accident? Angela must have been angry. The woman to whom she had given Laker had proved not to deserve him. Had she lied not to Laker but to Paula, to protect her friend from the guilt of knowing that she was responsible for the crash?

'We're getting near London,' said Laker's son. 'Are you going right in?'

'Keep straight on for the moment.' Paula began to rethink her plans for the day. Instead of arriving early at Angela's house she must wait until evening, after Tom had left – and must phone up in advance to specify the earliest time when she could be expected, so that the day would not be spoiled for mother and son.

That was an easy decision to make. But it implied that Paula was prepared to abandon her own definition of friendship – a relationship of complete honesty – and adopt the different definition by which Angela had been living for years: that loyalty could be founded on lies; that friendship was a relationship for which anything could be sacrificed. Not only truth, but perhaps even life. Once the thought had touched Paula's mind, she could not free herself from it. Angela was in mourning for a man who didn't know she existed – who for years before the crash had hardly known she existed, surely, except as a pleasant and hospitable friend of his wife. Or had Laker, in that last drunken telephone call, said something to make her believe that he loved her? Paula thought back to the anxious conversations of a year before. Angela had suspected that there was some kind of bet between the men – that Simon and Clark were listening to find out whether Laker's wife was where he claimed her to be. Pouring out endearments in an effort to convince his friends that Paula was on the line Laker would have been careful not to address his listener by name. Had Angela, already angry about Paula's marital disloyalty, wondered whether Laker was remembering their brief moment of closeness so many years before? Had she since then been grieving for a man she believed might love her?

If so, she must learn the truth – that Laker would never recover. Paula, who for twelve months had refused to believe this, accepted the reality without hesitation now that it was her friend's life which was perhaps affected by an unjustified optimism. She hoped that Angela had not been too definite in sending Henry Peacham away.

'No, I'm not going right in,' she told Tom. 'Pull in somewhere where you can pick up another lift.' She waited until she was once again in the driving seat before allowing herself to take one last long look at Laker's son.

'Will you do me a favour?' she said, putting on a necessary act. 'I shouldn't really be driving today. I've been disqualified for speeding. I wouldn't want to stop you telling your friends how well you managed a Porsche, but perhaps you could transform its owner into a twenty-year-old blonde, could you? Just in case there happens to be a policeman or a magistrate listening. There aren't too many black women who own expensive cars, and I'm rather too well known in the south of England.'

'My mother's a magistrate,' said Tom. Paula, of course, did not need to be told. He grinned at her in gratitude and conspiracy. 'You're the most beautiful blonde I ever met. Thanks a lot.'

He waved goodbye as she pulled out on to the road again. For a few seconds she could see him in the driving mirror. Then, reaching a roundabout, she changed direction and headed west. To Oxford.

2

'Mr Franklin can see you now, Mrs Laker-Smith.'

The hospital was the only place where Paula was called Mrs Laker-Smith – the only place where she was not herself but somebody's wife. Slowly she rose to her feet. Her hand stroked along her husband's arm. For a few seconds longer her fingertips traced the shape of his face, imprinting it on her memory by touch as well as vision. When the contact broke at last, it was with a wrench so great that she cried aloud with the pain of it. She turned towards the wall, banging her head against it as though to give herself a physical reason for tears. She had never before, in the twelve months since the accident, broken down like this.

The nurse who had come to fetch her waited sympathetically. 'Sorry,' said Paula. She bent slowly to kiss her husband goodbye. He was too clean to be real; he had lost the smell of a human body. The soft flesh of his cheek gave a little beneath the touch of her lips, but there was no flicker of the eyes, no stirring out of sleep, no arm flung up in sudden gaiety to pull her down and into the bed. Paula straightened herself and followed the nurse along the corridor.

Mr Franklin stood up behind his desk to shake her hand. The secretary to whom he had been dictating made no move to go. Did the surgeon already know what Paula was going to say? Why else should he want a witness in the room?

'Please sit down, Mrs Laker-Smith. You've been in to see your husband?'

'Yes. There doesn't seem to be any change.'

'No. No change, I'm afraid.'

'This is what I came to ask you, Mr Franklin. Is there any hope at all of any improvement? Ever?'

'I believe you know the answer to your question.' He tapped a pencil on the desk in front of him while his eyes looked seriously into hers. 'When I saw you first, Mrs Laker-Smith, I had to tell you that there was very little hope of your husband's recovery from his accident. Within eight weeks I tried to make it clear that the damage to the brain made any return to normal life impossible. Eight weeks, a year – the time makes no difference, except to confirm the situation. There will never be any improvement. I'm sorry to have to say this, Mrs Laker-Smith, but I think you know it for yourself.'

'Yes,' said Paula. 'But I had to be sure.' She stood up. 'I came in to say that I don't intend to visit my husband any more.'

The surgeon, on the other side of the desk, seemed to be considering something. Paula spoke more quickly, justifying herself.

'I have to earn my own living, Mr Franklin. I must – '

'Please!' The surgeon put up his hand. 'Please sit down again, Mrs Laker-Smith.' He leaned back in his own chair, looking at her compassionately. 'You don't have to give me reasons. You have a perfect right to take this decision, and no one here will feel anything but sympathy. I've never believed that the living should sacrifice themselves to – to the dead. You remember that I hoped you would make this choice ten months ago. Then there would have been no element of convenience, and so no feeling of guilt. But you are right now, just as you would have been right then.'

There was a long silence.

'Well,' said Paula. 'That's all. I just wanted to tell you.' She was sweating. Everything that was alive inside her had drained out through her pores, leaving her limp and shivering.

The tapping on the desk began again. 'I understand what you are trying to tell me,' Mr Franklin said. 'But though *you* have taken a decision, *I* have to accept a responsibility. I believe that your decision is correct, but I must ask you to spell it out.'

'Is that necessary?'

He raised his eyebrows, questioning himself. 'There are some people who need to confuse their consciences with euphemisms. I don't believe you are one of those. Also, there are many people who are incapable of looking the facts of death in the face. You yourself, in the first shock of the accident, had this difficulty. Some relatives of my patients never escape from it. I have to grope my way through the fog of their minds. But you're an intelligent woman and you have, now, thought the situation through. Is it asking too much that you should put your thoughts into words?'

'To dictate them to your secretary?' asked Paula. 'You told me once that every doctor has to be prepared to play God. Does God require an indemnity?'

'Men have been known to curse their gods for granting their wishes.'

His sympathetic understanding – of a situation which he couldn't possibly understand – combined with Paula's anger that he should force her into explicitness to give a cold edge to her voice. 'All right,' she said. 'You told me last year that if my husband should develop some secondary infection this could either be treated or allowed to take its natural course. I asked you to treat him. Now I withdraw that request. Is that enough?'

'It's enough for me,' said Mr Franklin. 'It might be better for you if you finished the thought off.'

'I want you to let him die,' said Paula. 'Is *that* enough?' She could feel her voice rising hysterically. 'It's my turn to play God today. You have my permission to let my husband die.'

Mr Franklin stood up again behind his desk. 'It's only in a technical sense that your husband is alive,' he said. 'He's been dead to you for a year already. It would have been better if you'd been able to grieve and recover a long time ago. I hope most sincerely that you'll be able to make a new and happy life for yourself now.'

It would never be mentioned again, Paula realized as she shook hands. 'Let him die,' she had said to the surgeon, because years earlier she had said casually to the man she loved, 'Look after Angela.' It was hard to believe that such a trivial remark should have had so many consequences but now, at last, the chapter must be closed. She would walk out of the room and in a few months a letter would arrive or the telephone would ring. And that would be the end of that. There would, as Mr Franklin had said, be grief and recovery. For Angela.

3

Paula guessed that Helen would use her London flat rather than her house in Cambridgeshire as the starting point of the trip to Wetherly. Asking her for a lift solved two problems at once. There would now be no risk of Angela discovering that her friend had acquired a Porsche; whilst Paula herself, exhausted by emotional strain and lack of sleep, knew that she was unfit to drive.

It would be necessary to behave as though nothing of importance had happened in the course of the day, but Paula's heart sank at the thought of the evening to come. Reunions of any kind were a mistake. Even supposing Helen to be right in saying that Ingrid and Lindsay did not hold Paula herself responsible for the death of their husbands, there was no pleasure to be anticipated from their company. It would be artificial to pretend to a special friendship now just because they had genuinely been friends twenty years ago. They had grown out of each other long before the accident.

Paula was clear-sighted enough to understand why they had drifted apart. Her work brought her daily into contact with successful men and women and even before she became a journalist she had found success an attractive quality in itself. She had no interest in the unambitious and little use for those who were ambitious but had failed. Failure would never have spoiled her friendship with Angela, because her affection went too deep for that – but in fact she genuinely admired the businesslike confidence with which Angela ran both her charity and the health hydro. Helen, too, had the self-confidence of a woman organizing her life successfully, although on a more domestic scale; and in her case friendship had been reinforced by the family link. But Ingrid and Lindsay . . .

Ingrid had never become a professor. Simon wanted a large family and his wife had provided it for him. For almost eight years she had been either pregnant or breast-feeding and then had settled down happily to cope with the brood in a house which rapidly became an academic slum. She had no interest in cooking or interior decoration or even basic comfort, and her policy of encouraging the children to express themselves did not make for peace or tidiness. Paula had once dropped in uninvited, to find Simon writing an article on heresies at one corner of the kitchen table while his five-year-old daughter created a picture with finger paints at another; the youngest child was performing on his pot in the centre of the floor, the eldest squeaked away on a violin in the corner, and the others tackled their homework with one hand while eating fish fingers with the other. Paula, who had a methodical mind, had found the chaos and babble impossible to endure.

Ingrid at least was happy in those days, and could take a vicarious pride in Simon's academic success. Lindsay, by contrast, had proved to be a loser. She had never come near to winning Wimbledon. Her best effort was to reach the quarter-final of the mixed doubles at the age of twenty-four, and she had hopes of doing better the next year. But when that June arrived she was five months pregnant.

The effect of the pregnancy had been greater than merely the interruption of a tennis career. Lindsay had tried to free herself from the trap first by a series of gin-drinking sessions and later – too much later – with outside help. Instead of getting rid of the baby this had caused it eventually to be born spastic.

There were other results of that episode. She had retained a taste for too much gin; and just as she had never forgiven Clark for the baby's inconvenient conception, so he had never been able to forget her disastrous handling of the situation. He had bought a prep school and became its headmaster himself. But he was lazy and unbusinesslike, perpetually struggling to keep up with loan payments; whilst Lindsay, who taught athletics and maths in the school, did not really like small boys in the way which was necessary if she was to understand their problems, and soon became as bored as her pupils. Drinking had become the only hobby which she and her husband shared.

'Dead on time,' said Helen, drawing her Jaguar to a halt in front of Wetherly Hall. 'That's to say, if a time had been appointed, and if the appointment were for seven-thirty, we could claim perfect punctuality.' They walked together up the wide stone steps, rang the bell, and asked to be shown to Lady Angela's flat.

They were expected. Paula, of course, had known that this would be the case, but she did her best to join in the smiles of delight and relief – on Helen's part as well as Angela's. Then it was time to greet the other two, who had already arrived.

Ingrid's manners were perfect. Tomorrow would be the first anniversary of her husband's death, but she expressed her pleasure at Paula's presence with a politeness which made it clear that there would be no mention of the subject from her. In less than a year she had transformed herself from a housewife into a breadwinner. She taught in a local sixth form and earned extra money by marking O-level examination papers. It was good of her, she implied, to take an evening off at this time of year. She held herself very straight and dressed with severe smartness. Her long black hair, strained off her face, was sleek and well-groomed. She had become cold, in the way which Paula, twenty years earlier, would have expected her always to be cold. The warm and surprising years in which she had been happy to be a wife and mother had slipped away. This, Paula supposed, was what Mr Franklin meant when he talked of recovery after grief.

Where Ingrid had turned a sharp corner, Lindsay had continued a descent. They were all five the same age, but Lindsay looked by far the oldest. The corners of her mouth were pulled down by petulance; she had tinted the first grey hairs, with patchy results, and her eyes wandered discontentedly. It was hard to know what could be safely discussed with her – there seemed no subject which might not touch some sore point, some frustrated ambition. She had achieved nothing. Even the spastic child had died.

The worst subject of all, thought Paula, was the past. She fought against it through the meal, but the past was all they had in common. They were assembled to celebrate Angela's fortieth birthday because they had been friends on her twenty-first. No amount of gossip about politics, holidays, television, theatres, could put off the moment when somebody would say, 'Do you remember?'

In the end, modern fiction was the subject which opened the door to reminiscence. 'A month ago I noticed a review of a book by Isabel Blair,' Angela said. 'Isabel Trent married someone called Blair. It was in the college record. It must be the same Isabel. Do you remember, at my twenty-first birthday, how we wrote her off? I never thought she'd make it. But here she is, after all these years, getting her first novel published at forty.'

‘It shows how important it is to choose an ambition which doesn’t have to be realized too young,’ Paula commented. ‘If you’re frantic to be an Olympic swimming champion, then by the time you’re twenty you’ve either succeeded or else you know you never will. Terrible to be a loser at twenty. But if you plan to be an archbishop, or a prime minister, or governor of the Bank of England, presumably you can’t even dream of success before you’re fifty. So you can’t be disappointed before that. Writing novels must be even better. No limit at all.’

Too late she realized that this was one of Lindsay’s many vulnerable points. Ingrid, coming to the rescue by a change of subject, succeeded only in hitting a second one.

‘It’s the thing we weren’t taught at Oxford,’ she said. ‘Isabel seems to have managed it, and I’ve been forced into it. The most important thing in a woman’s education, one might think. How to change directions, and when. How to have one life, and end it, and start another. And what the timing should be. Do you have children young and then start to work when they’re all at school? Or get established in a career first and hope you’ll be allowed back if you take ten years off in the middle. It’s not simple. The rest of you have dodged that choice by making another one, not to have children at all.’

‘You’re taking two things for granted,’ Lindsay pointed out. ‘That we all want to work. And that it’s impossible to work and bring up children at the same time.’ She had not, it seemed, noticed any lack of tact. Perhaps she – like Ingrid – had forgotten that she had ever had a child.

‘Bringing up young children is a full-time job.’ Ingrid was as definite now as nineteen years earlier in the way she stated her views. ‘But after that, yes, I do think we ought to work. We spent a lot of our time and other people’s money having our minds trained. I think we should make use of them, not just sit at home.' Now she did perhaps realize that she was being tactless, although with a different target; her eyes flickered guiltily in Helen's direction. 'Isabel seems to me to be a success,' she went on. 'She's had a job and a husband and perhaps children as well, for all I know. But all the time she's kept her vision clear. Ambition modified, I've no doubt, but ambition realized.'

So they were back at the twenty-first birthday party. By now Paula was too tired to contribute to the discussion as her companions worked their way through the whole undergraduate intake of their year. Lindsay was catty, Angela was kind, Ingrid was dogmatic. Only Helen, who had willingly sacrificed all thought of an independent career but had failed to have the children she longed for, was as silent as Paula herself. It was all too complicated for Paula, whose head was heavy with more than her sleepless night. Her body was sitting at Angela's table, but her emotions were still in a hospital room and now her memory was being dragged back to yet another room, in which she had been young and happy and supremely confident at the prospect of controlling her own life. There seemed no bridge between that girl and this woman, and yet every inch of the way was locked securely to the one before – just as the past nineteen years of Angela's life were locked to the moment in which Paula had given Laker a loving push: 'Look after Angela.'

'A dangerous game to play,' said Lindsay's voice through the haze. 'We seem to have arrived at ourselves. As a quintet, we don't come very well out of it, do we? I'm a straight loser. Helen and Angela have both failed to notch up the families they hoped for, although they seem to have acquired satisfying substitutes. Ingrid obviously values her children more than her lost professorship, but in terms of ambition . . .' She let the thought die away. 'Paula's the only one who's got what she wanted.'

The sound of her own name jerked Paula back into the present. 'No,' she said.

'You may not be prime minister. But you wanted to be a political journalist. I remember you saying so.'

'I was fibbing,' Paula admitted. 'That was only a secondary ambition. A kind of showing off. What I wanted then was what most girls want at that age – to spend the rest of my life with the man I loved. Laker. Laker for the rest of my life. That was what I wanted.'

She buried her head in her hands. Beside her, Helen stood up. 'We must make a move, Angela. It's a long drive back, and Paula didn't get to bed at all last night.'

Angela followed Paula out of the room as she went to fetch her coat. She had long ago ceased to put her question into words, and always before it had been enough for Paula to shake her head. No. No change. Tonight, though, Angela was clearly disturbed by the way her friend had spoken. 'Paula? Has something – ?'

'No,' said Paula. 'Nothing's happened.' To describe her visit to Oxford would be too brutal and too revealing. All the same, she ought to give Angela a warning hint. 'Nothing good is ever going to happen, Angela. He won't recover. Mr Franklin tried to tell me that a year ago, but I wouldn't believe it. Now I've had time to see . . . There's no use hoping any more.' The mistiness of her eyes prevented her from seeing the expression on Angela's face. She said goodbye quickly and was once again relieved that she did not need to drive herself.

Helen handled the Jaguar with her invariable competence and was glad to have a passenger for conversation. 'Angela's an incredibly loyal soul, isn't she? A result of not having a husband, perhaps. She treats friendship like marriage. A friend is a friend for better or worse, till death us do part.'

'Not many people treat even marriage like that these days.' Paula was not disagreeing with the tribute to Angela's loyalty. She, more than anyone else, had cause to recognize its wholeheartedness.

'Don't they? I know one reads all the gossip about affairs and divorces, but most of the people I actually *know* seem to stick together quite happily. Like Bernard and me.'

'Have you ever been unfaithful to Bernard, Helen?' It was an inexcusably personal question, but Paula needed reassurance. Had her own behaviour on the night of the accident been uniquely unforgivable, or was it the way in which everyone behaved. Was she merely unlucky to be caught out? But then, she would never be sure whether she *had* been caught out or whether Angela's loyalty had been great enough to survive even this test.

'No,' said Helen. 'And Bernard's never been unfaithful to me.'

The second statement was more difficult than the first to accept, though no doubt Helen believed it herself. Bernard was a loving husband and shyness might make him unadventurous. But Paula's experience was that all husbands took advantage of anything on offer, and it seemed unlikely that Bernard had never been exposed to temptation.

'It goes with not having children,' Helen went on.

To Paula's tired brain, this did not make much sense. 'You mean that you've never risked neglecting your husband in order to care for kids?'

'More than that. I wanted to have children, you know. I wanted it very much. You chose not to, so I don't expect you to sympathize. But I would have had a sort of pride in turning a baby into a civilized human being.

Bernard knew how I felt, though he's never felt it himself. It was a kind of silent trade between us. If I didn't cheat on him by having an "accidental" pregnancy, he wouldn't cheat on me by having love affairs. I don't expect you to believe me. But I trust him. Like Angela, he has a loyal nature.'

'I haven't seen him since he got back from India. Did the trip change him?'

'Change him?'

'Don't you remember, when you were in hospital, he was talking about the way in which his father had fallen under a spell. He wondered whether the same magic would work for him.'

'Oh, that. No, no magic. I think he was shocked by some of the things he saw. Overcrowding and poverty and famine. It must have confirmed everything he's ever believed about over-population. He was pretty shaken when he arrived home, and every week he reads out some paragraph in the paper about the drought in India. Wells drying up, bullocks dying so that the fields can't be ploughed, starving families forced to eat the grain that should be kept for seed. He's given a lot of money . . .'

Helen continued to talk: about charities and her own open day in the garden in aid of a special project. But Paula was not sufficiently interested in India to struggle any longer against her weariness. As the car wound its way along the country roads she closed her mind to sounds and thoughts, and slept.

Bernard

Siva Dancing 1973

1

Where was Helen? Emerging from the customs hall into the reception area of Heathrow's Terminal Three, Bernard set down his bag while he looked around for her. He was tired and irritable and more than a little queasy at the end of a bumpy flight. November was not a good month for flying.

He had not wanted to go to Washington in the first place. But in the late autumn of 1973 an anti-monopoly suit there would, if successful, have threatened one of his drug patents, and his lawyer had recommended that the company chairman should appear in person. The proceedings had dragged on – not longer than he expected, since his expectations had always been gloomy – but longer than he liked to be away. When at last he was free to fly off, he had celebrated his successful defence with rather too much of the champagne which was on offer in the first-class cabin. Later he regretted this as storms tossed and delayed the plane, which was then forced to circle Heathrow in buffeting clouds for another half hour before it could land. When at last they touched down, it was two hours after the scheduled time.

There was no sign of Helen, who was always punctual in meeting him. Perhaps she had gone off for a cup of coffee until the 'Baggage in hall' notice should click up against the number of his flight on the arrivals board, forgetting that Bernard had travelled with only a large cabin bag and would not need to wait. He stood still for ten minutes before making a quick inspection of the bar and the coffee room, and then asked for a message to be broadcast on the Tannoy, but without result. He rang first the flat and then the Cambridgeshire house, but there was no answer from either. To his tiredness and impatience as he continued to wait was added anxiety lest she should have had an accident on the way to the airport. Only when an hour had passed did he take a taxi into London.

The flat was dark and empty. On the hall table was a neat stack of letters which had been addressed to him in the country and must have been brought from the house by Helen. Bernard looked quickly to see whether they included any message from her. Then, exhausted by the strain of his negotiations in the United States as well as by the journey, he lay down on the bed to wait with his eyes closed until Helen returned to explain how she had missed him.

He was awakened by the sound of a closing door and found that he had slept in his clothes for ten hours. His head ached and his whole body was stiff and dirty. Helen would need all her charm to soothe away his feeling of neglect and malaise. But no one called out in greeting or came into the bedroom. Instead, there was a sound of scrubbing in the kitchen. Rubbing his heavy eyes awake, he went to investigate.

The intruder was Jenny, who came in twice weekly to clean. Bernard had never before been in the flat during her working hours, although he had communicated with her by notes. She proved to be a young black woman with elaborately braided hair who looked up, startled when he appeared.

'I thought it might be my wife,' said Bernard, although he could not seriously have expected to find Helen scrubbing the floor. 'You don't know where she is at the moment, I suppose?'

'She was here Thursday.' Jenny's voice was soft and pleasant. 'She left to stay with some friends. She didn't say where. Shall I make you some breakfast?'

'A cup of coffee is just what I need.' He needed a bath even more, but that could come afterwards. Picking up the pile of letters from the hall, he carried them to the table.

Within five minutes Jenny had produced fried eggs and fruit juice and toast as well as the coffee. Bernard ate appreciatively as he looked through the mail. All the envelopes had been opened. It was understood between them that Helen would deal with his personal correspondence whenever he was away for more than a week; they had no secrets from each other. On the top of each letter or invitation was a neat note in her handwriting to say how she had answered.

At the bottom of the stack was a card which, unlike the others, had been replaced in its envelope. It had originally been addressed to him at the registered office address of his company and forwarded to his Cambridgeshire home from there. An unfamiliar handwriting had addressed the envelope and marked it 'Personal'. The Irish postmark was also unfamiliar. To the outside of the envelope Helen had paper-clipped a brief note: 'When you read this one, you will know why I am not here to greet you.'

Bernard stared uneasily at her message for a few seconds. Helen's absence was deliberate, then. There had been no accident, no mistaking or days of times. Whatever it was that he was going to read now, he was not going to like it. Worried, he drew the card out of the envelope. The note it bore was as brief as that clipped to the outside, and as menacing.

‘A shout of joy! Your child is born, perfect. I will send you an invitation to the christening.’ It was signed by Gitta.

Gitta? Gitta Clyde? Bernard’s first reaction was one of disbelief. She was too old. Surely she was too old to have had a baby. He tried to remember how Gitta had looked, and uneasily the suspicion grew that he could feel sure only that she was not young. Because she took no pains with her appearance, because she was ugly and lacking in any sort of sex appeal, she could be in almost any other period of her life except that of youth, moving without change between thirty and fifty. And women even in their forties were able to bear children, even if not many of them chose to do so.

As disbelief faded, a feeling near to panic invaded his mind at the thought that he was responsible for the existence of a child. He had spoken to Gitta about the dangers of world over-population, but that had never been more than a rationalization of his real belief: that to inflict life on a human being was as unforgivable a crime as that of taking it away. When he had taken such care to avoid that responsibility inside his marriage, it was monstrous that he should have been trapped into it in such an accidental way.

But of course it was not an accident. Panic gave place to anger as he realized that Gitta must at some point deliberately have chosen to have the child. Although abortion was doubtless illegal in Ireland, she could have come to London; she could have asked Bernard for help. To remain silent until it was too late was a positive action. Perhaps not even the conception had been accidental. Gitta had said more than once during the holiday that women needed to create. Wasn’t it likely enough that she wanted a child herself and that Steve had proved unwilling or inadequate?

Rage closed Bernard's throat. He stared with disgust at the congealing egg on the plate in front of him and stood up, sweeping the whole of his breakfast to the floor with a furious gesture. It had been humiliating enough to know that in the caves of Ellora he had been the fortuitous instrument of Gitta's need for a man. But to realize that she had not expected pleasure from him, but had only demanded a stud, was insupportable. When Jenny knocked softly at the door to see what the crash had meant, he stood in her way, blocking the doorway so that she could not come in.

'You can go home now.'

'I come for two hours.' Her eyes looked past him to the sticky mess of egg and marmalade and broken china.

'I said you can go.'

'Thank you, Sir Bernard. I'll just clear this floor first.'

'Get out!' shouted Bernard, shocking himself, since it was his habit to be polite to employees. He could tell from the hurt and indignant expression on her face that she would not come back.

As the front door closed behind her, Bernard picked up the note to read it again. His eyes were unfocused by anger so that the words this time were illegible. It didn't matter. He remembered them clearly enough.

For perhaps ten minutes he paced up and down the flat, flinging open doors because no one room was large enough to contain him. He prided himself on his ability to handle difficult situations smoothly, but he had no idea how to deal with one woman whose motives he did not understand and another who had run away. Outraged and at a loss how to deal with the situation, he went back to bed.

He was awakened by the telephone. In the few seconds which he needed to clear his head, someone in another part of the flat answered the call. Bernard picked up the bedroom extension in time to hear Helen's voice telling his secretary that yes, he was back, but very tired: she would ask him to ring the office later.

Bernard lay still, needing a moment in which to be sure that neither Helen's earlier absence nor her return now was a dream. Then he got up and opened the bedroom door.

Helen, the telephone call concluded, was clearing up the mess he had made. She looked up, not smiling, and waited for him to speak.

'Ten minutes,' said Bernard. 'I'll be with you in ten minutes.' He was unshaven and, after sleeping in his clothes at the end of a long journey, suspected that his body was smelly as well as dirty. It would be a mistake to embark on the inevitable argument at such a disadvantage.

After a quick shower, he shaved and dressed in clean clothes, choosing a smarter suit than the probable routine of the day required, as though it would be helpful to present himself to his wife as a prosperous, well-dressed, confident businessman. But still she did not smile. Sitting straight-backed on a dining-room chair, she needed no words or gestures to make it clear that he was not to kiss her.

'One makes the gesture of walking out,' she said. 'But then one has to be practical. There are always details to discuss.'

'I hope not,' said Bernard. 'Not the sort of details you seem to imply. I agree that we need to talk.'

That was easy to say but difficult to do. He sat down opposite Helen, hoping that she would speak first so that he could answer specific accusations rather than make a general speech in his own defence. His silence was to some extent successful.

'I take it I don't need to apologize for opening the letter,' she said.

'Of course not. It's what I expected.'

'I worked out the dates. This Gitta, I take it, is a girl you met on that trip to India.'

'Yes. Not a girl, though.'

Helen waved the irrelevance away with her hand. 'Have you always used your trips abroad like this?'

'No. And I didn't that time. I'd like to tell you what happened.'

'I don't want to know,' Helen said. 'Good God, you can't think that I want to hear the details. I just want to be sure that you understand why I'm going to leave you. I wouldn't like you to think that it was anything as petty as jealousy about a holiday affair.'

'Helen, you don't mean that. You mustn't leave. It wasn't an affair. I understand that you're upset, and I'm sincerely sorry about it. But this wasn't anything important. There's no need to be dramatic.'

'Not important! There's a baby, and you say it's not important!'

'The baby hasn't got anything to do with you and me. Gitta's a married woman. If she had the baby, I presume it's because she wanted to.'

'But she told you about it. She intended you to be involved.'

'I don't precisely understand why. Perhaps she wants money. Well, she can have money. I've got enough.'

'My God, Bernard, this is your child! You're its father. You can't simply cut it out of your life with cash.'

'I don't understand what's upsetting you. In particular, I mean. I've said I'm sorry about Gitta, and I am. Terribly sorry.'

'I wanted children,' said Helen. Her voice was pitched lower than usual, as though she were controlling a wish to cry; she turned her head a little away from him. 'When I was young, you knew how much I wanted children. But you didn't. You had strong views, if you remember, about the wickedness of forcing life on to someone who doesn't ask to have it. My views were strong as well, but I could only argue a personal need, not some great moral principle. In a conflict like that you were bound to win. How could I bring a baby into our family if I knew that you wouldn't love it, that you'd be angry with me for forcing it on you?'

'You make it sound as though I sprung it on you. I made it clear what I felt before we were married. You can't pretend – '

'Yes, all right, I had to choose. You or children. I was in love with you and I chose you and until now I've never complained about that. Now it's too late to re-open the argument. The choice doesn't exist any more, not for me. But if you were going to have a child after all, it should have been mine.' She turned to face him at last, shouting slightly. 'Do you understand me? It should have been my child.'

'It wasn't intended,' said Bernard. 'An accident.'

'There were never any accidents between us, were there?' Helen said bitterly. 'You were careful enough with me. No passion without protection. But you can take a risk with a stranger.' She brought her voice under control and continued more calmly. 'Can you blame me for being jealous? Jealous of a woman you loved enough to be careless with. Every time I look at you I shall think of the child you refused me and gave to her. That's why I'm leaving you. Now. I shall go to the house. You can phone me up when you want to fetch your things and I'll keep out of the way.'

'Helen! Be reasonable!' But as he moved towards her she too stood up, ready to step back if he came nearer.

'No,' she said. 'I can't be reasonable. This hits me in the stomach, not the head. When I think of you creating that baby, I want to be sick.'

Bernard took no notice. He understood his wife's distress, but it was time to convince her that he loved her, that nothing else was important. He put his hands on her shoulders. Helen pulled her right arm back and then swung it sharply to slap him hard on the cheek.

The blow was a fierce one, and painful, but it was a different kind of shock which made Bernard drop his arms to his sides and stare in incredulous silence at his wife. In all the years of their marriage they had hardly ever quarrelled even in words – certainly there had never before been any blow struck on either side. For a moment it seemed as though Helen were equally shocked by her own action. But she did not apologize. Instead, she picked up the tray which she had loaded with the debris of his own earlier loss of temper.

'How do I make it clear?' she asked. 'I'm not in a civilized mood. If you touch me again you'll get this lot in your face.'

She moved away quickly, not wanting him to accept the challenge. Bernard watched as she carried the tray out of the room. He stood without moving until he heard the front door close behind her. Then, oppressed by the impossibility of solving his private problem, he abandoned it and went into his London office.

In the course of a busy day he made one domestic decision. He would not attempt to get in touch with Helen for a week. This would allow her anger and disgust to fade a little. When jealousy had moved from her body to her mind it might be possible to offer an explanation. And perhaps by that time she might be feeling lonely enough to imagine what it would be like to spend the rest of her life alone.

In the course of that same day he asked his secretary to discover Gitta's address from the agency which had organized the tour to India. What he should do with it was another matter. She was apparently not on the telephone and he could not spare the time to travel to a remote country district of Ireland. If he were to write, Steve might see the letter, and it was no part of Bernard's intention to cause Gitta the same kind of trouble that she had already brought on him, angry though he might be. If the baby was to be kept out of his way, nothing must happen to disturb its mother's marriage. The Gitta problem was, for the moment, as insoluble as the Helen problem.

The next day's post brought him a printed invitation to a private view. An exhibition of new sculpture by Brigitta Keenan was to open at a gallery in Grafton Street in a week's time. Bernard stared at the card in puzzlement. He had little interest in art and was on no gallery's regular mailing list. He was just about to throw the card away when the name which had been on his mind for the past twenty-four hours thrust itself out from the black italic letters of Brigitta.

So the card explained itself and might also explain a good deal about Gitta. At last she was answering the question he had been trying to ask throughout their holiday together. Sculpture was, presumably, the ruling passion which he had so signally failed to identify in her personality. But by now he was no longer interested in her tastes and talents. The invitation represented only an opportunity to meet and ask for explanations, and an excuse to postpone any decisions until the meeting had taken place. Bernard noted the date of the private view in his diary and propped the card up on a ledge in the flat as though there were a danger that he might forget the occasion. The real message which it bore him, he had completely failed to understand.

2

The gallery was crowded with sleek young men and expensively-dressed older women, each holding a glass of champagne; the high-pitched sound of their chatter bubbled out through the double glass doors. Bernard paused on the pavement outside to amend his expectations of the evening. The card of invitation had been a printed one. It had been ridiculous of him to suppose that Gitta had been proposing a private rendez-vous when she addressed it to him – or, rather, added his name to a list. But art exhibitions were not an ordinary part of his life. He had not realized that a private view would be a party.

Lingering for a few moments before taking the plunge, he studied the single exhibit displayed in the window of the gallery: a bronze hawk. The almost invisible perspex rod on which it was mounted gave it the impression of swooping through space. To express so much power and movement in a stationary object was an extraordinary achievement, thought Bernard. As he stared into the window he could feel himself subconsciously amending all his earlier opinions of Gitta and beginning for the first time to understand her – but he was not prepared to let admiration for her skill mitigate his resentment of her behaviour.

He opened the door, and the noise shrieked round him. One of the suave young men pressed a glass of champagne into his left hand and a pen into his right so that he could enter his name and address in a book. Then he was free to make his way down a spiral staircase to a lower floor. He paused halfway down to look around for Gitta, but she was nowhere to be seen in the main exhibition room of the gallery.

Once he had established that, he allowed himself to consider the exhibits, sipping his champagne as he moved through the crowded room. Even his untutored eye was able to recognize that Gitta's strength lay in her talent for suggesting movement. There were a great many birds: sweeping, darting, hovering birds. He recalled how he and Gitta had watched birds together on the balcony of the hotel at Aurangabad and how the three crows had posed for them. It was a visual memory which until that moment had quite vanished from his mind.

As he moved from one work to another he forgot for a little while the anger which he had so justifiably borne towards Gitta. She had behaved thoughtlessly; but perhaps that could be explained by the strain of pregnancy and the birth of a baby which her husband might have good reason to disown. Instead, for a few moments, he felt sympathy for a woman who, during all her adult life, had been unable to move freely – and who had directed her talent instead to depicting movement in more fortunate creatures.

Had he been honest with himself, Bernard would have recognized that he had almost forgotten his earlier impression of Gitta. Now that she had revealed her true self, it was difficult to remember how reserved, even secretive, she had been. Seeing her talent on display, he forgot that he had found her dull. He remembered, certainly, that she was not beautiful, but not that she used her unattractiveness as a positive defence, to keep away all those for whom she had no use.

So he experienced an unexpected feeling of warmth towards her as he moved into a second room. When he encountered Gitta, as he was bound soon to do, he would not quarrel, but merely arrange a time and place where they could talk privately. He looked round from the doorway; but she was not in this room either.

Here, the work was in a different style; not birds, but playing children – groups of small bronze figures bursting with energy. One in particular caught his eye. Four spiky runners were bunched together in a race while the fifth with a desperate effort breasted the tape to win. Bernard stared at it for some time and was interested enough to wonder how much it would cost. There was no price on the bronze itself. He looked round the room again and saw Steve approaching.

It was interesting to notice what a difference the surroundings made. Standing by Gitta's side at Heathrow, Steve's appearance had seemed odd, but here he was in his proper element. His stylish blond hair was fairer but not more elaborately waved than that of most of the other young men who leaned languidly against the walls; his purple velvet jacket and matching bow tie looked restrained beside the extraordinary outfits worn by some of the middle-aged women. And his handshake, as he caught sight of Bernard and came across, was firm and businesslike.

'Is Gitta here?' Bernard asked him.

'No. She'll come tomorrow. She can't stand these occasions. She hates the people who only drink the champagne and don't look at her work, and she hates the people who do look but pass on. It all hits her as a personal rejection. But that's only a first-night reaction. After this, everything will be more relaxed and she won't mind about people who come in to look round and then go out again; she'll just hope they enjoy it. Tonight I'm standing in for her. I act as her agent, as you probably gathered earlier.'

'No,' said Bernard. 'I didn't gather anything. I didn't even know about this – ' he waved an arm to take in the whole exhibition – 'until I saw the preview card.'

'It's true that she doesn't like to talk about what she's doing. I think she feels that to discuss it would waste the energy which should go into the actual work.'

There was an awkward pause. Bernard wanted to ask about the baby, but saw clearly that he must wait for Steve to mention it first: equally clearly Steve's mind was only on the exhibition. 'Do you like the show?' he asked.

'It's most impressive. In qantity as well as quality.'

'She doesn't bring her work to London very often. Ireland suits her. Plenty of space. Peace and quiet. No distractions. Favourable tax laws for creative artists. She gets dug in and doesn't want to move. I have to bully her from time to time, or no one would know she existed. This exhibition represents about five years.'

'I like this one.' Bernard pointed at the racing children. 'Is it still for sale? And how much would it be?'

'Didn't they give you a catalogue upstairs? Here you are.' Steve produced a list of titles and prices from his pocket. 'This is Number 24.'

Bernard studied the price, which seemed reasonable enough to someone who had no idea what such objects normally cost. 'If I think about it and come back tomorrow, what are the chances of it still being available?' he asked. The excuse for returning when Gitta would be on the premises was probably unnecessary, but Steve accepted it as easily as it emerged.

'Two gone out of an edition of twelve,' he said, and Bernard saw now that two small red spots were stuck on to the base of the group. 'It's not likely to sell out tonight. But before you think too much about this one, Gitta told me that if I saw you here I was to make sure that you had a look at her Siva. It's in the tiny room through the arch.

Nice to see you again. If you decide that you are interested in anything, have a word with the girl at the desk.'

Bernard watched him move towards the stairs, smiling to welcome a new arrival. He himself pressed on through the lower gallery towards what was little more than an alcove. No one else had come as far from the champagne as this and as he turned a corner the high-pitched chatter was cut off as abruptly as if a door had been closed. He took one more step and stopped in amazement.

The walls of the alcove were black and a ceiling spotlight pointed down at the single exhibit. There was no need to look at the catalogue to know that the statue would be called Siva Dancing. Here, re-created in three-dimensional bronze, was the stone relief which had so greatly moved Gitta at Ellora. It was also Gitta herself, her body strained back over the lingam, her arms stretched over her head – but now there was no supporting stone, so that the figure was held in the dancing pose only by the strain and strength of its own muscles. The tension in the movement was so great that Bernard found it painful to study. In any case, he was not at this moment capable of considering the bronze as a work of art. The sight of it seemed to have winded him not only emotionally but physically. He leaned against the wall until his heart should stop pounding.

At first it was memory which overcame him – the memory of that ludicrous and ecstatic moment when he had seemed to be under a spell, unable to free himself from the mysterious bondage of the shadowed temple at Ellora. But as he struggled to bring his emotions under control, the remembrance of that extraordinary episode was banished by a new thought – was it a supposition or a hope? He stared more intently at the statue, and the supposition became a certainty. This bronze, this Siva, was the child which had been conceived during that second dark visit to the Kailasha temple.

Everything fitted. Gitta's card must have referred to the perfect casting of the bronze. Tonight's preview was the christening to which she had promised to invite him. Steve had not mentioned a baby because there was no baby. With a deep sigh, Bernard let out the breath he had been holding.

Chief amongst his emotions was relief that there was not after all a living child – it did not occur to him to doubt his certainty that he was right now and had been mistaken before. Later he would no doubt be angry again with Gitta for misleading him, and for the damage she had done to his marriage. But at this moment the memory of the desire he had felt for her in the darkness was so vivid that Helen's jealousy seemed justified, even if she had founded it on a misunderstanding. At the same time he was conscious of another and less familiar feeling. This was a statue which he longed to possess.

By comparison with the intensity of this need, his earlier interest in the racers revealed itself as merely a casual whim. If he had bought them, it would have been only through a sense that he ought to purchase something, and that piece was as good as any. The little bronze group had pleased his eyes, but Siva hit him below the belt. This, he felt as he circled the solitary figure, this was perhaps how a father felt at the first glimpse of his child. He no longer wondered why Gitta had chosen such an unfortunate metaphor as he acknowledged the same reaction of awe at perfection, of pride in being partly responsible, and of a deep determination to protect.

Before anything else he must find out if he could own the work. He looked anxiously to see if it carried any red spot: none was visible. In respect of this item the catalogue was unhelpful, giving neither the size of the edition nor the price. Details, it announced, could be obtained from the desk.

As he turned to go, the entrance to the alcove was blocked by a small group: two young men and one elderly woman with straight blonde hair, wearing a silver trouser suit. They, like Bernard earlier, seemed transfixed by the quality of what they saw.

'That's quite something,' said one of the young men to the woman; while the other wrote in a notebook. 'If you're seriously interested, this would be the one.'

'Excuse me.' Bernard pushed rudely through the trio and hurried up the stairs to ask the price of Number 49. The girl at the desk studied him for longer than seemed necessary before she answered with another question: 'Are you Sir Bernard Lorimer?'

'Yes. What's that got to do with it?'

'The price of Siva Dancing is three thousand pounds, sir.'

Bernard stared at her unbelievingly. 'But that's ridiculous!'

'The bronze that you've seen is the only one that will be cast, apart from Miss Keenan's own,' explained the girl.

'But even so. Compared with the others . . . I mean, you presumably know about prices. Don't you agree that this is exceptionally high? She's not Henry Moore, after all.'

'I believe there are special circumstances, Sir Bernard. The money from the sale of this bronze is going directly to a famine relief fund in India, to buy a machine for deepening wells.'

'You asked my name,' said Bernard suspiciously. 'Is that price a special one for me?'

'Only in the sense that I'm not giving anyone else a price at all. Miss Keenan told me to say that it was reserved, until you'd had time to see it and decide whether you were interested.'

That made some sense. Bernard swallowed his indignation while he considered what to do. 'So you could hold it for a day or two while I think about it?'

'Of course, Sir Bernard.'

'I'd like to have a word with Miss Keenan before I decide. When will she be here?'

'Tomorrow afternoon.'

'And what time does the gallery close?'

'Half past five.'

'I'll try to come before then. But would you be kind enough to ask her if she could wait here until six, in case I'm held up?'

'I'll give her the message.' The girl wrote it down, making no promises on Gitta's behalf. Steve came up to stand beside him.

'Did you see the Siva?'

'Yes,' said Bernard. 'It's very powerful.'

'The best thing she's ever done. It ought really to be kept available for a museum. The Tate. That's why we haven't put any details in the catalogue. Gitta thought that you might like it but only if you didn't have to share it with anyone. If she's wrong about that – the not sharing – we could have a normal edition cast; twelve copies, say. It would help to spread her reputation, and of course it would enormously reduce the price to you.'

'I hope to talk to her tomorrow,' said Bernard. 'Tell me. She works at this sort of thing all the time, does she?'

'Seven days a week,' said Steve. 'Ten hours a day. It's her life. The only thing that has the slightest importance for her.'

'It was something I wondered in India. How she spent

her time. But then, I never understand what women do with themselves all day.'

'This particular woman would make any good trade unionist throw up his hands in horror at the length of her working week.'

'I'd like to take another look,' Bernard said. 'And then I'll hope to see Gitta tomorrow.'

He went down the spiral staircase for a second time. The alcove was crowded now with people circling the bronze. Bernard stod in the archway, listening to their comments.

'Is it male or female?'

'Neither, darling, it's divine.'

'What, with that nasty mischievous look on its face?'

'The god of destruction, that's why.'

'I suspect that gods don't have backbones, then. Could you bend like that, pet?'

'You'd have to hold me up.'

'Come on, then. Back you go.'

Bernard turned away. He was not going to have his statue gooped over in museums by people like that. By the time he reached the top of the stairs he had already decided to buy the Siva.

3

Deliberately the next evening Bernard waited until after half past five before returning to the gallery. In the brightly lit window the hawk still swooped on its unseen prey, but the reception hall was in darkness. Angry at the possibility that Gitta had chosen to evade the meeting, he rapped sharply on the glass door. A dark figure rose from an invisible seat and came to let him in.

'Hello,' said Gitta. She was wearing the same black sweater and trousers in which Bernard had first seen her at London Airport, but there was a brightness in her eyes which had not been present at that earlier meeting. 'You've come to see Siva again, have you?'

She led the way down the spiral staircase and through the dark exhibition rooms. The spotlight in the alcove was already switched on. Someone had set two stools side by side in the entrance, but Bernard remained standing.

'You're expecting compliments, I suppose,' he said, staring at the creature's odd, mischievous face. 'Well, of course it's good. Marvellous. But you've made me very angry.'

'Why?' asked Gitta; and then answered her own question, revealing the sphere in which her conscience must at some point have troubled her. 'You mean that I've used an experience that ought to be private and transformed it into something public, on display? If that worries you, I'm sorry.' She did not sound very sorry.

'I don't think you understand how it feels to be really angry. If you did, you wouldn't dismiss it so lightly.'

'Oh, I understand well enough. The anger I feel at being crippled is what flows into the movement I carve or model. Other sculptors may be inspired by touch or eye, but I need an emotional stimulus to set me off. In a way, you were right in one of your first guesses, when you realized that I wanted to dance. This is the only way I can do it. Siva moved on my behalf. So something positive comes out of an old frustration. Anger is a creative emotion.'

Bernard contradicted her, not troubling to be polite. 'You've done a lot of damage. Anger is destructive.'

'Is there any difference? Those old Hindus with their three-headed gods saw creation and destruction as aspects of a single whole, and I agree. Destruction is a part of creation. An essential part. I break down the clay before I can begin to model. Or I destroy the shape of a piece of stone in order to carve a new shape from inside it. Something had to be heated and pressed out of shape to form that quartz I showed you. And no one could make use of it, or even see it, until its shell had been broken.'

'You destroyed a good deal more than clay or stone to make the Siva Dancing, didn't you?' he accused.

'Your peace of mind, do you mean? I'm sorry if you think so.'

'Rather more than that. My marriage. My wife read your note – and not unnaturally misunderstood it.'

'I sent it to your office,' said Gitta, disturbed as she recalled what she had written. 'And I marked it Personal so that your secretary wouldn't open it.'

'I was away from the office when it arrived. The details of what happened aren't important.'

'They are to me, if you're accusing me of meddling deliberately.'

'No, not that.' Bernard's anger was changing as he put it into words. Had Gitta after all been right in describing it as a creative emotion? He could no longer tell the difference between fury and passion. Gitta's closeness excited him even while he was unable to forgive her.

'Well, I really *am* sorry,' she said. 'But surely the misunderstanding can be put right easily enough.'

'It's too late for that. Because of course it was founded on the truth. And *I* misunderstood what you wrote as well – took it literally. So I admitted more than I can explain away by suddenly pointing to a piece of bronze. The situation has the essential ingredient of destruction – that what has been destroyed no longer exists. The trust has gone.'

Was he complaining? Did he still care about Helen's

feelings? Too many details now reminded him of the evening in Ellora – the same cave-like darkness broken by the single beam of light; the enigmatic Siva; and a woman who, now as then, was not the dull tourist he had first met but someone who sparked with an inner electricity. Impulsively Bernard stepped forward and took her into his arms.

There were differences as well as similarities. It was good that the gallery was empty, with no guard to watch or interrupt. But it was not good that Gitta was unresponsive. More than that, she fought him off – and she was strong. 'Not in front of the children,' she said.

Instinctively Bernard looked up at the statue. Then he turned back towards Gitta; but she held herself rigidly, willing him not to come nearer. It attacked his pride that she should have had her own way in Ellora but should refuse now to accept his initiative. In the end it was his own anger that restrained him, and he allowed it to show in his eyes as he stared at her.

Gitta lifted her hands and shoulders in what was perhaps a gesture of apology. 'Some things can't be repeated,' she said. 'The atmosphere at Ellora was – unusual; and we were both sensitive to it, just for a moment. But here in England we have nothing in common.'

'Don't you think that any two people can make a relationship work if they both want it?'

'Perhaps.' Her voice was flat. 'But I have no interest in relationships. None at all. I use Steve to protect me from them. I'm not interested in anything but my own work. I have a need to create, and for that I have to be emotionally free. I take what I require from other people and I have nothing to give in return. I told you all that in Bombay. You should have believed me.'

'Yes.' Bernard was suddenly tired. He would not have

expected that Gitta would hold the power to hurt him so deeply. Staring at the Siva, he experienced again the protective emotion that had overcome him on the previous evening. If this was only a part of how a parent felt towards his child, he could understand Helen's anger at her deprivation. She would never forgive him. His loneliness made Gitta's attitude even less tolerable. 'It doesn't occur to you that you might owe me something?' he asked.

'We never made any kind of bargain.'

'You think it was fair simply to use me?'

'As fair as the way in which millions of men use millions of women. As you've used your wife, to have sex without children. Well, that's not my business. I took what you gave me and this is what I made of it. For you, if you want it. And *only* for you, if you want that as well. If I put a price on it, that's so that a few hundred people can perhaps stay alive for a little longer. Vishnu, the preserver – wasn't that how you saw yourself?'

'Yes,' said Bernard. 'I'll send you a cheque.' He would have liked to have had the last word, to leave with some stylish phrase which would restore his own self-esteem or damage hers. But the selfish concentration of her interest made her invulnerable. Nothing he could say would emerge as more than spiteful. For such an extraordinary relationship to end with a triviality only increased its oddness. He felt his way up the twisting staircase and let himself out of the dark gallery.

4

'But I'm going to Paula's party,' said Helen.

'Going where?' asked Bernard. The telephone connection was distorted by clicks and crackles.

'To Paula's party.' The crackling stopped without warning just as Helen shouted to overcome it, making her voice sound untypically strident.

Paula's party would be in London. The invitation would certainly have included Bernard, but Helen had not told him about it. 'Come and dress for it here,' he suggested. It would be a step back towards normality if Helen were to change at the flat, as she had always done in the past before an evening out in London. 'There's something I need to talk to you about. And something I want to show you. Could you call at the office at five o'clock. You'd have time to change afterwards.'

'All right.' The answer came grudgingly. And Helen's reluctance to allow him much of her company showed itself again when she arrived at his office already dressed for the party. The fact that she had done her hair and made up her face and put on jewellery and a long dress all before leaving the country house at three o'clock in the afternoon was in itself a snub, telling him that she was not prepared to visit the flat even for her own convenience. She made it clear that he was not to kiss her, even in the way which she would have let the most casual of her male acquaintances kiss her at the beginning of a social evening.

Making the best of the situation, Bernard took her out to a taxi and gave the address of the gallery in Grafton Street.

'You're not interested in art,' Helen said.

'There's something I want you to see. I'll explain afterwards.'

They reached the gallery ten minutes before it was due to close. Helen looked round curiously as Bernard hurried her down the stairs.

'I'd like to know what you think of this,' he said when they reached the alcove, empty but for the dancing Siva. He stood back in the archway while Helen, still puzzled, walked slowly round. The red spot which signified that he owned it of course meant nothing to her.

'Well?' he asked.

'I don't like it. It's evil.'

'Mischievous would be a better word, don't you think?'

Helen shook her head. 'It's nastier than that. Who is it?'

'Siva. The Hindu storm god. The destroyer.'

'I believe you. A horrid adolescent boy tearing wings off flies.'

'Not really. He destroys bad things more than good. Disease, for example, and infertility.'

'A fertility god? I can believe that too.' She circled the bronze again and this time Bernard kept beside her. 'I wouldn't want him looking at me in my own drawing room.'

Out of the corner of his eye Bernard saw Gitta walk past the alcove on the far side of the exhibition room, pause, and turn back towards them. He had not expected her to be here again this evening, and gripped Helen's arm in alarm and warning. 'That's the sculptor,' he whispered. 'Just so that you don't say anything rude too loudly.'

'Male or female?'

Bernard, who had once experienced the same doubt himself, was unreasonably annoyed that Helen should share it. There was no time to answer, for Gitta had already joined them.

'I brought my wife along to see the Siva Dancing,' he said. 'Helen, this is Miss Keenan, who made it.'

'Do you like it?' asked Gitta as she shook hands. Bernard wondered whether Helen would be polite or honest.

'It's very powerful,' she said. 'I don't think I can say that I exactly like it. I find it disturbing.'

'That's what I intended. As your husband may have told you, the idea for this came from an eerie temple in the Ellora Caves.'

'In India, you mean?' Startled, Helen glanced towards Bernard.

'Gitta was a member of the same party.' Bernard deliberately used the name with which Gitta had signed her note and waited to see what would happen. Nothing could make the situation much worse.

Helen's expression changed from puzzlement to incredulity. She stared speechlessly at Gitta, taking in every detail of her unbecoming hair, her weathered skin and flattened profile, and her unstylish sweater and trousers.

Gitta too was reacting to the unexpected meeting. 'Your husband did me a very good turn,' she told Helen. 'I expect he told you. We went to a temple with the guide, on the normal tourist timetable, but then I wanted to go back again at night. It was a spooky enough place even by daylight. I don't think I should have dared to go alone after dark, but I did very much want to see a particular carving again. So Bernard agreed to come along as protector, when he could have stayed comfortably in the hotel. I'm more grateful to him than I can say – I couldn't have made this without his help. I think of him now as a kind of godfather to it.'

By pretending not to know that Helen had read her

note, she presumably hoped to explain it away. Bernard stared at the two women as their conversation continued. In this trite social situation Gitta's electric vitality had disappeared. As well as being ugly, she was dull. Helen – at this moment stunned by the flow of irrelevant words – was not only beautiful, expensively dressed and carefully groomed, but human in a way that seemed not to apply to Gitta. Helen was a woman who could be hurt, who *had* been hurt. Bernard would have liked to hurt Gitta, but lacked the power to do so. All he could do – more to defend himself than to attack her – was to rid himself of any interest in her. His success in this was a victory for her, not for himself.

Gitta now was explaining the process by which the bronze was cast and the anxiety she felt as she waited for the mould to be opened. 'It must be rather like having a baby. Not that I ever have. But one hears that almost all mothers ask whether the baby is perfect before they bother even about whether it's a boy or a girl.'

Helen's mood had changed. She was no longer merely taken aback. From the way her hands clenched into tight fists Bernard could see that she was angry. The situation portrayed by Gitta was true, but of course Helen knew it in a deeper sense to be a lie. He had better separate the two women before the inevitable quarrel erupted.

'We must be getting along,' he told Gitta. 'I only brought Helen in to look at the Siva. I didn't expect you to be here.'

Even that last remark could not save him from Helen's fury. As soon as they reached the pavement she turned on him.

'How dare you! Do you think I'm an idiot? Did you really believe you could set up that oh-so-innocent explanation, so accidental, so spontaneous, and expect me to forget that you'd already admitted the truth?'

'Of course not.' Bernard took her arm and propelled her round the corner, so that the scene would not be visible to Gitta. A restaurant he knew was just opening for the evening there. It was too early to eat, but they could talk more peacefully over an aperitif.

'I don't want – ' began Helen; but Bernard insisted.

'Paula's party isn't for hours and we need somewhere to sit. I can explain what happened then.'

Reluctantly she went in and waited while he ordered drinks.

'You've answered your own question,' he suggested. 'Of course I'm not such a fool as to ask someone to tell you a lie after admitting the truth myself. I didn't expect to see Gitta there. I didn't *want* to see her. I never want to see her again, and I don't imagine I ever shall. I certainly didn't ask her to tell you anything.'

'Why should she bother to lie, if you didn't ask her to?'

'It wasn't a lie. That bronze, the Siva, is the child she mentioned in her note.'

'I certainly gathered that was what I was supposed to believe.'

'It's true,' said Bernard.

'You mean there's no baby?'

'No. Just the Siva. That's why I took you there to see it.'

'When did you find out?'

'At the private view on Monday. I realized what Gitta had meant as soon as I set eyes on the bronze.'

'But until then you'd assumed she was talking about a real baby, just as I did. So it wasn't impossible. You did make love to her while you were in India.'

'Just once. In that temple, on the night she described.'

'Then she was lying about that.'

'Implicitly, yes. Not in so many words. When I met her again, I told her how furious I was because her note had caused so much trouble. Meeting you unexpectedly, perhaps she thought she could put it right.'

There was a long silence. Then Helen let out the deep breath of her anger in a single sigh and picked up the drink which until then she had ignored. 'I don't really understand,' she said.

'I'm not sure that I do either. It was odd, what happened in the temple. Gitta called the atmosphere eerie, but it was stronger than that. As though centuries of magic and ritual were trapped in the air.'

'It's an original excuse. I can imagine the headlines of a divorce court report. "Enmeshed by magic, says drugs boss."'

Bernard let that go and pressed on with his own argument. 'She used the atmosphere – to get her idea of the statue straight. She used me as well. To say it straight out, she seduced me.'

Helen's laughter, loud enough to make the waiters turn towards them, mocked his humiliation. There was no sympathy in her voice as she asked for another drink. 'I don't know that it makes much difference,' she said when it arrived. 'There's no baby, but there could have been. You seem to have conducted your private fertility rites without regard to the consequences.'

'As people have done for thousands of years. It's only within comparatively recent times that any choice has existed.'

'It's a comparatively recent time that we're discussing. The fact that Gitta's baby is made of bronze instead of flesh owes nothing to any forethought on your part.' She paused as a waiter appeared with menus and lingered within earshot.

'Since we're here, we might as well dine,' Bernard suggested.

'I don't want anything. There'll be food at the party.'

'You won't see it before eleven at the earliest. Have something light to be going on with.' Since she did not seem prepared to choose, he ordered trout for them both, knowing that she liked it. 'Couldn't you look at this in a different way?' he asked as the waiter moved off. 'You'd have had more cause for indignation if I'd planned this, or hoped for it; if I'd taken a packet of contraceptives out to India and remembered to slip them in my pocket before setting out for the temple that night. Surely you must realize – I mean, you've seen Gitta now. Do you really believe – ?'

Helen's laughter was higher in pitch than usual, suggesting hysteria rather than amusement. 'You're not exactly gallant. But I accept your point. You found her sudden irresistibility as startling as I do.' She pushed her glass forward for a refill. Bernard tried to fathom her expression. Was the storm over? Had she forgiven him for his holiday indiscretion? But then, Gitta had been almost irrelevant to the real cause of their quarrel.

'Would you like to adopt a child?' he asked. He spoke abruptly, but the thought had been in his mind all day. If it would solve any problem for Helen, it need create none for himself. He had enough money to keep the inevitable disruption under control.

Helen's face, which for a few seconds had seemed amused and almost friendly, froze into a white mask. '*What* did you say?'

'We could adopt a child. More than one if you liked. I realize that I've been selfish about this. And since it's too late . . .'

'What makes you think that you'd like other people's children when you didn't want your own?'

'They'd be children who existed already. I wouldn't have to feel responsible for bringing them into the world.

I do see, of course, that for you it would only be a second best, but . . .'

'Do you?' Helen buried her head in her hands.

'Yes. It's odd. When I saw that statue . . . Well, I know it's only a piece of metal. But I had a queer sensation. Almost as if it were my own child. It made me understand how perhaps you felt.'

'Seventeen years,' said Helen. As she lifted her head, Bernard saw that she was crying. 'We've been married seventeen years, and in all that time you've never sympathized with how I felt. It was children of my own that I wanted. Now it's too late. I tried to convice you years ago how strongly I felt that children were a necessary part of a marriage and a home. But one can't go on arguing the same point for ever. If there's a deep disagreement inside a marriage, someone has to give in. I did give in. I accepted the situation. I could have continued to accept it indefinitely – but only if you were consistent. If you change your mind, you make all those years a waste.'

The tears were running down her cheeks. She dabbed at them with a table napkin. Then she stood up.

'Where are you going?' asked Bernard.

'To put my make-up straight. And then to the party. Paula won't mind if I'm early.'

'But stay and have dinner first. Look, it's just coming.'

'For seventeen years,' said Helen, 'you've been making all the decisions. I've been living your life. It's my turn to be self-centred now. I've made it clear that I don't want to have dinner with you, and you haven't bothered to listen. For the third time: I shall be eating at the party.'

'May I come with you?' asked Bernard, standing beside her.

'I'm going with Tommy. And I shall probably get drunk. You wouldn't enjoy watching.'

'Will you come back to the flat tonight?' he asked.

'That depends what address Tommy gives to the taxi.'

It was a moment before Bernard could control his voice. 'You're certainly rubbing my nose in it.'

Helen shrugged her shoulders. 'I may be sorry tomorrow. I'll come round and talk again if you want me to. But I don't think you realize how angry I am. I have to work it out. I can't just calmly tell myself to forget it.'

'Do you think I'm not angry too?' demanded Bernard. 'To be used as she's used me?' He choked on the thought and then forced himself to be calm again, quoting what Gitta had claimed, although he had been unable to believe it. 'Anger can be a creative emotion. We could use it to make something new out of our marriage, not to destroy it.'

'I take no responsibility for what has happened to our marriage,' said Helen. 'And if anything new is coming out of it, it's a life in which I make my own decisions.'

'All right. I accept that.'

'Yes,' she agreed bitterly. 'You'll let me make my own decisions as long as they fit in with your plans.'

'Helen, I'll try.' The head waiter came questioningly forward as they moved towards the door. 'Just a moment,' Bernard said to reassure him; and then, to Helen, 'I'll get you a taxi.'

'Even hailing a taxi is something I can manage for myself if I try very hard.'

Bernard gripped her hand. 'Come back to the flat afterwards,' he pleaded. 'Please. Even if you're drunk. Even if it's not until after you've been home with Tommy. I don't care about any of that. If I can just feel sure that you'll come.'

'It's a snag, isn't it,' said Helen, 'when people take over their own lives. You can't be sure that you'll get a happy ending when you only have the power to write half the script, because the other person's happiness may lie somewhere else. I don't promise anything. I haven't decided anything.' She moved away and then, remembering something, turned back and took a small object from her evening bag. It was the quartz stone, the two halves fastened together with sticky tape. Bernard had kept it in the house as an ornament, open on a shelf to catch the light: a holiday souvenir. 'I brought this,' she said. 'I don't want anything from India in my home.'

The door of the restaurant swung behind her as she walked away. Bernard, no more hungry now than Helen had been, paid the bill and went outside. A need to quarrel took him back to the gallery, closed by now. He rattled at the door, but no one came. Frustrated by the absence of anyone on whom he could vent his anger, he clenched his hand around the knob of quartz, squeezing it as though that pressure might be enough to sublimate his aggression. Then he took it from his pocket and hurled it with all his strength against the window in which the bronze hawk swooped.

The glass was of a quality strengthened to keep out burglars and bullets. It was the quartz which shattered, littering the pavement with its tiny crystal teeth. Bernard stared at the mess and at the smoothness of the unharmed window, almost wishing that a policeman would appear to accuse him. At least then he would have the chance to explain his feelings. But no one was interested. More tired now than angry, he went back to the flat.

Sooner or later, he believed, Helen would return. Only someone who loved him deeply could have felt so deeply a hurt which a different woman might have shrugged away. In a permissive age they were curiously old-fashioned in their views. Other couples took marriage more lightly, or did not trouble to marry at all. Bernard and Helen had married for life. It was because they each set such a high value on the other's continuing loyalty that what in a different relationship might have seemed only a minor peccadillo had presented itself as an unpardonable betrayal. Illogically, it was at this very moment when he most desperately feared that she might leave him that Bernard was more sure that Helen would come back in the end – as though the fear were the price he must pay for eventual forgiveness.

It would be a long wait before he learned what she had decided. Paula's parties always continued far into the night. Even if Helen did not after all carry out her threat to go home with Tommy, she was unlikely to leave before two or three in the morning. Jealous and unhappy, Bernard settled down to wait. It was the longest night of his life.

5

Every December for more than ten years Paula and Laker had declared themselves to be At Home on an evening shortly before Members of Parliament dispersed to their constituencies for Christmas. Such occasions were useful in Paula's work, and for this reason she continued to act as a hostess even when she no longer had a husband able to appear as the host. It was at other people's parties that she was able to sniff out hints of coming change or make new acquaintances whom later she could approach for information and comment. Her own invitations paid off debts and kept her in the swim.

One of her guests this evening was John Lorimer. It would be amusing, she had thought, to re-introduce him to the cousin he had apparently only met once or twice in his life at funerals or weddings. But Bernard had not been able to come. Helen's apologies on his behalf were vague and unconvincing – and Helen herself appeared to be under some kind of strain. Paula, though, was too busy welcoming and introducing her other guests to have time for personal questions.

Midnight was the noisiest and most crowded moment of the party. Everyone had arrived and no one would think of going for a long time yet. Paula, no longer needing to keep an eye on the door, was talking to John about Jamaica, where he owned a villa. He was worried about the reported increase in violent crime in the island, and Paula was suggesting explanations and possible solutions to the problem.

She had been giving her native island a good deal of thought recently, for more and more frequently she considered the possibility of returning to live there. When she first left home, at the age of eighteen, it had been her declared intention to return as soon as her education was completed. Her father had always laughed at her teenage determination to become prime minister of Jamaica one day, but it had been a serious ambition at the time. Oxford and London had seduced her by their certainty that they represented the centre of the civilized world, but now their charm was fading. She could make no changes in her life while Laker was alive, but ever since her visit to Mr Franklin in June she set herself regularly to think about a world in which Laker did not exist, and to make plans for her part in it. A return to Jamaica might provide the kind of break and the kind of opportunity necessary for making a fresh start.

She was still discussing the island's problems with John when Helen came up to join them.

'Helen, your cousin-in-law, Sir John Lorimer,' she said; but before doing more than acknowledge the introduction, Helen had a message to deliver.

‘Your phone was ringing, Paula,’ she said. ‘I guessed you couldn’t hear above all this chatter, so I answered it. Someone’s holding on to speak to you. I couldn’t catch the name.’

‘Thanks. I’ll take the call in my bedroom. Would you be an angel, Helen, and put the receiver here down again. Otherwise the background noise will make a conversation impossible.’

Two cabinet ministers were holding an earnest discussion in the bedroom – hatching a plot, to judge by the excessively jaunty grins with which they moved out to leave her alone. Paula picked up the receiver. The noise of the party surged along the extension line and battered against her ear-drum until it was cut off with a click. ‘Paula Mattison speaking.’

‘Mrs Laker-Smith?’

There was only one man who called her Mrs Laker-Smith, and only one reason why Mr Franklin should telephone in the middle of the night. Yet Paula’s first reaction was one not of distress but of shame. It must have been all too clear to Mr Franklin as he waited for her to come on the line that a lively, merry party was in progress, that she was enjoying herself while Laker, while Laker . . . Paula sat without moving, as though she had lost the knack of breathing, as Mr Franklin told her that her husband was dead.

Half an hour later she returned to the party, amazed that the laughter and babble of voices should be continuing as though nothing had happened. No one had missed her. At a large party like this, nobody expected much of his hostess’s time, and the caterers had provided waitresses to keep the food and drink in circulation. She had decided to keep the news to herself. If she were to make any kind of announcement Laker’s friends would be upset and those who knew him less well would be embarrassed;

the evening would collapse into awkwardness. For an hour or two more she could sustain an act. If anyone noticed that her smile was a little forced, or her attention not wholly on a conversation, that too might be expected of a hostess.

John Lorimer was one of the first to leave. He had told her earlier in the evening that he was not an enthusiastic party-goer and had come only for the pleasure of seeing her again. On his arrival, ignoring the privileges of cousinship, he had merely shaken her hand – but since then had obviously noticed the warmth with which most of her guests kissed her as they came into the room. So now he too, uncharacteristically, kissed her on the lips. Paula found the small gesture endearing. She liked this cousin about whom she knew so little; and at this moment above all, when she needed comfort, was glad to know that he liked her.

With his hands still on her shoulders he looked into her eyes. 'You look . . . is it only tired? Is anything wrong?'

Paula shook her head, not wanting to put either the truth or a lie into words. But when his departure inspired a gradual movement towards the door, she did not try to check it in what would have been her normal manner. Soon after two o'clock – far earlier than usual – the party was over. Only Helen, it soon appeared, remained behind.

'I'll help you to clear up.'

Paula shook her head. 'I'm not going to do anything now. In fact, I'm not going to do it at all. It's all part of the caterers' contract.'

'Oh.' Helen seemed disappointed, although Paula would not have expected her to risk spoiling her frock by washing up. She hesitated for a moment and then, speaking more jerkily than usual, asked, 'Could I stay here for the night, Paula? I'd meant to drive back to Cambridge, but I don't think I'd pass the breathalyser.'

'Why not take a taxi to the flat? You could pick up the car tomorrow.'

'I can't go there. Bernard's there.'

Unlike her friend, Paula was completely sober; but she was tired, and that remark did not make sense to her confused mind.

'We've separated,' said Helen. 'That's why Bernard didn't come tonight. I expect he'd have liked to, but I didn't tell him about the invitation until today.'

More than anything else in the world, Paula wanted to be alone with her unhappiness. But Helen's need to confide was so obvious and so deep that it would have been a heartless act to send her away. Paula smothered her sigh and sat down.

'I've never known two people more happily married than you and Bernard,' she said. 'I simply don't believe you.'

'He's been having an affair. Well, a sort of affair.'

'Is that so important?'

'I trusted him,' Helen said. 'It hurts.'

'Of course it hurts. But is that any reason for hurting yourself even more? How did you find out?'

'Accidentally. I opened a letter from the woman while he was abroad.'

'So he didn't tell you himself?'

'No. But he didn't deny it.'

'That's not the point,' said Paula. 'The important thing is that he didn't want you to know because he didn't want to spoil your marriage. I can remember being in the same kind of situation once, and when I thought about it . . .' What she thought about now was that she had had almost this same conversation once before, defending her night with Ben Townsend in the moment before Angela told her about Laker's accident. And that thought in turn led to another. She had been able to forgive Laker his affair with his constituency secretary – had forgiven him so completely that she never even let him know that she had discovered it. But Laker, if he had guessed at her infidelity, had had no time to forgive it. 'Go back to the flat,' she said. 'Wake Bernard up. Tell him he's a heel, if he is. Slap his face if it makes you feel any better. Accept any promises you can get out of him. And then tell him that you'll never mention it again. Never think of it again. It's not important, Helen. Not compared with having someone to love. Someone who loves you. You don't know how lucky you are.'

'Paula . . .'

'Laker's dead,' said Paula. 'Not dead like the last eighteen months. Absolutely, clinically, finally dead.' She put her clenched fists up to her eyes and began to rock backwards and forwards. She was aware of Helen's arm round her shoulder, of Helen's voice trying to comfort her, promising to stay, and managed for one moment longer to hold back the tears.

'I don't *want* you to stay. I want you to go back to Bernard. Now, this moment. In case he dies in his sleep tonight, and leaves you with the sort of regret that can never be put right.'

Startled by the force of her words, Helen stood up, accepting orders. 'You said you were in this situation yourself once, Paula. You mean that Laker was having an affair? Did you have time to put things straight with him? To tell him that you still loved him? Or was that the night . . .'

'I had time,' said Paula briefly as she kissed her friend goodbye. Helen had asked the easy question and could be given the easy, truthful answer. She might have put it another way. 'Were you having an affair? Did Laker know? Was there time . . . ?' And if she had, she would have been answered with a lie. Angela knew the answer to that question, and because of that Paula was not sure that she would ever be able to face Angela again. What was certain was that there was no one else in the world to whom she could ever confess the truth. On the night of the accident Laker had had too much to drink, and that was his own responsibility. But it had been the suspicion of his wife's infidelity which made him hurt and angry, and it was anger which led him to drive while he was drunk. That responsibility was Paula's own, but no one except Angela must ever know.

John and Isabel

The Small World Game 1973

1

A thunderstorm in the early evening had snarled up London's rush-hour traffic and the rain was still falling steadily, covering the streets with a glistening film of water which resembled the surface of a lake; in it the lights of the city reflected and trembled. Cocooned in the comfort of his Daimler, Sir John Lorimer allowed himself a moment to enjoy the shimmering pattern. Then he looked at his watch.

Ten past six. He was late. But the thought did not disturb his patience. Paula Mattison's party on the previous evening had been a sparkling occasion; he had looked forward to it and had not been disappointed. But tonight's party was a business occasion, holding no promise of pleasure. Although formally he himself was the host, it was Lance who was actually in charge, and Lance would already be waiting at the boardroom door to welcome the first guest. John opened his evening paper.

As usual, he looked first at the city pages. Only as he flicked through the rest of the paper did a familiar name catch his eye. James Laker-Smith was dead. John put the paper down and thought back to the previous night. Had Paula known, he wondered? Not, he felt sure, at the beginning of her party. He had watched with admiration the easy, smiling manner with which she had welcomed her guests and made the first introductions before leaving them to mingle as they chose. She had chatted to him about Jamaica, and there had been nothing forced about the way she expressed her opinions and listened to his enthusiastic description of his villa. But he remembered that she had been called to the telephone – and remembered too that when he said goodbye later her eyes had seemed bloodshot and lacked their usual sparkle. Yes, by that time she must have known.

The sympathy he felt surprised him by its force. In spite of his lack of family feeling he had from the time of their first meeting had a special interest in Paula, a special wish that she should do well and be happy. He made a mental note to write to her at once and later – but not too much later – arrange a meeting. No doubt she had already been lonely during the eighteen months since Laker's accident, but she would be feeling a different kind of loneliness today.

Only now that he had stopped reading did he become aware that the Daimler was no longer moving even at its previous snail's pace. Both in front and behind, the road was jammed with other stationary vehicles. The pedestrians whose heads or umbrellas bent into the driving rain might well be wishing that they, like himself, could enjoy the shelter of an expensive car – but unlike him, they were making progress. He leaned forward to speak to his chauffeur. 'Can you find out what's going on?'

Connor switched off the ignition and disappeared into the rain. 'There's a fire in Kingsway, Sir John,' he said when he returned. 'A bad one. The area's closed to traffic. The police are trying to clear this jam from behind.'

That would be a long job. 'I'd better walk,' John said. It would only take ten minutes, and after his last heart attack the doctor had recommended fresh air and careful exercise. Not that the air here was particularly fresh, but wet and heavy with exhaust fumes. The rain, drumming against his umbrella, was heavier than he had realized from inside the car. He increased his pace – but then slowed down again. No over-exertion; the doctor had said that as well. John turned a corner and the tower came into sight at the end of the street; the skyscraper which he owned and which he had helped to design.

There had been glimpses of the tower earlier in the journey, but now he could see it whole. He paused for a moment, ignoring the rain as he studied the building with an approving pride. Only a few rectangles of light were scattered through the lower storeys, but the wide windows of the penthouse floor blazed like a cruise ship seen on a dark horizon, or a space craft hovering. The party would be in full swing by now. Walking steadily he came to the foot of the tower and pushed open the heavy glass door.

Of the eight lifts clustered on the far side of the lobby only two went right to the top of the building. Both were standing at the twentieth floor, having presumably just taken guests up to the party. John pressed the call button and waited.

The lift arrived and, as its door opened, so did the outside door of the lobby. A woman's high heels clicked across the floor. Stepping inside the lift, John pressed the Hold button.

'Thank you.' The woman came past him to stand at the back of the lift, while John continued to face the control panel at the front. She might well be on her way to his party; but she would not recognize her host any more than he expected to know his guests. The smiles and smalltalk could be postponed for a few more moments.

'Which floor for you?' he asked.

'Seventeenth, please.'

So she was not after all a guest and potential customer.

'Will there be anyone there?' He still did not turn to face her.

'Someone to hand me a packet. I'm expected.'

It was none of his business. The lift shot smoothly upwards. John watched as the light above the door moved over each number in turn. He was not altogether at ease with the speed and silence of the new lifts – although he had hated those in the old building for precisely the slowness of their creaking journey from one floor to the next, with its inescapable impression that sooner or later they would abandon the effort and crash to the bottom of the shaft.

The light passed ten, eleven, twelve. There was no thirteenth floor. They were half way to the fourteenth, moving at full speed, when the lift stopped dead with a staggering jerk. At the same moment the lights went out.

John heard the woman stagger and fall, but at first he could neither move nor speak. Only after a few seconds was it possible to breathe again. They were not going up, but neither were they falling down. 'Are you all right?' he asked.

'Yes, thank you.' To judge from the level of her voice she had already picked herself up. 'I lost my balance. What happened?'

'Damn lifts,' said John, angry because he had been afraid. 'We've been in this building four months now, and there hasn't been a week pass without a breakdown. Because of overcrowding, the engineers always say. They won't be able to use that excuse this time. Are you carrying any kind of light? I can't remember where the alarm is.'

He heard a click and rustle as she opened and explored her bag. Her hand, feeling the way round the wall, rubbed briefly against his elbow; then he felt her close beside him. She was taller than he, so that her shoulder touched his cheek.

'Only book matches, I'm afraid,' she said. 'They don't last long. I'll strike and you press.' She held the flickering light close to the panel while John put his finger on the alarm and held it there. 'How do we know if it's working?' she asked, stamping or the match. The renewed darkness seemed blacker than any ordinary night.

'It rings in the caretaker's two offices,' John told her. 'Of course, it's intended for use if something goes wrong with the mechanics of the lift. But the light shouldn't have gone out as well. This may all be caused by something outside – a power failure.' The emergency generator which he had ordered for the tower had arrived, after a strike-extended delay, only three days earlier: it had not yet been connected to the system.

'You mean that the alarm may not be working either?'

'It may be on a battery. I don't remember. Anyway, someone who wants to use the lift will notice and tell the caretaker.'

'If it's a general power failure, none of the lifts will be working. People will use the stairs without thinking of any possible prisoners. In any case, there can't be many people left in the building at half past six.'

'There's a party on the penthouse floor. *My* party, as a matter of fact. I should have arrived for it half an hour ago.'

'So your guests will be queueing at the door.'

'My brother will be there.' Because of that, no one – except Lance himself – would worry about the lateness of the official host, which would seem to be explained by the traffic chaos outside. If there had been a complete power failure, someone would produce candles. The party might even become animated by the unexpected excitement. No one would be sure who was and who wasn't wandering in the shadows. John, his anxiety returning, banged with his fists against the door.

'There's an axe up there in a glass case,' said the woman. 'I noticed it. In case of emergency, it says. Is this an emergency?'

'We're stuck between floors in a shaft made of pre-stressed concrete. There's a weak panel above our heads which we can't reach. If we hack a chunk out of the floor we can certainly get out of the lift, but the only place to go is down.'

'Sorry.' She moved away, no doubt annoyed by the snub.

'No, *I'm* sorry.' His own hammering at the door had been equally unreasonable and he was relieved to have a companion: it wouldn't do to be impolite. 'But I don't think we can do much but wait. My name's John.'

She laughed: an attractively low, amused laugh. 'What a very anonymous name,' she said.

'Anonymous?'

'You might have said something like Montmorency. Either one knows a Montmorency or one doesn't. Or you could have gone the whole hog and said John Smith or whatever. Then I'd have had some chance of pinning you down. But there are so many just Johns.'

'How would you expect to pin me down? You don't know me.'

'How do I know that I don't know you? I might at least have heard of you. You smell of riches.'

'You mean the party?'

'On the penthouse floor. Partly. I was speaking literally, though. Most of us carry around all the mustiness of other people's sweat and cigarettes. But you haven't been on the Tube since the last time your overcoat was cleaned. At the end of a working day you smell of after-shave and slightly scented soap. And even if you're not a well-known millionaire, I'm a dab hand at playing the Small World Game.'

'What on earth's that?'

'I once read an article on coincidence and probability. One conclusion was that any two people from the same national group – in our case a mere fifty million or so – would only need to go through a maximum of four stages of knowing someone who knows someone else before reaching a point of contact. Whenever I'm bored, I test the theory out. The game is to open a conversation with a complete stranger and within half an hour get him to the point where he remarks spontaneously, "It's a small world, isn't it?"'

John laughed, forgetting his anxieties. 'Does it really work?'

'If I were prepared to tell the occasional fib, it would work every time. But I reckon that would be like cheating at Patience. So I always tell the truth, which cuts me down to about an eighty per cent success rate. But I shouldn't have told you about the game, should I? Even if I could get you to think it was a small world, you wouldn't say it now. Anyway, since we're moving straight on to Christian name terms, mine's Isabel. And I'm going to sit down. If this *is* a power failure, I suppose it may go on some time, and I've had a long day.'

'The floor will be filthy. Use this as a cushion.' Taking off his coat, he moved carefully across the lift until he could touch her with it. He approved of the momentary hesitation which indicated that she remembered the coat as being an expensive one, but equally he approved of the common sense which on second thoughts accepted it as an object to be put to whatever use its owner chose.

'Thank you very much. You'll share it, won't you?'

'Thank you.' He laid the folded coat along the floor.

When Isabel had settled into a corner, he lowered himself to sit beside her. Now he was sufficiently close to be aware of every breath she took, but silence and the black darkness combined to make him feel alone and uneasy. 'Let's talk,' he said.

'Fine. Let's talk. Talk away, John.'

'Well, you. I'm not good on small talk.'

'Nor am I. I'm a journalist, with a passion for finding out about people. My only idea of conversation is to ask questions.'

If only . . . An unexpected thought flashed into John's head; if only the voice could have been that of another journalist, a different woman. With Paula as a companion, instead of this stranger, he might even have been able to enjoy his imprisonment. But he must make the best of the real situation, not a fancied one. 'All right. Ask questions. I don't mind.'

'You will,' she said. 'The sort of questions I ask may begin innocently enough, but they always end up by being impertinent. If I do ask, will you answer truthfully?'

'I don't expect so.'

She gave a gasp, only half of laughter, and John smiled to think that he had surprised her. 'Surely that's a journalist's occupational hazard,' he suggested. 'And even lies can be revealing.'

'Of course,' she agreed. 'But only if one starts off from something known. There has to be a baseline of probability. Why should you feel that you might want to lie?'

'Because I have a high regard for truth. To tell the truth is a compliment: to hear it, a privilege.'

'And you don't think I deserve it?'

'I don't know yet. I was reserving my position.'

'But you answered that first question truthfully.'

'Did I?' he asked.

2

Isabel's laughter revealed the amusement of a woman intelligent enough to see two moves ahead. 'I've had a hard day,' she said. 'I don't feel intellectually equal to a debate on logic and ethics. I note that you are a man so high-principled as to be completely unscrupulous. So.' He was conscious of her wondering where to start. 'Tell me about your journey here this evening. The journey that you certainly didn't make on the Tube. Exactly how did you get here?'

'I came in a Daimler. Chauffeur-driven.'

'And what did you think about, or talk about, on the way?'

'I read a report. Looked at the evening paper. It mentioned the death of a family connection. I thought about that for a minute. Then – well, I stared at this building we're in now. The office lights were beginning to go off.'

'I saw that too, from the bus,' said Isabel. 'There was a dark stripe across the middle, so that the top half of the tower seemed to be floating in the air.'

'An insurance company has the eleventh and twelfth floors. Its staff go home at five-fifteen sharp.' It gave John an unexpected feeling of companionship that they should have shared a visual experience even before they met. 'And after that, the pattern kept changing. A black square here and another there, joining up in odd shapes.'

'I was imagining the people behind the windows as each light went off,' Isabel said. 'Well-lunched managing directors with company cars to take them to their week-end cottages. Grey-faced married men locking their drawers and heading for Waterloo and the suburbs. Red-faced bachelors making for the pubs. Office boys taking their pay packets home to Mum. Pool typists back-combing their hair ready for their evening dates. All glad that the working week was over. I expect you're an employer. Doesn't it depress you, the thought of millions of people who are bored with their work?'

'You talk like a writer,' John said, and was pleased to realize that he had disconcerted her for a second time.

'Like everyone who earns a living from words, I spent years believing that I was a novelist manqué. Until I finally produced a novel and realized that it wasn't worth reading. You dodged my question. About all the bored office workers.'

'They're fools to let themselves be bored,' said John. 'All those girls who don't want a career but just a bit of money until they get married! If they don't like typing in London, why don't they go off to Toronto or Timbuctoo?'

'The typing would still be dull. You're only suggesting a change of scenery outside office hours. And what about the man with a wife and children and mortgage? He can't just get up and go.'

'He could work at a job which interests him.'

'That remark suggests that you've created a career to suit your own talents. Not many people are as determined or as fortunate – or as talented – as that. Boredom comes from working for someone else's ambitions, so business is based on boredom. You don't want the girl on the addressograph machine to *think*. It's only the man at the top who can be trusted to make choices.'

'You're talking nonsense,' said John mildly.

'It's an unusual luxury, jabbering away to a stranger whom I shall never meet again. Anyway, as you watched the lights go off, you clearly didn't waste your time imagining people.'

'No,' agreed John. 'I just looked at the lights. At the pattern they made, and the way it kept changing. It occurred to me that something of the sort could be made to decorate a white wall, or a window after dark. Small rectangles of light to flash on and off in changing combinations, using a random selector. It would be perfectly feasible.'

'But hardly restful. Would you like it in your house?'

'Not mine, no. But not everybody wants to rest. My brother doesn't think he's still alive unless something's happening to stimulate him. I'll try the idea out on him when I get to the party. If I ever do get to the party.'

'Do you care whether you do or not?'

'I don't care about the party in itself. But having travelled so far, I prefer to think that I'm going to arrive.'

'One could say, having lived so long, I prefer to think that I shall soon be dead.'

'One could. But usually one doesn't. Have you run out of questions so soon?'

'I thought you'd probably had enough for the moment.'

'So what do you know about me now that you didn't know before?'

'Except that your name is John, I didn't know anything before.'

'And now?'

'And now I'll guess that you ought to be an artist. Instead of that, you work for a large company. Right at the top of it – managing director, probably: a high salary certainly. There are no women in the company of a status equal to your own. I'm inclined to suspect that you're not married – and that your company deals in objects, not people. You don't like people much.'

'You're off beam,' he said; although she had come

close enough to startle him. 'I'm not an artist. Never have been.'

'I didn't say you were. Only that you might have wished to be. I'm interested that you choose that point to quibble over.'

'I could quibble on the rest as well. I'm chairman of my company, for example, not just managing director.'

'My apologies, O Great White Chief. But that's what I meant, only more so. You like to be in charge. You haven't much use for ordinary people.'

'I respect anyone who knows what he wants,' John said. 'Most people just drift. They wait for someone else to take a decision and then merely approve or disapprove. The verdicts of democracy are usually either ignorant or retrospective. If you waited for ordinary people to decide, nothing would ever happen. Somebody has to act. In my company it's me.'

'My summing up wasn't so far wrong,' she pointed out. 'You've confirmed most of what I guessed. And I can tell you something that didn't need a question to find out. You're afraid of the dark.'

'What makes you think that?' he asked, not denying it.

'Englishmen don't talk to strange women in lifts. If the light hadn't gone out, you'd have made a single restrained comment on the inconvenience of being stuck here before retreating into your private thoughts. You wouldn't have let me bully you like this.'

'But you've already deduced that I'm not used to accepting women as working equals. Perhaps I retain the old-fashioned attitude of letting them get away with murder just because they *are* women.'

She laughed. 'I'll trade on it, then. *Why* are you afraid of the dark? When you were a little boy, did you always share a room with Nanny and a night-light?'

'When I was a little boy, a pit-cage cable snapped. My

father was killed. I've never felt quite safe in lifts. But it's a fear of falling, not of darkness.'

It was curious that he should find himself repeating the old lie in these circumstances. It had been his mother's lie to start with. Later, discovering and rejecting the truth, John had continued to feed the older version to journalists. Now, unexpectedly, the memory of a man in a wheelchair flashed through his mind: a different – and real – father who had fallen in a different and real way. But the nightmares had been genuine enough. 'Do you despise me for it?' he asked.

'Oh no. There's something curiously endearing about a rich man who's frightened.' Her voice, while mocking her own reaction, was sympathetic, making John grateful for her understanding. 'Your father was a miner, then?'

'In Leicestershire,' said John. 'An ugly county.'

'I remember holidays in Leicestershire when I was a child,' she said. 'My grandfather lived there, in the country. You're right, the villages were ugly. Bright red brick houses opening straight on to the pavement. Old women in black sitting outside on wooden chairs. And dozens of men in cloth caps leaning against walls.'

'If you were a child then, you must be younger than I am,' he said. 'That would be after the strike. Where the pits closed, there were men who never got off the dole until the war began.'

'I'm forty-one,' she said, making no fuss of the announcement. 'And the other thing I remember is that the women in the villages wore hideous steel curlers all day. I could have understood it if they wanted to look nice when their husbands came home in the evening. But these husbands were at home all day, seeing them at their worst. Did your mother go around in curlers?'

'She had to work, after my father died.'

'What did she do?'

'She sewed. Made dresses. Or worked by the day in some of the big houses in the country. Mending linen, embroidering initials, that sort of thing. Are you comfortable?' He could feel her shifting her position on the coat, leaning away from him so that she could fit her shoulders more snugly into the corner of the lift.

'Comfortable enough.'

After the off-hand remark it seemed that she had nothing more to say. The silence lengthened. It became heavy and tangible, as though the lift were filling with little cubes of quietness and darkness which divided and multiplied, crowding the empty space and advancing to smother them with soundlessness. John would have liked to touch Isabel, to put his hand on her own – not flirtatiously, but for reassurance. 'Don't stop talking,' he said. 'I like to hear you talk.'

'Even though I can't do anything but ask questions?'

'Just the sound of you talking. I don't care what you say.'

She drew in her breath and sighed in acceptance. 'All right. I need the questions to have a purpose, though. Since I've spoiled my chances of playing the Small World Game with you, let's pretend that I'm going to write your autobiography. I'm your ghost.'

'Without knowing who I am?'

'That will add a detective interest to the interrogation. It's a challenge. Shall I succeed in identifying you before the lights go on?'

3

'I can refuse to tell you my name,' John said. He spoke teasingly, not defensively, realizing that, in spite of her claim, she was going to attempt a version of her Small World Game, and enjoying the prospect of fencing with her. She shrugged the warning off.

'That's your privilege. But you won't refuse to answer any other questions, because that would mean allowing the silence to swallow you again. I even have a clue to start with. A relative of yours has died, you said: important enough to be mentioned in the evening paper.'

'A relative-in-law. Married to a distant cousin.'

'Mm.' She thought for a moment. 'A drug-crazy pop star? A lady-in-waiting to the Queen Mother? A Russian dissident poet?'

'You're very well informed about the possibilities.'

'It's my job. No one reads newspapers more avidly than the people who write them. I haven't come to the end of the list yet. There was a cardinal dying this morning; he might have gone. And a man who was tipped as a future prime minister until he went for a drunken drive eighteen months ago has lost whatever life he had left.'

'That's the one,' said John, knowing that he was not in fact revealing anything about himself by the admission. 'James Laker-Smith.'

'But he was married to Paula Mattison.'

'That's right. Paula's a cousin of mine. Do you know her?'

'We were up at Oxford together. A long time ago, and we haven't met since. But she's not someone easily forgotten. You could say that *everyone* knows Paula Mattison. And – '

'And she's black. True. It may seem unlikely – but all the same, her grandfather was the younger brother of my grandfather.'

Isabel's voice revealed her amusement. 'I might have guessed that you'd only give me a direct answer when you were sure that it wouldn't be of the slightest help. Well, I shall have to creep up on your identity. And whenever you dodge, I shall know I'm getting warm. I shall jump about, to prevent you from preparing your evasions. Tell me first of all, what was the most important thing that happened to you when you were ten?'

The directness with which she pointed her question at the most traumatic experience of his life almost took John's breath away. 'There was nothing special,' he muttered. Even to himself the lie did not sound convincing.

'There must have been. Even if it was only leaving your primary school.'

How foolish of him to think that she could somehow have known the answer to her question in advance. John collected his thoughts. At the age of ten he had discovered that his father, whom he had believed to be long dead, was not only alive but famous and rich. So great had been the shock of the discovery that John had concealed what he learned for the whole of his adult life, and he did not propose to reveal it now. But there was an alternative answer.

'When I was ten I went in for a newspaper competition – for painting a poster. I won first prize in my age group: a bicycle. It opened up half England to me. I used to cycle enormous distances.' It was eighty miles from his village to Blaize, but the prize bicycle had covered the distance to bring him face to face with his father.

'So I was right earlier on.' Isabel's voice revealed a trace of smugness. 'You *are* an artist as well as a company chairman.'

'One success as a ten-year-old hardly guarantees a talent. All the same, I agree, it did have an effect. I'd always enjoyed drawing, and the competition gave me confidence that it was something I could do. So when I was offered an apprenticeship in Bristol later as a draughtsman, it seemed a good idea to take it.'

'We haven't reached apprenticeship time yet. You're still ten. What else happened when you were ten?'

Why had she chosen that particular year to investigate in such detail? He was reluctant to answer, but even more unwilling to abandon the game and allow silence to creep over them both again. 'That was the year my brother was born,' he said.

'But you told me your father had died when you were a little boy. Do you think of a ten-year-old as – '

'Half-brother, I should have said.' By now John was beginning to feel uneasy. No one before had ever tried to elicit his personal life story. The foundations of the business career which made his fortune and reputation had been laid during the war, when he was in his twenties, and he had never encouraged questions about his earlier life. Whatever information he did from time to time reveal emerged in such a piecemeal fashion that no one in the past could have checked a single item against the rest. Anyone who tried to put the pieces of the jigsaw together, as Isabel was trying now, would soon discover that they did not fit.

'So your mother had married again by then?'

'I'm answering your questions about myself,' said John. 'But that's a question about someone else.' His choice of words gave a clear enough answer and he was grateful for the tact with which Isabel accepted it.

'Ten years is a big gap between two boys,' she said. 'Do you feel close to your half-brother?'

'Now, yes. He's my company's sales manager, as a matter of fact. But as boys we hardly knew each other. My mother was ill from the time he was born. He was brought up by friends of hers in the village, and they adopted him when she died four years later. I rescued him, you might say, when I first began to make some money. Made sure that he had a decent training, just as someone I hardly knew had done for me.'

'That was bad luck, being orphaned before you were fourteen.' But she did not explore the loneliness he had felt at that time. Her next question revealed instead a different pre-occupation. 'Do you mind if I smoke?'

He could hear the groping sounds in her handbag as she took his permission for granted. John himself, except for the usual schoolboy gestures, had never smoked. Even before the habit had been proved dangerous he had considered it dirty. He coughed automatically when he found himself in a smoky room, with an irritation both mental and physical, and never – unless business demanded it – acted as host more than once to anyone who lit a cigarette between the courses of a meal. But to a compulsive smoker, he supposed, this must be exactly the kind of situation in which a cigarette would be most soothing. One form of selfishness was in conflict with another – but he was entitled to fight for his own comfort. 'It might be better if you didn't,' he said.

'Why?'

'These lifts are tightly sealed. If something's badly wrong, we might be here for hours. We'll need all the oxygen we can get.'

Isabel gave a rueful laugh. 'Some people would regard death by suffocation as almost preferable to an attack of nicotine withdrawal symptoms. I take it you don't smoke yourself?'

'No, I don't.'

'You could have said so. No need to slink up from behind. If we're going to be forced into hours of each other's company, democracy will have to operate.' She paused, considering her own statement. 'That is a point which I don't remember seeing in any of my books on political science. One requisite for democracy is an odd number.'

'Or a chairman's casting vote.'

'Then who casts the casting vote to elect the chairman? Besides, decisions by casting vote are always negative, preserving the status quo.'

'Only when the chairman's a gentleman, or playing at law or politics,' he said. 'When it's something important, the casting vote means power. The smallest shift from an even balance tips the whole see-saw. Someone might get forty-nine per cent of the voting shares in my company if he tried, but I should still run it my way.'

'Is it a big company?' she asked. 'So many people are company directors these days. It sounds grand until you discover that the company's just some little back room with two men and a boy.'

'Mine's rather more than that. *Too* big, I sometimes think.'

'Are you a millionaire?'

'If somebody bought my company and paid cash, I'd be a millionaire then. There aren't many men outside the deserts of Arabia who can write a cheque for a million pounds on their current accounts. I have as much money as I ever personally want to spend.' That was enough about his financial state: he took a conversational step backwards. 'Do you read many books on political science?'

'Not nowadays. I took a degree in history once. Hobbes, Locke and Rousseau were required reading. Hegel and Marx were optional extras. I found it all very exciting at the time, but now I can hardly remember a word of any of them.'

'I've never thought that a degree in history was much use.'

'What's wrong with history in particular?' She did not sound annoyed: merely curious.

'It's inexact.'

'I don't agree. History is what happened. What could be more exact than that?'

'History isn't what happened,' argued John. 'It's what some historian says happened. A very different thing. Especially in time of dispute. War criminals are always on the losing side, because it's the winner who watches the history books being written. If Richard III had won the battle of Bosworth, who should we think had killed the princes in the Tower?'

'Oh, that. We're talking about two different things: fact and the relating of fact. The life you've lived comes before the autobiography you write about it. The history comes before the history books.'

'But it's what we learn from the history books which actually changes our lives. The world is full of liars – and a lie can have quite as much effect as the truth.'

His whole childhood had been dominated by a single lie: that his father was dead. When at last John had exposed this particular untruth, it had at once been replaced by another: that his father had deserted his mother when he himself was only a baby. How could a young boy, so deliberately deceived, be expected to find his way to the truth? By the time he learned part of it, his hatred of his father was too strongly entrenched to be capable of change. It was not the true facts about his parents which had influenced his life, but the lies he had been told. 'How can one ever hope to find out what really happened about anything?' he asked.

'You can try. I try. Anyone who believes that truth is important has to try.' She was silent for what seemed a long time. When she spoke again, it seemed that the problems of truth had ceased to interest her. 'At midnight,' she said. 'Could I at midnight?'

4

'Could you what?' John was bewildered by her abrupt switch from subject to subject.

'Could I smoke at midnight, if we're still here? It would give me something to look forward to for the next five hours. Just one cigarette.'

'Yes, of course. I've no right to stop you having one now if – '

'That's all right. Good for me.' She closed her handbag with a click. 'Perhaps the bomb's fallen.'

'A bomb?'

'*The* bomb. The one we've been waiting for and protesting against and shutting our eyes to and expecting all our lives.'

'There wasn't anything in the paper – '

Isabel tutted impatiently. 'The whole point of using the bomb is that the first one must come without warning. The first victims are bound to be surprised. I was thinking about the lift. Air-tight in a concrete shaft. The perfect shelter from radiation, I should think. A fortnight sealed up here and we could be London's only survivors.'

'Except that we'd still be sealed up – and would probably have starved to death before then.'

'It takes longer than a fortnight to starve, surely,' he said. 'Hunger strikers go on for two months.'

'They're kept alive with water and glucose.'

'It makes me thirsty just to think of it. What will your guests be swigging on the penthouse floor at this moment?'

'Champagne. Were you on your way to the party?'

'I was going to the seventeenth floor, if you remember. Wouldn't you have known if I were one of your own guests?'

'No,' said John. 'My brother sent out the invitations. It's a business party. People from all over the country. Town clerks, borough surveyors, housing officers, that sort of thing. We were taking advantage of the fact that they're all in London for a conference. I know some of the men, but I haven't met any of their wives.'

'Well, I'm nobody's wife. I have to earn my own invitations.'

'Are you divorced?'

'Widowed. Your party doesn't sound madly exciting. Or do town clerks turn into gay dogs when they escape from the mayoral eye?'

'No. It would have been dull.'

'I should have thought that one advantage of being chairman was the right to leave the dull duties to someone else.'

'Normally I do. But I go if it's important. According to Lance, my function is to stand and give an impression of financial soundness. Not so easy when you're only five foot three. But in fact I've never been the sort of company chairman who's only interested in the figures. I'm very much involved in design and presentation. I can make quite an enthusiastic speech about whatever it may be that we're trying to sell.'

'Lance?' There was an edge to her voice as she queried

the name. In an ordinary conversation John might not have noticed it. But the voice coming out of the dark, with no glimpse of face or figure to distract the attention, had developed an identity of its own and his ears were sensitive to the slightest change of tone. Lance's name had for some reason startled her.

'My brother,' he explained. 'You wouldn't think that a woman who christened her first son John would plump for Lancelot when it came to the second, would you?'

'I'm stiff,' said Isabel. Necessarily they had been sitting close together on the coat, so that when she stood up John was chilled by the emptiness all round him. The hem of her coat brushed his shoulder as she moved out of the corner. When she spoke again, her voice seemed to come from a long way away.

'Have you – has your company – been in this tower block long?' she asked, confusing him yet again by the sudden change of subject. 'Were you somewhere else before?'

'We moved here about four months ago, from Southwark.'

'You said you involved yourself in design. What exactly does your company make or do?'

He turned his head to speak in her direction. Her sudden withdrawal had left him isolated and anxious again. A factual statement helped to keep him calm.

'Pre-fabricated building is our main business – houses, hospitals, schools: anything that's needed. But one thing leads to another. We have factories to make and use concrete, engineering interests, overseas subsidiaries, our own financing system to give credit for big contracts. It's a complicated business. Do you have to do that?'

She was pacing up and down, three steps each way like a tiger in a cage. The lift rocked beneath her footsteps – only very slightly; but John, still sitting on the floor, felt every tremor in his bowels. His knees cracked as he scrambled to his feet.

'I'm tired of keeping still,' she said. 'I need the exercise. And if this thing weren't safe, we'd know by now. Are you frightened again, John? Do you feel safer standing up?'

'Yes.' Her mockery did not shame him. His pride, he realized, went with his name. Anonymous, he could not be humiliated. He stepped into the path of her pacing, as far as he could judge it, and put out his hands, stopping her so abruptly and so close that he could feel her breath on his eyes. As he gripped her arms, his right wrist pressed against the firm curve of her breast, and he could judge her slimness by the closeness of his own hands. 'Isabel!' he said.

She took a step backwards, twisting herself free. 'Isabel!' she repeated. 'My names's John. Call me John. How matey, and how modest. Are you ashamed of the handle, Sir John? I'm sorry, Sir John, that I'm not a Lady, Sir John, so that we could have swapped modesties.'

John's brief need to touch her, to feel himself not alone, was banished by the inexplicable bitterness in her voice. He waited to discover the reason for her attack. 'Do I gather that you disapprove of knighthoods?' he asked.

'Who am I to approve or disapprove?' It sounded as though she were sitting down again. The sudden fire had gone out of her voice, as though she had lost interest in him. 'I've no doubt you deserved yours as much as anyone. I only wondered why you kept quiet about it. And why you felt the need to fib. I'll accept the drawing office in Bristol. There was a big ship-building company there, wasn't there, before nationalisation? The Lorimer Line. Owned by a family who used to be little tin gods in the city in the old slave trade days. I can see it might suit you to pretend that you started at the bottom, with no special advantages: it makes a good publicity story. But why all the stuff about your father being a miner? I don't believe that for a moment.'

'Sometimes a lie describes the real state of affairs more accurately than the truth.'

'We've had this conversation before. The truth is what matters. The truth about you is that you're Sir John Lorimer, half-brother of Lance Tyrell and chairman of Lorico. That's right, isn't it?'

There was no point in denying it and no need to waste words on admitting it: her identification was definite, not questioning. How was it, he wondered, that she had come at the truth so quickly? He had not consciously given her any useful clues. Then something clicked in his mind. It could be that their paths had crossed before. Although she had not yet claimed a victory, perhaps she had made good her boast to be an expert player of the Small World Game. Her name, after all, was Isabel.

History Is What Happened 1973

1

Isabel. John repeated the name to himself in silence. He sat down again on the coat, careful not to touch her. Isabel. The name on a letter in a dead man's pocket. Not too unusual a name, but not a common one either. Not 'anonymous', as she'd say. Of all the Isabels in London, how many would be widows? And the age. He tried to remember what he knew about Isabel Blair, to work out how old she would be by now.

Once, many years ago, on his way to Barry Blair's office, he had passed in the corridor a girl who carried a clip-board, studying it so intently that he had to step aside to avoid a collision. A tall, slim girl with long, black hair and an intelligent, restless face.

Barry's offices had always been full of pretty girls, and the long-haired beauty might have been one of the art students who besieged every advertising agency with samples of their work. All the same, John had felt at the time that this must be the girl whose name was mentioned in the interview which followed.

'I'm doing the artwork myself,' Barry had said. 'And you can have Isabel for the copy. She's my newest find. Young, but very good. You'll have the first flush of her enthusiasm. She tends to produce a wild rush of ideas for every project. A responsible job like this is just what she needs to tame her imagination.'

'This is an important promotion,' John said drily. 'I

don't want it to be used as a training class. I'd like to meet her.'

Barry laughed. It was a standing joke of his that John – like himself, still a bachelor – was a wolf in perpetual search of a lamb.

'I'll bet you would. She's quite something. But she doesn't like talking to the client. She'll work through me. She'll study the product until she knows as much about it as you do. If you like to send her a memo on where you see the potential market, she'll weigh it in with the results of the market research. But she reckons it's *her* job, not the client's, to work out which points will actually do the selling.'

'She sounds a very self-opinionated young woman.'

'She's a very competent young woman. She's done some good work: people have been pleased. It's time she had a chance at something big. And naturally I shall be responsible overall for the campaign.'

'That's all I need to know,' John had laughed. 'Which head to chop off. Your excuses for keeping wild creatures on your creative staff are your own business. Just ask me to the wedding, that's all.'

The remark was made only half in joke, for even as early as that there had been a possessive note in Barry's voice when he spoke about Isabel. But when, a year later, the wedding did take place, John had been supervising an emergency scheme to rehouse earthquake victims in Chile and could not attend.

Barry had never invited John to visit him at home after he was married, any more than he had done before. The two men had been friends for many years, but it was a friendship well enough sustained by conferences, drinks and lunches. John himself rarely entertained at home, so he saw nothing unusual in the fact that Barry also chose pubs and restaurants rather than his own house for their social meetings. It had not seemed surprising or important that Isabel was never present on these occasions. Wives were evening appurtenances, not expected to be produced in daylight.

Naturally John asked Barry from time to time how his family life was going, and was given news of Isabel. She had baby trouble, John remembered now – pregnancies which invariably ended in miscarriage, so that over a period of several years she was often sick or depressed. Later, abandoning the attempt to start a family, she had returned to work full-time at her husband's agency. But by then Lance had taken over the duty of discussing Lorico's publicity, while John was travelling all over the world as his own best salesman, negotiating the overseas government contracts which steadily built his company into one of the leaders in its field. He still thought of Barry as a friend, but they saw each other less frequently, and he never met Mrs Isabel Blair. There was no real reason why he should have felt sure that she was the young woman he had glimpsed in the corridor.

Shifting uneasily in his coat, which seemed to be sprouting buttons in all the most uncomfortable places, John tried to visualize the woman whose breathing was the only sound in the lift. What did she look like? He had taken little notice of her when she first joined him. Their moments of contact since the light went out confirmed his glimpse of her as being tall and slender – which would fit with the old memory. He had an impression of high heels and slim ankles and a neat, smart coat: of hair piled high on her head – tidy, but beginning to go grey. Isabel Blair would be in her forties now. His present companion had said that she was forty-one.

If she were in fact Isabel Blair it would explain the speed with which she had identified him, and the anger in her voice. He remembered the note she had written to him after Barry's funeral. But she still had not volunteered her own full name. For him to ask, to check his deduction, would be to make a quarrel inevitable. And they were cooped up in this damn lift. He was curious, though. Earlier in their conversation she had accused him of having little interest in people and perhaps this was true. He had allowed her to explore his life without making any effort to imagine her own. Now he wanted to know all about her.

'How long have you been a journalist?' he asked abruptly. Isabel Blair had been a copywriter; but it was not an impossible change of career. 'It seems an odd choice of job for a history graduate, when you think how careless newspapers are with facts.'

There was a pause before she answered. Perhaps she had expected a more positive reaction to the venom in her identification. But when at last she continued the conversation it seemed that she, like himself, was not anxious to provoke a quarrel from which they would be unable to escape. Her voice was matter-of-fact as she said, 'Wasn't it you who felt so strongly that lies could have as much effect as the truth? Isn't it important, then, that mistakes shouldn't be allowed to get into print, and be repeated, and have consequences of their own? It's a good thing that a journalist should have some historical training before recording the sources for the next generation of historians? But actually, although I work on a newspaper, the job isn't what people first think of when they hear the word journalist. I'm in charge of obituaries.'

He couldn't help laughing; it was so unexpected. For a moment he forgot who he was trying to discover. 'You mean you write them?'

'Not necessarily. Mostly they're commissioned in advance from someone in the same field: stage, politics or whatever. But I'm responsible for keeping them up to date and making sure that the paper isn't caught napping by celebrities who die inconsiderately young.' Isabel laughed suddenly. 'Suppose the bomb *has* fallen. The whole of London lying dead. What a spring-cleaning I could have of my files! A complete edition. No one except the Queen or Prime Minister could have more than half a column. Knights of the stage and Nobel prizewinners would be cut down to shorties. Royal dukes and professors and pop singers would pile up in the waste paper basket. But you might be my only reader.'

'I suppose that was how you identified me, from your files.'

'No, it wasn't. But it was why I wanted to. From the moment I caught the whiff of wealth. It's always intriguing, the feeling that you may know more about someone than he's telling you.'

'But if I'm not on your file – '

'I didn't say that. I only said that wasn't how I recognized you. I usually won't tell people but yes, you are on the list. Only a shortie, though. I'd give you two inches more if your company crashed and you were next heard of in Brazil.'

'I'll settle for the shortie – and hope it doesn't end, "Died in a London lift during a power failure." Was that the only reason you were curious – to see whether I figured in your records?'

'At first, yes.'

'And afterwards?'

'Aren't all women curious?' she asked vaguely.

'Not more than all men.'

'You're not.'

'I'm interested in you.' He tried to make the remark sound merely flirtatious lest she should discover the strength of his wish to know all about her. And indeed, it was more than curiosity that he felt: there was an emotional need to establish some kind of relationship with this woman who might or might not be entirely a stranger. He was attracted by the darting intelligence behind her questions and by her low voice and husky laugh: he was grateful for the sympathy which had recognized his need for company in the dark stillness and had prevented her from holding herself aloof for more than a few seconds. He wanted to be allowed to like her.

'Your turn will come later,' she told him. 'I haven't finished *my* questions.'

'You've identified me.'

'That was only the beginning. It allows short cuts, that's all. I'm researching your autobiography, if you remember. What was the most important thing that happened in your forty-sixth year?'

John hesitated for a moment. Why did she wish to continue playing a game which she had already won? And why should she grope her way through his life now that she had the information with which to challenge him directly, if she chose? But his involvement in the game was by now as great as hers. He puzzled over the answer to her question.

'That's difficult. You know how it is. When you're young, events leave landmarks. But later on there's a routine. In your forties, life's much the same in one year as in the next. As far as I remember, when I was forty-six – '

'You're forty-five, not forty-six, when you're in your forty-sixth year.'

The sharpness of the snub annoyed him. Under any other circumstances he would have cut the conversation short: but then silence would spread its black blanket over him again.

'When I was forty-five I went to India. There was a plan to tempt the graduates back from the cities. I was invited to provide a building to serve as clinic and school for each village.' He laughed at the memory. 'It turned out that there wasn't any money. I was expected to raise it myself from either the Americans or the Russians.'

'Did you do it?'

'No. I let them have a design as my private aid contribution to the Third World. But I wasn't short of work and I wasn't looking for that sort of hassle. On the way out, though, I stopped off in Calcutta. It was an eye-opener. Thousands of people sleeping on the streets, with a patch of shade on a paving stone for a home. It gave me a new attitude to basic standards. When the floods came in Pakistan two years later I had a blueprint ready for an emergency housing pack – the minimum of shelter and privacy with the best possible safeguards for health. Low price and short construction time. The houses were meant to be temporary, but people are still living in them, I'm told, like Dayaks in long-houses. They've changed the pattern of society in some of the flooded areas.'

'Fifty-eight,' she said.

'In my fifty-ninth year London will burn to the ground and I shall produce a detailed plan for its rebuilding as the greatest city in the world. No one will take the slightest notice of the plan, of course.'

'Fifty-seven.'

He saw what she was doing and did not answer at once. In a few moments they might no longer be on speaking terms. When the last barrier of reticence was breached, the flood of truth was likely to drown the illusion of intimacy which had grown between them. He sighed, surrendering.

'Fifty-seven. When I was fifty-seven I found myself stuck in a lift with a woman called Isabel. I suppose you think like this all the time. As an obituarist, I mean. I find it a little frightening that everything I do in the present should be so promptly translated into the past tense. If I get married in the morning, I suppose that by lunchtime you've added another sentence. "In such-and-such a year he married so-and-so, daughter of . . ." How long does the present last?'

'The present has no existence,' said Isabel. 'It's gone by the time you're able to think about it. Jam was always yesterday.'

'You do have some extraordinary ideas! The present is all that *does* exist. Not because we're thinking about it; because we're living it. Anyway, you know what you wanted to know. I'm fifty-seven. You could even have asked me.'

'And when you were fifty,' she said. 'Did anything important happen when you were fifty?'

John worked out the dates and the answer left no room for doubt – only surprise that she apparently wanted him to incriminate himself rather than listen to her accusation. 'I was ill,' he said.

'Yes?'

'Quite seriously ill. I was away from the office for about four months. In hospital at first. Then on a health farm for a few weeks, convalescing. And a few more weeks in Jamaica, doing nothing. Just lying in the shade, listening to the waves roll and break. I felt weak and empty – almost as though I were dead already – and I enjoyed the feeling. There didn't seem anything that I needed to live for. I had no wife, no permanent attachments. Building up my business had always been the most important thing in my life, and I'd been very successful in that. But if I'd died when I had the first heart attack, and if the company had crashed, it obviously wouldn't have mattered to me. So why should it matter when I was alive? I discovered how to relax. Wasting time. Closing my eyes and feeling the warm air wrap itself round me like a shroud. And yet getting better without noticing it.'

'But when you went back to London you were still chairman: still in charge of your company.'

He agreed with a nod and then, remembering that she could not see him, said 'Yes.'

'So what else happened that year?'

'I took things easily for quite a long time. The doctors had been stern. No more flying off all over the world. Apart from that heart attack, my fifty-first year was reasonably uneventful.'

'Are you sure?' she asked. 'Isn't there anything else you remember?'

John turned his head towards her voice, taking his time to answer. How much did she know, he wondered; how much did she need to know? In the moment when Isabel identified him he had felt the force of her recollected anger – restrained only so that she should not betray herself before she had forced him into some kind of admission. Should he try to head her off with evasions? An hour or two earlier he might have continued to dodge her pressure. But by now he felt an overwhelming interest in the woman who was quite certainly Isabel Blair. He could use silence only as a protection. If he was to tempt back her earlier warmth and sympathy he would have to take a risk and open the floodgates to let the truth pour through. But there was no need to start with more than a trickle.

'Yes,' he answered. 'I remember one more thing. That was the year when the company decided to move its advertising account.'

2

Neither of them wasted any time in formally confirming her identity. John heard Isabel's breath go out in a long sigh and waited to find out what it was that she hoped to prove. Barry Blair had killed himself with a mixture of drugs and alcohol on the day he was formally notified that his agency would be losing the Lorico business. No one at the inquest had challenged the assumption that his mind had been temporarily unhinged by business anxieties; and his widow, in her letter afterwards, had made clear her view that Sir John Lorimer was little better than a murderer. But she had had time since then, surely, to consider that a minor business set-back would hardly be enough in itself to drive a man to suicide.

Her tone of voice now contained no indication that her opinion had changed. 'The company!' she exclaimed. 'Companies don't make decisions. People make decisions. Your company is you.'

'I didn't – '

She interrupted him angrily. 'It was Lance who decided: I know that. But he couldn't have put the decision into effect by himself. Illness or no illness, you were the man with the power.'

'He was in charge of marketing,' said John. 'When I give a job to a man, I believe in letting him get on with it.'

'You can delegate work, but you can't delegate responsibility.'

'I'm not trying to. You interrupted me a moment ago. Lance made the decision that the account ought to be moved. It was part of his job to evaluate the effectiveness of our publicity, and its cost. He went into it thoroughly and was shocked by what he discovered. He knew that Barry was a friend of mine, so he sent the report to me before putting his recommendation to the board. I read the report and was convinced by it. I have no intention of evading responsibility. The decision may not have been mine originally, but it was correct.'

'A friend of yours!' Isabel repeated bitterly. 'What does friendship mean, then?'

'Barry would have found out if he'd lived. What it doesn't mean is that the affairs of a large company should suffer because one man is out of step. Tell me, Isabel, did the report really come as a shock to you and Barry?'

'We knew that Lance was making an investigation, of course. He asked Barry to go through everything with him. To put him in the picture after he took over the marketing department, he said, and at first Barry thought that was all it was. Then Lance wanted to see some other figures, and – '

'And you realized that he was in the picture with a vengeance already.'

'I was never involved with the business side,' admitted Isabel. 'I only knew what Barry told me. I think he did expect that he'd have to make some changes. But I'm sure he didn't anticipate losing the account altogether.'

'We'd tried to make changes before, you know,' John told her. 'Sometimes Barry didn't seem to recognize the difference between advertising soap powder directly to the consumer and selling our kind of product, where the purchaser is likely to be a government or a large organization. We tried to remind him that he needed to reach the men who signed the contracts and the cheques. But – '

'You said you believed in letting people get on with their own work.'

'Then I'll put it bluntly. Barry wasn't efficient at that side of the job. He would have done better to go on working in a big agency instead of starting his own.'

'But it was cruel!' she burst out. 'To wreck his whole business so suddenly! You could at least have cut down gradually.'

'You know, surely, that one can't move gradually in the advertising world. The moment we'd given the first piece of business to somebody else, the whispers would have started and Barry's other accounts would have begun to slip away. But I had my own plans to help him.'

'Barry didn't know that.'

'It's one of the things I regret, that he didn't wait to be told. But you know how stubborn he could be. If I'd put an alternative plan in front of him while he was still handling our work, he'd have turned it down. He wouldn't have believed in advance that we'd refuse to renew the contract. He had to go right down to the bottom before he'd be willing to accept a position somewhere in the middle.'

'Well, you certainly sent him to the bottom.' Her voice betrayed a bitterness which must presumably have faded in the years since Barry's death, to be resurrected only by this unexpected meeting with the man she regarded as an enemy.

John wondered how much of what he could tell her, if he chose, would come as a shock. Three hours ago he would not have cared about her reaction, but now he was anxious for her to understand. 'Barry came to see me after he received the formal letter from Lance,' he told her.

'I know about that meeting. He said you'd refused to intervene.'

'It wasn't quite as blunt as that. I promised that we wouldn't announce that we were moving our account. He could put out his own version – say that he didn't want to handle us any more.'

'As if anyone would have believed that!'

'A stout lie and plenty of confidence go a long way when no one is going to deny the story. As well as that, I told him that I had a positive suggestion to make and that I'd call at his office to discuss it over a drink that evening. He knew I was coming. It was his own choice not to wait.'

'And *did* you go?'

'I was the one who found him, if you remember.' She must have been told that by the police who broke the news to her: but no doubt she had been too shocked to register anything but the fact of her husband's death. 'And your other point,' he went on. 'About wrecking Barry's business. Barry wasn't a businessman, you know. There was no one better for catching the eye with a good design. But an agency is better off being run by an accountant than by an artist. Barry's business was a mess.'

'It was profitable,' Isabel said defensively.

'The Lorico account was profitable,' John corrected her. 'And we hadn't been as strict as we should have been in investigating campaign costs, not until Lance took over the marketing. Over the years we'd been gradually landed with a good many of Barry's overheads.'

'You were the biggest account.'

'And by God we were paying for the privilege! For media advertising, of course, the agency had the normal commissions. But a good deal of the Lorico publicity took place on the road – presentations to housing committees, exhibitions in town halls, elaborate sets of material to go overseas. Naturally we expected to pay the bills for that. But what Lance discovered was that – for example – we were carrying the whole costs of an exhibition design department and a specially equipped van, although they were only working for us part of the time. When the agency looked for new business, it was able to give very competitive quotes because so many of the overheads were covered already. That might have been only inefficient accounting. But I think Barry must have known, or he wouldn't have been so quick to realize that when we withdrew he'd have to fulfil his other contracts on what would then be an uneconomic basis. An agency which loses a big account often has to shed staff. But it's only if the costing for the account hasn't been properly done that the whole agency is in danger.'

Isabel took a moment to consider this and chose not to argue the point further. 'You said you were going to put a suggestion to Barry,' she reminded him. 'What was it?'

'I was going to offer to buy the agency. He could have stayed in the firm with whatever job he liked as long as he accepted my nominee to take control of administration and finance.'

'Why should you have been willing to do that?'

'Because whether or not you believe it, Barry *was* my friend.'

'That's what he thought. He couldn't believe you'd desert him.'

'I wouldn't have done. He was the one who deserted.'

'But why?' she asked herself. 'If he knew you were coming, why didn't he wait to hear what you had to say?'

'Can't you answer that question?'

'I? Why should I know?'

'Just a matter of timetabling.' Accepting her reaction as genuine, he tried to keep his voice vague. 'You must have seen Barry after I did. He came round to my office as soon as he read Lance's letter – at about half past nine in the morning. It was almost twelve hours later that I called at his office and found him dead. Didn't you see him during that time?'

'Yes,' she agreed. 'I had an outside job, but his secretary phoned me and I went to the office in the afternoon. Barry had been drinking. I tried to get him to come home, but he said he had an appointment to see Lance at five. He still hoped it could all be talked out somehow.'

'Did you stay for that meeting?'

'No. He told me to go home. Perhaps he felt that if Lance was going to humiliate him, he didn't want me to hear. And I thought that if he was going to lose the business, it was important that he should feel cared-for at home. I wasn't always a good home-maker. When you're working full-time, it's not easy. But for this one evening I tried to get everything right.'

He could guess from the break in her voice how closely she still grasped the memory of that evening. 'Tell me,' he said gently.

Isabel made an unsuccessful attempt to mock herself. 'I bought flowers on the way home. I lit a coal fire and put his slippers out to warm. I'd never done that before – I thought it might make him laugh. Then I cooked a proper meal – herbs, wine, the lot. It smelt the house out, but at eight o'clock it was a good smell. By ten o'clock the smell was stale and I was cross because he hadn't phoned. I took it for granted that the meeting with Lance had gone badly and that he was stopping at every pub on the way home. I was angry about a spoiled meal when I was already a widow. I cried about that later. But by then I was angry about other things as well. With Barry himself, for walking out on me. And with you and Lance, for driving him to it.'

'Do you still hate me now?'

'You mean now that I know what happened? How Sir John Lorimer, chairman of Lorico, intended to do the decent thing?' Isabel sighed. 'Somehow you don't seem to have much to do with the man I hated.'

'Why did you need to know that I am who I am?' John asked. 'Why did you have to press it right to the end?'

'It was curiosity at first,' she said. 'Playing the Small World Game. But as soon as I heard Lance's name and guessed . . . It was you who needed to know about me, really. I could feel you beginning to get interested. Perhaps you thought it would be safe to involve yourself with a stranger who would never know who you were. But we were involved with each other already. It didn't seem fair to keep quiet.'

'Ah yes, the history graduate. The truth and nothing but the truth.' He waited, but she did not comment on the incomplete quotation. 'I'm tired,' he said. It had been two o'clock in the morning before he had arrived home from Paula's party. 'Let's go to sleep.'

'I'm not sure that I can,' she said. 'But use me as a pillow if you like. Make yourself comfortable.'

He took her at her word, stretching himself along the floor of the lift and then settling his head on her lap. At first he lay flat on his back, but the position was uncomfortable. His main weight fell on a thick ridge made by the collar of his overcoat, and his neck was strained at an awkward angle. Anxious not to fidget, he considered possible improvements before he moved. Then he turned on one side so that his face pressed into Isabel's smooth coat, while his lower arm encircled her waist. To fall asleep at will was an art he had acquired during his journeys round the world. Within seconds the blackness of the lift had invaded his eyes and his mind. Peacefully, he slept.

3

'Are you awake?' John whispered the question.

'Yes.'

He sat up stiffly, flexing and relaxing his numbed muscles. The darkness seemed even more oppressive than before. He stifled a yawn and then, stretching and sighing, gave a second one its head. 'Have I been asleep long?'

'I don't think so. Though it always seems a long time when you're trying not to disturb anyone.' Isabel too was stretching herself, taking advantage of her freedom to move.

'I'm sorry.' He needed only a short time to throw off his heaviness: travel had made him as efficient at collecting his thoughts for a new day as at relaxing. 'What were you thinking of while I was asleep?'

'I was trying to recall what's in your obituary.'

'You must have hundreds of people on your files. You surely can't remember all of them.'

'I have a photographic memory. Given time, I can work out like a jigsaw anything I've studied once. And at the time when I took the job I had a personal interest in you. I looked up your file specially. I remember feeling that as a record it wasn't complete. There were two large omissions. For instance, it didn't say how you started.'

'Started what?'

'To make a fortune. I've never understood how people acquire capital. It may not be too hard to come by the second quarter million, but how did you get the first?'

'I worked on the Mulberry project during the war. One of my colleagues was a specialist in concrete. I learned from him what could and what couldn't be done, and we became friends. I already had a plan for building a small house from prefabricated sections round a central core which would come ready equipped to provide all the kitchen and bathroom services.'

'Just what was needed, I suppose, to replace bombed homes.'

'Exactly. The two of us went into partnership. Unequal partnership, really. All I brought was the ideas. He provided materials and credit. But it was only a sideline to him and he was happy enough when his concrete business found that its bills were being paid. As soon as we had one success behind us, the banks queued up to lend us money. That's probably the answer to your question. All that you need to make a fortune is the confidence of people with money to lend – and the ability to use the borrowed money at a higher rate of profit than the interest you're paying on the loan.'

'You make it sound very simple.'

'One thing follows from another when you're actually doing it. What was the other omission?'

'Your father. You don't seem ever to have mentioned any facts about him to anyone. I would have thought you'd be proud of coming so far from being a miner's son.'

'I didn't want to have it on the record.'

'But why not?'

John took his time to answer. If Isabel had been interviewing him across a desk, he would have repeated the old lie. But she had been right to suggest earlier that he had become interested in her. If he were hoping to establish any kind of relationship, it ought not to be founded on deceit. Besides, talking in the dark created an atmosphere in which it was easy to exchange confidences. Would he regret it later? He shrugged the doubt away. 'Somebody might have checked and found that it wasn't true. My father wasn't a miner. Nor did he die when I was three.'

'But you said . . .'

'Yes. I wasn't telling the truth then. I am now.'

She took a little while to consider his confession. 'So there wasn't any pit-cage cable to break,' she said at last. 'No falling and no blackness to explain why you should be terrified when the lift stopped. What was there instead? What was the mining business supposed to cover up?'

'My father did fall. In an aeroplane, not a pit-cage. He was shot down by the Germans in 1917. He wasn't killed, but he spent the rest of his life in a wheelchair. And as a result my mother washed her hands of him.'

'Did that make you afraid that she might wash her hands of you as well?'

'As a small boy I believed what she told me. If I claim to be a miner's son, brought up by a miner's widow, it may not be strictly accurate, but it fits with the way I had to live then. I was ten before I found out that my father was still alive.'

'How did that happen?'

'Every birthday and Christmas I used to get a present from someone I'd never met. My mother told me it was from my Uncle Matthew – she always managed to get to the parcel first and take out my father's letter. But my tenth birthday came just after Lance was born. My mother was still in bed, so I was able to open the parcel myself. It was a fishing rod. "From your affectionate father," the card said. And there was an address. This was just after I'd won the bicycle in the painting competition. I cycled down to see him.'

Even after so many years he could recall his feelings as he leaned the new bike against a cedar tree and stepped on to the terrace of Blaize. Looking round for his father, he had not recognized the heavy man in a wheelchair.

The garden was full of people with posh voices which seemed to mock his own flat Midland vowels. They were expensively dressed, making him conscious of the shabbiness of his own handed-down clothes. In the shock of that first encounter he had come near to running away. They had all done their best to be kind once his name was revealed; but the memory of that confrontation could still bring a flush of humiliation to his cheeks.

'He must have been surprised. Was he nice to you?'

'Pleasant enough. I was invited to stay the night. The next day someone took me out to buy new clothes. My father asked me about school. He said that if I ever wanted to train for anything I was to let him know and he'd try to make it possible. He gave me a five-pound note. I didn't know what it was at first – just a bit of paper, it looked like. Money he could spare by then. Why should he let his life be complicated by a grubby, tousled boy whose accent you could cut with a knife?'

'You've still got it,' said Isabel. 'Just under the surface. That way of giving every syllable its full value.'

'It's a business asset,' John told her. 'The backbone of England, that's what we peasants are – to be trusted because we so obviously haven't been to Eton.'

'So you weren't adopted into your new family?'

'I suppose I could have asked to live with them. But I was angry that my father had never bothered to get to know me. Two presents a year – that seemed to be his idea of fatherhood. I blamed him for the fact that my mother and I were so poor while he was living in luxury. Even after I challenged my mother, you see, and told her that I knew my father was still alive, she only changed her story very slightly: well, no, he hadn't died, but he'd deserted her – and me.'

'Why didn't your father tell you the truth?'

'I suppose he thought it kind not to upset my view of

my mother if I was going to go on living with her. And kind to her not to steal me away. I didn't tell him about the new baby. If I had, perhaps he'd have seen it differently.'

'When *did* you find out what really happened, then?'

'When my father died – twenty years after that meeting – his aunt sent me the details of the funeral arrangements. I wrote back that I wasn't interested – and she came to see me; furiously angry and very upset. She wanted me to know that my father was a marvellous man who would never have deserted me. He was the one who'd been abandoned when he was too poor to support a family and too badly injured to behave as a normal husband. My mother had turned him out of his own home and looked for company elsewhere. In other words, my mother had been an immoral, unfeeling, deceitful woman.'

'And you believed that?'

'Yes.' Lady Glanville's anger had carried conviction. 'But it was too late by then for me to love my father. All that Great-aunt Alexa achieved was to make me hate my mother as well.'

'For cutting you off from what ought to have been your family?'

'For being dishonest. For lying. A child should be able to trust his parents. When you discover that the foundations of your life aren't what they seemed, it makes the whole edifice rocky.'

'Is that why you've never married?'

'Perhaps. I see children as victims. Knowing how easily they can be hurt by their parents, I've never wanted to risk that relationship. And if I don't want children, why should I bother with a wife? Though I might have married if I'd ever found an honest woman.'

'You mean that because you shouldn't have trusted your mother, you're not prepared to trust anyone else?'

He shrugged his shoulders in the darkness. 'It's simply that, in my experience, all women deceive.' He heard her draw in a breath, probably in protest. 'Do you think of yourself as honest?'

'I try to be. In this conversation, *you*'re the one who's been telling lies. Why did you need to do that? It must be more than twenty years since your father died. Why should anyone be sufficiently interested in what precisely he did for you to invent someone completely different?'

'My father had become a famous man by the time he died. Matthew Lorimer.'

She had to think for a moment, but her mental filing system was efficient. 'The portrait painter?'

'That's right. I imagine he notched up a fair ration of obituary space on his day.'

'That would be before I was concerned with it. But I do remember. He had a fashionable clientele, didn't he – all the aristocratic babies! Are you ashamed of him? Artistically, I mean.'

'He was an extremely competent artist. To pin down something as unformed as the expression of a child needs a great deal of technical ability. I respect that in any field.'

'Then I still don't understand.'

'It happened that he died – a couple of years after the war – just about the time that my company was getting off the ground. A reporter who interviewed me when I went public made a guess and connected me with Matthew Lorimer. He suggested that I'd inherited a fortune and used it to start myself off. When you've hauled yourself up from nothing by your own bootstraps, it riles you to see half the credit calmly assigned to someone else. I didn't owe my father anything but my name, and I didn't see why I should admit even to that. So I denied any relationship.'

'You were talking about reporters making mistakes, putting things wrong for ever,' Isabel said. 'This is why it happens. People like you lie to them.'

'Of course it happens. That's the point I was trying to make. All you can hope for is a version of the truth.'

'One version *is* the truth,' she pointed out. 'You're the son of Matthew Lorimer.'

'But as a fact, you see, that's misleading. Anyone reading that statement in print would draw certain conclusions – generalizations from what can normally be expected of a father-son relationship. In this case the conclusions would be inaccurate. Sometimes one can approach nearer to the truth by telling a lie.'

'A moment ago you were blaming your mother for the same lie that you've adopted yourself.'

'She told a lie to someone who had the right to know the truth, deliberately intending to give a misleading impression. When I repeat the lie, I'm giving an impression which in most respects is accurate. And using it as a polite alternative to saying, "That's none of your business".'

'You talk as though you were the only one who mattered. Hasn't Matthew Lorimer the right to be recognized as your father? When you die, I ought to be able to put in your obituary that you were the son of Matthew Lorimer: because you were.'

'When I'm dead, I shan't care. But if you tell me now that you're going to do it, I shall care about that. Matthew Lorimer is dead. He has no rights.'

Isabel made no comment on that statement. Instead, she said, 'It isn't long since you asked me whether I still hated you. As though hearing a different version of past events should have changed my feelings within minutes. Yet you've known the truth about your father for years, it seems, without ever being able to forgive him for something he didn't do.'

'Yes.'

She gave a quick, incredulous laugh before moving on with her questioning. 'So you didn't move in with him when you first discovered he was alive. What about after your mother died?'

'She died just before Christmas, in December. My father didn't come to the funeral.'

'How could he if her friends in the village thought she was a widow?'

'I see the difficulty now. When I was fourteen, it wasn't so clear. He invited me to stay for Christmas and I had to go because there wasn't anywhere else. Lance had lived with foster-parents ever since he was born, but they didn't have room for me as well.'

'So you turned up at your father's house in a state of sulks.'

'He lived on a huge country estate,' said John. 'Lady Glanville's place, Blaize.' He had revealed so much to Isabel by now that there seemed no need to keep any names secret. 'I was swamped by the size of it, and the style. Servants. Food that I'd never had before. There were other children there, but they didn't know how to treat me. They'd all been given presents to give me, but I couldn't give them anything back. I was a stranger on the outside of a tight family circle. I've never been so unhappy.'

'Poor little lad!' The sympathy in Isabel's voice warmed the darkness. Her hand stretched out to touch John's as though, forty years on, she could comfort the bewildered boy who had briefly stepped into his father's life and found no place for himself. The approach made John's heart beat faster. Throughout this ordeal of dark confinement he had increasingly felt the need to move close to

Isabel. But even stronger than his wish to touch, to stroke, to embrace this stranger whose presence had brought him such comfort had been his wish that she should be the one to make the first move. Now, feeling her long, cool fingers slip between his own, he turned his hand to enclose them.

The small gesture snapped his self-control. He moved his other hand up the line of her arm, shoulder, neck, until he was stroking the back of her head. She made no attempt to twist away when he kissed her. And then the lights went on.

4

At the same moment the lift, its mechanical memory untouched by time, shot upwards like a rocket from its launching pad. Its two occupants, taken by surprise, rolled – still mouth to mouth – sideways on the floor.

Isabel, disentangling herself, was the first to recover. She laughed in relief and amusement. 'Like Sleeping Beauty – one kiss from Prince Charming and the world returns to life again!' Then her tone changed. 'John, are you all right?'

John was not all right. The sudden shock of light and movement had jerked his heart with panic: there had been a moment in which he could not tell whether the lift was rising or falling. Now he was attacked by a pain in his chest, a tightness which increased with every moment that passed, as though a nutcracker were closing on a shell which must inevitably soon shatter. Unable to move, he remained hunched up around his heart.

Smoothly the lift stopped. Silently the door opened. John struggled to push himself upright, to escape from the prison. Isabel was speaking. Her voice seemed to come from a great distance, and yet her arms were around him, lowering his shoulders so that he lay along the floor without twisting.

'Lie still, John. Keep quite still.'

'I want to get out.' Even to his own ears the words sounded blurred. The doors were beginning to close. He stretched out a hand to stop them, but they took no notice. Of course, he was at the back of the lift. His eyes were not focusing properly: distances closed up on him and then receded. The lift began to move again.

'That was my stop,' Isabel said. 'The seventeenth. Three more floors to go for you.' Even as she spoke they came to a halt again. Once more the doors opened. Isabel stood up to move a switch on the control panel. 'That will hold the lift here,' she told him.

'I want to get out,' he repeated, between gasps of pain. 'Out.'

'There's plenty of time.' Isabel's voice, although anxious, was soothing as she returned to kneel on the floor beside him. 'The lift won't move. Lie still and relax. Breathe deeply and let all your muscles go.' Her hand smoothed his forehead back as he made one more effort to sit up. 'Trust me, John.'

There was no choice. For a few moments longer he remained tense. But Isabel's hand, moving above his face as she gently continued to stroke his forehead, had a hypnotic effect. He felt his body becoming heavier on the floor; his fists unclenched and his ability to speak returned. 'Jacket pocket,' he whispered. 'Two pills.' He felt her hand searching. Then she put two tablets on his tongue. They both waited without moving until little by little the pain slipped away, leaving him almost light-headed with relief.

His recovery must have shown in his eyes, for Isabel

smiled and put an arm round his shoulders, supporting him as he sat up. After only a few moments more he was able to smile back.

'It's all gone. Quite all right.' He allowed her to help him to his feet, and then there was nothing more to worry about. The sudden withdrawal of pain left him feeling young and fit – he could have danced! Within seconds even the memory was fading. It was Isabel who seemed reluctant to shrug it off.

'Does this sort of thing happen often?'

'It started seven years ago. The first attack was the worst – that was what I was convalescing from just before Barry died. The attacks I've had since – like this one – haven't been so bad. The old arteries are furring up, apparently. There's a new kind of operation which may be able to help, and if things get really desperate I'll try it. But as far as I can gather the surgeons are still practising it. I prefer to wait – if I can – until they're out of the experimental stage!'

He stepped out of the lift and began to walk towards the boardroom door. Isabel lingered, her face still worried.

'Wouldn't it be better if you went straight down and got a taxi to take you home?'

'A taxi at three o'clock in the morning? Anyway, nothing would induce me to get back into that lift again. And we can freshen up here. There's a director's flat. Having my own place in town, I don't use it much. But any executive member of the board can sleep here for the odd night.' He took her arm and they walked slowly along the corridor. Departing in darkness, no one had bothered to turn off light switches, so that the whole of the penthouse floor was brightly lit.

'There may be someone in the flat now,' Isabel pointed out. 'London must have been in chaos for the past nine hours. Think what happens when only a single traffic light packs in. One of your party guests may have decided to stay.'

'Then he's due to be disturbed,' John said cheerfully. The exhilaration of being able to breathe freely once more had gone to his head. He was in control of his own life again, and excited. 'This is our boardroom. You'll find a cloakroom just through that door. Would you excuse me for a minute?'

He made for the bathroom in the flat almost at a run. The second form of relief within a short time left him breathing deeply with pleasure. There had been a time after he awoke in the lift when he had feared that he might not be able to control his bladder until they were released. He washed his hands and face and opened the door into the bedroom, nodding with satisfaction as he saw it to be unoccupied.

Returning to the boardroom, he surveyed the wreckage of what had been a party nine hours earlier. Empty glasses perched on every available surface, sometimes precariously near the edge. On the long buffet table candles had burned right down to their holders. The party must have continued for a little while after the power failure, then. But not for as long as expected – for a whole crate of champagne bottles was still tucked under one end of the table and more than a dozen bottles stood forlornly in ice buckets, up to their waists in water.

Lance, unable to display his models or show his films to the assembled housing officers, would have been furious. But the power failure might have added a touch of animation to what had all the promise of being a socially sticky occasion. People would remember the Lorico party, if not quite in the way intended. And if Lance had had time to find out which of his guests were the most likely prospects, he had been given the ideal excuse for a follow-up.

Isabel was taking a long time. John wandered along the buffet table, picking at the food which remained on many of the plates. He was not at the best of times attracted by the bits and pieces which were invariably produced on such occasions, spoiling the appetite without providing a proper meal; and by now the vol-au-vents were soggy with sauce, the pastry of the sausage rolls had become cold and greasy and the sandwiches were stale. But he was hungry. With no one to see, he licked caviar off wilting triangles of toast and unrolled smoked salmon from its stodgy overcoat of brown bread.

He had had no chance to study his companion of the darkness after the light went on in the lift; for at first his eyes were clouded and afterwards she was too close beside him as he held her arm. And in the lobby downstairs he had not bothered to look round at the sound of high-heeled footsteps on the marble floor. But now as the same footsteps approached over the polished parquet he turned quickly, unashamedly staring.

How did she manage to look so elegant after so many hours of restless confinement? John himself felt crumpled and dirty; but Isabel had taken off her overcoat and her slim, sleeveless dress was uncrushed. She had twisted her long hair smoothly into a chignon at the back of her head and her fresh make-up, colouring her eyes but leaving her lips pale, was fashionable and flattering. In twenty years her face had changed only in being no longer young. The high cheekbones, the intelligent eyes and the wide mouth, a little unsure of itself, were all as he had remembered them. He had been right to suspect that he had seen her before. But he could not expect her to remember the unimportant occasion. 'Let's go outside,' he said. 'I need to spring-clean my lungs.'

'*Is* there an outside?' She put on her coat again.

'A roof garden. Brand new – only planted a week or two ago.'

He unlocked the door and switched on the concealed lights as he stepped through to the penthouse terrace. The garden had been his own idea, laid out to his design. Hexagonal containers of different sizes, clustered to provide an impression of statuary even when they were empty, were planted with shrubs and trees. Against the outer wall of the boardroom was a white trellis, at whose foot were roses and clematis, neatly cut back after planting. A flower bed beneath the parapet was golden with late chrysanthemums. Isabel laughed softly.

'Joke?'

'Only just planted! And the lord says, "Let there be flowers!" and flowers in their season bloom. Don't you ever feel that you're missing something when life's made so easy for you?'

'One of the benefits of civilization is the division of labour. Can't you enjoy an evening at the theatre without feeling guilty that you didn't write the play yourself?' He breathed deeply, stretching his arms wide, and felt the cold air washing out his lungs. 'That's better. It was almost worth being shut up for the sake of being able to appreciate freedom and fresh air.'

'You're a Pollyanna!'

'What on earth's a pollyanna?'

'The heroine of a book I read as a child. She always managed to feel glad about the most unpromising situations. When she was given a pair of crutches for Christmas by mistake, she was glad – because she didn't need them.'

'I'm certainly prepared to take a pollyanna view of the power failure. If it hadn't been for that, you'd have gone off on your errand to the seventeenth floor and I should never have met you.'

'Would that have been such a disaster?' Isabel's smile suggested that she was enjoying her freedom as light-heartedly as himself.

'Yes.' John surprised himself by the certainty of his feelings as well as of his voice. 'And just think how small a chance might have kept us apart. If I'd arrived half a minute earlier, or if the power failure had been ten seconds later, after you'd left the lift – '

'I don't believe in chance,' Isabel said. 'There was a reason why the power was cut off at precisely that second. I don't know what it was – fire, flood, human error? – but whatever the reason, it was the result of something that made the stoppage inevitable – and inevitable at that time. And if you could have arrived half a minute earlier, you would have done. But hundreds of tiny circumstances pressed you into a particular timetable, and each of those circumstances had itself been influenced by something else. You and I and the lift were each programmed to reach the same point at the same time.'

'What a gloomy viewpoint! You're not only saying, "History is what happened": you're suggesting that it all happened inevitably. I'd prefer a more optimistic definition: history is what happens next. Whatever I do now influences the future. I have the power to make choices.'

'When you make a business decision, you weigh up all the facts you know. It's an automatic process. You can't control either the facts or the prejudices you bring to them. Where's the freedom of choice there? I'm agreeing, in a way, with something you said yourself earlier. You believe that children are the victims of their parents. I believe that all of us – children and adults alike – are victims of circumstance. There's not much difference.'

'So you think we're all defeated before we begin?'

'Not all,' she said. 'There are winners as well as losers.

What I *do* think is that the winners were always bound to win and the losers never had a hope. The past is always too powerful for the present. You've never escaped, have you, from the attitudes to family life which had their roots in your childhood?'

'Yes, I have,' replied John, more confidently than perhaps was honest. 'I've cut myself off from my father's family. They simply aren't part of my life.' Except for Paula, he suddenly thought. But the warm interest which he felt for his black cousin was rooted in the belief that she was as much an outsider in the Lorimer family as himself.

Isabel, meanwhile, was smiling as though the statement proved her point. But it seemed to John that her theory could be used to absolve anyone from responsibility for his own actions, providing too easy an excuse for inadequacy. Was it an excuse which she would use for her own past behaviour? 'How much do you think about your own past, Isabel?' he asked her. 'About Barry, for example?'

'I keep a photograph of him beside the bed,' she said. 'A snapshot that I took on our honeymoon. Sometimes it reminds me of the time when I was happy – when we were happy together. And at other times, when I'm lonely and miserable, I can look at it the other way. I point out to myself that if Barry had lived, then by now he'd be nursing what he'd call an alcohol problem. I might have stopped loving him.'

'Why did he kill himself?' John put the question abruptly.

'I told you. The account – the business.'

'I knew Barry for twenty years,' said John. 'He was a good chap. Not a smart businessman, but a good fellow. He wouldn't have left you on your own just for business matters which weren't really matters of life or death.

Suicide was too drastic an escape from a mere financial problem. Did you push him? Did you make him think that the business was more important than anything else?'

'No!' she cried. 'That was what hurt most of all, that he should have forgotten about me in his despair over a few columns of figures.' John could not doubt that she was telling the truth as she knew it, although his own version was different. She gave a rueful laugh. 'He was one of life's losers, I suppose.'

'Am I?'

'How can I know that?'

'I thought my life was an open book to you by now.'

Isabel shrugged her shoulders. 'A winner is someone who gets what he wants. You're rich and successful. Is that enough? Or is there something else that you've wanted all your life?'

'Yes,' said John. 'Someone I could trust. A modest ambition, but unfulfilled. Someone more honest than my mother and more caring than my father. Someone who would always tell me the truth. Someone I could talk to. That's what I've always wanted.'

5

Isabel took John's hand in a light-hearted gesture. 'Yes,' she smiled. 'I've noticed your addiction to conversation.'

She moved away from him, across the terrace. The wall which surrounded the garden area was waist high, with glass above it, strengthened by steel mesh. As she looked down through the glass John joined her, putting his arm round her waist. The staleness had vanished from his head and his skin felt clean again, and cool. He no longer remembered how it had felt to be in the lift: at first afraid and later in pain. Being careful not to move too fast for her or too slowly for himself, he could begin now to make clear to Isabel how attractive he found her. His inability to discover anyone who met his criterion of an honest woman was the reason why he had never married. But it had not condemned him to a celibate life. He enjoyed the kind of affair which was accepted by both parties as temporary even before it began. Was that, he wondered, a relationship which Isabel would be willing to accept and enjoy? He stood very close to her as they looked out over London.

Lights were blazing in the windows of offices and flats. Lance had not been the only one to forget about turning off switches in unlit rooms. Anyone flying in from another country would have wondered what crisis or celebration was keeping a whole city awake in the small hours. The curve of the river was charted by a deep, rich blackness, but on either bank ribbons of light marked out the streets of the capital. John stared down, enjoying the pattern woven by the threads of colour: yellow, white, green, dotted with the red rear lights of cars.

'One can see the fascination,' Isabel said.

'Fascination of what?' John's mind, like his eyes, was preoccupied with light and design.

'The fascination of throwing oneself down. For the people who do that sort of thing, I mean.'

John tightened his arm around Isabel's waist, although there was no way in which she could fall. 'Is it something you've ever considered?' he asked.

'Yes.' Her answer was matter-of-fact, as though he ought to have taken it for granted. 'I had to identify Barry.'

'I'd already done that.'

She shrugged her shoulders, not remembering or understanding the reason for her summons. 'The police sent a car to pick me up, but afterwards I said I'd walk home. I was dizzy – the smell and the shock. I can remember stopping on a bridge over the railway and looking down. I could see the whole of my life stretching ahead. No husband, no children. Just a woman on her own getting older and older, with no one to care whether I lived or died. I started to cry again. Sheer self-pity this time. It's one of the traps about being married – and the more you love your husband, the tighter the trap closes. You honestly forget that it's possible to be independent – to live alone and still be happy. I looked down at the railway tracks and felt as though I was rushing along one of them myself. Last stop, an old people's home. Terminus, death. Straight ahead, with no chance of branching off. And then I thought, "Well, now, before the train starts moving again, this is the time to get off. If there's nothing but unhappiness ahead, I might as well jump now, while I'm still too numb to care."'

'What made you change your mind?'

'As soon as I realized it was possible, and easy, it didn't seem necessary any longer. It was the time that had frightened me – the sheer length of time of growing old and ill and waiting to die. What comforted me then – and it's comforted me ever since – is the realization that I don't have to wait if I don't want to. Even if I live for another forty years, those years are made up of only one minute at a time, and between any two minutes I can stop the clock. It's the most reassuring discovery I've made in the whole of my life.'

John did not feel it to be reassuring. He shivered as the picture of the woman on the dark bridge came vividly in front of his eyes.

'You think too much about death,' he told her, turning her back towards the boardroom door.

'It's my job,' she reminded him. 'Golden lads and girls

come daily to dust on my typewriter. That time in the lift has left my throat very dry. Is there anything to drink?'

'Only champagne, I'm afraid.'

'Only champagne!' Her voice was amused as she repeated the words. 'Then I'll settle for only champagne. Please.'

He took a bottle out of its bucket of melted ice and opened it. Each of them drank the first glass quickly, as though it were fizzy lemonade.

Somewhere in the boardroom there would be a machine equipped to provide background music at the start of the party. John found it and switched it on. A selection from *The King and I* emerged from concealed loud speakers.

'Shall we dance?' asked John, quoting. He led her into a brisk polka, which within only a few seconds switched to the waltz-time of *Hello, Young Lovers*.

'Should you do this sort of thing?' asked Isabel. 'Prancing round a dance floor half an hour after having a heart attack?'

'That was a very minor affair,' he told her, continuing to move smoothly over the polished floor. 'And you and I have made the same sort of discovery. You've discovered that you can stop your own clock. I've had to recognize that mine may stop of its own accord at any moment. So I appreciate all the more the moments while it goes on ticking. In that sense, I don't allow my heart to rule my life. In any case, it was sitting still in the lift for so long which was bad for me. And feeling anxious. A few sedate dance steps are just the exercise I need.'

The music changed again, this time to a rhythm which defeated him. With one hand still on the cool, smooth skin of her arm, he led her back towards the champagne.

'You're very beautiful.' He looked into her eyes as he poured a second glass and handed it to her. It required an effort of politeness not to sound surprised. Except for the moment when he had remembered the girl in the office corridor, the sharpness of her voice and the definiteness of her opinions in the dark lift had distorted his guess about her appearance. He had not expected her to be beautiful.

'Women in their forties aren't beautiful. Mature, or gracious, or well-preserved, or occasionally even handsome. But not beautiful.'

'You must allow me the right to choose my own words. But if you insist, I'll delete beautiful and substitute desirable.'

Isabel looked into his eyes with a steadiness equal to his own as she sipped her drink. But instead of commenting on his choice of adjective, she turned away and began to wander round the boardroom. She was not yet ready for him to approach her more closely: but now that he had given notice of his intention, she would be preparing her reaction as she studied – or pretended to study – the displays on the walls. John watched her without interrupting her exploration, excited by the need to wait and curious to see what would catch her interest.

In the centre of one of the long walls hung a temporary exhibit, part of Lance's promotional material: photographs of completed housing projects set askew on triangles of bright colour. 'Fussy,' commented Isabel.

'It was a party, remember. To put up a price list might have been thought in bad taste.'

She moved on towards the picture at the far end of the room. 'Lowry?' she said; and then, approaching more closely, 'But it's a print!'

'Yes.'

'I should have thought you could afford the real thing.'

'I don't believe in company ostentation. In any case, the original of this is locked up for life in a municipal art gallery, and it was this special picture I wanted.'

Isabel studied the relentless lines of grey houses marching over a hill into a white dead sky. 'As an awful warning,' she suggested, 'of what happens when you build a hundred houses which all look alike?'

'Of what happens,' he corrected, 'when you build houses and expect them to last for ever. And also as a hint, a reminder. People come in here straight from their modern picture-window flats or their garden suburbs. They may think my product looks a bit cramped. So it is by their standards, no doubt – especially when they set it up on the cheap and don't allow any room for trees and lawns. But these hundred-year-old houses in the picture are what you see by the thousand from the train as you draw into any big city. These are the houses in which people are still living.'

'What about your own home?' She turned back towards him. 'Or homes. What do you hang on your own walls?'

'Not a great deal. Not more than one good picture to a room.'

'Prints, or the real thing?'

'The real thing. I like to see the paint.'

'Whose paint, for example? Considering how freely you've been talking all evening, you're making me dig for your taste in art.'

'Because I fight against my taste in art,' John said. 'I fight against everything I inherit from my father. I try very hard to make myself appreciate accidental art, undisciplined pictures. I've stood for hours in front of a Jackson Pollock, willing myself to admire it. But the effort's too much for me. When my father painted, he was meticulous to the last detail. I find that my eye is meticulous too. I can enjoy a Picasso because I know that Picasso was technically capable of painting a Rembrandt head if he'd ever felt like it. But the blot-and-trickle men haven't any standards by which I can judge them. At least, I suppose they have standards, but I don't know what they are. And the new men, with their nails and black panels, are meticulous enough, but they frighten the eye away.'

'So what have you got, for instance, in your London flat?'

'A Braque.'

'Oh!' It was not, perhaps, what she had expected. Looking round for somewhere to sit, she chose the armchair reserved for the chairman of the board. 'And are you suggesting that your father would have shared your liking for it? I've seen some of the Matthew Lorimer portraits. I wouldn't have thought . . .'

It had been easy in the darkness to release his memories of childhood. Now they emerged more painfully, but he did his best to answer the question.

'I remember, when I was visiting him – it must have been the Christmas when I was so unhappy, after my mother died. He did his best, I suppose, to amuse me. One day he let me look at all the pictures which he'd painted but never sold. They were in a kind of loft. He couldn't get up there himself, not in his wheelchair. There was one painting – I'd never seen anything like it before. I'd never know before what it was like to be *excited* by a painting. This one was entirely in tones of grey and green. On the face of it, a mass of triangles and other geometric shapes, but underneath . . . I couldn't believe that Matthew Lorimer had painted it. It was so different from all the others. I carried it down to ask him about it.'

He paused, remembering the only moment of his life when he had understood what it could feel like to have a father.

'My father told me that years before, when he lived in Paris, he and Braque had been friends. The name didn't mean anything at all to me, you understand. They'd experimented together, shared all the excitement of new ideas. That was when my father painted his green picture. He and Braque were both badly wounded during the war. Afterwards, Braque went on experimenting, but my father changed direction. He was very successful, of course; but just for a moment, while he was talking to me, I understood that he despised himself for it. He recognized, I think, how exciting I found that picture. It must have been surprising to see a fourteen-year-old with no artistic education at all bowled over like that – exciting for him as well, perhaps.'

'Did it bring you closer together?'

'He asked me if I'd like to have it for my Christmas present. I longed to say yes. But I was a stupid, sulky young puppy who'd decided never to accept anything from the man who hadn't even come to his own wife's funeral. I turned it down. Crazy. And cruel.'

Isabel nodded in understanding. 'Children can hurt their parents as badly as parents hurt children, can't they?'

'Yes. I may not have realized that at the time.' John stopped to consider. 'I think I did. I think I wanted to hurt him. You were talking earlier about winners and losers. My father earned a good deal of money and finished up with a knighthood, but he was a loser, all the same. The whole of his adult life, I believe, he was in love with a woman he couldn't marry; the woman he *did* marry threw him out; he didn't honestly value the work he produced; he spent thirty years of his life in a wheelchair; he released whatever right he had to a son's love in the interests of a wife who didn't deserve such consideration; and he wasn't able to recover it even when both he and I – ' Suddenly upset, John broke off in mid-sentence. 'Oh, damn my father! Why are we talking about him?'

'Because you've spent all your life wishing that you could love him,' suggested Isabel. 'When you were a boy, he was a stranger. And when you became a man, you kept him a stranger by refusing to admit that he existed. Now I've made you talk about him, and he's not a stranger to you any more. You should be grateful to me. I've given you back a place in your family.'

'I'm not interested in my family. Only in you.' He reached out to touch her bare arm again, thrilling like an adolescent at the smoothness of her skin. Gripping her hands, he tried to pull her up into his arms. 'Isabel!' His need for her was too great to be expressed in words. She had come into his life as a gift from fate, and now it was time to enjoy her. His voice was husky with emotion as he repeated her name. 'Isabel!'

But Isabel did not move. She made no gesture of rejection or pretence of surprise, but her steady look reflected none of his own eagerness.

'Sir John-Bloody-Lorimer,' she said. 'That's how I've thought of you all these years. Sir John-Bloody-Lorimer. And now you come along and tell me that I'm beautiful. Desirable. That wipes out all the past, does it?'

'The past is your own invention.' John tried urgently to escape from the prison of talk and move into action. 'You were angry with a bogeyman of your own creation. Now you've met me for the first time and I'm real. Not quite the villain you thought. And you find me interesting. Don't you?'

Earlier in the evening she had said that she was honest. Now, unwillingly, she gave support to her claim. 'It's true that I find you attractive,' she admitted. 'But that's not enough. I may have been wrong to think that you deliberately intended to ruin Barry's life. But whatever your intentions, it *was* ruined. Finished. I can't forget what happened. As you've discovered yourself, memory is an obstacle. The biggest, because you can't fight it.'

Doing his best to restrain his impaticnce, John accepted

the need to convince her. 'Are you sure, though,' he said, 'that all your memories are true?'

6

'What do you mean by that?' asked Isabel.

John took his time about answering. Both his mind and his body were restless with disappointment. In the past he had discovered that the traditional aphrodisiacs of wealth and power worked a rapid effect on the women who attracted him. This argumentative approach to an affair was a new experience – but then, he was already beginning to hope for something more than a brief relationship. He needed to persuade Isabel not merely to sleep with him but to love him. It was worth a little time and patience. He refilled her glass and his own and applied himself to bringing this brief chapter of the past under the same scrutiny that Isabel had already applied to the trauma of his childhood.

'Tell me honestly, what happened seven years ago between you and Barry and Lance?' He did not reveal how much he already knew, hoping that she would have the courage to volunteer rather than merely confirm the truth. 'You knew, Barry and you, that Lance was investigating the efficiency with which our account was handled. Did you do anything about it?'

Isabel's pause was an answer in itself, but John waited for the words.

'We had to decide at the beginning whether to keep out of Lance's way while he poked around, or actively help him, or tell him to go to hell. That was what Barry really wanted to do, the last. After all, Lance had no real right to pry.'

'If you sent him to hell, he would have taken the account with him.'

'Yes. So it seemed to me that if we were helpful, we could find out early on if anything was wrong, while there still might be time to do something about it. I didn't know, you see, any of the details you were talking about earlier.'

'You persuaded Barry to go along with that?'

'Yes. And I acted as a sort of liaison officer for Lance. If he wanted a file, I found it. If he wanted to talk to a member of the staff, I fixed it. That way, no one else in the office realized quite what was going on. Lance was in and out of the place over a period of several weeks. Not every day – certainly not all day – but off and on. I saw quite a lot of him. He was very friendly. I don't suppose he wanted me to know how important the investigation was.'

'Did he flirt with you?'

'Yes. At first it was nothing serious – just the way a man does flirt with a woman who happens to be on the spot and giving him her full attention. I didn't mind. He was good company, and right from the start it seemed to me that we needed to get him on our side. So whatever you're thinking is quite right. I set out to – to charm him, you might say.'

'I'm sure you were very successful.'

'Yes. Yes, I was. I'd never behaved like that before. And I wasn't a glamorous young girl. It almost took my breath away to find how easy it was.'

'How much of all this did Barry know?'

'It started as a joke between us. We were happy together, you see; we could take that kind of risk. I even think it was Barry who said it first: "You'd better go and vamp him." We both laughed, and I went off to do it. I find it incredible, looking back, how unsophisticated I was. Those were the Swinging Sixties, after all. And if you asked most people to imagine a female copywriter in a smart ad agency they'd be likely to envisage a tough bit of paintwork having one affair after another. I expect that was how Lance saw me at first. But although I'd flirted with people before, and laughed at dirty jokes and made flip remarks at parties, I always went home with Barry. I didn't see anything unusual in the fact that I'd been faithful to my husband ever since we married. It came as a shock to Lance, though.'

'So what happened.'

'Lance flirted with me, casually. I flirted back. When he asked me out for an evening, I went. I must have seemed – well, available. The next time he made a date, the evening was scheduled by him to finish up at his flat. And I didn't expect that. Isn't it ridiculous! I thought I could get away with kissing him goodnight on the doorstep.'

'Do you blame Lance for trying?'

Isabel shook her head. 'Not for that, no. I ought to have stopped him long before. I ought never to have let him start.'

'You say you didn't blame him for *that*. For what, then?'

'For letting his pride affect his business decisions. I know I behaved badly. But he had no right to take it out on Barry.'

'He might have thought Barry was encouraging you. And would that have been so far from the truth? In any case, you must have skipped something. Lance was never a chap to take No for an answer. Something else must have happened.'

'There were two things,' Isabel said. She finished her champagne and put the glass down on the floor. 'Lance fell in love with me. He'd started off by thinking of me as a bit of fun. Easy. If I'd gone home with him when he first asked, it would have been a one-night stand and goodbye. And if I'd been pretending – playing hard-to-get – when I said No to the invitation, he might not have bothered any more. But he recognized that I meant what I was saying, and that seemed to change his view of me. It mattered much more to him when I said No the second time. And that was when *I* fell in love with *him*.'

'That happened, did it?' John spoke almost to himself.

'I was one stage behind all the time. I'd thought he was only doing what was expected of a bright young bachelor – that his feelings weren't involved at all. I hadn't noticed that there was a difference between the first time of asking and the second, until I realized that I'd hurt him.'

'So the third time he asked . . .'

'He didn't need to ask again. The look in his eyes – I kissed him, and he knew. I wish you'd sit down, John. It fidgets me, having to watch you pacing up and down like that.'

John turned a chair to face her and sat down. His hands clasped and twisted between his open knees and he found it difficult to keep still. He could hardly wait for the conversation to end, yet it seemed important not to leave anything out. 'So you slept with him,' he checked.

'Yes.'

'I remember that letter you wrote,' John said. 'To Sir John-Bloody-Lorimer, murderer. You've hated me for seven years. Because I was disloyal, you said, to my friend. And after all you were the first one to rat on him.'

'It was only a week – and a week in which Barry was worried about the business. He didn't know anything about what happened between me and Lance.'

'Disloyalty lies in the action, not in its discovery. Weren't you the one who said, "History is what happened"?'

'Yes, I did say that and yes, I was disloyal. But you were right earlier when you said that what has an effect is what is known. My disloyalty was a private affair.'

'You didn't tell Barry, then?'

'Why should I hurt him by confessing. It *would* have hurt him. He loved me. And I still loved him. That was what caused the trouble.'

'We haven't reached the trouble,' John pointed out. 'You're happily in bed with Lance.'

'That was more than I'd intended to start with. But it wasn't enough for Lance. He asked me to marry him.'

'Now you do surprise me!' John exclaimed.

Isabel frowned slightly as she looked at him. 'Did you know the rest before, then?'

'Part I knew and part I guessed. There were clues. But I doubt whether Lance has stretched out his arms very often towards the hand-cuffs of matrimony. Like me, he was brought up in a distorted version of family life. He's never seemed tempted to find out whether he could do better himself.'

'He wouldn't have got much of a family out of me. I'd already discovered that I was no good at producing babies. Anyway, I was married. He must have known that it was impossible.'

'Marriages have been known to come to an end. And your behaviour could have suggested that this particular marriage was shaky.'

'Yes.'

'But it wasn't?'

'Lance was a marvellous lover,' she admitted. 'But I loved Barry too, and I was his wife. There was never any possibility that I'd hurt him by walking out.'

'I don't suppose Lance liked that much.'

'He tried to blackmail me.' It was Isabel's turn now to be restless. Hugging her arms round herself for warmth, she began to walk up and down the long boardroom. Her voice receded, and then approached again as she turned. 'He told me that if I'd marry him he'd somehow make it all right about the account. Barry was to save his business by losing me.'

'I'm even more surprised. I thought I could trust Lance to be honest in his report.'

'I don't think he was going to lie. He chose his words carefully when he spoke to me. He said he'd have to make it clear that there had been mistakes in the past: but if he could appoint someone from his own department to liaise closely with Barry, he could make positive recommendations for the future. As though Barry would have accepted favours from a man who stole his wife!'

'The plan wouldn't have worked, then?'

'I thought, I really thought, that if Barry had to choose between his wife and his profits he'd choose me. I believed that if I walked out on him, he'd feel that life wasn't worth living: but that he could cope with any business problems as long as I was behind him. I was wrong, wasn't I? In those last few minutes he must have forgotten all about me.'

She held her chin high as she looked towards John, as though the memory of that betrayal could still tempt her to tears.

'You said that Lance blackmailed you. He told you, did he, what kind of report he'd write if you didn't co-operate?'

'I shouldn't have used the word blackmail. Presumably he wanted me to marry him from love. It was more a kind of bribe, I suppose.'

'So you knew the verdict before Barry did?'

'Yes. I tried to warn him. But he was still sure that he could rely on you – until he saw you that morning. When I heard about that, I thought it might be easier for him if the reason didn't seem to lie in himself. He'd still be losing your business, but he wouldn't need to think it was his own fault. I told Barry that the report was a bad one not because the firm was inefficient but because Lance had made a pass and I'd brushed it off.' She flushed as she met John's eyes. 'It was half true. Things would have been different if I'd gone off with him. He *was* being spiteful – paying me out.'

'No. The figures were on his side. He might have skated over them to please you, but he didn't invent them to hurt you.'

'Well, I won't pretend that I'm proud of that period of my life,' Isabel said, sitting down again. 'Anyway, now you know it all.'

'Not quite. I still don't understand why you went so far with Lance if you were happy with Barry.'

'There's no easy answer to that. Partly I drifted. It's easy for a woman to fend off a man if she's single-minded about it right from the start. But once he's got his foot in the door . . . Whether it started as a joke or a business ploy, I did encourage him to begin with, and it's not easy to catch the right moment for a change of direction – especially if you genuinely don't want to hurt somebody. And then – ' she drew a deep breath, sighing for words. 'I'm not sure that a man can understand how I felt.'

'Try me,' suggested John.

'Well, when I was young, I was good-looking. There were always plenty of young men around. Then I married Barry and I wasn't interested in anyone else. But after twelve years . . . There comes a moment when you don't feel young any more – not old, but not young – and you guess that no one is ever likely to fall in love with you again just because you're a pretty girl. Even though you're happily married and you don't *want* anyone else to fall in love with you, the belief that nobody will – ' She threw her hands angrily outwards. 'It's too trite for words. You *know* what's happening. You know that it isn't even special to yourself. Probably all women feel it at some time or other. Yet all that knowledge doesn't make the temptation any less – because you're amazed that the chance has come and sure that it will never come again. The last fling! It's despicable, and even at the time you know it.'

'But you said that you fell in love with Lance.'

'Falling in love doesn't excuse anything. It's only a form of words which people use to claim that the rules of decent behaviour need no longer apply. I was Barry's wife. I had no right to fall in love with Lance.'

'But then Barry died. Did you go on seeing Lance?'

'How could I? It would have made me feel dirty. He did try, but I was so angry with him and with you . . . No.'

'So you're – what's the word – unattached now?'

Isabel looked at him curiously. 'All this business about Lance and Barry is past history,' she pointed out. 'I haven't spent seven years in solitary mourning.'

'More specifically, then. You haven't married again? And you have no current relationship with Lance?'

'No.'

'Do you recognize now, when you think about it honestly, that you never had good reason to blame me for Barry's death. Hating me may have been a comfort to you, but I didn't deserve it. Did I?'

'Why should you care what I believe?' asked Isabel.

'You know why. I want to have everything straight between us before – I want – I want you. Now. Come to bed with me, Isabel.'

Isabel looked neither surprised nor shocked, but her answer was as definite as it was unwelcome. 'Sorry, John,' she said. 'But no.'

7

So surprised was John by Isabel's answer that for a moment he could not believe it. Although he had known her for less than twelve hours, their exchange of confidences had inspired, he had thought, a closeness which in other circumstances might have taken many months to grow. The total indifference to a stranger with which his journey up the tower block had started had very quickly given way to gratitude for companionship; and from that moment onward curiosity had carried him rapidly through all the stages of discovery. He had found her challenging, interesting, sympathetic and attractive. He wanted her as a friend: he wanted her to be part of himself. To delay the moment of love, to keep her talking, to make her strip away the shield of her old resentment, had all increased his desire, and he had felt sure that Isabel shared his growing excitement. She had allowed him to kiss her in the lift and there had been time before the light went on to feel sure that she took as much pleasure in the embrace as he did.

Unexpectedly upset by the rejection, John held out his hand towards her. It made her refusal even more confusing when she grasped it with what appeared to be a warm affection.

'Not now, not at this moment, that's all I mean,' she said. 'It doesn't imply . . . I'll give you my phone number. If you're still interested enough to call me tomorrow, I'll be glad. But this isn't the right time.'

'Why not?'

'I don't know what the state of your heart is,' said Isabel. 'But it's less than an hour since you were looking distinctly groggy. Oughtn't you to take things easy for a little while?'

'Isn't it every man's ambition to die in bed with a beautiful woman?'

'Is it? It wouldn't be much fun for the woman, would it?'

'I suppose not. But all the same . . .'

'That's not really it,' Isabel confessed. 'Your health is your own affair and you can make your own decisions about it. What I feel is that we're in danger of falling into a kind of cliché situation. A man and a woman imprisoned together, getting to know each other, suddenly released, falling into each other's arms – it's all somehow too predictable, as though it might happen to any man with any woman. I'd like to feel more special to you than that. Besides, in a few hours you'll be back in your chairman's office, running your company. When you remember all the things you've told me, that you've kept secret from everyone else, you may be sorry you said so much. You may not want to be reminded of it by seeing me again. If that's going to happen, I'd prefer you to find out before rather than after.'

Disappointed, John stared at her, his body trembling with indecision. If he stepped forward now to take her in his arms, could he sweep away her doubts? The temptation was great, and it was not the erratic pounding of his heart which held him back but the surging certainty that if he waited, she would be waiting as well. To the sum of all the other pleasures which her body promised him he could add the anticipation of them. He kissed her, accepting her conditions.

'But you'll spend the rest of the night here, I hope,' he said. 'This is no hour to be struggling across London.' It was easy to interpret the questioning look she gave him.

'Twin beds,' he told her. 'I won't . . . I'll phone you tomorrow.'

'Thank you,' said Isabel.

Politely, like a conventional host, John showed her the bedroom and bathroom, checked on soap and towels, withdrew tactfully for the period in which she might hope for privacy. It was possible to control his behaviour, but less easy, later on, to curb his imagination. Lying only a few feet away from her in the bedroom, he found her nearness and separateness almost unbearable. Was she lying naked in her single bed? Imagination and hope combined to keep him awake; not because he was unable to sleep, but because he did not want to try. Earlier in the evening he had confessed that he had never found a woman he could trust. Isabel had claimed that she tried to be honest and gradually, as the long conversation continued, she had convinced him that she was telling the truth. Had he at last, after so many years, found someone with whom he could fall in love?

'I want to talk to you, Isabel.' He kept his voice low, so that if she were asleep he would not disturb her. 'Don't say anything. I don't want to know whether you're awake and listening. Even if you hear what I say, you can pretend in the morning that you didn't.' He could not, all the same, resist the temptation to listen for a second; but detected no change in the steady rhythm of her breathing.

'I think you've been honest with me,' he said, so softly that he could hardly hear the words himself. 'You've told me what you knew about Barry's death. But you didn't know everything. On the day he died, Barry was drunk, fighting drunk, by the time Lance arrived to keep his appointment. You'd given him a weapon, and he used it. He accused Lance of behaving spitefully because you'd turned him down. So Lance pointed the same weapon back at him. He told Barry that you hadn't turned him down all the time.'

There was the very slightest of silences before the sound of Isabel's breathing resumed with slow regularity. John was almost sure that she had heard; but, if so, she was disguising the fact sufficiently to face the morning without referring to it. A peaceful satisfaction invaded his body. Within only a few seconds he was asleep.

Isabel's light touch awakened him after what could not be more than two or three hours. Startled into alertness, he saw that she was fully dressed, her overcoat already buttoned against the cold outside.

'It seems cruel to disturb you,' she said. 'I must go, though. After yesterday, everything's going to be chaotic. I need an early start to the day. But there's something I must ask you first.' She was nervous. 'John, I wouldn't have expected Lance to tell anyone what he said to Barry at their last meeting. How did you find out?'

John's heart gave a leap of excitement. She was admitting, then, that she had heard what he told her. Last night he had been hopeful, but now he was sure: Isabel was a woman he could trust. 'It was Barry who told me,' he said.

'But he was already dead when you called at his office that night.'

'Before he killed himself, he wrote you a letter.'

'And you read it!'

'Don't sound so shocked.' John pulled himself up into a sitting position. 'A suicide note is public property. If the police had found it, the whole world could have heard it read out in a coroner's court.'

'Why didn't they find it?'

'I destroyed it.'

'Because he blamed you?'

'Quite the opposite,' said John. 'If I'd realized you

were going to think that, I'd have kept the letter in my own defence. He blamed himself for being a failure, as a businessman and as a husband. The letter made it clear what he'd learned from Lance.'

'I still don't see why you destroyed it.'

'He was drunk as well as angry when he wrote it. It was a wild letter – and unfair: it gave you no chance to defend yourself. I couldn't do anything to help Barry by then. But I didn't see why you should be made to feel guilty about his death for the rest of your life.'

'I could have argued that Lance was entirely to blame, if he told Barry.'

'Lance reported the fact. The fact already existed.'

'And had done no harm by existing. When Lance told him about it, that was when Barry killed himself. Lance can't have told the whole truth. He can't have made it clear that the affair was over, that I'd already made the decision to stick with my husband.' She gave a short, almost bitter laugh. 'So all these years that I've hated you for driving my husband to suicide, you've blamed me for exactly the same thing. You're telling me that I was responsible for Barry's death. Why come out with it now, after hiding it for so many years?'

'I want you for a friend,' John said simply. 'More than a friend. I don't want to have secrets from you. So that we can love each other.'

'You whispered very quietly last night.'

'That was for your sake, so that you could pretend you hadn't heard.' He smiled at her, exhilarated by all that had happened. It was a miracle that a chance meeting with a stranger should hold the antidote to all the fears and hatreds of his childhood. Isabel's honesty went so deep that she not only spoke the truth but could accept the truth she was told. He had allowed her the chance to pretend, but she had not pretended. It was too late now for him to forgive his mother for her lies, or to bridge the gap between himself and his father. But, freed overnight from the insecurity which had narrowed his happiness for so many years, he felt his body to be as light as his spirits. That was why he did not notice at once that Isabel was not smiling back at him.

'It won't work, John,' she said. 'The blame for Barry's death will always stand between us. Not attributed to Sir John-bloody-Lorimer any more, but to Isabel-bloody-Blair.'

'That's all over long ago. Finished. Forgotten.' Suddenly alarmed, he struggled out of bed; but Isabel stepped backward, not allowing him to touch her.

'Perhaps one day I shall be able to forget,' she agreed. 'But never with you. I'm ashamed of what happened. Too deeply ashamed ever to be at ease with someone who knows all about it. I can't accept forgiveness from you when it was someone else who was hurt. I'm sorry, John. Sorry in more ways than I can tell you. But it's better to stop before we start, isn't it?'

'No!' Convinced that he could argue away her doubts and make her happy if she would only give him time, John lunged towards her. But already Isabel was moving fast, closing the door behind her. She must have run down the length of the boardroom, because by the time John reached the outer door of the company suite she was already stepping into one of the lifts. The doors closed and a light danced across the figures on the panel above. Going down, going down, safely past the level on which they had spent half the night together, going down to the ground floor.

He stood in the doorway, breathless and frustrated. He could hardly chase her through the streets of London wearing only his underpants. But it was not as though she had vanished irrevocably. He knew where she worked:

he could trace her through the paper. As he returned, more slowly, to the directors' flat, he was already mentally rehearsing his arguments, planning his courtship.

The flat did not tempt him to linger. Its central heating, controlled by a timing device which had been frozen by the power failure, was not yet operating. The hours in the lift had made all his clothes dirty and crumpled, so that he needed to change in his own flat before starting the day's business. Besides, he was extremely hungry. It was not yet seven o'clock when he closed the door of the boardroom behind him, walked towards the lifts and pressed the call button.

At once a door opened – the door of the lift which had been his prison for so many hours of the night. Isabel had taken the only other lift which served the penthouse floor down to street level. John stared uneasily at the cube of space and could not bring himself to enter it. He pressed the call button again: but the lift mechanism, applying its programmed reasoning to the situation, decided that the caller already had a lift on offer and refused to summon an alternative. The doors, which had begun to close, opened silently for a second time.

It was ridiculous to hesitate. There had been an explanation for what happened thirteen hours earlier and he had no reason to anticipate a second power failure. But if anything did go wrong, he would be alone. Well, why should that matter? There was no good reason why John should feel afraid, and yet his feet refused to carry him into the lift.

Once again the doors closed. Furious at his own superstitious cowardice, but unable to overcome it, he turned away and pushed open the heavy fire door which led to the staircase. A much larger number of lifts came as far up as the seventeenth floor. There he could choose between two clusters in two different parts of the building. He set off briskly down the shallow stone steps.

After only a single flight he was forced to slow down, even to stop for a moment, to fill his shuddering lungs with air. This shortness of breath was something new – but not surprising after such a confined and stuffy night. He gave himself pause to recover and then began to descend the next flight more slowly.

Before he had gone more than three steps down he knew that he was making a mistake. In the stillness of the stairwell he could hear the slow, erratic thumping of his heart as the blood forced itself through his inelastic arteries. He turned to go back to the nearest landing, but with the abrupt movement one foot slipped on the polished surface and he jerked to correct his balance. Panic snatched away whatever breath was still left in his lungs. The pain which steadily crept across his chest commanded his body to freeze, to crouch without moving until its grip was relased. But his brain was frantic with the knowledge that if he were to collapse here, on the staircase which nobody used, it would be hours, days, before he was found. Using all his strength, he dragged himself up the three steps to the landing, pulled the door open and staggered inside.

There were some pills left in his pocket. He fumbled for them and swallowed two, panting with the effort. Now all he needed to do was wait. All this had happened before, and he had survived it. It had been just as bad as this before – but even as he tried to make himself believe that, he realized that something different was happening. It was not the first time that he had heard himself cry out in agony, but always before the pain had receded under the attack of the pills. This time it was increasing, and he recognized that in a moment he would be unable to bear it any longer.

The shock cleared his mind of panic, rousing him to draw on one last reserve of strength. He stabbed with his finger at the call button of the lift, which came quickly from the storey above and waited silently for his command as he fell forward through the door. But by now John was doubled up on the floor in pain, his arms crossed over his chest. He was not conscious of the shuddering which signified that the lift had begun to move.

Second Chances
1973–74

1

It was unclear to Bernard exactly why Helen had, after all, returned from Paula's party to the flat and to him: at the time he was too greatly relieved to ask questions. From her careful walk he recognized that she had had more to drink than usual. Perhaps for this reason, she made it clear that she was in no mood to embark on the kind of discussion which would be necessary at some point if they were to mend their marriage. But her single question, or statement, gave a welcome clue to her intentions. 'This Gitta. You won't ever see her again?'

'No. Of course not. Never.'

'Then we won't ever mention her again. I'm going to bed.'

Bernard knew better than to follow her there. Gitta, in the role of the Other Woman, was hardly important at all. Helen's quarrel with him had gone far deeper than that. He waited until the next day, but found her still reluctant to talk. It was as though she needed time to think before beginning to put her thoughts into words. Remembering the conversation over their abortive meal, Bernard suspected that she was preparing some kind of ultimatum; a plan for her future life which she would allow him to take or leave, but not alter.

It was in the course of that day that she told him Laker was dead. Bernard took time off from his own anxieties to try and comfort Paula, but there was no answer from either her telephone or her doorbell. He could only write, hoping that she would accept his sympathy and affection and also his offer of help in dealing with the financial and legal complications of her husband's death. He was genuinely anxious to support her, and planned to call every day until she was ready to open the door. Nevertheless, when Helen dropped a hint that he could, if he wished, return with her to their country house for the weekend, he accepted the indirect invitation at once.

Over the car radio as they drove towards Cambridge they heard news of a power failure which had brought half London to a standstill. 'We were lucky to escape before the traffic lights packed in,' Helen said. Her voice was light and pleasant – normal, in fact. Bernard, searching her every word for significance, wondered whether their quarrel was to be forgotten, never mentioned again. Although that in a sense might come as a relief, he was not sure that it would be wise to take the easy way out. He had hurt her, and must find some means of healing the wound. He still did not understand what had happened to assuage her anger.

The answer was revealed a day later, following an unexpected telephone call. Helen, who took the call, appeared – after some hesitation – to recognize the speaker. 'Oh, Isabel *Trent*! Yes, of course I remember you. I'd forgotten your married name, that's all. I don't read the college record as carefully as I should. Yes. Hold on.' She covered the mouthpiece with her hand as she passed the receiver to Bernard. 'Mrs Isabel Blair. She was at Oxford with me, but that doesn't mean I owe her any favours. Says she wants to speak to you but that you don't know her.' Helen did not quite succeed in keeping a note of suspicion out of her voice. For years, Bernard was sure, it had never occurred to her to question his relationships with other women; but now that he had shattered her trust, she would perhaps never feel sure of him again.

'I'm sorry to trouble you, Sir Bernard.' Isabel Blair's voice was low and attractive, but troubled. 'I've been trying to find out from the Middlesex Hospital how Sir John Lorimer is, but they'll only give information to the immediate family. So I wondered . . .'

'John? Is he ill? I didn't know.'

'He's had a heart attack,' Isabel said. 'His secretary was able to tell me that much. He collapsed in a lift and was found by a group of office cleaners arriving to start work early yesterday morning. There was a power failure in London that night. He spent the night in the Lorico tower and – and – ' She sounded on the point of tears.

'Is it bad?' he asked.

'I'm afraid it may be. He was rushed into an intensive care unit. That's all the hospital will tell me. I don't know who his nearest relative is, but I wondered if you – '

'Of course,' said Bernard. 'Give me your number.' The news that he passed on to her five minutes later was not encouraging. 'In a serious but stable condition, they say. He was found just in time. Another half hour, and it might have been too late. I'm sorry there's nothing more cheerful to report. You're a friend of his, I take it.'

'We hadn't known each other long,' she said. 'But I had – unfinished business, you might say. A letter that I wanted him to read. You've been very kind, Sir Bernard. If there's any more news . . .'

'I'll ring you straightaway.' As he put down the receiver he was struck by the pallor of Helen's face.

'John? What's wrong with him, Bernard?' She listened, shocked, to his explanation. 'But I was talking to him. Only twenty-four hours or so before. At Paula's party. He looked perfectly fit. Lively and charming. And now you say . . .'

Bernard looked at her in surprise. Helen seemed genuinely upset. Yet she hardly knew this remote relation by marriage, surely. Eighteen years ago John had – surprisingly – come to their wedding, but Bernard could recall no social contact since then.

A possible explanation occurred to him. Helen had gone to the party without a husband in tow, and John was a bachelor who perhaps used this kind of occasion as a hunting ground. He had no family feeling to make him decide that a cousin's wife should be off limits – indeed, he might be mischievous enough to enjoy the prospect of causing trouble inside the family circle. And Helen had made it clear earlier in that evening that she was in no mood to refuse invitations. To start some kind of affair might have seemed a good way of working off her anger and returning to normality by way of revenge. 'Did he flirt with you?' Bernard asked cautiously.

'Of course not.' Helen's shock now was of a different kind. 'It's just that – well, he looked so healthy. No one could have guessed . . .'

'He's not dead yet,' Bernard reminded her.

'No.' Helen took a deep breath. Bernard waited, watching her. Now she was going to tell him what she had decided to do. It was going to be all right. He was sure of that: it was going to be all right. But he still did not understand why.

'There was something Paula said,' Helen explained. 'After she'd heard that Laker had died. He'd been like that for so long, it was expected in his case, of course. But she wanted me to remember that it could happen to anyone, any time. You might step under a bus, or I might. And then we'd be apart for ever, with one of us left to regret . . . She made me think whether that was what I wanted, even when I said I did. And she tried to make me see that I might not always be able to change my mind. I'm not sure that I believed that part of it. There seemed to be plenty of time. And I thought you deserved . . .'

'To suffer?'

'Well, to wonder. But she was right, wasn't she. John's just proved that. It *could* happen. And then how would one live with the feeling – ?' Unexpectedly Helen laughed. 'And I'm a missionary's daughter. Brought up on a text for every occasion. Never let the sun go down on your anger. I should have remembered.'

'So?'

She looked him straight in the eyes. 'So what I do remember is that we were married for better or worse. You've given me a lot of the better, and not much of the worse. I ought to be able to work my way through it. If you want me to, that is.'

Bernard did not waste time in answering, but took her into his arms. 'Oh God!' he said. 'God, Helen, I love you so much. I'm sorry. Really sorry. Not just about Gitta. About – well, everything.' Was she ready, he wondered as he kissed her, to let him take her to bed? Yes. Whatever she had or had not decided, she was going to approach the decision with love. 'Thank God for Paula,' he said.

2

As soon as she had settled Laker's affairs, Paula went home. Home was Bristow Great House in Jamaica, where she had been born and brought up. Her father, before he died, had sold off the fields of sugar cane and groves of bananas which originally supported the plantation and instead developed a holiday hotel in the gardens and pleasure grounds of the old house. In the eighteen years since she inherited it Paula had rarely returned, being content to leave the hotel in the hands of a manager. But Laker's death, more decisively than she had expected, ended not only her marriage but her pleasure in being at the heart of British affairs. She needed to make a break, to begin a new life – and where better than in Bristow, where as an earnest schoolgirl she had dreamed her first ambitious dreams of helping her fellow-islanders to escape from poverty?

In spite of its name, Bristow Great House was not large or grand. The eighteenth-century trader who designed it for himself had kept the domestic quarters at a decent distance and so needed in the main house only a few entertaining rooms and three modest bedrooms. The most important feature of the house had always been the wide covered verandahs which encircled it at each of the two levels. On its own it could never have served as a hotel. So Paula's father had left it unchanged, building a restaurant and open-air bar along one of the terraces and a scattering of individual holiday bungalows throughout the grounds. Paula could return to her own bedroom as though it were only yesterday that she had set out for Oxford as a bright-eyed eighteen-year-old.

Sooner or later she planned to take an active part in Jamaican politics, but long absence had made her a stranger, even a foreigner. She was not arrogant enough to expect her opinions to carry weight immediately, but she had no false humility either. In due course she would decide whether she could wield most influence as a journalist writing in the local paper, as a television or radio commentator, or as a consultant to an influential politician.

She was still making a preliminary investigation of the possibilities when Bernard and Helen arrived at Bristow

Great House, laughing happily at her amazement as she saw them stepping out of a taxi.

'Why didn't you warn me?' she exclaimed.

'If we'd told you in advance that we thought of coming, you'd have felt bound to invite us as personal guests,' said Helen. 'We weren't going to have that. But you've always made Bristow sound such a heavenly place. It seemed silly to ignore a personal recommendation when we were looking for somewhere to flop.'

'I didn't think Bernard knew how to flop,' Paula laughed – and although she was teasing, she was genuinely surprised by their choice of destination. Helen's idea of a perfect holiday was to toast herself in the sun, but Bernard was a red-head whose skin burned rather than tanned. He was prepared to visit a hot country when there was sightseeing to be done, but enjoyed neither sun-bathing nor idleness. It was for this reason that Paula had never suggested a Jamaican holiday to her cousin.

Bernard provided an explanation later. While Helen rested after the journey, he strolled with Paula through the shady grounds. Tropical lushness and the brilliant blossom of native flowers and trees had not wholly overwhelmed the original plan of an English country garden, laid out two centuries earlier by the same slave-trader who built the house. Paula's father had added a swimming pool to the amenities of the Great House, but the lake by which she and Bernard walked now could have been designed by Capability Brown, so perfectly was it positioned.

'There's a special reason for this holiday,' Bernard said abruptly. 'It's not an ordinary trip. A second honeymoon, you might call it. And I owe it to you that it's happening at all.'

Paula looked at him questioningly. 'How come?'

'Helen and I had a quarrel just before Christmas. A

bad one. It shook me, I can tell you. We don't normally have even trivial tiffs, so when she told me she was walking out . . . She went to your party; do you remember? And I didn't know if she was ever going to come back.'

Paula remembered. She had done her best to put that unhappy evening out of her mind – and her only subsequent meeting with Helen and Bernard had been at Laker's funeral. They had said merely what a widow would expect a cousin and a friend to say, and Paula had been too overwhelmed by her own grief to ascribe any significance to the fact that they arrived and left together. But now that Bernard reminded her, yes, she did remember. 'So she did go back to the flat?'

'Yes. And it was because of what you said to her. She made it clear that she was acting on your advice – your instructions, almost. I'm grateful to you. I'd like you to know that.'

'I'm delighted that all's well,' Paula said. 'But as for needing to be grateful, fiddlesticks! I'm sure you'd have worked it out between you.'

'Well . . .' Bernard sounded less sure. 'Let's just say that you're definitely my favourite cousin.'

'Have you any others?' But of course, Paula reminded herself, there was John. She had been talking to him about his house in Jamaica at the very moment the message came through from the hospital, and since then he had come near to death himself. 'How's John getting on?' she asked. 'He still wasn't well enough to have visitors when I left England.'

'He's had that horrific operation on his heart. Putting in a bypass. Makes it sound as though he were part of a traffic control scheme. Pretty hairy for a time, I think, but he's come through remarkably well. They allowed him out of hospital in a wheelchair for Angela's wedding, just for the day; we had a word with him then. I gather he plans to come out to Jamaica to convalesce. He's got a place of his own here somewhere, is that right?'

'Angela's wedding?' queried Paula.

'Yes. He's an old friend of Henry Peacham's. He knows Angela as well, of course, from staying at Wetherly.'

'Talking about the wedding?' Refreshed by her siesta and shower, Helen arrived to join them. 'It was a pity you couldn't get back for it, Paula. But we thought of you as we toasted absent friends. Ingrid and Lindsay sent their love.'

Paula didn't believe that, but she no longer listened as Helen described the occasion. It was startling enough to learn that Angela was married. But that she should marry without inviting her best friend to the wedding, without even *telling* her . . . As soon as she could politely do so, Paula steered Helen and Bernard in the direction of the swimming pool, arranged to meet them for dinner, and escaped.

Alone at last, she climbed to the highest part of the grounds. From the bench she had placed at the summit of the hill she could look down over the grassy terraces to the old house and its cluster of new buildings. But today she was not conscious of the view. She was thinking about Angela.

Although she had managed to disguise her astonishment at Bernard's revelation, the news left her hurt and angry. Did Angela despise her so much that she could not bear to meet her old friend again, or even correspond with her? At first there seemed no other possible explanation. Laker was dead and it was Paula's fault and Angela could not forgive her for it. But the Angela she had loved for so many years had never shown any sign of such bitterness – and if she had felt unforgiving, she would have demonstrated this after Laker's accident, not after his death. Little by little, as her feelings calmed, Paula realized that there could be another explanation.

Angela could not possibly have expected to keep her marriage secret from Paula; she would have known that Helen would carry the news. Either she was delivering a direct snub to Paula, or else she was sending indirectly an opposite message: that Paula herself need never be ashamed. No one else would ever know exactly why Laker had staggered drunkenly to his car on the last night of his conscious life, and Paula herself need never again be reminded of it by the sight of the woman who could have accused her of being responsible for the accident. For twenty years Angela had sacrificed her own happiness in the cause of friendship. Now, loyal to the last, she was sacrificing even that friendship for the sake of her friend's peace of mind.

The longer Paula considered this alternative interpretation, the more convincing she found it. Her first instinct was to fight Angela's decision, risking a small quarrel for the sake of a continuing affection. While writing to say how much it had hurt her to hear of the marriage indirectly, she could make it clear that she accepted her responsibility for Laker's accident; there was no need for her feelings to be protected. But she remembered in time that the secrets were not all on one side – and Angela did not know that one of her secrets had been discovered. Paula now could make a small return for all her friend's sacrifices.

She must write to Angela – at once, while she still had the courage. A letter of congratulations and good wishes. With, at the end, an unequivocable statement that the two of them were never likely to see each other again. Angela could take that in whatever spirit she chose – that Paula was either upset at receiving no invitation to the wedding, or else did not intend ever to leave Jamaica and return to Europe. It was the definiteness of the declaration which would be important, not the reason for it. Once Paula had made her position clear, there would be no further need for Angela to continue with whatever cover story she had invented for Tom. Instead, she could settle down to a happy family life with her husband and her son.

That was that, then. The decision closed the last door on her life in England. Paula stood up and prepared to make her way down the zig-zag path which led back to the hotel. A movement below caught her eye and she saw Helen and Bernard appearing through the screen of trees which concealed the swimming pool. At this distance one fair-skinned woman in a bikini top and wrap-around skirt was not easily distinguishable from another, but Bernard's floppy sun-hat made him instantly recognizable. They were walking hand in hand and, as Paula watched, Bernard pulled Helen into his arms and kissed her. Then they began to run towards their bungalow.

There was a moment after they disappeared from sight in which Paula was overcome by desolation. For almost two years – while Laker lay in hospital, and after his death – she had lived a celibate life. Even while her body ached for the comfort of being loved, the numbness of her emotions prevented her from seeking that comfort and at the same time made the ache tolerable. The despair which she felt in her heart at this moment, though, was less easily endured.

She had experienced the anguish of loneliness before – once when she was shown into Laker's room on the day after the accident, and again at the funeral, when she was forced to think of herself as a widow. But in losing Angela she would lose a very special relationship. For twenty years, until Tom smiled at her in a motorway service station, Angela had been the friend to whom she always spoke the truth. Who now could play that role in her life? The desire to confess stabbed into her mind with an almost physical pain. But there would never again be anyone who would be interested in whatever truths she wished to tell.

As Paula made her way down the hill she remembered the reunion on Angela's fortieth birthday and forced herself to laugh. On that occasion she had accepted the reminder of her ambition to become a political journalist and perhaps to go directly into politics. Under the pressure of distress she had revealed the more personal hope, that she would spend the rest of her life with Laker. But she had never repeated to anyone except Angela the deeper decision which she expressed to Laker when he asked her to marry him. It was an ambition which had come true in an unhappy way. She had wanted to live her own life, to be responsible for herself; and that was exactly what she would have to do from now on. She was on her own.

3

Across the dazzling silver surface of the Caribbean Sea a corridor of rippling orange beckoned the way towards the sun. John relaxed on a chaise-longue as he waited for the sunset and for Paula. Sunset was a daily treat, but his pleasure was doubled when Paula shared it with him.

The room in which he was lounging was cantilevered out from the cliff of a headland. John had designed it himself when he first commissioned the house, in such a way that the wall of glass at one end seemed to float in the air above the bay. As he looked down in the water it was possible to watch the shoals of fish which meandered like a black curving river through the sea – fish so small that he could distinguish them individually only when the barracuda arrived. Then, with a heave and sparkle of silver, the shoal scattered, leaving a circle of clear water around each elegant predator.

In a second or two the barracuda would surge forward again, and again the water would flash with the silver panic. But now John's attention was distracted by the sound of a car. He did not move, but smiled to himself. Weeks of convalescence had taught him to savour the pleasure of anticipation. He sat without moving, listening to the slamming of a car door, the jangling of a bell, the sound of a woman's footsteps. That sound reminded him of Isabel, the stranger who with equally firm steps had approached a waiting lift in the Lorico tower block. But Isabel had stepped out of his life as suddenly as she had entered it. More decisively than he would have thought possible in the space of only a few hours she had changed his whole attitude towards women, but had not in the end had the courage to take advantage of the change.

The confrontation had left him restless. In the past, impermanence had been the only constant factor in his relationships with women. He had never promised or expected fidelity, never held out the slightest prospect of marriage. He enjoyed bachelor life in London, and on business trips found that more was accomplished if he travelled alone.

There had, nevertheless, been exciting holidays in the past. In particular he had always – until this convalescence – brought a companion with him to Jamaica. Perhaps that was why for the first time he felt lonely here. Or was the reason to be found in the new energy which the by-pass operation had brought him now that he had recovered from the surgery? No: the most probable explanation of his craving for company was the liberation which Isabel had provided from his life-long view that all women were deceitful, not to be trusted.

He could have trusted Isabel: he could have surrendered his life to her in a way he had never even contemplated before. But, unable to sweep aside her feeling of shame about events long past, he had by now accepted the fact that he would never see her again. It was that acceptance which opened the door to a new relationship with Paula.

He had not revealed his feelings to his Jamaican cousin – indeed, he had not acknowledged them even to himself, so perhaps they were no more than insubstantial dreams. The women who had been his temporary companions during past Jamaican holidays had always returned to England when the holiday was over. Sometimes they had remained friends, sometimes they drifted apart; it was all the same to him. But Paula lived in Jamaica; it was now her permanent home. He must take care not to spoil the island for himself by creating a situation which he might not be able to resolve.

More than his own doubts restrained him from speaking his mind. Paula too was holding something back: he was sure of it. He remembered that during their first encounter he had deliberately refrained from revealing her relationship to himself and the other Lorimers. She had been aware then that he was concealing something. Now it was his turn to be conscious of a reticence on her part. Only very recently had he succeeded in identifying the subject. She never mentioned Laker's name.

Now she came swiftly into the room, her white teeth and brown eyes both sparkling in a smile. 'Don't get up.'

'How shall I ever persuade you that I'm perfectly fit?' Disobeying her instruction, he walked over to a concealed refrigerator and poured glasses of fresh lime juice. For different reasons he and Paula had both given up alcohol.

'I haven't been so healthy for years. All that blood pumping its way round and round! All that oxygen stimulating my brain! I feel twenty years younger. My only terror is that someone in the company will discover that all this talk of convalescence is a sham, and summon me home.' He laughed. No one in Lorico gave orders to the chairman.

'When that time comes I shall produce an excuse for you to stay,' Paula told him. 'There's a project under discussion for Kingston which would be right up your street.'

'Tell me now.'

Paula shook her head. 'I'm here to enjoy your company and your sunset,' she said. 'When I need to see you as an emissary from the government, I'll make a business appointment.'

'Since that means I can look forward to an extra visit, I won't argue.' There was a hint of flirtatiousness in the exchange, but instead of developing it he changed the subject as he sat down again. 'Did I tell you that I wrote to invite Henry and Angela here? For an extension of their honeymoon?'

'Have they accepted?' Paula asked the question not in the casual manner which might have been expected, but as though the answer were of great importance to her.

'No. It sounded as though Henry might have liked to come; but Angela couldn't get away, he said.'

Paula sat down on the end of the chaise-longue, staring out of the window as intently as though the sunset show had already begun. 'Angela won't come while I'm here,' she said.

'But you're such great friends,' protested John.

'Angela has ended her friendship with me for my own sake.' Paula gave a short laugh which combined regret and reminiscence. 'I can remember Angela herself – years ago, when she was an undergraduate reading English – quoting a bit of a poem at me. "Yet each man kills the thing he loves." That's what's happened.' Without warning Paula ceased to laugh and buried her head in her hands.

John stared at her, trying to understand. A casual conversation had changed its character. Something important was happening. 'Are you still talking about Angela?' he asked.

'Partly.' Then Paula lifted her head and looked straight at him. 'No,' she said. 'I'm talking about Laker.'

'I notice that you never do talk about Laker.'

'Because I'm ashamed,' Paula said. 'Because I was responsible for Laker's death. Angela knows that.'

'In what way responsible? Did you have to authorize the doctors to turn off a life support machine?'

'That comes into it. But my responsibility was more direct.'

'You weren't driving the car when it crashed, were you?'

'Nothing so straightforward,' Paula told him. 'At the time of the accident I was in bed with another man. It was because he discovered that – or guessed it, at least – that Laker decided to drive off in search of me even though he knew he was drunk.'

'That was his decision. His mistake. Not your fault.'

'Legally I'm not to blame, agreed. But I know the truth. And that's why Angela's cutting off. She thinks I can't face her because she's the only other person who knows.'

'You've told me now.' John found it difficult to speak calmly. In an almost unbelievable manner this discussion seemed to be running parallel to the conversation he had had on the morning after the power failure. From the facts he had put before Isabel then she had been honest enough to accept and brave enough to admit her share of responsibility for her husband's death; but she had not dared to remain with the man who knew about it. Now Paula, using almost the same words about a remarkably similar situation, was confessing to an involvement which he could never have deduced for himself. She was proving to be braver than Isabel, and more honest. John found himself praying silently that she would not continue the parallel by withdrawing from his company.

'I need to say it.' Paula stood up and walked across to the huge wall of glass. 'Angela obviously doesn't understand that need, and there are special reasons why I can't have it out with her. With most people, I don't care about their opinion of me, and so it doesn't matter. But with you . . . I realize that you didn't need to know. I don't even expect you to be interested. But there has to be someone in my life to whom I can always tell the truth. I can only test that by doing it.'

'Why me?' asked John. 'I understand what you mean, but why – ?'

'I like talking to you. I like being with you. But I have this feeling of being a phoney. Of putting on an act because I want you to – well, to admire me.'

'I do admire you,' said John. He paused for only a second, amazing himself with the realization of what he was about to say. 'I love you. I want you to marry me.'

4

Paula stared out of the window without moving or speaking, not wishing John to realize that he had astonished her.

It was only the last part of his declaration which

surprised her. During the course of the past few weeks she had realized that he found her attractive, and the realization had excited her, stirring her body from the celibate lethargy of the months since Laker's accident. She was ready for love again.

For most of the time she took pains to conceal this, playing the part of the single-minded career woman with as much energy as the island's hot and humid climate allowed. She had needed to cultivate many new working relationships since returning to Jamaica, and had not allowed the fact that she was a woman to complicate any of them.

John, though, was in a different category from any of the men she needed to impress: the radio producer, the newspaper editor, the members of the government. She already had a relationship with him, of friendship as well as family. As soon as she learned of his arrival in Jamaica she had called on him and – as at every previous meeting – had been warmed by his obvious liking for her. If, as time passed, she had been careful not to make too obvious the increasing depth of her own feelings, it was not because she feared a snub or held old-fashioned ideas about always leaving a man to take the initiative. She genuinely did not know how strong John was, how fully he had recovered from his operation; it was as simple as that.

So had he merely swept away that doubt by making a straightforward proposal that they should go to bed together, she would not have hesitated; it was an invitation which, sooner or later, she expected. But the suggestion of marriage took her completely aback. She reckoned herself to be a good judge of character and had thought it certain that her cousin would never marry. Whatever his original reason for remaining a bachelor, it was hard to understand why he should contemplate such a radical change at the age of fifty-eight. Was there something she herself had said which had prompted a change of heart?

Thinking quickly back on the conversation, she was able to pinpoint the moment. 'There has to be someone to whom I can always tell the truth,' she had said, and by telling him had chosen him to be that person. To that extent she had made a commitment – but without expecting such a small declaration to elicit a proposal so much more far-reaching. She searched for words which would organize her undisciplined thoughts into an opinion, a decision; but certainty eluded her. 'The sun's setting,' was all she could think of to say.

He came to stand beside her at the window; very close, with one arm round her waist, one hand resting on her hip. Together they watched as the sun, huge and red, hurtled towards the horizon as though it were falling out of the heavens. The sea flushed with fire and from behind the thin evening clouds spread a pink glow which gradually suffused the delicate turquoise of the sky. Then the thick black canopy of night rolled dramatically above their heads, swallowing all colour and making land and sea invisible.

Neither of them moved away. The first sunset was beautiful enough, but it did not mean that the day had died. In ten minutes or so there would be a second and even more spectacular display. But for the moment, while they waited, they were standing in darkness. All Paula knew for certain was that she must accept the lesson she had learned from her marriage to Laker. She drew in her breath, but it was John who spoke first.

'That housing project you mentioned. I know about it already. I've been considering the possibility of setting up a company here. The government will favour a tender from a company that's more or less local.'

Paula, startled, couldn't resist laughing. Had John forgotten what he was talking about only a moment earlier? It seemed that she need not have wasted time puzzling over the difference between independence and selfishness, the nature of commitment or even the reason for John's sudden interest in matrimony. But he too was laughing, as if knowing that he had disconcerted her.

'My surgeon gave me a lecture before I left England,' he said. 'On the subject of stress. Physical exertion is OK, it seems. Sex is particularly OK. What I need to cut out is anxiety. He suggested that I should ease my way out of the Lorico powerhouse. It's true that for thirty-odd years I've taken all the important decisions there, and there can be a great deal at stake. Are you listening?'

'Of course I'm listening,' Paula assured him. 'I've no idea what you're getting at, but sure, I'm listening.'

'I realize that I couldn't ask you to leave Jamaica,' John said. 'You've got your radio programme, you've got your column in *The Gleaner*, and my spies tell me that your honorary appointment as research assistant on health and education is actually an opportunity for you to give advice to the government which you're pretty damn sure will be followed. You have a lot to offer the people of this island. I don't see that I'd have the right to interfere with that.'

'So?'

'So I think it's time for me to take the doctors' advice and plan for early retirement. I *could* stay on at Lorico as non-executive chairman, but it wouldn't amuse me to see someone else doing things the wrong way. What I have in mind is to sell out. That, incidentally, will make me an extremely rich man. Since a wife is the only person who could inherit my millions without paying any tax on them, it's clearly essential for me to acquire a wife before I die.'

'Oh John, really . . .'

He laughed. 'Don't worry. Money isn't part of the argument. The scenario is this. I retire from Lorico. I come to live in Jamaica because I like the island, I happen to have a house here already, and the woman I love happens to live here. I buy myself a small business just to give me an interest, because I'm not used to doing nothing. But mainly I support you in whatever you're doing. If possible, I do it openly. But if it wouldn't be to your advantage to be Lady Lorimer – or to have a white husband whoever he is – then we have a secret wedding and no one here need ever know.'

'Is a wedding necessary?' asked Paula. 'We're friends already, and cousins. We could simply become loving friends. Kissing cousins.'

'Marriage is a gesture of commitment. That's what's necessary.'

'It's supposed to be a public gesture. Here you are offering to change your whole way of life for my sake. What do you expect of me?'

'I expect you always to tell me the truth,' said John. Paula felt his grip tightening round her waist. 'But most of all – whether you show it in public or not – I want to feel sure for the rest of my life that you think of me as the most important person in the world. Just that one little thing. Could you do that?'

He laughed, but Paula knew that he was not joking, and shivered with excitement. John was demanding loyalty as well as passion and she was mature enough now – as she had not been twenty years earlier – to give him what he wanted. She could love him not only as she had loved Laker, but as she had loved Angela as well, and as Angela had loved her. She had lost the two people dearest to her through her own fault, but John was offering her a second chance.

The black cloud-curtains of night parted in preparation

for nature's second display of pyrotechnics. An arch of crimson and black was licked by tongues of yellow, like lightning shooting upwards. Paula did not even notice the spectacle. Turning her back on the sunset, she smiled into John's eyes, pledging herself to a new life. This time there would be no mistakes, no deceptions, no secrets.

'I could do that,' she said.